LADYKILLER

LADYKILLER

A NOVEL

KATHERINE WOOD

BANTAM | NEW YORK

Published in the United States by Bantam Books, an imprint of Random House, a division of Penguin Random House LLC, New York.

BANTAM & B colophon is a registered trademark of Penguin Random House LLC.

LIBRARY OF CONGRESS CATALOGING-IN-PUBLICATION DATA
Names: Wood, Katherine, author.
Title: Ladykiller : a novel / Katherine Wood.
Description: First edition. | New York : Bantam, 2024.
Identifiers: LCCN 2023039784 (print) | LCCN 2023039785 (ebook) | ISBN 9780593726440 (hardcover ; acid-free paper) | ISBN 9780593726457 (ebook)
Subjects: LCGFT: Thrillers (Fiction) | Novels.
Classification: LCC PS3619.T2484 L33 2024 (print) | LCC PS3619.T2484 (ebook) | DDC 813/.6—dc23/eng/20231214
LC record available at https://lccn.loc.gov/2023039784
LC ebook record available at https://lccn.loc.gov/2023039785

Printed in the United States of America on acid-free paper

randomhousebooks.com

2 4 6 8 9 7 5 3 1

First Edition

Book design by Susan Turner

For Sierra and Jade

"Love all, trust a few, do wrong to none."

—WILLIAM SHAKESPEARE,
All's Well That Ends Well

His stories were good because he imagined them intensely, so intensely that he came to believe them.

—PATRICIA HIGHSMITH,
The Talented Mr. Ripley

LADYKILLER

PROLOGUE

—

THE NIGHT BEFORE HUGO TORRES'S FUNERAL, A CHEETAH ESCAPED
its enclosure at the Bronx Zoo and devoured a warthog. Had the
victim been a more charming animal—say, a koala or a monkey—
perhaps there would have been some level of outrage directed at the
cheetah, but as it was, the whispers among the mourners assembled
in the cathedral on Park Avenue the next morning were of sympathy
not for the warthog, but for the cheetah. After all, cheetahs were
predators not meant for a life in captivity; the cat had only done what
it was born to do.

The turnout for the memorial service was impressive, the church
packed to the gills with Manhattan's finest decked in their best be-
reavement attire, rendered antlike by the towering stone pillars and
soaring vaulted ceiling. Diamonds glittered on beds of black lace as
mourners craned their necks to get a glimpse of the mahogany cas-
ket, their morbid curiosity stifled by the closed lid draped in more
roses than a Kentucky Derby winner.

The invitation had said nine-thirty, but it wasn't until the church bells struck ten that the family stepped through the massive doors, ushered inside by a gust of bitingly cold wind that chilled the back third of the church. Everyone turned to watch the spectacle, carefully concealing their fascination as the solemn group proceeded up the marble nave.

First in line was the third and current wife, Melodie, a waxy-looking French Canadian of fifty, who had a frigid personality and a frosty relationship with her husband's exes and their children. Her bone-thin frame was draped in black wool and ivory-colored pearls, the hand of the six-year-old son she shared with Papa Hugo gripped tightly in hers. Everyone murmured how awful it was for the poor boy to lose his father at such a young age, but such were the risks of a May-December romance.

It's fair to say the congregation was universally disappointed that the crazy second wife wasn't in attendance. Of course, they knew it wasn't okay to call people who had been institutionalized for mental illness *crazy*—could you even say that word anymore?—but privately, that was how they thought of her. In her day, Caroline had been a talented painter, not to mention very beautiful, with a habit of flirting with husbands who didn't belong to her. Now she lived in a sanatorium in Switzerland, like it was the nineteenth century or something, neatly packed away for unbecoming behavior.

Her daughter, Gia, was just as stunning as her mother had been. *And just as much trouble*, elite circles would say. She was a staple of the society pages, flitting from boyfriend to boyfriend between various creative endeavors that included a salacious but surprisingly well written memoir and a perfume she loved too much to sell to the public.

Today she was wearing a skin-tight black satin dress with long sleeves and a completely open back, her eyes hidden by giant black sunglasses, her long brunette locks gathered into a bun at the nape of her neck, clutching the arm of her brother, Benecio.

Benny had wavy dark hair like his sister's, almost long enough on top to tuck behind his ears, and they both shared their father's deep-set eyes and olive skin and their mother's artistic sensibilities. The mothers in the crowd registered Benny's bare ring finger and pinched their eligible daughters, who blushed but for once didn't protest. Sadly, ever since Benny's first screenplay was turned into a runaway hit film, he was perpetually accompanied by some actress or other, and to the chagrin of all the mothers, his current girlfriend, the star of a television show about witches, would be stapled to his side by the time he reached the reception.

Notably missing were the British first wife and the three grown children she shared with the deceased. It was no secret that she regarded Americans as gauche and had elected to hold a competing memorial service in London. Which was, ironically, rather gauche.

When the family reached the first row, Melodie allowed Gia and Benny to sit first, then took her place at the end of the pew, leaving a discernible gap between herself and her stepchildren. Gia's best friend, Abby, the daughter of the family's former chef, leaned forward from the second row and put her hand on Gia's shoulder. Thanks to Papa Hugo's generosity, Abby had gone to boarding school with Gia and the daughters and sons of many in the congregation. She was petite and reserved, pleasant-looking but not gorgeous, an unobtrusive interloper in their rarefied circles, and though she was better turned out than she had been in high school—her mousy hair now a smart shoulder-length blond, her glasses replaced by contacts that revealed large green eyes—her middle-class clothes and bearing would have rendered her nearly invisible to this set, were her face at eighteen not burned into their minds.

"Scandal" was the wrong word for what had happened. Shocking violence was more like it. The assault Abby had suffered at the hands of Gia's stalker was shocking, that much was certain, and violent. But real tragedy had been narrowly averted when Gia stepped in, saving Abby's life by extinguishing that of her attacker.

The news cycle seized on the story: HEIRESS KILLS HOMICIDAL MANIAC AND SAVES BEST FRIEND'S LIFE. They'd all seen the television interviews Gia gave and read the memoir she wrote about it afterward too, of course. Though some accused her of profiting off tragedy, the book had been a moderate success and would have provided her the opportunity for a career as an author if she had so desired. Alas, ten years later, her publisher was still waiting on her follow-up.

Everyone stared at the gold-framed oil portrait of Papa Hugo displayed on an easel next to his coffin as the priest rightly declared him an icon, beloved by those close and far. It was warm in the church, and minds began to wander as the priest went on to summarize how Papa Hugo had made his money in oil but poured it back into green energy, turning Cleanergy Corp. into one of the largest clean fuel companies in the world before he retired to focus on the nonprofits he supported.

"... and that is why Hugo chose to donate his entire five-hundred-million-dollar fortune to the Torres Foundation."

This got their attention. The Torres Foundation had been founded by Papa Hugo and his second wife, the crazy artist, and therefore the main causes it funded were the environment, which was his passion, and the arts, which was hers. Donating his fortune to the foundation was admirable, of course. But what of his children?

Suddenly the congregation's focus was once again on the front row of the church, as they desperately tried to make out from the tilt of a head or the side of a face whether his family had known they would be cut out of the will. Husbands and wives gave each other meaningful glances as they bowed their heads for a final prayer before everyone—even those who had thought five minutes ago they might skip the wake in favor of a round of golf—headed over to the ballroom at the Waldorf for the reception.

ABBY

CHAPTER 1

FIVE MONTHS LATER

THE INVITATION ARRIVED IN THE MAIL WITHOUT NOTICE, AS WAS CUS-tomary for missives from Regina "Gia" Highsmith Torres. My best friend had always enjoyed the element of surprise, which paradoxically meant that nothing she did was all that surprising—to me, anyway.

The battered red envelope was marked Air Mail and covered in stamps, the return address that of her family's Greek islands home. I felt a wave of nostalgia, picturing the view from the balcony of what had been my bedroom when I used to visit, rocky hills tumbling down to an azure sea. I could almost hear the song of the cicadas, smell the leather of the couch in the dusky library, taste the earthy olive oil pressed from the trees in the grove.

An icy blast of air conditioning brought me back to the present as I stepped into the elevator of my modern high-rise apartment building. The August heat was no joke in Atlanta no matter the time of day, but the air conditioning was always shockingly cold. I caught a glimpse of myself in the mirror, my blond hair dark with perspiration from my early morning run through steamy Piedmont Park. Dry shampoo wasn't going to cut it this morning, which meant I needed to rush if I wanted to make it to work on time.

As the elevator whooshed me up to the fourteenth floor, I pried the flap of Gia's envelope open with damp fingers, slicing my thumb in the process. I sucked the stinging cut, muttering expletives under my breath as I extracted a postcard from a hotel in northern Sweden. The picture showed a stunning wood and glass structure nestled in the mountains overlooking a lake, beneath the vibrant green and pink hues of the aurora borealis. On the back of the postcard, I recognized Gia's looping scrawl:

Abby,

Please join me and Benny (just us three!) for my thirtieth at this incredible hotel where we can see the northern lights. I'm so sorry about the things I said the last time we talked. I love you and really hope you can come. Please come.

Love,
Gia

I turned the envelope over in my hands to see there was something else folded inside. A first-class plane ticket to Kiruna, Sweden, departing on September 8.

I exhaled through pursed lips, touched, but also annoyed. I'd told her a million times that as an associate at a law firm pushing hard for partner, I worked twelve-hour days at least six days a week. While it was true Gia and I had fantasized about seeing the northern lights since we were teenagers, there was no way in hell I could just drop everything and jet off to Sweden in a month's time. But Gia never planned anything in advance.

Hell, she'd only known her husband four months, and they'd been married three.

Even for Gia, that was reckless.

I'd tried to caution her before they tied the knot, but Gia was too busy playing the heroine in her own love story to listen to the advice of her boring best friend. Which was why we hadn't spoken in as long. I stood by my refusal to bear witness while she exchanged vows with a man she'd known only a month, but I did regret the wounds we'd inflicted on each other over their nuptials, and this invitation told me she did as well.

IT DIDN'T HELP THAT IT had been five-thirty in the morning when she called to relay the news.

"We're getting married!" she'd squealed into the phone when I answered, worried that something terrible had happened.

"Who's we?" I grumbled, rubbing the sleep from my eyes.

"Garrett," she answered with a laugh. "He's The One, Abs. It's magic."

Garrett. It took me a minute to picture his face. I'd met him only once, about two weeks after they'd gotten together. I'd been in New York briefly for work and Gia had brought him along to our dinner, foisting him upon me like a gift. I could see why she liked him; he was charming, handsome, and erudite. I, however, found the way he fawned all over her a little nauseating. But adulation was Gia's sunlight.

"That's great." I rolled over and turned on the bedside lamp, squinting in the sudden light. "But isn't it a little fast to be getting engaged?"

"None of that matters when it's right," she declared. "I wish you were here already. I'm shopping for dresses now, I need your opinion."

"It's five-thirty in the morning. My opinion is it's too early."

"Can you come tomorrow? Just send me your passport number and I'll book your ticket."

"Tomorrow?" I asked, alarmed. "When is the wedding?"

"This weekend!"

"*This* weekend? Gia, no."

"Yes!" she said, giddy, her words tumbling over each other. "I'm in Copenhagen. You can get married fast here, it's like the Vegas of the E.U. I mean, I'll have to buy a dress off the rack, obviously, but I think I can find something. It'll just be us, anyway. Maybe we'll do something big in a few months, but for the moment—"

I was up now, pacing into the kitchen to make coffee. "Gia, I know with your dad gone, you're probably wanting stability right now, but marrying a man you just met is not—"

"It doesn't have anything to do with that. I'm in love!"

Panic rose in my chest. I felt like I was watching a runaway train, and though I knew logically there was nothing I could do to stop it, I had to try. "Please don't take this the wrong way, you know how much I love you and your enthusiasm . . . but you've been in love before."

Gia was always in love passionately—and briefly. She was obsessed with the idea of finding her one true love and thought that any reasonably good-looking man who showed interest in her was The One until she got to know him properly. I never knew, when meeting her latest beau, whether I'd be introduced to an intensely cerebral professor, a whiny viscount, a coked-up stockbroker, or an artist who refused to wear shoes—in New York City. I was still scarred from a road trip we'd taken with the latter, during which he put his nasty feet on the air-conditioning vent of her G-Wagon to "refresh them."

"It's different with Garrett," she declared. "It's like we were made for each other. Can't you just be happy for me?"

"I am happy for you. But you've known him less time even than you knew—"

I broke off, Noah's name hanging in the silence between us.

"Please don't," she said after a moment.

"I'm sorry," I said, kicking myself. "I just get protective of you."

"I know what he did to you was awful," she said sincerely. "And I know it's my fault for bringing him into our lives. I will forever be sorry for that. But I was eighteen. I've grown up. My judgment is better now."

I didn't point out that her decision to marry a man she'd known a month made me highly doubt that. "Have you told Benny?" I asked instead.

"I'm not asking my brother to stand beside me, I'm asking you," she pleaded. "You're my best friend; we always promised we'd stand beside each other."

My heart pinched. I bided my time as I filled the coffee maker with water, searching for the right answer. "Okay," I said finally, with as much diplomacy as I could muster. "If you really want me to stand beside you, you're going to have to wait at least six months. I have a job. I can't just take off to Denmark at the drop of a hat."

"Your job you hate?"

"I don't hate it—"

"You complain all the time that they take advantage of you," she pointed out. "So, fuck 'em."

I could feel a tension headache coming on. "That's not how it works."

"If it's about money, I can send you money."

"I don't want your money, G."

"What do I have to do to get you here?" she begged.

"There's nothing you can do," I snapped, my irritation flaring as the coffee machine hissed. "I can't come this weekend. And even if I could, I wouldn't. I love you too much to let you marry a man you just met."

We'd gone back and forth like that, our exchange becoming more barbed with each volley, until she finally hung up on me, and we hadn't spoken since. We'd texted and emailed a few times and commented on each other's social media posts, but three months had passed since I'd heard her voice—a record for us. I knew we'd make up eventually, though; our friendship was too deep to be ended by one fight. And while I was wary, I really did hope things would work out with her new husband.

———

THE ELEVATOR DINGED AS IT reached my floor, and I replaced the post-card in the envelope. As I stepped off the elevator, I was so caught up in my own thoughts that I nearly tripped over my octogenarian neighbor, dragging a full bag of trash down the hallway. "Mrs. Lee," I said, shaking my head, "that's my job."

"I don't want to bother you, dear," she said, smiling up at me. "I just let it get too full."

"It's no bother at all," I said, taking the bag from her.

As I hoisted the garbage bag, Gia's red envelope dropped from my fingers, and before I could stop her, Mrs. Lee had bent to pick it up.

"A red envelope is good luck," she said, handing it to me.

"Is it?" I laughed. "Unfortunately, it's not an invitation I can accept."

She clucked her tongue. "A word of advice from an old lady. Accept all the invitations. One day they'll stop coming."

I opened my mouth to protest, but all that came out was a small, strangled noise.

Mrs. Lee patted me on the shoulder. "Have a nice day."

"You too."

I trudged down the hallway to the trash chute, her words echoing in my mind. I recognized that this invitation to Sweden was Gia's olive branch, but as I'd told Mrs. Lee, it wasn't one I could accept. Not because I didn't love her, but because unlike her, I lived in the real world.

We were opposites: I craved rules and structure, while she was allergic to the very idea of coloring inside the lines. Which was why I had become an attorney and she was . . . well, Gia was more concerned with living than making a living.

Her indolence wasn't for lack of brains, that much was certain. The girl never studied a day in her life and managed to score straight A's at every one of the fancy schools we attended, throwing rowdy flapper parties in our shared room while I crammed political theory at the library. Her father had enough money that she needed at least a handful of strikes to get uninvited from a school, but she'd eventually get kicked out for a third or fifth infraction, blatantly hotboxing the dorm, cussing out the drama teacher when he cast another girl in the role I'd been so desperate to play in the spring musical, or filling the foyer with flyers made from the unsolicited dick pics Scott Thurston sent her, his phone number and class picture printed at the bottom.

She was always divisive, beautiful and brash, unable to keep her opinions to herself, while I was the mild, diplomatic one, negotiating our way out of whatever messes she got us into. It was a symbiotic relationship and I never minded being in her shadow—in fact I found it freeing. No one paid any mind to the diminutive, pale-eyed girl with the mousy brown hair and glasses reading in the corner when a goddess was setting off fireworks on the soccer field, which meant I got to finish my book in peace. I never liked a lot of fuss.

I'd had enough therapy now to realize her reckless behavior was a bid for attention from the father who was never around and the mother who was too consumed by her own psychosis to pay much notice to the lives of her children. But that father was dead now, the mother was in an institution, heavily medicated, and Benny was preoccupied by his own high-pressure life. There was no one left to stop her from marrying a man she'd known a month. No one but me, and I'd failed.

I'd just dumped the bag down the trash chute at the end of the corridor when my phone started to ring. Extracting it from the pocket of my leggings, I was surprised to see Gia's name. I didn't have time to talk to Gia right now—but then I never did, and with her invitation in my hand, I felt guilty sending her to voicemail. Dry shampoo would have to do this morning. "Hi, G," I said as I answered.

"It's seven your time, I'm guessing you just got back from a run through Piedmont Park."

"You know me well."

"How's Colin?"

I sat on the bench in front of the picture window at the end of the hall, looking out over the sea of green treetops sporadically inter-rupted by towers of steel. "We broke up."

"I'd say I'm sorry, but he was never good enough for you."

I snorted but didn't disagree. "Where are you?"

"Greece." She sighed dramatically. "Preparing to sell the house on Miteras."

"Really," I said, taken aback. Even after all the things that had happened in that house, it had always been Gia's favorite, and she spent nearly every summer there.

"Didn't you get my email?" she asked.

I felt a stab of contrition, remembering the email she'd sent shortly after our fight over her wedding three months ago, inviting me to come to Miteras. "You didn't mention you were selling."

"I can't afford to keep it," she said. "Now that Dad's gone, I'm poor."

I couldn't help it—I laughed.

I was intimately acquainted with what poor was. A person who could sell the espresso machine she rarely used for fifteen grand on eBay was not poor.

"I'm serious!" she said.

"How poor?" I asked.

"I don't know," she said. "You know how bad I am with money. But my accountant assures me I have to sell."

"What about Garrett?" I asked. "He owns a shipping company, right?"

"It's complicated right now. Not with him, just his business. Any-way, I didn't marry him for his money, Abs."

"No, of course not," I said. "I'm so sorry, G. Are you okay?"

"I'm fine. Change is good, you know. I'm writing again."

"Oh?" I asked, surprised.

The memoir she'd written about the summer that ended in our shared misfortune had been cathartic for her, allowing her not only to work through her trauma, but to tell her side of the story, silencing the haters who doubted her version of events. She was remarkably talented, her descriptions vivid, her voice candid—and in true Gia fashion, she hadn't shied away from the salacious bits, recounting her sexual adventures in juicy detail as if daring readers to pass judgment on her.

The book had been well received, though she hadn't been inspired to write anything since. She feared she wouldn't be able to tell other people's stories with the same flair, she said, and believed she wasn't creative enough to write novels—which was horseshit, I assured her. While I didn't doubt Gia had full confidence in her recollection of the events that unfolded that fateful summer, suffice it to say our memories . . . diverged. Whatever the parameters for "memoir" might be, I was pretty sure her book didn't fall within them. Of course, Noah was dead, and I wasn't going to say anything. So a memoir it was.

"What are you working on?" I asked now.

"I'm not sure yet," she said. "I'm kind of just writing things down as they happen. More like an elevated form of journaling than anything else, to be honest."

"I'm glad to hear that," I said. "But why now?"

"I told you, I'm poor," she said with a laugh.

"I don't know that writing books is really going to—"

"I know, I know. I'm joking. Or half-joking, you never know. At any rate, I promised Dad before he died that I'd start writing again, and I'm a bit bored here, so it seems like the right time. Anyway, it's fun being creative again. I've missed it."

"I can't wait to read it," I said.

"Thanks." The line was silent for a moment, and I could picture her sitting at the outdoor table of the house on Miteras with a sweating gin and tonic in her hand, her eyes focused on the sea below. "So . . . have you received something in the mail?"

"Something in a red envelope?"

"Are you coming?"

"I really want to," I said earnestly. "But you know how hard it is for me to take off work on short notice. Most people apply for leave a year in advance."

"Benny's coming."

My heart involuntarily swooned a little at the idea of a vacation with Benny, but I wouldn't allow myself to indulge that fantasy. There was a moment when our friendship might have evolved into something more, but that ship had sailed a long time ago.

"It's just a few days," she pressed. "I miss you."

"Me too. I'll do what I can."

As I hung up the phone, I felt the old familiar cocktail of emotions Gia always stirred up in me. Love for the friend who'd always been there for me and gratitude for everything her family had done for me, obligation due to both, frustration at her inability to see past the end of her own nose, and perhaps just a touch of envy for the freedom with which her circumstances allowed her to live.

But none of that changed anything. It wasn't that I didn't want to go to Sweden, it was that I couldn't.

GIA'S MANUSCRIPT

CHAPTER 1

THE LIGHT ON THE WATER IS DAZZLING THIS TIME OF DAY, AFTER-noon sun glinting and flaring like a fire of diamonds on the sea. If I stare at it long enough, I can almost feel the pricks of brilliance tickling my salt-crusted skin. The breeze that ruffles my loose cotton dress is like dragon's breath, the flagstones warm under my bare feet even beneath the shaded archways that run around the stark white house, which stands high on the hill looking across the bay toward the mountains of Naxos and Kampos that stud the horizon.

After two months on the island, my hair is long and perpetually tangled, shot through with highlights from the sun, my body sinewy and strong from swimming in the ocean daily, and the freckles that disappeared in the city smog have returned in a constellation across my nose. I'm bronzed as a local—which I suppose I am; I've got nowhere else to live—and healthy as when I was a child, deposited on the island with my brother for the summer months to be half-watched by girls too young and distracted to be of much help.

I feel like a child too, barefoot most of the time, physically ex-hausted by the end of the day, well rested and well fed. I've hired a girl from the village to cook and clean who doesn't speak a word of English. She's beautiful—she looks a little like me, to be honest, but softer and sweeter. The me I might have been if I'd had a wholesome upbringing on an island in Greece instead of shuttling from one boarding school to another while my father tried on women like hats and my mother progressively lost her grip on reality.

The girl's name is Aristea, and she's a wonderful cook.

She uses the cucumbers from our garden to make fresh tzatziki, grills whitefish and octopus and zucchini with a side of tart dolmas and slices of cold feta as thick as my finger with red onions and juicy tomatoes. I could drink the olive oil straight, and I use it in my hair too, just a bit to nourish the ends before a dip in the sea, leaving my dress in a pile on the hot sand and running into the bay naked as the day I was born.

The first few days I wore a swimsuit but it felt so unnatural, having a strip of wet fabric between my skin and the water when there's no one around. Anyway, I've never been a big believer in rules, and it's a long way down to the sea from the house where the workers I hired to fix up the place hammer away in the beating sun while my husband lazes on one of the many shaded porticoes reading Plato and Aristotle.

Husband. The word still feels strange in my mouth.

"What better time to revisit the classics," Garrett said shortly after we arrived, plucking a dusty leatherbound copy of *The Republic* from a shelf in the library. He's done it, too, and kept me apprised, sweeping a hand through his wavy blond hair as he waxes poetic about the meaning of justice over glasses of ouzo. His passion for Plato was so contagious I'd straddled him before he was half finished and we'd fucked like animals on the kitchen island, shattering a platter of roasted eggplant on the tile floor in our haste.

Everyone cautioned me not to get married so fast, warned me things would change once we were legally bound, but it's been three months now and I do still like to fuck my husband. I worry sometimes about how much I like to fuck him, and I wonder how long this honeymoon will last. What is it they say? For every beautiful woman, there's a man who's tired of screwing her. I swore I'd never be like my mother, looking the other way to preserve the peace. Though that's the least of the reasons I don't want to be like my mother.

But Garrett and I are not like my parents. We're like two parts of a whole; so in sync that sometimes I wonder if he can actually read my mind. I never knew what it was like to be loved—really loved for who I am—before Garrett. Sure, I'd had boyfriends, but none of them understood me the way Garrett does, appreciated me for my flaws, not despite them.

I know I'm a lot. *Too much,* some people say. But with Garrett, I don't have to make myself smaller.

Still, I notice things sometimes that make the back of my neck prickle. I see the way he eyes Aristea when she's bent over a pot, her skin glistening with the steam from the boiling water. I wonder if he thinks about her when he's inside me.

It doesn't matter. I think about her too. And Dimitrios, the builder I hired, who has a habit of shedding his shirt when it gets hot. My lust is indiscriminate. I think about my junior year history teacher and the guy down at the docks who sells fish, about exes and celebrities. It's the heat, I think. That, and all the sex I'm having.

Yes, I think marriage suits me.

I dip my toes into the pale blue infinity pool; it's early August and the water is as warm as bathwater. In the driveway on the far side of the house an engine fires to life and wheels crunch over gravel, signaling the end of the day for the workers. I toss my dress onto a lounger and dive in. Light flickers across my closed eyelids as I glide through the water, washing the salt from my skin and hair.

A lightness rises inside me.

If only I could float in this pool forever, staring up at the birds soaring in the cobalt sky. Ditch regret and anticipation, refrain from any thought of yesterdays and tomorrows, turn my back on the memories that gather like thunderheads on the horizon. But that's easier said than done, especially when your lion of a father has just died and left his entire fortune to charity.

Poor little rich girl.

I can't say I wasn't warned; his intention was never a secret. But it was hard to imagine that a man with as much life force as my father would ever actually die. In his last days, I asked him what I should do once he was gone, and he made me promise I'd pick up the pen again. So here we are.

Only it's not a pen—my handwriting is atrocious—it's a typewriter. The same vintage black machine that faithfully printed my words ten years ago sits on the desk at the end of the hallway upstairs, overlooking the sea. It's been taunting me ever since I arrived two months ago, inviting me to sit in the smooth wooden seat and rest my hands on its keys.

So I have begun committing my days to paper, hoping that a story will appear. This morning as I was typing, a ladybug landed on my finger. A sign of luck.

See, it's not all gloom and doom. My bank account may be rapidly dwindling but I have this property—Dad did give his fortune to charity, but not before taking care of all three of his wives and dividing his properties among his children—and his last wife has offered to buy the place at full price. Lord knows I've never liked Melodie, and I'm not excited to sell this house to her, even less excited about the caveat that I fix its myriad problems before the sale goes through. But push has come to shove.

After the roller coaster of the past few months, the stillness of the big house on tiny Miteras in the Cyclades islands is like walking out of a rock concert into the quiet night, ears still ringing. It was jarring at first; the sameness of every single day, blue sky over blue sea, dusty shrubs tumbling down to a rocky beach with coarse golden sand, protected from the wind by the mountains on either side.

The week we arrived, I was cleaning out a drawer in preparation for the move when I came across the handwritten bucket list Abby and I had made at eighteen, designed to turn us into interesting people with compelling lives:

- Learn to sail
- See the northern lights
- Get a tattoo
- Go on safari
- Fall in love
- Live abroad
- Swim with dolphins
- Write a book
- Make a difference in someone's life

To my knowledge, Abby hasn't completed any of the tasks, but I've been slowly working my way through each one. The book was the first thing, of course; I have tattoos on my rib cage, wrist, and ankle; and I am deeply in love with my new husband. I both swam with dolphins and learned to sail during the winter I spent in St. Barths. I asked Abby to join me, but she was focused on the LSAT. Nor did she join me on safari in South Africa—too busy studying for the bar exam.

Which is why ten years later, she's a successful attorney and I'm floundering around in Greece, preparing to sell the only thing I own so I won't go broke.

I haven't seen the northern lights or made a difference in anyone's life, but I've invited both Abby and Benny to spend my birthday with me in Sweden next month. I hope Abby recognizes the invitation as the olive branch I mean it to be. In deference to her, I haven't invited Garrett. It'll be just the three of us, like old times.

Though I haven't seen Abby regularly for years, I miss her terribly since we fell out. Most people look at us and wonder how the hell we're best friends, her so sensible and virtuous, me so impulsive and brash—but each of us is strong where the other is weak. Even though we live on different sides of the globe with very different lives now, every time we see each other it's as though not a day has passed.

I feel a spray of water across my face and open my eyes to see Garrett at the edge of the pool, evaluating me over the top of his aviators with a crooked grin that displays a dimple on one side. It's a boyish grin, mischievous and inviting, the kind of grin that makes men pass cigars and women drop their panties. Or vice versa. He's barefoot in faded blue shorts, his rumpled linen shirt unbuttoned to display his toned chest, a bottle of Mythos dangling from his hand. "Hello, gorgeous," he goads. He speaks English with a sexy British intonation, though his first language is Danish. "Putting on a show for the help?"

"They're gone," I say, flipping onto my stomach to swim to his feet.

"Not all of them." He cuts his eyes to the guesthouse a hundred yards down the slope, where I can just make out a dark head bent over a cactus.

"Which one is it?" I ask.

He sips his beer, his blue eyes flashing in the reflection off the water. "The young one with the Adonis body."

Dimitrios. Without a backward glance I place my hands on the side of the pool and push myself out of the water, rising to stand dripping naked before Garrett, my chin raised in defiance.

"You are a showoff, aren't you?" he asks.

It's true, I like to remind him how lucky he is to have me.

For a moment I think he might actually be jealous, before he cups my ass in his hand and kisses me deeply.

I bite his lip and push him back, relishing the feel of the wind drying the water on my skin as I stalk over to my dress and slip it over my head.

"Let's go into town."

He takes a swig of his beer. "I just got back from town. It's very hot."

"So we'll go to the harbor. What's the word on the permit for decommissioning the well?"

"Still in process," he says, shaking his head. "They couldn't tell me a damn thing about when it might come through. You sure you don't want to use the well to irrigate the olive grove? It would be so much cheaper than running another water line . . ."

I cross my arms across my chest, stopping him with my glare.

Closing the old well between the barn and the olive grove was at the top of my list from the moment I inherited the property, and we'd applied for a permit the first week we were here, but that didn't stop the contractor from going behind my back to try to persuade Garrett to recommission it.

"I know, the goats, I get it. But this isn't for drinking water—"

"Seven goats, Garrett. Dead within hours. And we're damn lucky it was goats. That could have been my entire family."

"Okay," he says, raising his hands. "I will continue to stalk the permits office. Shall we go to dinner?"

"Yes," I say, kissing him. "We shall."

ABBY

CHAPTER 2

THE MORNING OF MY FLIGHT TO SWEDEN ARRIVED HOT AND HUMID, the lingering summer almost tropical in its intensity. As I rushed from the dry cleaner's to the pharmacy to the post office in the sultry sun, it was hard to imagine that the highs in Sweden would only be in the fifties. I couldn't wait.

The month since Gia's invitation had flown by in a blur of late nights at the office as I worked to compensate for the days I would miss. I still couldn't quite believe my vacation time had been approved. Perhaps it was because my case that was supposed to go to trial had just settled; perhaps it was because I hadn't taken so much as a day off since I started at the firm three years ago. Or maybe someone in HR had simply pressed the wrong button. Regardless, I was going.

While I'd stayed in nice hotels with Gia before, I'd never been anywhere like the Two Pines Arctic Hotel, and I'd clicked through the pictures on the website so many times in the past few weeks I had them memorized. I imagined myself having a glass of cabernet in front of one of the gigantic fireplaces in the soaring wood and iron lobby; getting a much-needed massage in the luxurious spa; enjoying the mouthwatering offerings in the sexy cave-like restaurant, where a jazz band played on Saturdays.

And to be in such a place with Benny and Gia . . . it would be like old times, the three of us together again.

I'd known them more than half my life at this point, ever since my mom began working as the Torreses' chef when I was thirteen. She'd toiled in restaurant kitchens for most of my childhood, fighting her way up the chain in subpar dining establishments on the ragged edges of Los Angeles, never making quite enough to pay our bills. While she'd always done her best to hide from me how insecure our life was, I knew she didn't want to be pulling double shifts, leaving me home alone at the age of ten. Though I didn't remember my dad, I hated him for hitting the road with his band shortly after I was born, never to be seen again. When people asked me about him back then, I told them he was dead, though there was no evidence that was the case.

Things started to turn around for my mom and me when a friend of hers who worked as a private chef moved away and suggested my mom replace her. Everyone loved her upbeat, flexible personality as much as her healthy, flavorful meals, and as her client list grew, she was able to quit her restaurant jobs and move us into an apartment with air conditioning and a communal pool. But working for the Torreses was a whole different level. I felt like Cinderella at the ball when the two of us moved from the Inland Empire to take up residence in the guesthouse overlooking the sea on the Torreses' Montecito property, where Gia promptly befriended me, inviting me into her life with open arms.

We clicked immediately and in no time were more like sisters than friends, trading books, clothes, and secrets. The first year, she was in private school and I was in the local public school, but after Papa Hugo got to know me and became convinced I was a good influence on her, he sent us to boarding school together, with my mother's blessing. She wanted more for me, and so did I. I supposed

I did have my dad—or rather, his absence—to thank for my drive to succeed.

Benny was two years younger than Gia and me, but our personalities were similar, and we had a natural rapport, both of us introverted and even-keeled, content to read about drama or watch it on television rather than creating it in our own lives like Gia.

The three of us spent the summers at their property on the small island of Miteras, in the Cyclades, gleefully unsupervised. The summer after I graduated from high school, I had a job waiting tables at a tavern near the harbor to earn money for college—Papa Hugo was paying for my tuition and housing at Georgetown, but I needed to earn my own spending money—and I split my downtime between Gia and Benny as though they were my divorced parents. Benny and I holed up in the library reading through all the classics on the shelves, a book club of two, while Gia and I beach-hopped on their boat *Icarus Flies* and danced the night away at the one disco on the island.

It was hard to imagine now how carefree we'd all been then, blissfully unaware that summer would mark the end of our innocence. None of us were the same afterward, though I can say with certainty the fallout was hardest on me.

But I'd worked hard to be better, to be normal, not to lose my breath if I glimpsed a boy who looked like Noah, or conjure up a phantom pool of blood when I saw someone sleeping with their head just so. This would be the first time in a decade the three of us had been alone together, and I was excited to spend quality time with my friends, hopeful we could enjoy one another's company without the pall of the past hanging over us.

AT FOUR O'CLOCK, I BLEW into my building, elated that I'd finished everything I needed to do and would have time for a quick run before my nine-thirty flight. I stopped in the lobby to check my mail, tucking the stack under my arm as I asked the doorman to hold any packages until I returned in five days.

I hadn't spoken to Gia since the day I received her invitation, but we'd traded texts and voice messages, and I knew how thrilled she was that I'd agreed to come. She needed a break too, she said, and she knew Benny did as well. She insinuated he could use some time away from the girl he'd been seeing, but she didn't specify whether they were still together, and I didn't ask.

I had, however, finally caved and indulged in some light Instagram stalking the night before. Benny's account was private, and he obviously didn't keep up with it—his last picture was three weeks old and featured him in conversation with the director of the film he was working on behind the scenes at the Colosseum in Rome, with the caption "Can't believe we're shooting here. So surreal."

The previous picture was from two weeks before that, showing him shirtless on a beach, kicking a soccer ball. Though I'd been alone in my apartment, I'd felt embarrassed as I zoomed in on the picture, studying his toned physique. I hadn't seen him with his shirt off since long before those muscles had developed. It was true what they said: Gia's little brother had turned into a total thirst trap. Feeling suddenly like I'd just been handed a hot potato, I'd clicked off his page and tossed my phone onto my bed.

He and I hadn't spoken since I'd accepted Gia's invitation to Sweden either, though we'd traded text messages about logistics. He was flying through Amsterdam while I was flying through Stockholm, but we were both getting in to Kiruna around the same time, and he'd rented a car to drive us to the hotel, which was another hour outside the city. Gia would be on a later flight and had arranged a driver to take her to the hotel in time to meet us for dinner. Between the two of them, they'd taken care of everything; all I had to do was get on the plane.

In my light-filled apartment, I opened my email to check in for my flight, and my eye immediately went to a message that had just popped up from an account I didn't recognize, titled simply URGENT.

Assuming it was spam, I was about to delete it without opening when I noticed the preview line: *You're a liar.*

My blood ran cold as I clicked on the message.

But that was it. No attachments, no signature, no further information. Just a long email address containing letters and numbers, and those explosive words.

Was it blackmail?

I could count on one hand the number of lies I'd told in my life, and it wasn't hard to pinpoint which would be worth blackmail.

But the sender hadn't asked for anything.

I felt immediately claustrophobic, the walls of my carefully constructed life suddenly oppressive. I closed my eyes and practiced the box breathing method my therapist had taught me, forcefully slowing my heartbeat.

Perhaps it was nothing, a phishing scam. But as much as I wanted to believe that, my gut told me differently.

Who was this person, and what did they know? Was it simply a coincidence that this email had arrived the day I was to leave to meet Gia?

Suddenly I couldn't get out of my apartment—out of the country—fast enough. If whoever sent that email had somehow learned my secret, it stood to reason that person could also discover where I lived, where I worked, what my routine was. Screw going on a run, I decided. I'd go to the airport early.

GIA'S MANUSCRIPT

CHAPTER 2

Ammos restaurant is bustling this evening. The place is nothing posh—a simple open-air dining room overlooking the promenade lined with shops and restaurants that runs along the emerald water. Smaller boats drift in and out of the marina visible across the glinting inlet as seagulls call to one another overhead, while out on the sea the larger yachts wait for their human cargo, who shop in port or play at one of the island's spectacular beaches, ferried to and fro by tenders that skip over the tops of the waves.

Miteras is not big or fancy, but in recent years the island has become popular with the yachting set for just that reason, known for its "authentic" fishing village, unsullied golden beaches, and quaint windmills. The architecture is consistent with the rest of the Greek isles, boxy buildings with flat roofs painted white to reflect the heat, accentuated with bright blue doors. In the center of the promenade stands a stone statue of Io, the maiden turned to a cow when the goddess Hera caught her husband Zeus making love to her. According to local legend, Io stopped in Miteras as she was chased through

Greece by a gadfly, and the local sea nymphs took pity on her, giving her directions to Egypt, where she finally became human again.

The current of the past is strong here, the myths so tangled up in the real history that it's hard to separate fact from fable. Looking out at the sea, it's easy to imagine the ships of Agamemnon or Odysseus on the horizon, to conjure up Poseidon racing over the waves with his team of snow-white horses. Abby and I used to pretend to be Sirens, screeching into the wind as we flew over the water in *Icarus Flies*.

I wish she had come to visit this summer, but at least I'll see her in a month in Sweden for my birthday. If she agrees to come, that is. Surely she'll agree to come. I'll have to get Benny on the case. If anyone can persuade her, it's him.

This evening, Helios has finally guided his glowing chariot downhill to its resting place beneath the sea. Garrett and I are freshly showered and dressed in our uniform of white linen—mine a pristine sundress, his, long pants and a button-down, the sleeves rolled up to display his watch. I let my wet hair dry naturally on the trip down the hill on the back of the ATV so that it falls down my back in loose curls, and I'm wearing the gold necklace with a diamond key that Garrett gave me on our honeymoon.

He inhales my hair as he leans past me to open the door, ever the gentleman, and I playfully bite his warm neck, leaving a pink lipstick stain on his skin. "God, I love the smell of you," he says.

I always wear cologne, even when I'm alone. The smell of my signature scent *Gia* calms me and grounds me, helps remind me of who I am. It's a scent I created a few years ago when I toyed with the idea of producing a perfume. But in the end I fell so deeply in love with *Gia* that I didn't want to share it. I couldn't stand the idea of strange women walking around out there smelling like me. Now I'm the only woman in the world who wears it, my scent truly one of a kind, an intoxicating blend of orange blossom, vanilla, and musk.

"Ms. Torres, you are celebrity," the young maître d' says with a smile, pulling a magazine from beneath his stand. "It come yesterday," he says as he hands it to me.

It's the latest issue of *Luxe Life Mediterranean*. I excitedly flip to the table of contents and locate the For Sale section, flicking the pages until I land on a picture of me in a long white dress with Greek blue piping, standing barefoot by the fountain in front of the house, the sea visible in the background. I consented to the shoot hoping a more palatable buyer might come along before my deal with Melodie closed, but my accountant Leon has disabused me of that notion; the deal has been set in motion and there's not much I can do to stop it without incurring legal action on her part. Once the repairs are completed—or before, if she decides it should be sooner—the property is hers.

"My goddess," Garrett growls in my ear.

I remember how bright it was the day the photographer came, how worried I was that I'd look like I was squinting or frowning, but the shot is beautiful, the light catching in my hair and illuminating my eyes. I'd asked Garrett to pose with me, but he'd demurred. It was my home and my turn to shine, he said.

"Take it," the maître d' says. "We have more."

"Thank you," I say, tucking the magazine in my bag to read at home.

The low sun bounces off the glassware on the tabletops, coating the restaurant in its golden glow as the maître d' leads us to our usual table beneath the arch that looks over the brilliant sea. I feel the eyes of the men chomping on cigars, the women swilling fluorescent orange Aperol Spritzes, the children playing with their iPads beneath the tables. Everyone notices us, even if they pretend not to. We're a striking couple, and they like having us around. We laugh too loud and drink too much and get the grandmothers up and dancing to the traditional Greek music played by the man with the guitar, who raises a hand in salutation as we pass.

I allow Garrett to pull my chair out for me, and I sit, leaving my sunglasses on for a moment so that I can scan the crowd unobserved. It's a mostly older group this evening, a few families with teenage children whose eyes seek one another out when they look up from their devices, though sadly it never seems to be at the same moment.

I remember so clearly being that age, annoyed with my little brother, who engaged with adults as if he were one of them, and hating my parents, who sparred like boxers whenever they were together, clearly headed for divorce. Of course, once my mother went away, everything changed.

I was my most authentic self those summers after my parents split when Abby, Benny, and I were deposited on this island to fend for ourselves, before everything fractured the last year. Some things change you, cleaving your life into a before and after, and that summer was that for all of us. We each held it together differently afterward; Abby threw herself into her schooling, Benny into his writing, and once I'd exorcised my demons with the book, I threw myself into living, fully aware of how quickly it could all be over.

GARRETT AND I MET SHORTLY after my father's funeral, at a Clean the Beach event in Santa Barbara, hosted by one of the charities sponsored by the Torres Foundation. It wasn't a great place to host a Clean the Beach event, seeing as the beaches in Santa Barbara aren't terribly dirty, but the people who wanted to participate (i.e., donate) didn't want to visit a truly dirty beach.

The real beach cleaning wasn't done by the participants, of course, but by crews paid with the dollars pledged by the donors. My father had first tried simply having a regular charity event on the beach, no cleaning involved, but attendance was disappointing. There were so many charity events, all of them the same. But I knew this crowd; they didn't want to stand around and drink champagne and make small talk, they wanted to feel like they were getting their hands dirty, wanted to post pictures of errant Aquafina bottles on their Instagram with sad emojis and pleas to "Save the beach!" . . . and then drink champagne. So I suggested we let them do the "work" and give them a party at the swanky hotel across the street to celebrate themselves afterward. The event in the Hamptons went off so well that we added Palm Beach, Santa Monica, Santa Barbara, and San Francisco.

That day, the girls we'd hired to work the check-in booth hadn't shown up, so I was alone at the table, madly crossing off names in yellow highlighter as eco-conscious socialites checked their Rolexes, making plans to scrap the whole thing and go have brunch somewhere if this took much longer. I'd just dropped my gaze from the strikingly blue eyes of one Garrett Baker to cross his name off when a man's hand—tanned and golden-haired—reached over and took half the list from me. I opened my mouth to protest just as Garrett asked the sour-faced woman in front of me, "A through L or M through Z?"

"Tania Carlton," she said, and he grabbed a highlighter to cross her off the list. I warmed to him immediately.

"Garrett, what the hell?" a perfectly proportioned blonde demanded. "We have to clean the beach."

"She needs help," he responded, glancing up from the list only briefly. "I'll see you later."

I smiled to myself as the girl rolled her eyes and stomped away. Garrett gave me a shrug, then crossed the following person's name off the list, and we worked side by side for the next thirty minutes until the last of the participants had proceeded to the beach with their garbage bags.

"Thank you," I said, finally turning to face him. My stomach did a little flip as our eyes met. "I was drowning there."

"I could see that," he replied, his lips quirking into a smile. "I'm Garrett." Garrett wasn't my usual type—he was too gentlemanly, while I typically preferred rockers and surfers—but as his eyes caught on mine like magnets locking into place, I saw a glint of mischief beneath the surface of those clear blues, and I grew flushed.

"Gia," I introduced myself.

He offered me a garbage bag. "Wanna hit the beach?"

"Not really," I answered. "I had to put trash out there this morning so they'd have something to clean up."

He laughed. "You're joking."

"Sadly, no. You should probably rejoin your girlfriend, though. She didn't seem too happy."

He licked his lips, holding back a smile. "She's not my girlfriend."

"Does she know that?"

He nodded. "I travel too much to have a girlfriend. I'm only in town for a few days."

He was becoming more attractive by the second. "Work or pleasure?"

He held my gaze, his dimple deepening. "Work. But I take my pleasure where I can find it."

Yeah, there was something undeniably seductive about him. This was a man—yes, a man, I placed him somewhere in his midthirties—with secrets. And I loved a man with secrets. I suddenly felt lucky that the girls who were supposed to be working the check-in hadn't shown.

"What do you do?" I asked.

"My family's in shipping," he answered. "And you? Is this your job?"

It dawned on me then that he thought I was poor. That I was some young girl hired for fifteen dollars an hour to cross names off a list. I was thrilled. "Sort of," I answered, vague enough that I wasn't lying—I did in fact help with my father's charities. "Wanna get out of here?"

"Won't you be fired?"

I shrugged. I'd been there since seven. The event manager could handle it from here. "There's a house a few miles down with a private beach and I know the owners are out of town," I suggested.

He nodded. "We can take my car if you like."

His eyes caught on my YSL bag when I draped it over my shoulder and I laughed, glad I wasn't wearing any flashy jewelry. "They make great fakes these days." It was true, just not true of my bag.

I had him park the black Range Rover he'd rented at the base of the driveway of the house I grew up in, a sprawling Spanish Colonial mansion overlooking the Pacific. I was the only family member in town, and the maids and groundskeepers didn't work on Saturdays, but I slunk along the path that ran along the edge of the property behind the rosebushes all the same, just for show. When I arrived at the iron gate, I reached over the top to unlatch it and pushed it open, revealing the path that led down to our private cove.

Beaches in California can't technically be private, but our little slice of heaven was surrounded by cliffs, the only access point through the gate on our property, so it was as close to private as you could get.

Garrett's eyes danced. "You sure they're not home?"

I nodded, starting off across the sand toward the cabana nestled on a rocky shelf just off the sand. "And I know where they keep the towels."

I slid up the roller door, revealing the nautical-themed sitting room, complete with a television and air conditioning. "Beer?" I asked, opening the mini-fridge and taking out two local IPAs.

He nodded and I handed him one, then grabbed two oversize blue-and-white-striped beach towels from the shelf and headed onto the sand, placing the towels a few feet from the lapping waves. He cast an uncertain glance up toward the house as he unbuttoned his shirt, and I laughed. "Really, it's okay. Only thing is, I don't have a swimsuit." I took off my Clean the Beach T-shirt, revealing my sheer white mesh bra. "You don't mind?"

He watched me, amused. "No, I do not."

I stepped out of my shorts, glad I was wearing a matching thong. "I'm just gonna take a dip."

"In that ice bath?" He laughed. "You're crazy."

"That's what they tell me."

I threw my shirt at him as I ran into the frigid midnight-blue sea and dived beneath the surface, enjoying the shock of the cold water on my skin. I emerged refreshed and covered in goosebumps to find him propped on his elbows watching me stalk across the sand, his athletic chest gleaming in the sun.

"Aphrodite, born of sea-foam," he mused, looking up at me as I squeezed the excess water from my hair. "Created by the castrated cock of the sky god."

"What?" I guffawed. Garrett wasn't the first man who had compared me to Aphrodite, and I'd always had a soft spot for her—I even had a framed print of Botticelli's famous painting of the goddess hanging in my bathroom. I knew of her marriage to Hephaestus, the god of fire, her affair with Ares, the god of war, and her feud with Persephone over Adonis, but I had never heard anything about the castrated cock of the sky god. I definitely would have remembered that.

"The sky made love to the earth, creating Kronos, who promptly hacked off his dad's genitals and discarded them in the sea. *A white foam spread among them from the immortal flesh, and there rose a maiden, an awful and lovely goddess.*"

I tossed my head back in laughter. "'Awful and lovely,' I like that," I said, dropping to my knees on the towel beside him.

"Goddess," he said, his eyes roving down my body as I stretched out on my stomach and handed him the sunscreen, then reached around to unclasp my bra.

He rubbed the coconut-scented cream into my wet back slowly and sensually, his touch igniting a fire within me, then worked his way up my legs to my buttocks, his fingers slipping beneath the band of my thong as he massaged the lotion into my flesh.

When I couldn't stand it anymore, I rolled toward him onto my back, discarding my bra. "You should probably get the front of me as well."

He hovered just above me, his bare chest brushing mine as he caressed my breasts with the sunscreen, drawing circles with his fingers lower and lower until his hand was between my legs and I was panting, unbuttoning his shorts.

Yes, I had sex with my husband on the beach within three hours of meeting him. And for that I am not sorry.

"GIA," GARRETT SAYS, CALLING ME back to the present. "G and T?"

I look up to see the waiter hovering over us. "Yes, thank you."

"Where were you?" Garrett asks.

"I was just thinking about the day we met."

"When you convinced me you were just a poor girl, breaking into a cabana and stealing towels to make love to me on the beach?"

"I don't know that I'd call what we did that day *making love*," I tease.

"We're always making love," he growls into my hair.

"The look on your face when you came down from the cabana with that picture of me and my brother in your hand . . ." I laugh.

"I don't know how I didn't notice it before," he says. "It was huge."

I smile. "Because you were looking at me."

"I'm still looking at you, darling."

But he's not. He's looking past me.

GIA'S MANUSCRIPT

CHAPTER 3

I GLANCE OVER MY SHOULDER, FOLLOWING GARRETT'S GAZE TO THE good-looking couple threading their way through the restaurant, straight toward our table. Their faces are not familiar, but I feel like I know them. She's sun-kissed with long blond tresses, pillowy lips, and high cheekbones, clad in a sleeveless floral print dress that I recognize as Gucci because I have the same dress in my closet in green. Her other half is caramel-skinned with thick black hair swept off his high forehead, the collar on his pink polo popped, sunglasses slipping down his prominent nose.

A collection of Cartier Love bracelets jangles on her wrist and a giant pear-shaped diamond sparkles on her finger as she dumps her oversize Chloé sunglasses into her summer print Louis Vuitton shopper and slings it over the back of the chair at the table next to ours, accidentally knocking my seat in the process.

"Sorry," she says, flashing me a smile.

"No worries," I tell her. Garrett seems annoyed they've been seated so close to us, but I'm glad for the distraction.

"Can you please tell the waiter to send over two Aperol Spritzes as soon as possible?" she asks the maître d' before he departs. "We've had quite a day." She has an accent I can't quite place, perhaps Northern European or German.

I take a swig of my drink, refreshing and cold. "You guys new on the island?" I ask.

"We didn't even intend to come here," she says with a sigh. "Our boat is a piece of shit."

"Excuse my wife, she is very dramatic," the man apologizes, and I notice his diction is British—posh British. "The boat hasn't been used in a few years and is in need of some unexpected repairs."

"Nothing your father does is without strings," the wife says, waggling a finger manicured tastefully in the palest pink.

"This is true," the man agrees.

"I can understand that," I chime in. "My father just gave his entire fortune to charity, so . . ."

"My wife is also very dramatic," Garrett speaks up.

I give a little wave. "Hello, yes, I'm Gia, the dramatic wife."

"I'm Emelia," the woman echoes, "and this is my very undramatic husband, Timeo."

"Emelia," Garrett repeats, eyeing her in a not entirely friendly fashion. "And Timeo. I'm Garrett."

The waiter arrives with their drinks, and they raise them to us. "Cheers," Timeo says.

"I love your dress," Emelia says.

"Thanks." I smile. "I got it at this little shop in town."

"So what's the deal with your boat?" Garrett asks.

"My father got a new boat and gave me his old one," Timeo says.

"It's a thing he does," Emelia cuts in. "Giving Timmy his castoffs then acting like it's his fault for not being careful when they break." She eyes her husband. "It's like he thinks you're still sixteen, wrapping Ferraris around poles."

"That was only one, and I was very young and stupid," Timeo clarifies as Emelia draws deeply on her Aperol Spritz. "This boat is not terribly old, and we had it thoroughly inspected before we set sail, but they told us last night it's having engine trouble and will need repairs. Just bad luck. But we're very fortunate we were close to this island, where the boat can be fixed. So here we are."

While Miteras is only a few kilometers in diameter, the island's fishing tradition means there's a larger port beyond the small marina visible across the inlet, with skilled boat mechanics able to address the needs of the bigger boats that dock there.

"We were supposed to be meeting friends in Mykonos tomorrow," Emelia says, resigned.

"There's a ferry to Mykonos," I offer. "Well, not directly to Mykonos, but you can catch the interisland to Naxos, then the hydrofoil to Mykonos."

"Sounds delightful," she says dryly, then closes her eyes and shakes her head. "My apologies, I am letting a bad day get the best of me."

"Bottoms up," I instruct.

She obliges expertly, sucking down her drink in one long gulp, finishing with a sigh.

"Anyway, Miteras isn't such a terrible place to be stuck, I promise," I say. "We are known for some of the most mesmerizing beaches in all of the Cyclades."

"In that case, should we order a bottle of bubbly to celebrate?" she asks.

I shake my head. "The wine here is terrible, but the ouzo is delightful."

Timeo signals the waiter and orders a bottle of ouzo and we all put in orders for grilled octopus, merging our tables and adjusting our chairs so that we can talk more easily.

"What brings you two to the island?" Emelia asks.

I throw Garrett a glance before he can answer, letting him know with my eyes that I don't want to put on an act for these people. Our favorite game is fabricating wild stories about who we are and where we come from for strangers, but I like Emelia and Timeo, and it looks like they might be on the island for a while. I'd like them not to remain strangers. I could use a girlfriend, no matter how resistant Garrett seems to the disruption of our peace.

"I have a house here," I answer truthfully. "A family home. I'm readying it for sale."

"Why?" Timeo asks.

"My dad passed recently and there are a lot of properties that my brother and I now have to manage." Golden rule of the wealthy: Never let on when you're having financial trouble. "This one's a lot. It's over fifty hectares with horses and an olive grove . . . We're trying to simplify. I love the place but it's so remote, we don't spend enough time here."

"Where are you based?" Timeo asks.

Garrett and I exchange a glance. We haven't actually lived anywhere together but here. When we met, I was in New York and he was traveling so much that he'd put his things in storage and was staying in short-term furnished rentals. Once we married, we spent a month in London before heading to Greece. "Here, for now," I answer. "We've only been married a few months and we're still deciding where to settle."

"You look so familiar," Emelia says to me.

I used to get that a lot when my face was in the press more often. But that's the last thing I want to talk about tonight, so I simply shrug. "I don't think we've met."

"Maybe we have mutual friends. Where did you go to school?"

"America," I answer. "I did high school mostly at boarding schools in the Northeast, though there was a year in Northern California. Getting kicked out was kind of my hobby, so I bounced around a lot. What about you guys? Where are you based?"

"Mostly Zurich," Timeo says, "but I went to school at Harrow, so I spent a good deal of time in England, and we're in Dubai a lot because I have family there."

"How nice," I say. "You know I've never been to Dubai?"

"You have to go," Emelia says, her eyes lighting up. "It's incredible. The views, the restaurants, the shopping! It's unmatched. Really."

"Where did you grow up, Emelia?" I ask.

"Germany and Switzerland, though I did two years in England as well."

The waiter arrives with our bottle of ouzo and pours us each a glass. When he's gone, we raise our glasses, and this time I offer a toast. "To new friends."

THE SUN IS LONG GONE, as are the bottle of ouzo and all the other patrons of the restaurant, by the time we call the waiter over to settle the tab.

"Your friend has already taken care of it," the waiter says, indicating Timeo.

"Timeo!" I exclaim. "You didn't have to do that!"

"Really," Garrett adds. "You shouldn't have."

"It's fine," Timeo says, waving off our protests. "You turned our shit day around. It's the least I could do."

"Thank you," I say, coating my tongue with the last of the licorice-flavored alcohol in my glass.

"Where are you guys staying while you're in town?" Garrett asks.

"The only room we could find was at this little motel in the village." Emelia grimaces briefly, then covers with a smile. "It's fine. Hopefully the boat won't take too long to repair."

Timeo pulls out his phone and checks the screen, frowning.

"What is it?" Emelia asks.

"They told us they'd call when the room was ready, but they haven't."

Garrett checks his watch. "It's nearly eleven. Seems a bit late."

Timeo looks up the number for the hotel and puts the phone to his ear. "Yes, hello," he says into the phone. "This is Timeo Khan. We left our bags this afternoon, and you were going to call when our room was ready, but we haven't heard from you."

He frowns as he listens to the response on the other end of the line. "What do you mean, not available?" He meets Emelia's eye and shakes his head, his face tense. "You said we'd have a room . . . I understand, but as I told you earlier, we don't have anywhere else to stay . . . Look, we're willing to pay double, triple . . ." He closes his eyes and rubs his temple. "Yours is the only hotel on the island that has any availability. We would have taken a ferry to another island if you'd told me this in the afternoon, but now . . ."

He covers the phone with his hand. "They gave away the room," he whispers to Emelia. "She says she tried to call."

"I didn't get a call," Emelia says, checking her phone.

Timeo turns his attention back to the phone call, frustrated. "You're putting me in a very bad position right now . . . One moment."

He turns to Emelia. "She's offering us cots in the manager's office."

Her mouth forms a small o of disbelief before she nods, trying to stay upbeat. "Well, okay, then. I guess that's what we're doing. It'll be like camping."

I appreciate her spirit of adventure, but it doesn't sit right with me that she's forcing optimism about what we all know will be a terrible night of sleep, while I have a comfortable house with plenty of available beds simply going to waste. "No, no, no," I butt in, shaking my head. "You'll come stay with us."

"We couldn't possibly," Timeo demurs.

"Don't be absurd," I insist. "I know we just met, but I promise we're not axe murderers."

This elicits a laugh from Timeo, who murmurs, "Wouldn't that be something?"

"Really," I go on, "you're both so lovely, and I haven't had this much fun in weeks—no offense, darling." I squeeze Garrett's hand. "We have five bedrooms and we're only using one. You're our friends now, and friends take care of friends. Right, Garrett?"

Garrett nods, though I can tell he's less enthusiastic than I am. But my father always taught me generosity was a virtue. And really, what's one night of hospitality?

Timeo and Emelia trade a glance. "Perhaps just one night," Emelia says. "We don't want to impose."

"Really, it's no imposition," I promise.

Timeo and Emelia again look at each other, and he shrugs. "All right, if you insist."

"Then it's settled!" I clap my hands. "Let's go get those bags!"

ABBY

CHAPTER 3

ON THE PLANE TO STOCKHOLM, I FOUND IT HARD TO SLEEP, MY anxiety ratcheting up the moment I closed my eyes, the words of the email ricocheting around my brain like gunfire.

Who had sent it, and what did they want?

By the time my connecting flight landed in Kiruna at just after two in the afternoon, I was a wreck. I shivered in my jeans and T-shirt, pulling on my jacket as I hurried down the airstair and into the red-sided building to collect my bag.

Not two minutes had passed at the baggage claim before I heard my name and turned my attention from the conveyor belt to see Benny in jeans and a pullover hoodie, dragging a beat-up roller bag behind him.

He was tan and fit, his thick, wavy hair mussed, and he had a five o'clock shadow I hadn't seen before. He grinned when he saw me and dropped his bag to embrace me, squeezing me so tight I could feel his voice reverberating in his chest as he told me how glad he was to see me. "I think you're shrinking," he teased, setting his chin on top of my head.

I'd never been very big, topping out at five foot three, which made his wiry five-foot-ten frame seem tall. He pulled back and held me at arm's length, his eyes warm as they caught mine. "You look great. It's nice to see you. Really nice."

"Nice use of adjectives, great writer."

His smile widened. "What can I say, I'm rendered speechless by your presence."

"More like inarticulate," I specified.

"Dumbstruck."

I smiled. "It's nice to see you too. And you also look great."

It was almost laughable now, to think of how infatuated he'd been with me that summer in Greece when I was eighteen and he was sixteen. He was just a puppy then, earnest and not quite grown into himself. Sometimes on long hot afternoons when we were holed up in the arctic cool of the library of the Miteras house at opposite ends of the leather couch, engaged in philosophical conversations about the books we were reading, I would see flashes of the man inside the boy and experience confusing pangs of attraction to him. But he was my best friend's brother, not to mention too young for me.

One such afternoon, we were standing shoulder to shoulder in front of the bookcase debating which book to read next when he looked over at me—or down at me, he was already a head taller—and something about the way the light glanced off his cheekbones combined with the tenderness of his gaze ignited one of those inconvenient flares of yearning within me. He must have seen it because he stopped midsentence and kissed me.

It wasn't awkward or clumsy, as I had imagined, but soft and sweet and surprisingly sexy. Shocked by the rush of desire that came over me, I pulled away immediately. "Benny, I can't," I whispered.

He didn't drop his gaze, the passion in his eyes weakening my resistance. "I love you," he said.

"You're sixteen," I returned.

"My parents are seventeen years apart," he said, threading his long fingers through mine.

"I don't want to ruin our friendship," I said.

"It's more than friendship," he said. "I love you."

I felt the tug toward him, the temptation to let myself be loved. But I felt it would be a mistake in the long run. "I'm going to college in the fall, and you'll meet other girls—"

"I don't want them," he said. "I want you."

"Maybe when we're older," I said gently, disentangling my fingers from his. I took a breath, rebuilding the invisible wall between us. "For now, all I want is to be friends, and I have to ask you to respect that."

He nodded, understanding. "Of course. Just know, when you're ready, I'll be here."

I often wondered what would have happened if I'd let Benny love me that day instead of shutting him down. How differently things might have turned out if the following week I'd stayed home with him instead of going to the full moon party with Gia. Little did I know how costly the consequences of that choice would be; how heavy the weight of regret for every stupid decision I made the night of Bacchanalia. But the past couldn't be changed no matter how much I wished it could.

While we remained friends, Benny, Gia, and I were never quite as close after that summer, our feelings too big and complicated for our young minds to process. I moved to the East Coast to attend college while Gia took a year off to write and Benny went back to boarding school outside San Francisco. Their mother, Caroline, had been institutionalized by then, and there was no one left in Montecito for my mom to cook for, so she followed me to D.C., taking a job working for a family in Bethesda, a quick twenty-minute drive from me at Georgetown.

Over the years, Benny grew into the man I knew he'd become—handsome and clever and successful—and never mentioned our kiss again. It was as I'd predicted: He met girls at school, at work, in restaurants and bars, on planes, online, on set. I was sure he was glad I'd had the foresight to stop our ill-fated romance before it began.

Still, looking at him now, I couldn't deny I felt the sting of regret for what might have been.

Out of the corner of my eye I saw my bag slide down the chute. "My bag—" I started for it, but Benny beat me to it, lifting it easily from the belt. "Thanks."

As we rolled our suitcases past the customs agents and out the automatic doors into the chilly afternoon, I felt happy for one heedless moment, until I felt my phone buzz in my pocket. I stopped in my tracks, raising it with a racing heart to read the urgent notification on the screen.

GIA'S MANUSCRIPT

CHAPTER 4

IN THE MORNING, I AWAKE TO SEE GARRETT SITTING ON THE CHAIR BY the window, putting on a pair of work boots I've never seen. I rub my eyes, sleepy. "Where are you going?"

I don't recognize the T-shirt he's wearing, either. It's boxy and made of thick fabric, emblazoned with the name of a bar on Naxos. He must have found it in a drawer somewhere. It's not the kind of thing he wears, and paired with his oldest jeans and those boots, he looks like a different person. He looks like his father.

"To the old well."

I push up to sitting. "What? Why?"

"They're evaluating it to see whether it can be reopened for irrigation of the olive grove."

I frown. "But we're closing it as soon as we get the permits."

"I know. But the permits to decommission it still haven't come through, and neither have the permits to build a new one. From what I hear from the workers, those permits can take years to be approved."

"Years?"

"Yes, years," he confirms, bending to tie his boot laces. "And without some source of water, we can't complete the irrigation project for the olive grove, which not only means we may lose some of the trees, but we also can't complete the sale to Melodie. So right now you should really be hoping it works so we don't have to dig another well. It could save us a lot of money."

"It won't work," I say, getting out of bed and going to the closet. "It's a waste of time."

"How do you know?" he asks.

"It's contaminated." I pull on a pair of jean shorts, my throat tight. "I told you about the goats." He crosses his arms as I step into my dusty riding boots. "I'm coming with you."

"When was the thing with the goats?"

"Twenty years ago," I say, rising to face him. "When I was a child. But once a well is contaminated, it's done. I don't know why my dad didn't close it properly a long time ago."

Garrett nods, considering.

"This is why everything needs to go through me," I continue, marching for the door. "I have history with this place."

"Well, you better cough it all up," he says. "Because we're about to sell, and we can't have any surprises killing the deal."

Tears spring to my eyes. "What do you think I'm trying to do?"

"Hey, hey," Garrett says, wrapping me up in his arms. "I'm sorry. I'm on your side." I lean into him, and he kisses the top of my head. "Let's go meet the contractor and hear what he has to say. Then we can tell him no."

"Okay," I reluctantly acquiesce.

The cicadas drown out any chance of conversation as we trudge along the washed-out gravel road that leads up and over the hill from the house, the leather of my boots rubbing against my sweating shins. The day is already so blisteringly hot that the air burns as it goes down my throat, leaving me immediately parched.

As we crest the hill, the olive grove spreads over the rolling knoll before us, the horses standing still as statues beneath the silvery-leaved trees. A hawk soars overhead, buoyed on the breeze as it hunts for unsuspecting prey. The shade is a welcome respite as we follow the dusty road through the grove and past the barn, but I turn off before it reaches the caretaker's cottage.

"It's this way," I say, locating the overgrown path beyond a jumble of rusted-out farm equipment.

The wind whips my hair into my face and dry brush scratches my bare legs as we follow the trail to the flattened clearing where the old well rises from the ground. The stone cylinder is about four feet in diameter and perhaps three feet tall, the last relic of the village that once stood where the olive grove is now. Pieces of the rocks that made up foundations still pockmark this side of the estate, jutting up between the olive trees like partially submerged shipwrecks.

Legend has it that sometime during the late nineteenth century, a young woman set the village on fire in the middle of the night after she found out her husband was cheating on her with her sister, killing everyone in the town, then threw herself down the well. The story scared me to death when I was a child. I used to lie awake nights thinking of the ghosts wandering our land. After the goats died, I started making gifts to the woman in the well so that she would leave my family alone: flowers, fish, beads. I wasn't sure I even believed in ghosts, but it seemed a small sacrifice to placate a restless spirit.

The summer I was eighteen, I decided all that was silly; I was an adult and would no longer indulge in childish superstitions. I made no more gifts to the woman in the well; no sprays of bougainvillea, no half-drunk bottles of wine, no broken necklaces or unmatched earrings.

Was it a coincidence that Noah became obsessed with me that summer? That he found his way into my guesthouse like a man possessed and assaulted my best friend?

And why Abby? It's always bothered me. The toxicology report found large amounts of drugs and alcohol in his system, but could he really have been so fucked up he mistook pint-size Abby with her light hair for me? It didn't seem likely.

I know it's not possible that the woman in the well could have possessed Noah. But still, late at night, I think about it.

I shade my eyes against the beating sun as Garrett and I enter the clearing to find three sweating construction workers gathered around the well, its heavy metal cover resting against its wall. Even in this heat, the sight of the stone shaft sends a chill up my spine.

As we approach, I notice a scorpion crawling out from under an overturned stone at the base of the well. "Careful," I say, pointing.

One of the men scoops the scorpion up with his shovel and tosses it into the long grass.

"What are you guys doing?" I ask.

"We investigate if the well has water we can use," volunteers their leader, Yiannis, a scruffy, bearded man with graying hair. His eyes shift to Garrett. "Your husband agree."

The wood-framed pulley system is long gone, but I notice one of the men is steadily pulling a long rope that's coiled in the dry shale at his feet, the other end of it dropped into the depths of the well.

"I don't want to use this well."

"If the well work, you save much money," Yiannis says.

"I don't care," I say. "I don't want to use this well."

Yiannis looks to Garrett as though expecting him to overrule his foolish wife.

"The water was responsible for the death of some goats they had," Garrett says.

"The water is for trees, no animals," Yiannis says.

"I don't care," I say. "What if our caretaker's dogs drink from puddles, or the runoff gets into our drinking water? It's not safe."

The man pulling the rope cries out as the blue plastic bucket at the end of it reappears over the lip of the well. He hoists it onto the ground and we all converge around it to see it's full of clear water.

"See?" Yiannis asks, mopping the sweat from his brow with a dirty rag. "Is good. We install pump at bottom, connect to irrigation system."

I cross my arms over my chest. "Do you know the story of this well?" I ask, hoping his superstition is as strong as that of some of the other older Greek islanders I've met over the years.

He shakes his head.

His face changes as I recount the legend, his eyes searching for signs I'm telling the truth.

"It's all true," I say. "Ask anyone who knows anything about this island. To pump water from this well is to desecrate her grave."

He again looks to Garrett.

"What she says goes," Garrett says with a shrug.

"This is my property," I say, forcing Yiannis to look at me, not my husband. "From here on out, when you need something, you come to me directly. Understand?"

Yiannis nods.

"We'll let you know when the permits have come to close it up," Garrett says, slapping him on the shoulder. "Thanks, man."

Garrett laces his fingers through mine as we walk away, his thumb stroking my palm.

"I know it may seem silly," I say when we're out of earshot. "But after the things that have happened here, I just . . . I'm not taking any chances."

"I understand," he says, stopping to face me. "You've been through a lot."

He kisses me, his lips salty, and I make a mental note to throw a good bottle of wine down the well later today. I'm not taking any chances.

"DAUGHTER OF THE LATE HUGO Torres, Gia Highsmith Torres has the same charisma and quick wit her father was known for."

Garrett's eyes dance with mirth as he reads from the magazine at the head of the outdoor dining table, gesturing so wildly with his Bellini that it splashes onto the stone.

It's eleven in the morning and we've had nothing to eat but have already finished one bottle of champagne—the island may have terrible wine, but my father's cellar is nothing to scoff at—and are halfway through our second, our Bellinis becoming more champagne and less peach juice as the day warms up.

Emelia raises her glass. "To charisma and quick wit!"

"The article was supposed to be about the property," I start, lifting my hair off my sweating neck and twisting it into a bun atop my head.

"But the writer obviously fell in love with you," Garrett says dryly. "No surprise. Everyone falls in love with my wife."

I laugh. It's true, the article is very flattering, and the pictures they printed of the property are gorgeous. It's a little embarrassing, though, how they have me in every shot. If I'd known that that was their intention, I would have worn more than one dress.

At the bottom of the hill, the sea glints in the tireless sun while a hot, dry breeze tinkles the wind chime. "Who wants to go down to the beach before the sand becomes lava?" I ask.

Garrett's cellphone rings, and his face drops when he sees the number. "Excuse me, this is work," he says, putting the phone to his ear as he walks away.

"I need to call the marine mechanic and start looking for some kind of house rental," Timeo says.

"Stay another night, it's fine," I say, topping off my champagne.

"Are you sure?" he asks, casting a glance at Garrett's back.

"We're glad to have you," I assure him. I may be a little buzzed, but it's true. Timeo and Emelia are fun, and we've had hardly any social life all summer.

"It would be helpful," Timeo says. "We're not sure how long the boat's going to take, so it's hard to know how long we'll need to book a holiday house."

"Give yourself some breathing room," I encourage.

"Thank you," he says.

Emelia throws her arms around me from behind. "Yes, thank you. I'm so glad we met."

"Me too," I say, giving her a peck on the cheek as Timeo heads inside. "Come on, I'll show you around." I refill her glass and rise, sweeping my arm out at the pool and the ocean beyond. "This is the pool, down there is the boathouse."

She squints at Kampos, the island across the bay. It's clear enough today that you can see the turrets of the abandoned development glimmering between the mountains that rise from the sea. "What's over there?" she asks. "The spikes."

"The Palaces at Kampos," I say. "It was a development that was abandoned when it went bankrupt years ago. There have gotta be hundreds of little identical castles over there in different stages of completion. It's super eerie."

"And it's just abandoned? No one lives there at all?"

I nod. "Only the model home ever had electricity or running water. The whole island is pretty desolate. There are some nice beaches, though."

"Nice beaches everywhere around here," she agrees. "That's what's so great about traveling by boat."

"We have a boat," I say. "A speedboat. We'll take it out later, you'll like it."

I point past the pool about fifty meters down the hill where three shirtless men are stacking marble outside what is to be the renovated guesthouse. "Down there, they're in the process of modernizing the kitchen in the guesthouse."

As we watch, Dimitrios rises, hefting a slab of marble that swells his muscles as he carries it up the hill.

"Jesus," Emelia mutters under her breath. "I'd like a piece of that cake."

"Dimitrios," I call, waving my arm overhead.

Emelia sucks through her teeth as he sets the slab of marble next to the others and saunters up the hill toward us, his tanned skin glinting in the sun. My husband is handsome but there's something raw about Dimitrios, something that makes me want to taste his sweat. Obviously Emelia feels it too.

"Does the boat have gas in it?" I ask as he approaches.

I know it does, but I wanted Emelia to experience him up close, to smell the tang of him, see the line of dark hair running from his belly button down his flat stomach, feel the pull of his pheromones.

He nods. "I fill it the day before."

The fact that his English isn't great only adds to his allure. "Yesterday?" I ask.

He nods, his eyes catching mine for just a moment too long, and I can't help but imagine all the things I might do with him if I weren't a married woman.

"This is Emelia," I say. "She and her husband Timeo are staying here for a while."

His dark eyes take her in as his tongue flicks out to lick his thick lips. "Dimitrios."

She nods, extending her hand.

"The dirt," he says, referring to his hands.

"I don't mind," she answers, never dropping her gaze. He grips her hand gingerly, her skin pale and delicate in his dust-covered paw. "Nice to meet you, Dimitrios."

"Dimitrios has been kind enough to help me with a few extra things around here, like the boat and the four-wheelers," I say, smiling at him. "My husband is useless as a mechanic. I might have to pay you to teach me a thing or two, Dimitrios."

"Okay." He looks back toward the guesthouse.

"Don't want to keep you," I say. "I know you have a lot to do."

He nods at us, then trots off down the hill to rejoin the others. Emelia sips her champagne, watching him go. "Pay him to teach you a thing or two," Emelia teases under her breath.

"About mechanics." I smile innocently, and she laughs.

"I'd love for him to teach me a thing or two about . . . mechanics," she says suggestively, reaching out to pluck a spray of fuchsia flowers from a nearby bougainvillea bush. "Ouch," she cries, pulling her hand away to show me a spot of blood blooming from her finger.

"Careful," I warn her. "They have bigger thorns than roses."

She sucks on her finger as I lead her beneath the archways that surround the house and through the French doors into the great room. Like the exterior of the home, the walls inside are white and the floor is stone, softened with woven rugs. Between the fireplace and the wall of windows overlooking the sea, a giant white sectional couch surrounds a glass coffee table featuring a vase of wildflowers. "The great room," I say. "And you saw the kitchen this morning."

I gesture to my right, where the stone and wood kitchen centers on a large island and a breakfast bar separates the cooking area from the farmhouse dining room, which opens to the covered poolside table where we were just having our liquid breakfast. I lead her to the opposite side of the great room, up two steps and through the arched doorway to the master suite. "This is the sitting room," I say, passing the white couch looking out toward the pool to reach the door to my bedroom. "And this is the master." I press open the door, revealing the heavy wooden king-size bed facing the giant windows that look out over the guesthouse to the ocean.

"It's beautiful," Emelia gushes, just as the bathroom door opens and Garrett enters, stark naked.

The three of us freeze for a moment before Garrett shakes his head with a slight smile, cool as a cucumber. "If you ladies don't mind, I'm going to put on my swim trunks."

"Sorry, honey," I say, ushering Emelia from the room.

Once the master door has closed behind us, she catches my eye and we collapse in giggles. I pull her through the door of the library so he doesn't hear us. The room is a shift from the rest of the house, red Turkish rug and dark wood shelves lined with first editions, illuminated only by the one window above the leather couch, an oil painting my mother did of my father mounted on the wall above the antique secretarial desk. "Well, he may not be much of a mechanic, but from the looks of him, he's good at other things," Emelia titters.

"Oh my God, were you ogling my husband's dick?" I snort.

"I mean, we have to acknowledge the elephant in the room."

"Shit." I grip her arm, laughing so hard my champagne spills onto the rug as tears stream down my cheeks. "I have to stop laughing before he hears us."

"I don't think he'd mind," she says, changing her expression to imitate his. "*If you ladies don't mind, I'm going to put on my swim trunks.* I see now where he gets his confidence."

I wipe my eyes and take deep breaths, forcibly controlling my laughter. "Now I'm just going to have to catch your husband with his pants down so we'll be even."

She sighs. "Not nearly as exciting as yours, I'm afraid." She trails her fingers over a row of books, plucking a first edition Hemingway from the shelf. "But then, I didn't marry him for his dick."

"How sweet," I say, downing the last of my champagne.

She shrugs. "I was a virgin when we married, I didn't know the difference. But he spoiled me rotten. I knew I liked that."

"You can't have been married long," I say. "You're so young."

"Four years," she says. "How about you guys?"

"Three months," I answer.

She raises her brows. "This really is your honeymoon. Enjoy it." She smirks. "*All* of it."

"Believe me, I do."

She snickers. "How often do you have sex? If you don't mind my asking."

"I don't mind," I say. And I don't. Some people might be put off by her frankness about sex when we've only known each other less than twenty-four hours, but I find it refreshing. Also, we're both a little drunk and she's just seen my husband's dick. "Pretty much every day," I answer. "Sometimes more than once. We're both very sexual people."

"That must be nice," she says dreamily, but as she looks away, I see something that looks like pain cross her face.

"What about you guys?"

She puts the book back on the shelf and leans on the arm of the couch. "I try to get him interested, but most of the time he's too tired, or too stressed, or his stomach hurts, or he's not in the mood."

"I'm so sorry," I say.

She shrugs. "Makes it hard to get pregnant."

"You want to have a baby?"

She nods. "I've always wanted children. What about you?"

I shake my head. "I don't know. Not yet. My own parents weren't exactly cut out for it, so . . ."

"What do you mean?"

"Oh, nothing terrible. Just my dad was never around, and my mom—well, she struggled with mental illness. She's in a sanatorium now."

"I'm so sorry," Emelia says, her blue eyes full of concern.

"It's fine." I wave it off. "I just want to make sure I'm up to the task before I become a mom, you know?" I pause. "You saw the upstairs last night, right?"

She nods. It had been late by the time we collected Emelia and Timeo's bags from their hotel and returned to the house, so I'd shown them to the stairs and told them to choose whichever of the four upstairs bedrooms they liked. "Which room did you choose?"

"The big one on the end, facing the sea."

"I used to stay in that one when I was a kid," I say. "It's right above the master with an even better view. I'm gonna check on lunch. Are you hungry?"

"I'll eat whenever you want, but I should find Timeo and see what the boat mechanic said."

She pauses on her way out, her gaze landing on the glass case displayed on a shelf beside the door. Inside is an antique revolver. "What's that?" she asks.

"It belonged to my great-grandfather."

"Does it work?"

"I don't know. It doesn't have any bullets in it."

She shivers. "I hate guns."

She opens the door, heading for the stairs as I cut across the great room toward the kitchen. I feel sorry for the poor girl. To be married to someone who won't have sex with you . . . I can't even imagine how crushing that must be.

The sound of voices in the kitchen stops me before I reach the archway that leads into the kitchen. I stand out of sight, listening to Garrett teaching Aristea English.

"Tomato," he says. "Toh-mah-toh."

"Tomato," she repeats.

"Or, as Americans say, toh-*may*-toh."

She giggles. "Toh-*may*-toh."

"Very good," he says. "Knife."

"Knife," she says, laughing, though I can't see what about.

"Sharp," he says.

"Sharp," she repeats.

I start for the kitchen again but draw up in the doorway when I see the two of them face-to-face, the knife held in his hand between them as he watches her run her finger down the blade. "Sharp," she whispers.

"How's lunch coming?" I ask loudly, breaking up the moment.

She starts, cutting her finger on the blade.

"Sharp," I say coolly, before turning my attention to Garrett. "Why don't you fetch her a Band-Aid, love?"

Garrett's eyes catch mine and he runs his tongue over his bottom lip, roguish. Almost as though he wanted to be caught flirting with Aristea. In fact, I'm nearly sure he did. Games are his way of saying *I love you.* He opens a drawer and sets a pack of Band-Aids on the counter, then grabs my hand and pulls me to him, planting his lips on mine as Aristea busies herself applying a Band-Aid to her bloody finger.

He likes to keep me on my toes, pushing the envelope just enough that the voltage between us remains high. I didn't know it was what I needed until I met him, but he had me figured out from the beginning. His ploys would likely make most girls feel insecure or threatened, but they make me feel special, kindling for the blaze that burns between us.

But that evening after dinner, Garrett begs off when I invite him into the shower with me, and I start to second-guess myself. Is this part of his scheme, or is he losing interest already? My heart beats faster as I picture him with Aristea in the kitchen this afternoon, the blade of the knife between them catching in the light through the windows.

She is very young, and very pretty.

I was okay with him looking at her when it was us appreciating her beauty together. It was a tease, innocuous, like my flirtation with Dimitrios. But what he'd been doing in the kitchen today was his alone. His and hers. I'd assumed the performance was for me, but perhaps I've become overconfident. After all, I was nowhere in the picture until I walked in unexpectedly.

I cut the water and wrap myself in a towel, strategizing. I need to turn the tables.

In the bedroom, I find Garrett reading in bed with the windows open to the night air. I shed the towel, enjoying the breeze against my damp skin as I pull the covers back and climb onto the bed. It's not genius, but it's reliable. "Gia," he protests.

"Shh." I pull down his boxer briefs and take him in my mouth, doing all the things I know he likes until he puts the book down with a groan and pulls me on top of him.

Our property is large enough that we don't have any neighbors, so we've grown accustomed to not bothering to turn off the lights or close the windows, but tonight Garrett reaches for the light switch as I straddle him. "Timeo and Emelia went to look at stars down by the water," he says.

"Leave it on," I say, stopping him. "They're not having sex, maybe he could use some inspiration."

"That's too bad," he says, running his hands up my back.

"I saw the way you were looking at Aristea in the kitchen today," I say, thrusting my pelvis hard against his. "You wanted to fuck her."

"It was just a flirtation," he says with a flicker of a smile that tells me my jealousy was unwarranted.

I lean over him, dangling my breasts in his face as I ask, "Do you want to invite her into bed with us?"

I can guess his answer when the question pushes him over the edge.

GIA'S MANUSCRIPT

CHAPTER 5

I DIDN'T MEAN IT, WHAT I SAID LAST NIGHT ABOUT INVITING ARISTEA INTO bed with us. It's not that I'm a prude or I don't find her sexy—as anyone who read my first book knows, I've always been fairly adventurous, and while I'm partial to men, I don't discriminate. I enjoyed my fair share of women before Garrett, and Aristea is a woman I'm certain I would enjoy. Sleepy-eyed and sensual, comfortable in her own skin.

In fact, she reminds me of the girl Garrett and I had a memorable threesome with in Ibiza during the first month we were together. I wouldn't have chosen to bring someone else into bed with us, but when he suggested it, I felt challenged to show him I was as adventurous and open-minded as I'd claimed to be. It took some mental gymnastics to let go of the jealousy I felt watching him with her, but I got through it, and in the end it made us stronger.

But she was a one-off, someone we'll never see again. Aristea is a different story.

I was relieved when Garrett murmured after we finally turned out the light, "We can't fuck the help. Then who would cook for us and make our beds?"

I smiled in the dark, gratified that my strategy had worked. It had been a risk, but I'd defused the situation and taken the power back by placing myself in the center of his fantasies about Aristea. The idea of Aristea in bed was no longer his, but ours.

I can tell she admires us. We're kind to her, and she always seems a little dazzled by us. Even our fights are spectacular. Though she likely didn't enjoy picking up the shards of cocktail glass Garrett smashed against the wall a couple of weeks ago when I suggested to him that if his business needed this much bailing out, perhaps he should find a different line of work.

As the words left my mouth, a darkness I'd never seen before had passed over him like storm clouds appearing suddenly on the horizon.

For a moment, he looked so startlingly like Noah I had to blink to make sure I wasn't hallucinating. The same blond hair and blue eyes, the same angry vein pulsing in the center of his forehead as his handsome face turned ugly with rage.

"What do you know?" he snarled. "You've never worked a day in your life."

"I'm a writer," I reminded him.

Garrett had the gall to laugh in my face. "You've written one book, ten years ago." Clearly the tequila we'd been drinking all afternoon had made him mean, the same way it had transformed Noah all those years ago.

But this was Garrett, my husband who loved me, I reminded myself. I wouldn't cower; my past trauma would not dictate my future.

"So far," I returned, raising my chin.

"You've monetized your misfortune, I'll give you that," he scoffed, rattling the ice in his nearly empty cocktail glass. "But to be a success requires a work ethic, which I think we both know you don't possess."

I was shocked. He'd never spoken to me that way before, never been anything other than kind and complimentary—flattering, even.

"Says the man who spent the past three weeks reading Plato," I snapped. "Perhaps if you spent as much time tending to your business as you did lazing around my house, you wouldn't need another bailout."

His eyes turned from light to dark blue before he hurled the glass into the wall, scattering a sad display of ice, glass, and tequila across the floor, then roared into town on one of the ATVs.

He was repentant when he returned around midnight. He hadn't meant any of it, he swore. He was sensitive, and I'd hurt his feelings, so he'd lashed out. He smelled like cigarettes and beer and perhaps just a hint of cheap perfume as he held on to me like he was drowning, begging for forgiveness until I finally caved.

"We had our first fight," he murmured as he trailed kisses down my stomach. "And I love you even more."

I haven't told him yet that I'm writing again. After his harsh words about my work ethic, I've wanted to wait until I'm further along to prove him wrong, so I've chosen the moments he's out of the house to sit clacking away on the typewriter. I'll have to tell him soon enough, though. Emelia found me out yesterday—the keys are so damn loud it's impossible to keep it from anyone in the house—and it's better I tell him than someone else.

AS USUAL, I'M THE FIRST to rise this morning, early enough that Aristea hasn't arrived yet. I throw on a cotton dress, quietly closing the door to the master as I exit, phone in hand. I pad across the sun-drenched great room to the spotless kitchen, the stone floor cool against my bare feet as I stand before the brass espresso machine, watching the dark brown liquid drip into the small white cup.

When my espresso is ready, I carry it with me out the sliding glass doors into the brilliant day, swiping a wide-brimmed sunhat from the outdoor dining table before continuing up the spiral staircase to the roof deck, where I don the hat and settle into the blue and white pillows of the built-in couch, looking out over the calm cerulean sea. The morning is still and full of promise, the sea breeze warm and gentle.

A lizard scuttles over the wall as I unlock my phone and scroll through the day's news headlines. On Instagram, I click on a notification from Emelia Müller Khan, requesting to follow my private account. I approve her, then click on her profile, which is unlocked for all the world to see. We have two friends in common, a girl I went to boarding school with but didn't know well because she was a few years younger, and a daughter of one of my father's friends, a snobby bitch whom I hate. I take a sip of my bitter, strong espresso, hoping Emelia's not actually friends with her as I scroll.

Most of her pictures are of food or cocktails or vistas, but there she is by my pool yesterday, and with Timeo in front of Ammos restaurant just before we met the previous evening. There she is on what must be their yacht, drinking a smoothie, and on the deck raising champagne glasses to the sunset with two other girls, neither of whom is tagged.

I hear tires on the gravel drive and look up to see Dimitrios's four-wheeler. The island is small enough that most people use ATVs or mopeds to get around and the locals seldom wear helmets. The only trucks you see are for construction and delivery and are generally very old, like the 1990s-era Toyota Dimitrios's boss drives.

As Dimitrios gets off the four-wheeler, I see he's not alone. There's a girl on the back. A pretty girl with long dark hair like mine, wearing a sundress. Aristea.

I watch from above as he glances around furtively, then, satisfied we are all still asleep, takes Aristea in his arms and kisses her deeply. She responds to his kiss in the way I'd imagined she would to Garrett's, melting into him, made weak in the knees by his embrace. He brushes her spaghetti strap from her shoulder, placing little kisses along her neck and collarbone until she giggles and pushes him away, glancing up at the house.

I duck beneath the wall before she notices me, not wanting to deal with her embarrassment should she see me. Also, her secret is more useful to me if she isn't aware I know it.

I lie back on the couch staring up at the cloudless sky, wondering how long they've been sleeping together, how it started, and what it means to them. I imagine their first kiss, her coming out to give him a glass of ice water in one of those thin cotton dresses she never wears bras beneath. The rest of the crew has left for the day and the deconstructed guesthouse is dark and cool after the brightness of the outdoors, raising the goosebumps on her arms as she hands him the glass of water. He sets the water on an exposed stud and brushes his rough thumb over her prickled skin, their eyes locked as he draws her to him.

She wilts into him the way I saw her do just now as he kisses her, making no pretense of pushing his hand away when he runs it up her thigh beneath her skirt. I reach my own hand beneath my dress as I think about it, pretending I'm both of them, until a clatter in the kitchen blends with the crashing inside me and I return to myself appeased, if only momentarily.

Downstairs, I find Timeo drinking an espresso at the kitchen table while Aristea washes and slices fruit. She looks up from her task, a bright red strawberry in her hand, quickly covering the look of surprise that passes over her face as I enter.

"I woke up early so I went up to the roof, then I fell asleep again," I say with a laugh as I set my espresso cup in the sink. She relaxes, secure in the knowledge that I didn't see her arrive with Dimitrios. I pluck a wet strawberry from her cutting board and pop it into my mouth. "Mmm. Delicious. Timeo, you have to try these strawberries, they're perfect."

"Wait," Aristea says with a smile, showing me the knife and the fruit. "I chop."

I steal one more strawberry before I slip out of the room, across the great room and up the two steps to the master, where I find Garrett shirtless in gym shorts on the edge of the bed, madly typing away at his phone.

"Good morning," I say. He grunts without looking up and I go to the window, looking down the hill toward the mottled sea. "Beautiful day out there. I thought we might take the boat out."

Long prized by my dad, *Icarus Flies* is a speedboat with sharp lines and a monster engine, the boat my brother and I first learned to pilot and the one I enjoy the most. Garrett likes it too, and has quickly developed piloting skills to rival my own.

He shakes his head, his eyes still focused on his phone.

"Hello?" I call, waving my hand in front of his face. "What are you doing?"

He bats me away. "I'm trying to work."

I roll my eyes, returning to the window where I see Dimitrios and the two other guys down below, cutting the marble for the countertops.

The million I'm spending to fix this property up will leave me high and dry, but Melodie offered thirteen million as is, or fifteen if I did the repairs, so it was worth the extra million in the end to go ahead and do them. And the paperwork has already been approved, so once the repairs are completed, the sale will go through almost immediately.

There's a part of me that wants to simply downsize, to use the money from the sale of the house to buy a less expensive island home and live a simpler life, but I know Garrett would never be happy with that. He likes his cars and watches and wines too much to give it all up. I can tell the notion of a reduced budget is hard for him to wrap his head around. Sometimes I wonder if he would have married me if I were the simple girl I pretended to be the day we met.

He does make his own money, of course, and plenty of it—but his shipping business has been struggling in the months since we met, with supply chain issues throwing a wrench into his schedules and inflation hurting his bottom line. He swears up and down it won't always be this way, but for all practical purposes, I've been the one supporting us since we married.

Not that I'm complaining. It's fine. That's what you do when you're married; you support each other. I know how much it pains him to ask me for money.

Garrett chucks his phone into the pillows and balls his hands into fists, his mouth in a grim line.

"What is it?" I ask.

"I may have to go to Athens today."

"Why?" I ask, disappointed.

"The damn bank . . . One of our Panamax ships is late because it got stuck in the pileup in the Suez, so we haven't collected the payment on that shipment, but payment on the bridge loan I took out last month is due day after tomorrow. I've gotta go up there and get some kind of extension."

"What bridge loan?" I ask. "I thought the two hundred K I gave you last month took care of the shortfall."

The two hundred thousand euros I gave him in the wake of the smashed cocktail glass. Because of course I did. He's my husband.

"Part of it," he says. "We're still so behind from the bottlenecks at ports the past couple of years that we're redlining. Any missed delivery date sets us back."

I sit next to him on the bed, worried. "How long is this going to go on?"

"We should be caught up by the end of the year. Hell, we would have been caught up by now if I had all my ships on the sea. But I can't get the money to make the repairs to the *Suezmax* until I'm caught up with the bank. It's a shit sandwich."

"What happens if you miss your payment?" I ask.

"Then I'm in default. They can't seize my ships yet, but there are exorbitant compounding fees, and it goes on my credit record, which means I won't be able to get the money I need in the future."

"Have you talked to your dad?" I ask.

He lets out a harsh chortle. "He's no help. Says I'm too big for my britches, should never have tried to grow the fleet. Like it's my fault a global pandemic hit right after I expanded. Maybe he's right. Maybe I should sell the *Suezmax*."

"Can you?" I ask.

"I owe so much on it that I'd come out even, at best. What I need is for it to be out there making us money."

I go to the window, watching as a small brown rabbit hops from the shade of one bush to the shade of another. I wish I'd learned how to handle money when I was younger, but as terrible as I realize it sounds, I never even thought about it until my dad died. Money had never been something I needed to worry about. I hated the way people talked about it and lusted after it, compared themselves on the basis of it. I thought—still think—all of that is gross.

From a practical standpoint, however, I'm learning it's important to think about money, so I've tried harder recently to listen to my accountant. Leon has been with my family as long as I can remember, and he lights up like a toddler with a lollipop whenever any of us shows the least bit of interest in his advice. I've also taken to reading the business articles that pop up in my news feed (though most of them go right over my head), and Garrett has taught me about loans.

I'm not sure exactly how much money I have personally. I know the money from the book is long gone—after all, that was ten years ago, and as Garrett pointed out, it wasn't a bestseller. I know I have the money to repair the house in cash. There are brokerage accounts and a retirement account somewhere, which I'm not allowed to touch. But Leon warned me I needed to sell this property as quickly as possible if I wanted to keep living the way I do, which is why I've agreed to Melodie's offer, though the thought of her owning this house makes me sick.

Perhaps if Garrett's ships were all on the sea, we wouldn't have to sell this property. His success is my success, and I would love nothing more than for him to be successful.

"How much do you need?" I ask.

"It's okay," he says, palming my cheek with his hand and rubbing his thumb over my lips. "You've given me enough. I'll handle it."

"But it's not enough," I say. "You're still behind."

He sighs, his eyes resigned. "I promised you last month would be the last time."

"How much do you need?" I ask.

"A hundred fifty," he answers, dropping his gaze to his hands.

I take a deep breath and exhale through pursed lips. "Okay. I'll call Leon."

"You won't tell him—"

"I have to tell him the truth this time. He's getting worried."

"I know. It's just . . ." He picks at a hangnail on his thumb. "It's embarrassing, having to ask your wife for money. I've never been like this. I hate it."

"I know," I say.

"It won't be for long, I swear," he says. "Once I get the *Suezmax* up and running, it's all gonna come together."

I nod. "Of course."

"Thank you," he says, taking my hands in his own. "Just transfer the money to my account and I'll deal with the bank. I promise I'll pay you back."

"It's fine," I say, rising. "Come to breakfast. I'll tell Dimitrios to get the boat ready."

He kisses me then, and I feel a surge of affection for him as his lips meet mine. But I also think of an article I read recently, about throwing good money after bad, like a gambler on a losing streak. Is he the gambler, or am I?

ABBY

CHAPTER 4

H EAVY STORM CLOUDS GATHERED ON THE HORIZON AS BENNY AND I drove away from the Kiruna airport in our compact SUV rental, the two-lane road unspooling across the gently rolling hills toward the mountains rising in the distance. But I couldn't appreciate the scenery for the blinding fear swirling inside me.

The truth will out.

The words of the second anonymous email I'd received in as many days. This wasn't a mistake, or a scam. Someone out there knew my secret. And there was nothing I could do about it, other than wait for their request. Because that's what this had to be, right? Blackmail.

I added together my savings and checking accounts in my mind, combined them with my 401(k) and index funds. It didn't add up to much. I could sell my condo if necessary. I'd do what I had to.

Benny looked over at me from the driver's seat and I managed a stiff smile. "Are you okay?" he asked. "You seem tense."

I wanted so badly to tell Benny about the messages, to have him reassure me that everything was fine. That I was being paranoid. But if I told him about this, I'd have to tell him the rest. And he was the last person I ever wanted to share any of that with.

I widened my smile, willing it to spread to the rest of my face. "Just work stuff," I said. "It's hard to let go."

I brought my attention to my breath like my therapist had taught me. Wiggled my fingers and toes. I was in Sweden with Benny. I was okay. For now.

Benny was still looking at me, his face concerned.

"I'm gonna let it go. Right now. See?" I made a show of taking a deep breath and letting it out, then powered down my phone. "Bye, work."

I felt a hair better with the phone off.

As Benny rested his hand on the steering wheel, I recognized the worn tan leather band and smooth white face of the watch he was wearing as one belonging to his dad that he'd always loved. "Your dad's watch," I commented, to distract us both from my spiraling thoughts.

"Yeah." He ran a finger over the face. "I don't care about watches as much as he did, but I always liked this one. He only ever wore it when it was just our family around, which didn't happen much. It makes me think of those moments when he belonged only to us."

"How are you doing with him gone?"

"Okay, I guess. I mean, those last two years, he wasn't really there, and I know how hard it was for him to be a shell of himself. But still, I miss him."

"He was a force of nature."

"He always liked you. And your mom. I think he would gladly have made her his wife after he and my mom divorced, if she'd been interested."

I laughed. My mom was still in D.C., now happily married to a woman. She'd gained thirty pounds and let her hair go gray and had never been more content. "She brags about you like you're her son, you know. Tells everyone to watch *The End of Summer*."

The End of Summer was the screenplay of Benny's that had gotten Hollywood's attention. It was a coming-of-age story about a trust fund kid who spends the summer lusting after his big sister's best friend on Martha's Vineyard. He finally loses his virginity to her at the end of the summer, only for her to be killed in a car accident the following night.

Gia wasn't the only one to mine the events of that summer for inspiration.

"Does she tell them who it's about?" he asked, his eyes dancing.

I felt the heat rise in my cheeks as he looked over at me, memories swimming in the space between us. Our languid afternoon discussions of literature he turned into dialogue delivered by award-winning actors, the tentative kiss elevated to a tender love scene, the assault that became my death. He hadn't shown me the script when he wrote it, but he sent it to me after it was optioned to make sure I was okay with its being made into a film. He apologized for not asking me before, but he'd been embarrassed by the contents and had thought it would never see the light of day anyway. I could say no and he'd pull it, he said. He'd understand, and he wouldn't hold it against me.

But I loved it. The writing was simple and honest, the story both personal and universal. I recognized us, but I also recognized how we could be any young boy and girl at the end of innocence, making mistakes that were sometimes catastrophic as we hurtled toward adulthood. No one would ever know it was me—we'd decided he should say he was inspired by a friend's relationship, if asked—but I'd been bowled over by how well he understood me, touched by how he found beauty in the parts of me that I thought ugly.

By the time I read his script, five long, lonely years had passed since that fateful summer, but I was still trapped in some ways by the events that had transpired. Though I knew intellectually that the assault wasn't my fault, I still had scars from the trauma and felt guilty over the string of bad decisions I'd made that led up to what happened.

Benny's portrayal of me in his script did more for me than five years of therapy had. Seeing myself through his eyes helped me finally let go of the fear and self-loathing that had dominated my college years. I fell in love with him as I read it, but it was too late for us by then; I was no longer the person he'd written about, and neither was he.

He'd been relieved when I congratulated him and told him I'd be his biggest fan, and the script had done more for his career than either of us could have imagined.

"My muse," Benny said now, reaching over to squeeze my hand.

The sun through the window illuminated his dark brown eyes and I felt as though someone had placed a hot stone on my chest, the feeling fleetingly parting the clouds of fear that hung over me.

Should I tell him about the emails?

I couldn't. If I told him about the message, he'd ask questions I couldn't answer. Not if I wanted to preserve our friendship.

"You sure everything's good?" Benny asked, withdrawing his hand to shift gears as the road ahead of us sloped upward. "You still seem . . . pensive."

The light through the windshield glanced off the sharp angles of his face and caught in the fringe of lashes that framed his concerned eyes.

"Yeah," I said. "I'm just tired. But happy to be here."

"Me too," he said.

As we drew closer to the hotel, the mountains got taller and the shadows grew longer, the dark waters of a vast lake appearing every so often through the trees. I forced myself to focus on the view and the conversation, pushing thoughts of the emails from my mind. I'd never been to this part of the world, and was stunned by the natural beauty of the landscape.

When we reached the vast glacial waters of Torne träsk, the pines turned to mountain birches, their dying leaves an incredible blaze of orange and red. I'd read the seasons changed so fast here that all the leaves turned at the same time, making for a peak color display like nowhere else, but seeing it took my breath away. "Even if we don't see the northern lights, these trees are worth the trip," I said.

Benny grinned at me as he turned past a family of deer into a paved driveway with a massive guard house and modern-looking iron gates. He gave our names to the security officer, who checked our IDs before opening the gate. Inside, the road curved up the hill through the flaming trees toward the glinting light of the low sun reflecting in the glass siding of the hotel.

We circled around a modern bronze sculpture of two trees to park beneath a high portico in front of the valet, where a good-looking blond guy in a blue uniform opened our door with a smile. "Welcome to Two Pines," he said. "You can check in at the front desk. I'll send your bags to your room."

We thanked him and mounted the wide, low steps to the giant glass double doors, each etched with an image of one of the pines from the sculpture. Another handsome blond man swung open the doors and ushered us inside. "Welcome. Check-in is to the right."

The soaring lobby was inviting and warm with multiple stone fireplaces, its slate floors softened by conversation areas featuring plush rugs in earth colors and sleek ergonomic furniture. To our left was a long copper-topped bar backed by up-lit shelves, and the pine wall ahead of us was lined with three levels of open hallways, off which were the guestrooms.

"Welcome to Two Pines," said the woman at the reception desk as we approached.

I handed her my passport and she typed into her computer screen. "Oh, this is lovely. I have you in one of our luxury satellite suites. Those are our best rooms, you're going to love it." She pushed two key cards across the desk and indicated a door to our left marked SATELLITE GUESTS ONLY. "Use your key card to exit there and follow the hallway. Yours is number seven, the last door on the right. Your bags will be there shortly."

Benny raised a card to the reader beside the door and it swung inward. The wide hallway followed the curve of the building, the exterior wall made of floor-to-ceiling windows that looked out toward the lake at the bottom of the hill and the mountains beyond.

As we walked through the doorway of number seven, I felt I was leaving civilization completely behind. The glass hallway slanted slightly downward, following the slope of the hill, and cut into the rock so that the door of our cabin appeared to lead directly into a boulder.

As we entered the main room, I realized we were in a large clear igloo jutting off the hill, all of nature's glory spread before us, the lavender-and-tangerine-streaked evening sky drenching the room in rosy light.

Our bags were waiting for us in front of a stone fireplace on the wall to our right next to matching espresso leather couches that faced each other across a low-slung coffee table. To our left were a bar and two black Eames chairs oriented toward the view atop a large sheepskin rug. The entire place was incredibly sensual, designed for disconnection from the outside world, for connection with the simple pleasures to be found within these walls.

I couldn't fathom how much it cost, and we were staying four nights. I powered up my cellphone and shot Gia a text:

OMG this place is amazing! Can't wait for you to get here.

On either side of the sitting room were two large bedrooms, each featuring a giant fur-bedecked bed fit for the sexual exploits of a Viking king and a sexy slate bathroom with soaking tub and sauna, all beneath the same domed glass ceiling that covered the main room. I dragged my bag into the room on the left and Benny followed.

"Gia and I can take this one," I said.

"Sure." He flopped onto his back on the bed. "Not bad."

"Yeah," I agreed, walking to the window. "Have you ever been here before?"

He shook his head. "Farthest north I've been is Amsterdam."

We were high enough up on the mountainside that the view of the sky was uninterrupted in all directions, and I couldn't see the other rooms I knew must be just out of sight—there were no other signs of civilization at all. Only the fire-tipped mountain birches swaying in the breeze beneath us, interspersed with boulders and pines that tumbled down to the dark lake, beyond which the snow-capped arctic mountains loomed in the distance.

It was incredibly romantic, and for a fleeting moment, I wished Gia wasn't coming.

GIA'S MANUSCRIPT

CHAPTER 6

I T'S ONE OF THOSE SCINTILLATINGLY CLEAR MEDITERRANEAN DAYS, the sunlight dancing on the water so brilliantly, my polarized sunglasses do little to cut the glare as we speed out to sea. Garrett drives with Timeo in the captain's chair next to him, Emelia and I seated side by side on the padded bench at the stern. I've been piloting this boat since before I could drive a car, but I figured Garrett could use an ego boost after having to ask me for money again this morning.

I left a message for my accountant, though he's on London time and wasn't yet in the office. He's not going to be happy. This is the third time since my father's death that I've had to pull a six-figure sum from my account. The first time, I told him I wanted cash flow to feel comfortable now that dad was gone; the second time I told him it was for a painting, which he strongly encouraged me not to purchase. Leon sees himself as something of a guardian. His regard for my discretion will go only so far, and I can already tell that he's worried that I'm emptying my bank account so quickly.

Leon has been wary of Garrett since the beginning, though he would never say it outright. Even though Garrett signed without argument the prenuptial agreement Leon insisted upon, the only one of my accounts he's agreed to add Garrett to is the house restoration account, and that was only because Garrett's overseeing the repairs.

I wish that Garrett and I had met while Dad was still alive; I imagine Dad warming to him, the two of them sitting by the fire with Scotch, chomping on cigars. But that was never to be.

Emelia throws her hands up in the air and squeals, her hair streaming in the wind, and I follow suit, tossing my head back with laughter.

Garrett cuts the engine when we reach our favorite cove, a secret inlet protected from the wind below the turrets of the Palaces at Kampos, and I pop open cold beers and pass them around.

"Is that the abandoned development you were talking about earlier?" Timeo asks Garrett, casting a glance up at the spires.

Garrett nods. "I keep telling Gia we should buy it and finish it. The way prices are right now, we could make a killing."

"I'd be open to developing something down here," Timeo says. "It's prime real estate. We should go see it sometime."

I shake my head. Even if we could afford to buy the development—which we can't—the last thing I'd want to own is hundreds of identical castles. "It's eerie, and the houses are ugly."

Garrett holds up his hand. "Agree to disagree."

Timeo's phone rings, but he silences it.

"I'm surprised you get service out here," Garrett says.

"I wish I didn't." His phone begins ringing again, and again he shuts it off. "Sorry. I was going to offload one of my cars and now I've decided not to, but people are still calling about it, driving me mad."

"What car?" Garrett asks.

"A McLaren Spider."

"I love the Spider," Garrett says, swilling his beer. "What model?"

"Six hundred." Timeo smiles. "Lime green with black details. She's a beauty."

"Why were you going to get rid of it?" Garrett asks.

"Because he has too many fucking cars," Emelia pipes up. Off his look, she shrugs. "It's true, love, you do. It's either get rid of some or buy another storage garage, which is just silly when we don't ever drive half of the ones we have."

Garrett and Timeo exchange a knowing glance. "It's not about driving them, darling," Timeo says.

"I might be interested in that Spider if you do decide to sell it," Garrett says. "I had a 570GT a few years ago and it was—" He kisses his fingers. "Love to have a McLaren in my garage again."

"I, for one, am perfectly happy with my ATV, thank you very much," I say, covering my annoyance at Garrett's grandiosity. This is the first I've heard of his ever having had a McLaren, and he certainly can't afford one now, with me keeping his business afloat.

Not far from the boat, a silvery fish jumps out of the water, only to be scooped up by a dive-bombing gull, who flies away with it struggling in its beak.

"I forgot to ask yesterday," Garrett says to Timeo. "What's the word on your boat?"

"It's dry-docked at the marine mechanic's, but they're waiting on a part," Timeo answers. "Apparently there's a bottleneck at some canal that's slowing everything down."

Garrett winces. "I'm sorry, man. You're in for it. My whole shipping schedule has been thrown by that bottleneck."

"Don't worry, we don't expect to stay with you indefinitely," Timeo says. "I've already put out feelers for a holiday rental on the island. There just doesn't seem to be much that's . . . palatable, to be honest."

"Don't be ridiculous," I say. "We love having you. We were boring each other to tears before you came along, weren't we, darling?"

Garrett smiles. "Life with you is never boring, darling."

"Maybe I should sell the damn boat, buy a new one," Timeo muses.

"What kind of boat is it?" Garrett asks.

"It's a—"

"Men, *please* stop being so tedious," Emelia cuts in. "If you don't give it up, Gia and I are going to start talking about the finer points of bikini waxing."

Garrett gives her an impish grin. "Actually, that sounds fascinating."

"But only if it comes with a demonstration," Timeo adds.

"Ugh, you're the worst," Emelia says. With an exaggerated sigh, she climbs up onto the edge of the boat and strips off her dress, revealing a fluorescent orange bikini that leaves little to the imagination, and dives into the transparent water.

It's late afternoon when we return to the villa, salty and suncrisped. Emelia and Timeo retire to their room, where we've collectively agreed they will stay at least one more night, and Garrett crashes in our bed, while I take the opportunity to shower, then retreat to the library to try Leon again, closing the door behind me.

It gives me comfort to imagine the phone ringing on the giant desk in his wood-paneled office, the gray skies of London backlighting his silver hair. I can almost see the distressed look on his pale, dignified face as I tell him what I need.

"Gia, this is the third time since your father's passing that you've needed to withdraw a significant amount of cash. Is there perhaps . . ." I can hear his politeness getting in the way of the question he wants to ask. "Is there something going on? Something you need help with?"

"No," I say, fiddling with my diamond key necklace. "Everything's fine."

The line goes silent as he struggles with what to say to me. "I worry when I see an unexplained change in my clients' financial needs," he says. "Your father asked me to look after you, so I feel it is my duty to inquire as to the purpose of this transfer."

I bite my lip, weighing what to say. Garrett has understandably never wanted my family to know about his money troubles, not wanting to be seen as a failure.

"Gia," Leon continues after a moment, "I realize your financial needs have been taken care of until very recently, but you no longer have endless funds. To put it bluntly, if you keep spending money like this, you're going to run out."

"I've agreed to sell the Greece property to Melodie," I protest.

"A smart choice, but it's not a done deal."

"Do you think she'll back out?"

"I'm not saying she will, I'm just saying she could." He pauses. "I'm only telling you to be prudent. Don't count your money before it's in the bank."

"You're always so wise, Leon." I sigh. "Once I spend the budget for the renovation, how much will I have left?"

"That depends on the markets, but without selling any additional assets or dipping into your retirement accounts, you'll have about six hundred thousand."

Good God, not even a million.

When he puts it like that, the necessity of getting Garrett's business up and running is all the more pressing. "The money I need is for a business venture," I say.

"Okay," he says. "Tell me about it."

"It's not mine," I say. "You know my husband has a shipping company. They expanded right before the pandemic threw everything off, and they're still playing catch-up. He took out a bridge loan to keep things running while one of his ships is being repaired, and it's due this week. Once we get the ship back on the water, we'll be back in the black."

A cocktail of both guilt and relief swirls inside me as I wait for his reply.

"A bridge loan?" he echoes, a hint of confusion in his voice.

"I think that's what he said, yes."

"Maybe I should talk to him," he suggests. "I might be able to help. I have some relationships with banks that might prove beneficial."

"I'd love that," I say. "The only problem is, Garrett asked me not to tell anyone about his money problem. He's embarrassed by it."

"Gia, the other two money transfers since your father's death—were they for Garrett's business as well?"

My voice seems stuck in my throat.

"I won't be angry," he says. "But I do need you to be honest with me."

"Yes," I answer sheepishly.

"Do you have access to his accounts?"

"No, they're business accounts."

"Okay," he says, and I can tell he's writing something down. "What's the name of his business?"

"Hoegg Worldwide."

"Okay," he says. "You figure out what you need to say to him, and we'll set up a call."

"But the money is due day after tomorrow," I protest.

"So, the sooner the better," he says diplomatically.

I run my fingers over the spines of books, unsure whether I'm frustrated or glad he's slowing the transfer of the money. At least someone is looking out for my best interests.

"Okay," I say. "Thank you."

As we hang up, my fingers catch on the green spine of *The Talented Mr. Ripley,* by Patricia Highsmith. I pluck it from the shelf and open it to the copyright page to see that it's a first edition, signed on the title page. That's not surprising; all of the books in this library are rare and most are first editions, half of them signed. What's strange is that I've never seen this one before.

As I flip through the pages, a slip of paper flutters to the floor and I stoop to pick it up. It's a handwritten receipt from a shop called Olde Worlde Books, made out to Garrett and dated last week, for the amount of £10,289.

I frown, flustered by how angry it makes me. It's the kind of thing that in the past I might have bought my father for his birthday, but even then, a purchase of ten thousand pounds is not one I would have made thoughtlessly. Garrett didn't even bother to mention it to me, which, on our reduced budget, feels like an affront.

I shove the book under my arm and stomp out of the room, hardly acknowledging Emelia when she looks up from scrolling on her phone on the couch. I close the door to the master firmly behind me and march to the bed, where I toss the book onto Garrett's chest, waking him. He winces and rolls to the side. "What's happening?"

"What the hell, Garrett?" I demand. "You bought a first edition for ten thousand pounds and don't even bother to tell me?"

"I bought it with my money."

"So, your money is separate from the three hundred thousand I've given you in the past few months and the one-fifty you're asking for now?"

He sits up, rubbing his eyes. "What, do you not want me to buy anything at all until I've paid you back?"

"That's not what I'm saying. I'm just asking that you have the courtesy to at least let me know when you want to make a big purchase."

He snorts. "And ten grand is suddenly a big purchase."

"Yes!" I cry. "What part of 'reduced budget' don't you understand?"

"Shh . . ." He grips me by the shoulders, attempting to calm me. "We have guests."

"Wouldn't want them to know we can't afford to buy their McLaren, would we?" I snap.

He gets to his feet, shaking his head as if he's disappointed in me. "The money shortage is temporary," he says. "And this limited mindset you have is unhealthy. Once the *Suezmax* is up and running, you'll be spending ten grand on bags again and this will all seem silly."

"I have never spent ten grand on a bag in my life," I retort.

"Oh yeah?" He casts a pointed glance at my Louis Vuitton suitcase, sticking out of the closet.

"That's a suitcase."

"Okay, Gia." He crosses his arms. "You know, if you're so worried about money, you'd save fifty thousand euros by using the well we already have rather than decommissioning it and building a new one."

"I told you, that's out of the question."

"Because of superstition—"

"Because it's contaminated!"

"It's not for drinking water—"

"I'm not having this conversation with you again."

He laughs, not even bothering to glance over his shoulder as he goes into the bathroom and shuts the door calmly behind him.

I storm out of the room, fuming, to find Emelia staring at me from the couch, wide-eyed. "Everything okay?" she asks.

"I'm going down to the beach," I say, throwing open the sliding door to the pool deck. "Wanna come?"

I step into the pair of slides I'd discarded outside the door earlier and march across the stone to the sunbaked dirt path that leads down to the beach. The breeze has stilled, and without an inch of shade, the late afternoon is oven-like.

Emelia scurries to catch up. "What happened?" she asks.

"I don't want to talk about it," I say. "I'd rather not think about my darling husband right now."

"Say no more," she says. "Been there."

When we reach the beach, I see Dimitrios's four-wheeler parked outside the shed where we keep the boat things. I realize Dimitrios is likely inside and will probably emerge at any moment to clean the boat, but I don't give a shit. I strip off my shorts and shirt, then untie my bikini top and step out of my bottoms.

Emelia giggles, glancing at the ATV. "Are we skinny-dipping?"

"I am," I say, sauntering toward the water. "Suit yourself." I hope Garrett sees me out the window, I hope he notices Dimitrios's vehicle.

"I'm game," Emelia says with a grin, stripping down as well. She opens her arms wide as she runs into the sea, as naked as I am.

I cast a glance up at the house before I dive under, but I can't see anyone.

The sea has a soothing effect, tempering the fury boiling inside me. The money Garrett spent on the book wouldn't have made a dent in the three hundred—soon to be four-fifty—he owes me.

Still, the disrespect burns. I float on my back, focusing on the feeling of the cool, salty water buoying my body while the sun warms my skin.

"This is amazing," Emelia says, surfacing beside me. "I'm never swimming with a swimsuit again."

"I never wear one unless the workers are around." I glance over to see Dimitrios striding down the dock toward the boat. "Give me a sec. I'll be right back."

"Damn, girl, he must have really pissed you off," she says as I swim toward the dock, and I can hear the grin in her voice.

I know I'm acting out, but I don't care. Garrett could use a reminder not to take me for granted.

When I reach the strip of concrete that juts into the water, I can see Dimitrios inside the boat, wiping it down. Emboldened by my anger, I swim over to the ladder, where I hoist myself halfway out of the water, haphazardly covering my breasts with one arm while I wave to Dimitrios with the other. "Dimitrios," I call.

He looks up, pausing when he sees I'm not dressed, unsure how to act.

"Sorry to bother you," I say. "But Emelia and I came down to swim and forgot to bring towels. I was just coming to grab them out of the boat, but . . ." I look down at my naked body. "Well . . . we didn't bring swimsuits, either."

He grabs two towels and brings them over, our eyes locking as he realizes I'll have to get out to reach them. Electricity crackles between us.

"Can you just leave them on the beach?" I ask. "That would be perfect."

"Okay," he says.

I casually drop the arm covering my breasts, giving him just enough to remember before I sink back into the clear water and swim away. "Thanks," I call.

When I reach Emelia, she's laughing, shaking her head at me.

"You swam all the way over there and only gave him a glimpse of your tits?" she teases as we watch him walk across the golden sand with our towels. "This is Europe, tits are yesterday's news. Come on."

She swims for shore, splashing out of the water without shame as he stands on the beach with our towels. Not to be outdone, I follow on her heels, reaching the beach as she takes a towel from him. She doesn't wrap herself in it, though, she spreads it on the sand, then does the same with the one he's brought for me.

"The water's so nice," she says to Dimitrios, wrapping an arm around my shoulder as I approach. She throws her other arm around me so that we're face-to-face, her wet body pressed to mine. "You should come swimming with us sometime."

His dark eyes are unreadable as he considers us, his lips quirking into a smirk before he shakes his head. "Dangerous."

His gaze meets mine for just a moment before he turns and walks back toward the boathouse. Emelia and I stretch out on our towels, watching as he speeds up the hill on his ATV, scattering the gulls. "He'll think about us tonight," she says.

I cast a look up toward the house, where I see Timeo and Garrett sitting by the pool. "So will they," I mutter. I was bold before; now I'm not sure I should have been so brazen. I'm not ashamed, but I also don't want Garrett taking out his displeasure on Dimitrios.

"Yours will," she says. "Not mine. I tried to bring a girl into bed with us last year, hoping it would make him desire me, but it didn't work."

I raise my hand to shadow my eyes against the sun. "Surely he notices how beautiful you are?"

She shrugs. "He likes it when I dress up. Three months ago we went to the opera in Vienna for my birthday and I wore this red Valentino dress he'd bought me with a pair of Louboutins so high I could hardly walk. It was the first time in I don't know how long that he looked at me as if I was something to desire. That night when we got back to the hotel, he kissed me, and I thought it was going to happen. I unzipped his pants, then he pushed my head down and I gave him a blow job, thinking it was a warmup for the main event. But he came in my mouth."

"He didn't return the favor afterward?" I ask.

She laughs. "He's never done that, even in the beginning. Does Garrett?"

I nod, the thought of just how considerate he is in bed making me feel queasy about my behavior just now.

"Do you think maybe Timeo's gay?" I ask gently.

"I'd rather that than the alternative: that he's simply not attracted to me anymore," she says. "I did ask him once. It was the only time he ever raised a hand to me."

"Sounds like he doesn't want to admit it to himself," I say.

"In his culture, it's still very taboo. His money is all from his parents, and they would disown him if they ever found out he was anything other than straight."

"But what about you?" I ask. "Don't you want sex?"

"All the time." She rolls onto her back, stretching like a cat in the sun. "But I read a lot of smutty novels and I've become expert at taking care of myself."

I laugh. "But you can't be expected to be celibate your whole life." I draw circles in the sand, thinking. "Have you ever cheated?"

"I've thought about it," she says, "but never gone through with it. If he found out, he would divorce me and I'd have nothing."

"That's not fair," I say.

"Life isn't fair," she agrees. "But I can't go back to being poor."

"Have you ever tried bringing a man into bed with you?"

She shakes her head.

"Maybe if he had his and you had yours," I suggest, "you could stay together and both be happy."

"My greatest fantasy, one bisexual man to please us both." She reaches over, fingering my diamond key necklace. "This is pretty."

"Thanks. Garrett gave it to me on our honeymoon."

She casts a glance up the hill at Timeo and Garrett, deep in conversation, their chairs angled toward each other. "You ready?" she asks, pulling her swimsuit top over her head and tying it behind her.

I nod, but a creeping feeling of unease settles over me as I dress, knowing I'm going to have to confess to Garrett tonight that I've shared his money problems with Leon.

GIA'S MANUSCRIPT

CHAPTER 7

Hello, ladies," Timeo calls when we crest the hill. He and Garrett are seated at the outdoor dining table drinking gin and tonics, the sky reflecting tangerine in the pool. "Have a nice time torturing the help?"

"We were just having some fun," Emelia says, adjusting her bikini.

Timeo shoots a look at Garrett. "Girls just wanna have fun," he says, a note of sharpness in his voice.

I lock my gaze on Garrett. "Boys like to have fun too, I've heard."

Garrett runs his tongue over his bottom lip, considering me with unreadable eyes. "Aristea made lamb moussaka. Go get changed and we can eat."

Instead, I perch on his knee and take a long swig of his drink. "Mmm," I say. "Stiff, just the way I like it." I wipe my lips as he swipes it back from me and finishes it off. "Did she leave?"

"Who?" Garrett asks.

"Aristea," I say, overpronouncing her name so it falls off my tongue in four fat syllables.

"About twenty minutes ago," Timeo answers.

"With Dimitrios?"

I watch as Garrett stills. The change would be imperceptible to an outsider, but I've watched him enough to know his poker face.

"Are they together?" Emelia asks, thrilled.

"They arrived together this morning," I say blithely.

"He probably just gave her a ride, it's not our business," Garrett says.

"How gallant of you." I laugh. "Though I must say, from the way he was kissing her, he's giving her a ride on more than just his ATV."

Emelia squeals with delight. "Workplace romance, I love it."

Inside, the phone begins to ring.

"Don't let on that you know," I say, rising. "She would be mortified, I'm sure."

I pick up the receiver in the kitchen, knowing it must be either the contractor or a family friend; very few people have the number, and the phone rarely rings.

"Hey, Sis," says the voice on the other end.

"Benny!" I exclaim, my sour mood sweetening immediately. "Where are you?"

"Still in Rome filming," he answers. "How's the island?"

"Hotter than I thought it would be," I answer. The slanted evening sunlight bounces off the spotless countertops and catches in the yellow and purple wildflowers arranged in a vase atop the farmhouse table. "But beautiful all the same. I wish I didn't have to sell it."

"And that husband of yours?" he asks. "How's he?"

What with our living halfway around the globe from each other, Benny and Garrett have met only once, shortly after the wedding, when we linked up in London for a night, but they seemed to get along. Benny did express concern about how quickly we married, but by the time he met Garrett it was done, so he went with the flow.

Unlike Abby. I'm no longer angry, but I'm still hurt she wouldn't come to Copenhagen for my wedding. I understand intellectually that she was trying to protect me, but still, her refusal stings.

"Garrett's fine," I say, watching him through the glass. He's smoking a cigarette, something he only ever does when he's stressed. He'll need the whole pack once I confess what I told Leon.

"Trouble in paradise?" he asks.

"Nothing worth talking about," I return.

"We're going on hiatus starting tomorrow," he says. "I thought I might fly over and check on you."

"I'd love that." Just the thought of having my brother here loosens the knot in my stomach. "We have a couple staying here while their boat is being fixed, but you'll love them," I add.

"Okay," he says. "I'll take the ferry from Mykonos, should be in around five."

"I'll pick you up," I offer.

"I'm bringing a girl."

"The actress?"

"Not the one you met," he says. "This one's an actress too, though. She's in the film."

"Are you together?"

"No," he says. "Not really. She thinks we are, but . . ."

"But she's not Abby?" I tease.

"You're never gonna let that go, are you?" he asks.

"You know, deep down, you still love her," I say.

"She's a friend, Gia. A friend with a serious boyfriend, last I heard."

"Oh, Colin doesn't count," I say. "It would be a tragedy if she married that wet napkin." The sun is finally sinking toward the sea. "You got my invitation to Sweden?"

"I'll be there. It's right after we wrap, so perfect timing."

"It's only a month away and I haven't heard from Abby yet. Maybe you could reach out to her, make sure she comes?"

"I don't know that it's really my place. Especially with the boyfriend in the picture."

"Ugh, you are so diplomatic. I'll see you tomorrow. We'll come with two ATVs and the luggage rack."

I'm smiling when I hang up the phone, light with the prospect of seeing my baby brother.

IN THE SHOWER, I LUXURIATE under the hot water, turning my attention away from the tiff with my husband to mull over my encounters with Dimitrios this afternoon. I picture his face when I spoke to him in the boathouse, and again with Emelia on the beach. What was going on behind those dark eyes? Had I made a fool of myself?

The first time Dimitrios showed up to work, I came down to greet him and felt the familiar flicker of matched chemistry when our eyes met, but never considered doing anything about it; I'm married and he works for me. His presence alone was kindling for my libido, and I took all my fantasies about him out on my husband.

In the weeks since, I've left the windows open indiscriminately and skinny-dipped at will, daring him to look. Today was my most brazen indiscretion, though. I'd been angry and not thinking clearly.

Perhaps I shouldn't have gotten married so quickly.

But I'm being silly; it's just a lovers' spat. We're both stressed about money, which can't be good for any relationship. Anyway, divorce is off the table, seeing that he gets a million dollars I don't have unless there's infidelity. Not that I'm thinking about divorce.

I love Garrett; he made a mistake in buying the book, but it's not fatal. Surely he'll understand why Leon wants to talk to him— perhaps he'll even be grateful for his advice.

I dry off and massage lotion into my thirsty skin, then spritz myself with my signature scent and select a loose white dress, tying my hair back with a colorful scarf. I'll apologize, I decide. Emelia's complaints about her husband have made me newly grateful for mine. I won't let something as silly as a book come between us.

On the patio, I find Garrett, Timeo, and Emelia seated at the table beneath a lavender sky, silently staring into the pink spot where the sun has just slipped below the horizon.

"I made you a drink," Emelia says as I take my seat next to Garrett. "We're out of tonic so it's just gin on the rocks with a lemon from the tree." She gestures to the lemon tree on the far side of the pool.

"Thank you." The cut glass sweats in my hand, a single drop of condensation sliding down my thumb as I raise the drink to my lips.

Garrett smiles, and I'm glad to see that the alcohol seems to have lifted his spirits. He pushes a present wrapped in butcher paper toward me, the size and shape of a book.

"What's this?" I ask.

"An early anniversary gift," he says wryly. "It was meant to be a surprise, but Aristea found it while cleaning my closet and put it on the shelf in the library."

"Anniversary?" Timeo asks.

"Three months," Garrett says, catching my eye.

"God, you're good," Timeo chaffs.

"What is it?" Emelia asks, excited.

I tear open the paper, the tightness in my chest spreading down my arms to my fingers as I extricate the green book from its wrapping.

"Ooh, *The Talented Mr. Ripley*! I love that movie," Emelia gushes.

"So does Gia," Garrett says. "But she's never read the book, so I found this signed first edition to give her for our three-month anniversary." He smiles, and I feel like a complete bitch. "Happy anniversary, my love."

He leans in and kisses me. I put my arms around his shoulders, whispering in his ear, "I'm sorry."

He nods in acknowledgment and kisses me again. Emelia and Timeo raise glasses to us. "Happy three months," Emelia says, and we all drink.

"You see, that's a thoughtful gift," Emelia says, looking at Timeo.

He raises his hands. "No offense, darling, but you don't read."

She frowns. "I read."

"What was the last book you read?" Timeo asks.

"It was, um . . . There was the one I read in London, the romance with the murder mystery, set in a castle."

Timeo laughs. "That you left on the plane before you learned who did it?"

She shrugs sheepishly. "It's just hard to find the time."

"This is why I give you Cartier, darling. A rare book would be worth no more to you than a paperback. But Cartier . . ."

"Cartier is always a hit," I concur, clinking glasses with Emelia.

"A wise man once told me you can always count on the three C's," Timeo says to Garrett. "Cartier, Chanel, and carats."

Garrett laughs. "Seems like there's a good deal of overlap."

I furrow my brow. "Not really, though."

"Maybe to the untrained eye," Emelia agrees with a wink.

Timeo clears his throat, shifting his gaze to me. "Your husband did me the favor of showing me around your beautiful property this afternoon."

"Did you see the horses?" I ask.

He nods. "And the olive grove. And Garrett told me about the plans to deepen the approach to the dock to accommodate larger watercraft."

"We won't complete that before we sell," I say.

Timeo catches my eye and holds it. "What if you sold to us?"

I pause, my astonishment rendering me briefly speechless. "Are you serious?" I ask when I've recovered.

He and Emelia exchange a glance. "Very," he says. "We've been looking for a beach house, preferably on an island, and we love Greece. It's conveniently located for us, and your property is stunning. It's everything we want."

"Garrett told you we're asking fifteen million?"

He nods as though fifteen million is pocket change. "A fair price, I think. I'll have to talk to my father, of course, and my accountants, but I'm pretty sure they'll be as excited as I am. Properties like this don't come up all the time."

"Well," I say, fully aware it's unlikely we'll be able to back out of the deal with Melodie, "we have accepted another offer, but it's never a bad idea to have a backup."

"It's worth talking about, at least, I think." Garrett looks at me for approval, and I nod.

"I'll put you in touch with my accountant," I say.

"Let me talk to my father first and pull some things together," Timeo says. "Then I'd love to speak with him."

"Our meeting really was a stroke of luck," Emelia chimes in.

"Yes." I smile. "I believe this calls for champagne."

GARRETT PLAYS THE ROLE OF the devoted husband all night, pulling me into his lap for kisses and sneaking hands beneath my dress, making bawdy jokes and suggestive comments about our sex life. There's a performative aspect to it, but we're at our best when we have an audience, and Timeo and Emelia are keen spectators. Poor sex-starved Emelia laps up our chemistry with hopeful glances at her unreadable husband, who observes with impenetrable dark eyes.

I notice Timeo laughs loudest at Garrett's jokes, catches his eyes when he's talking, refills his glass first. I don't know whether it means anything. Timeo could prefer men, or simply be sick of his wife—though I don't know why he wouldn't divorce her if that were the case. According to her, the prenup she signed is ironclad. No, he needs her for something. I'm just not sure what.

Around midnight, I realize I'm drunk enough that if I have any more, I'm going to be ill, and I excuse myself from the table. I assume Garrett is going to stay with Emelia and Timeo, who have just lit cigarettes, but he rises with me, making a joke about how I keep him on a short leash.

Once the door to the master suite closes behind us, Garrett turns on me, pinning me against the knotted wood with the weight of his body, his lips on my neck. A dim light burns on the table next to the couch, giving the sitting room a golden glow, and the sheer curtains billow in the breeze. On the dining terrace, I can make out the silhouettes of Emelia and Timeo still at the table, the ends of their cigarettes glowing red in the darkness.

Garrett gathers my wrists in one strong hand and pins them above my head, pressing his pelvis into mine. "I saw you on the beach this afternoon," he says roughly.

I can't tell from his tone of voice whether he's angry or aroused. "I went for a swim," I say.

"You were too bold," he says.

"It was Emelia's idea," I return.

"I think I need to remind you who you belong to."

"Are you going to punish me?" I ask playfully.

He drops my hands and rips the scarf out of my hair. "Turn around," he says.

I comply, and he ties the scarf around my eyes. I'm breathing heavy as he unzips the back of my dress and lets it fall, leaving me naked and blindfolded. "Emelia and Timeo are still by the pool," I remind him in a whisper.

"Good," he says.

I let out a small cry as he enters me from behind, my hands pressed to the wood of the door. "You're mine," he whispers.

Then he bites my ear so hard he draws blood.

ABBY

CHAPTER 5

I'D THINK SHE WOULD HAVE TEXTED BY NOW." BENNY CHECKED HIS PHONE again. "Her plane should've landed in Kiruna forty minutes ago."

Benny and I were showered and dressed for dinner, him in dark jeans and a slate flannel button-down, me in black jeans with high boots and a soft cream cashmere sweater. The soaring lobby of the hotel was warmly lit and bustling with guests, but we'd managed to claim a clutch spot in front of the fire, where we'd spent the past hour chatting while we waited for Gia to arrive.

Even with the apprehension caused by the emails lurking at the edges of my periphery, it felt good to be with Benny again. We'd seen each other at his dad's funeral in March, but between his girlfriend, my boyfriend, and Gia's antics after being overserved at the wake, we hadn't spent much time together. I'd worried before this trip that perhaps we wouldn't have the same rapport that we used to, but our conversation flowed naturally, just as it always had. The thing that was different was the warmth that spread through my chest every time our eyes met. A warmth that had nothing to do with the fire or the wine.

The wood crackled in the massive stone fireplace before us as our waiter approached, noticing Benny's empty glass. "Another glass of cabernet?" he asked.

"Sure," Benny said, flashing a smile as he handed off his empty.

"And for the lady?" the waiter asked.

But I was already feeling a little buzzed and didn't want to get drunk and accidentally tell Benny about the emails I couldn't stop thinking about. "I'm okay," I said.

When the waiter departed, I took out my phone and pulled up my flight tracker app. "Do you have her flight number?"

He shook his head. "But I know she was coming from Stockholm. There aren't that many flights. It shouldn't be hard to find."

I opened the app and typed in today's date with flight origin: Stockholm, flight destination: Kiruna.

I saw my flight, arrived at 2:17 P.M. The only other flight from Stockholm had landed on time forty minutes ago, at 6:43 P.M. "It's landed," I said, showing Benny.

He pulled up Gia's number and put his phone to his ear. "Direct to voicemail," he muttered. "Hey, Sis, where are you?" he said into the phone. "Abby and I are here in the lobby waiting for you. Call me."

"Maybe she doesn't have service on the road," I suggested.

"Good point," he agreed.

I twirled the stem of my wineglass between my fingers. "Before she gets here, can I ask you something?"

"Of course."

"What do you think of Garrett?"

He wet his lips, gazing into the fire. "I don't know him well," he said diplomatically.

"But you've spent more time with him than I have."

"True. I was in Greece with them last month, you know."

I shook my head. Neither he nor Gia had mentioned it.

"It wasn't a good scene," he admitted. "She had this couple living with them, Emelia and Timeo. They were—I don't know—Swiss or something, stuck in Miteras because their yacht had engine trouble. But there was something about them that felt off to me."

"What do you mean?"

"They were just a bit much. He was kind of a douche and she seemed, I don't know, a little obsequious with my sister. But you know how Gia is. She loves a party."

"That she does. Are these people still there?" I asked, taking a sip of my wine.

"I don't know. I've been so busy the past couple weeks wrapping up the film in Rome, I haven't talked to her."

"And Garrett?"

"He's always perfectly nice to me, but I can't say we'd hang out if he wasn't with my sister. It's like he wants everyone to know just how smart he is. And as much as he talks a big game about his shipping company, Gia confided in me he's borrowed money from her. I feel a little better knowing she at least made him sign a prenup."

"Who knows," I said hopefully. "Maybe it'll work out."

He snorted. "If the way he was flirting with the girl I'd brought along is any indication, I doubt it."

The girl he'd brought along. If I were smooth, I'd ask him about her, but I wasn't, and was afraid anything I'd say would betray my disappointment that she existed. Thankfully, the waiter chose this moment to approach with Benny's glass of wine.

Our phones pinged at the same moment. "It's her," he said.

I opened the notification to read the text she'd sent both of us:

So sry I'm not there! Woke up today with fever & chills. Have been asleep all day. Hoping I feel well enough to come tmrw. Can't even think straight rn. Pls have a glass of bubbly for me. Turning my phone off & going back to sleep. Love you! G

As Benny and I lowered our phones and looked at each other, frowning, I felt a stab of regret for the desire I'd had earlier for Gia not to come. I hit Dial on her number, but it went straight to voicemail.

"Her phone's off," I said.

"What the hell?" He shook his head, rereading her text.

"She must be really sick not to come," I said. "She was so excited about this."

He didn't answer, the crease between his brows deepening as he stared at his phone.

"What?" I asked.

He shook his head. "I was just thinking maybe she didn't come because of Garrett."

"Did he strike you as jealous?"

"No," he said. "But *she* is. Maybe she didn't want to leave him alone on the island."

"Does he cheat on her, you think?"

"I don't know. I couldn't see her letting him get away with it, if she knew about it. But I could see him taking advantage of her not being there to have a . . . dalliance."

"A *dalliance?*" I teased.

"You know what I mean."

Across the lobby, the maître d' signaled Benny, and we rose and walked over to him, glasses in hand. "We'll just be two tonight," Benny told him.

The dining room was in what felt like a wine cave on a lower level, with vaulted stone ceilings, wood-burning fireplaces, and soft lighting that gave the space a cozy, intimate feel. The maître d' left us at a two top in the back corner and I settled into my chair, pushing the sleeves of my sweater up my arms. I hadn't had time to wash my hair, so I'd pulled it back in a low ponytail and slapped a dash of red lipstick on my mouth to dress up my simple wardrobe, but I didn't need to worry. Everyone in the restaurant was dressed as plainly as Benny and I were; this wasn't a place you came to show off, it was a place you came to enjoy.

"Do you think Gia's okay?" I asked as we perused the menu.

"Tonight or in general?"

"In general. Tonight she's obviously not okay, or she'd be here."

"Honestly, I think she's lost," he replied, looking up from his menu. "I think that's why she married Garrett so quickly. Dad was always her anchor, but now he's gone. And Mom is . . . well, you know."

Yes, I knew. "Is Gia happy?"

He shrugged. "Who knows. She always seems to be having fun, there are always people around. But most of them are transient. You're her only true-blue friend. Does she see how empty her other 'friendships' are? It's hard to tell."

"Ouch."

"Sorry, I got kinda burned out on that scene when I was there last month. All the dick measuring and sex games made me feel a little ill."

The waiter arrived to take our order, but as he reeled off the specials, I found it hard to pay attention for the growing knot in my stomach. Maybe I should have gone to Copenhagen, if only to persuade Gia not to marry Garrett. But she wouldn't have listened to me in person any more than she had over the phone.

"Abby? What do you want?" Benny asked.

I looked up quickly. But no, this was not an existential question. I glanced down at my menu. "I'll have the whitefish, thank you."

I handed the waiter my menu with a smile. "Sorry, I was just in my head," I said when he'd gone. "Worrying about her. Do you think he loves her?"

"He does pay her a lot of attention. And he knows how to handle her, that's for sure."

"That's a good sign," I said hopefully. I downed the last sip of my wine. "One of the things that bothered me most about my ex was that he didn't know how to handle me, even after I told him."

He smiled. "How does one handle you, Abby Corman?"

"Things like, when I'd had a long day at the office, the last thing I wanted to do was talk about work, and he'd find a way to turn it into a fight about how I didn't include him in my life."

"I've had that argument with girlfriends before. I think it's about compatibility, at the end of the day."

Meeting his eyes was like tapping into an electric current. I dropped my gaze to my empty wineglass, suddenly flushed.

"You like your job, though?" he asked.

"I don't know." I tore off a piece of bread and dipped it in olive oil, then popped it into my mouth as he did the same. "I wanted to be a lawyer so I could help people. Lately I just feel like I'm part of the problem."

"Abby, you will never be part of the problem. You have a heart of gold."

But he was wrong about me. I hadn't been the altruistic girl he'd fallen in love with for a long time. There was a reason I wanted so badly to be a part of the solution. It would take a lifetime of good to neutralize the wrong I'd done. And someone out there knew it.

GIA'S MANUSCRIPT

CHAPTER 8

I FEEL QUEASY WHEN I WAKE IN THE MORNING. PART OF IT IS THE amount of alcohol I consumed last night, but I'm also uneasy about the sex we had. I'd been turned on by the rough role-play when we began, but now, fingering the dried blood on my earlobe, I'm not so sure it was role-play at all. We've experimented with handcuffs and slapping, but all of it was consensual, planned. The bite on my ear was different. Painful. And the sex was too rough, even for me.

It reminded me of the last time I had sex with Noah. We'd already broken up by that point—if you could call it a breakup. We'd been hot and heavy for the first month of summer, until, to be honest, I got bored with him and told him I wanted to see other people, only to run into him at a party on the beach on Kampos the following weekend. He looked sexy that night, and I was drunk enough to think it was a good idea to hook up with him again, so we climbed the hill to the recently abandoned development, where hundreds of identical half-built mini-palaces loomed spectral in the moonlight, and entered the first one we came across. It was in the shell phase, with walls and a steepled roof but no doors or glass in the windows, dark inside but for the light of the moon through the window holes.

The scruff on his chin was coarse against my face as we started making out, his touch so rough he ripped my dress when he pulled it down to fondle my breast. I remember thinking it was funny at first, reminding him I was a girl, not a sex toy. We were on the hard floor, the weight of him on top of me pressing my bones into the cold concrete, when it stopped being fun. I told him I was uncomfortable, and he jerked me up, pushing me against the windowsill, pressing my face into the wall as he nailed me from behind. Through the hole where the window would eventually be, I could see a group of people smoking a joint down below, gazing up at us and giggling. It didn't take long for him to finish. I called him an asshole, and he laughed.

Little did I know that evening was just the beginning of my nightmare.

But Garrett is not Noah. Sure, he pushes the limits, but *I like that*. Who am I kidding, I would be bored otherwise. Last night might have been borderline feral, but it was exciting.

I roll over in bed to find that Garrett is gone, his side of the mattress cold. My head throbbing, I wrench myself out of the bed and lurch into the bathroom, where I take two ibuprofens and guzzle a glass of water. In the mirror, my eyes are bloodshot, my face puffy. But once I wash the crusted blood off my ear, I see that the damage isn't as bad as I'd feared.

In need of a jolt of caffeine before I can even consider a shower, I throw on a sundress and pad across the deserted living room to the kitchen, where I find Aristea hand-washing last night's dishes. No one else is around.

"Good morning," I say.

Her back is to me and she hasn't heard me come in over the sound of the water, so she starts at the sound of my voice, but strangely, she doesn't turn to greet me. "Good morning," she says, her voice strained.

"I'd like a macchiato," I say, taking a seat on a stool at the breakfast bar. "Please," I add.

She nods and turns away from me to dry her hands, briefly bringing the towel to her face before taking a deep breath, then moving toward the brass espresso machine with her head down. Even with her eyes lowered, I can tell her face is splotchy and more swollen than mine. She's been crying.

"Are you okay?" I ask.

She nods but doesn't meet my eye, focusing intently on the espresso machine.

Has Dimitrios broken her heart? Has Timeo said something insensitive to her? Or did something happen with my husband?

My mind swirls with the possibilities, most of them involving clandestine meetings between Garrett and Aristea. His hand up her skirt while she chops the vegetables for our dinner, his mouth on hers in the pantry, her head between his legs in the barn. The jealousy rises inside me like bile, and I run to the sink and throw up all over last night's dinner plates. Aristea hovers behind me, unsure, as I wash out my mouth and flush the vomit down the sink.

"Too much to drink last night," I offer with a weak smile.

She extends the perfectly crafted macchiato and I take it. "Is there bread?" I ask.

I return to my stool at the breakfast bar, resting my head on my arms as she pours a glass of water and sets it before me, then takes a half-eaten sourdough boule from the bread box and slices it, handing it to me on a plate with a pat of butter and a miniature jar of jam. I drink the water and the macchiato and eat the bread while she scrubs the sink, my stomach feeling more stable with every bite.

I'm nearly finished when I hear the front door slam and Garrett enters, shirtless and sweaty from a run, his athletic chest glistening in the morning light. Aristea drops her eyes as he brushes past her to fill a glass of water.

Inspired, I slide off my bar stool and wrap my arms around his shoulders, running my tongue over the salty skin of his neck. Aristea busies herself cleaning up my breakfast plate as Garrett pulls back to look at me, his gaze inquisitive. I trail my fingers down his slick chest, pausing to toy with his waistband for just a moment before I plunge my hand into his shorts, palming his balls.

"I think you need a reminder of who *you* belong to," I growl in his ear before I bite it, not hard enough to draw blood, but just hard enough so he knows I remember last night.

A smash, and we both whip around to see Aristea has dropped the saucer for my macchiato, shattering it on the tile floor. "Sorry," she says, bending to pick up the pieces with trembling hands.

Garrett kneels beside her, helping her gather the shards while I lean against the island, watching. Was that a furtive look that just passed between them?

"I spoke to Leon," I say lightly.

Garrett looks up at me, his brow furrowed. "We can talk about that later."

"We don't have to talk about it at all." I can feel my blood throbbing in my wounded ear, readying me for a fight. "You can just give Leon a call and explain to him what you need."

A look of displeasure contorts his handsome face as he rises. "What *we* need, for the amended house plans—"

"Yeah, he didn't buy that. He gave me a whole speech about how abrupt changes in clients' needs are often a signal of distress." I laugh. "I think he was afraid I'd gotten into drugs."

He places the shards of ceramic in the garbage and strides out of the kitchen without a backward glance, his fists clenched.

I don't follow, instead sliding the glass door open to step onto the veranda, where I settle into a white-cushioned couch beneath the shade of the portico, staring out at the tranquil sea.

Until now, Garrett and I have rarely disagreed over anything, much less fought, outside of the cocktail glass incident, so I don't know his anger patterns yet. I refuse to walk on eggshells around him, though. Childhood with my mother was like tiptoeing through a minefield, the whole household trapped by her moods as her bouts of anxiety and depression morphed into psychosis. At the time, I blamed my father for not being there for her, but I realize now he did all he could, trying every course of therapy offered before finally institutionalizing her when I was seventeen.

The place my mother has lived for the past twelve years is no *One Flew Over the Cuckoo's Nest,* with its dismal living quarters and padded cells. Vue sur la Montagne is a Swiss sanatorium with, as the name suggests, mountain views, as well as blooming flowers, elegant accommodations, and the utmost discretion. I feel guilty that I've been to visit only once since Garrett and I married.

I'd been meaning to introduce him to her since we exchanged vows, but I wanted it to be in person, and one thing after another got in the way until finally, just a couple of weeks ago, we were able to go and see her. The morning of our scheduled visit, however, Garrett woke up with a fever and a sore throat and couldn't come.

My mom had dressed for the occasion, changing out of her ubiquitous loungewear into a bright blue maxidress that brought out her eyes. She was rail thin, her blond hair sprinkled with silver, the color all but gone from her face, but her bone structure was still regal, her posture perfect. She smiled when she saw me across the garden, but I could tell she was disappointed I'd come alone.

She was gracious, though, when I explained the situation, and asked to see pictures of our wedding. I pulled out my phone to show her a picture of me in my white satin slip dress with flowers in my hair, paired with the diamond drop earrings my father had given me for my twenty-first birthday.

"Beautiful," she said.

I flipped to the next picture, this one of Garrett in his suit, and turned to her with a smile to see the blood had drained from her face.

"Who is that?" she asked.

"That's Garrett," I told her, flipping to a picture of the two of us together. "Isn't he handsome?"

She shook her head, her eyes wide with fear. "He's not who he says he is."

Oh no, I thought, resigned. *Here we go.*

"What do you mean?" I asked gently.

"That man"—she tapped the phone's screen with shaking fingers—"is not who he says he is. He's a liar, a fraud. He tried to steal from me."

"No, that's my husband, and we're in love," I said gently. "I think you may have him confused with someone else. Who are you thinking of?"

"That's him." Her breath was rapid now, and she'd begun to sweat. "His name is Brian. He wanted a grant from the foundation—"

"A grant from the foundation?" I asked, confused. While my mom started the Torres Foundation with my dad and was still technically on the board, she hadn't been active in over a decade.

"But I could see his true colors," she whispered, grabbing my sleeve. "My guardian angels showed me."

Oh, I realized. *That's where we are.*

"He's taking advantage of you," she continued, her eyes wild. "You have to get away from him."

By now the nurse had noticed her change in demeanor and approached with a concerned look on her face. "What's going on, Caroline?" she asked.

"My daughter has married a criminal!" she cried. She was growing more upset with every passing moment, her hands visibly trembling.

"I'm sorry," I said to the nurse. "I just showed her a picture of my husband and she thinks he's someone else."

The nurse gave me an understanding look. "I think it might be better if you came back another day. She's just started new medication, and—"

"It's not the medication!" my mother shouted, trying to rise from her wheelchair.

The nurse kindly but firmly sat her back down. "We're going to say goodbye for now," she said, spinning the chair back toward the building.

I could see my mother's raised fist as the nurse whisked her down the pathway, her wild accusations becoming less intelligible the farther away she got.

"It's the new medication," the coordinator assured me before I left. "Give her a few weeks, the paranoia will be gone and you can introduce her to your husband."

In the month since, she hasn't taken my calls, so I've stuck to writing letters. She doesn't write back.

I hear the sliding door and look up to see Garrett himself, fresh out of the shower in a T-shirt and board shorts, his laptop under his arm. He strides over to the couch and hovers above me, backlit by the sun, his face sullen. "What did you say to the accountant?"

"I told him the truth," I say, patting the seat next to me. "Sit down and we can talk about it."

He remains standing. "I asked you not to."

"I know," I reply, squinting up at him. "But Leon made it clear he's not going to let me pull any more money unless I tell him where it's going."

"It's your money," he says.

"But it's his job to manage it," I return. "He cares about what happens to us."

"No, he doesn't."

Sick of him towering over me, I shoot to my feet. "Well, I know he cared about my dad," I snap. "And my dad asked him to look after us."

Garrett snorts, looking down his nose at me. "Your dad wouldn't have given his entire fortune to charity if he'd thought any one of you was worth the paper it was printed on."

I stare at him for just a moment before I slap him.

He flings his computer to the couch, tensing as though he's about to return the blow, but I scuttle backward. "I'm sorry," I say, shielding my face with my hands.

"No you're not," he returns, his eyes dark with rage.

I back toward the door to the kitchen, praying Aristea is still inside—or, even better, that Emelia and Timeo have awakened. Surely he wouldn't lay a hand on me in front of other people. Surely he won't lay a hand on me at all. Has it really come to this? Fearing that my own husband will hit me? I've never feared him before, but then I've never crossed him before.

"You should probably be nicer to me if you want that money," I challenge.

"You really don't understand anything about the way the world works, do you?" He shakes his head as though he feels sorry for me. "Without that money, the bank will take the ship and you'll never get back the other three hundred thousand you gave me. It's up to you."

"So talk to Leon and explain it to him," I plead. "He'll understand."

"I'm not talking to Leon. It's your money. You want it back, you talk to Leon."

"Ours," I say.

"What?"

"It's our money. We're married." Though as I say it, I wish for the first time that we weren't.

As we stand there staring at each other with our arms crossed, a hole opens inside my chest and I remember our honeymoon in Paris, when I'd thought for a brief moment that I'd lost him.

IT WAS OUR FIRST NIGHT and we were having drinks in the dimly lit bar of our sumptuous hotel, feasting our eyes on the attractive clientele, when he turned to me, his eyes dancing with mischief. "You know what I would like for my wedding gift?"

"What?" I asked, bracing myself for what I was nearly certain would be another request for a threesome.

"I would like for you to secure an invitation back to another man's room, sealed with a kiss, then come home to me instead."

I laughed, unsure. "Why?"

"I want you to feel desire for someone else." He trailed his fingers up my leg, beneath my skirt. "And then I want you to choose me. While I do the same with another woman."

My breath caught in my chest. "I don't know if I can stand that."

"Do you think you won't be able to choose me with the taste of someone else on your tongue?"

I balked. That wasn't it at all. But was he serious? His eyes told me he was. "What if I don't want to?"

"You don't have to." He shrugged, withdrawing his hand. "It's only a game."

I rose, leaving my glass on the table. "I find myself in need of a drink," I said with a wink that was more daring than I felt.

I went to the bar, parking myself next to a dark-skinned Frenchman whose muscles rippled beneath his fitted button-down. His throaty laugh tickled me inside, and I felt a spark between us. I dispatched the absinthe he bought me and ordered another as across the bar, Garrett escorted a girl with a pixie cut to a booth.

The next time I looked, Garrett was kissing the girl, his large hand stroking her delicate neck. I turned back to my new friend and pressed my mouth to his. I felt a thrill as our lips met. He was a good kisser, slow and deliberate, but it felt different than kissing my husband and I pulled away, thrown. I looked back to where Garrett and pixie girl were sitting, but they were gone. I felt sick.

I grabbed my bag and beelined for the exit, stomping up the red-carpeted stairs all the way to the fourth floor, imagining all the terrible ways I was going to hurt Garrett if I ever saw him again. But when I burst into our suite, I found him sitting alone on the bed with a small red box in his lap.

"Where's your girl?" I spat.

"You're my girl."

He pulled me into his lap then kissed me deeply, the feeling of his familiar lips a relief. "You smell like another man," he whispered.

"And you smell like another woman," I returned. "Perhaps we should get in the shower."

"First I want you to have this."

He handed me a red box and I opened it to find a necklace featuring a delicate diamond-encrusted key. "It's beautiful," I said.

"You have the key to my heart," he said, clasping the necklace around my neck before he unzipped my dress.

We didn't bother to get in the shower first. I inhaled the other woman's intoxicating scent as we fucked, secure in the knowledge that he had chosen me.

"Do you remember our honeymoon?" I ask now.

He unclenches his fists. "Of course."

"Would you still choose me?"

Our eyes lock and the fury drains from his face. "Yes."

I wrap my arms around his waist and he circles his around my shoulders. We stand like that, my head on his chest as it rises and falls, for a long time, until Emelia slides open the door from the kitchen and emerges smiling, espresso in hand.

GIA'S MANUSCRIPT

CHAPTER 9

JUST BEFORE FIVE, GARRETT AND I FLY DOWN THE HILL TOWARD THE ferry landing on our ATVs in a cloud of dust. I've hardly seen him since our little tiff this morning and I'm not entirely sure where we stand, but we need both quads to pick up Benny and his girlfriend and whatever luggage they might have.

I spent the morning in front of the typewriter while Garrett and Timeo roamed the property on ATVs, going over the plans for the work that needs to be completed and the options for expansion, should Timeo have the opportunity to make an offer of his own. It's my property, but Timeo has warmed more to Garrett than he has to me, so when Garrett suggested he be the one to explore the sale with Timeo, I agreed.

Instead, I took Emelia into town, where we had a leisurely, boozy lunch at a little taverna overlooking the marina. We were on our second Aperol Spritz when she turned to me with a mischievous gleam in her eye.

"I broke my dry spell last night." She whispered, though the restaurant was sparsely populated and no one was seated next to us.

"Do tell."

"It's thanks to you, really," she said with a giggle. "And your husband. Perhaps more your husband."

I raised my brows.

"We were sitting out there at the table finishing our cigarettes when you went into your room." She took a sip of her drink, her eyes darting to me for approval. "There was a light on, and the window was open . . ."

I gave her a slight smile, acknowledging I was aware.

"I put my hand in his lap," she continued, "and for once he didn't move it away, so I unzipped his pants."

"Please tell me this wasn't one-sided again," I said.

Emelia shook her head. "He told me to stand up and bent me over a chair right there at the table," she said, flushed. "He's never done anything like that before."

"Good." I smiled. "So, are you hoping you might have gotten pregnant?"

She bit her lip, a blush creeping into her cheeks. "You can't get pregnant like that."

"Oh?" I asked.

"I mean, you know, it was the wrong"—she glanced around and lowered her voice even further—"entry point."

"Ah," I said. "And did you like that?"

She took another sip of her drink and nodded. "I mean, I would have preferred the other, but you know, at this point . . . I'll take what I can get."

I frowned, watching this beautiful woman contort herself to fit into the compartment her husband had designed for her. "Emelia," I said softly, "you know you don't have to stay with him."

She stared into her drink. "I have nothing without him."

"Because of the prenup?" I asked.

She nodded. "It's all his family's money. Nothing he owns is really his."

"How do you spend money?" I asked. "Don't you have a bank account?"

"I have his credit card, and he gives me cash if I need it," she said. "It's not like I'm on a tight leash or anything, he's generous. But if I leave him . . ."

"Do you have anything saved?" I asked her.

She shook her head.

"What about jewelry he's given you, or a car in your name?"

"The cars are all owned by the family trust, like everything else." She gazed down at her diamond engagement ring. "I mean, I guess I could get something for this. A couple pairs of earrings, a few watches, my Cartier Love bracelets, a Chanel bag . . ."

"That's a start," I said. "And if you're really serious about leaving him, you could start saving the cash he gives you, open your own bank account."

She looked at me with wide eyes, frightened by the very idea.

"Did you go to university?" I asked.

Again, she shook her head.

"So, have him pay for it while you're still together," I suggested. "Or go to some kind of trade school."

"I've always thought it would be fun to do hair," she mused, a far-off look in her eyes. "I looked into cosmetology school once a few years ago, but he laughed and told me he wouldn't have me working."

I shrugged. "Let him think you just want to do it for yourself because you're bored," I said. "My dad always gave his wives whatever they wanted when they got bored. He knew from experience that bored rich women tend to get into trouble."

Emelia laughed.

"I'm just saying," I went on, "you're young and beautiful with your life ahead of you, but that won't last forever. It's far easier to leave now than it will be later. Especially if you have children."

She took a deep breath and let it out through pursed lips. "Something to think about."

I nodded. "Let me know if you need help."

"Thank you." She smiled and covered my hand with hers. "I haven't had a girlfriend in a long time. It's nice."

My heart swelled with compassion for her. "It is," I agreed, thinking of Abby. When I'd spoken to her earlier today, she'd been noncommittal about my birthday trip. I knew how hard she worked, but that didn't change how much it stung. Still, we had nearly a month before the trip, so I was hopeful she'd find a way to come.

I paid for lunch, then we got gelato on the boardwalk near the statue of Io. Emelia stopped to read the placard, licking her spoon. "What's a gadfly?"

"It's like a horsefly."

She nodded in appreciation. "Hera was a bitch."

I laughed. "That's the least of her revenge plots. She caused Hercules to go mad and kill his whole family, she tricked Semele into incinerating herself . . . I can't remember the rest, but she was known for being a jealous and vengeful goddess. Io should have known better than to sleep with her husband."

In the dress shop around the corner, I picked up two more of the linen dresses I loved to add to my stable, and Emelia selected two for herself, but when we got to the register, her card was declined. "Oh," she said, disappointed. "It must be that we didn't let the credit card company know we were going to be staying here this long. They probably think it's fraud."

She thumbed through her wallet looking for cash but didn't have enough to cover the cost of the dresses.

"Just put them on my card," I told the shopkeeper.

"You don't have to do that," Emelia protested. "I can call the credit card company and come back another day."

"It's no big deal, really," I assured her. "Consider it a gift."

She laughed. "You've taken such good care of me, I'm the one that should be giving you a gift."

"Like you said, it's nice to have a friend," I said.

"You're too kind," she returned, squeezing my hand. "Thank you."

———

NOW GARRETT AND I MANEUVER the four-wheelers through the shaded whitewashed alleys of town and back into the full glare of the late afternoon sun. We park as close to the dock as we can and find a spot to sit on a nearby bench, facing the azure sea. The water is choppy today, refracting the sunlight into a million specks of light.

"How did it go with Timeo?" I ask, watching one of the island's ubiquitous hedgehogs dig for beetles in the dirt beneath a nearby picnic table.

"He's for real," he says. "His dad is interested, and it sounds like he wants to pay cash."

I nod. I'm glad that's the case, as it makes the whole process easier, but still it nags at me that he can afford to pay fifteen million cash for our property and won't give Emelia a dime of spousal support if they divorce.

"We should put his bank in touch with Leon," I say.

"Did you talk to him today?"

I shake my head. "I told you, he's not going to give me the money until he talks to you."

He breathes as if to calm himself, his gaze focused on the horizon. "I don't think you understand the gravity of the situation," he says slowly. "If I don't get this money by tomorrow, I'm in a lot of trouble."

"So they take your ship," I say. "It's not ideal, but at least it's off your plate. You downsize—"

"You're not the only one I owe money to," he cuts me off.

A gust of wind blows my hair into my face, and I gather it into a ponytail in my fist. "What do you mean?"

"Before I met you, I went to an associate of my dad's."

"Who?" I ask.

"It's better you don't know," he mutters.

"Garrett, what the fuck?" I demand. "Why didn't you talk to me about this? What do you owe this person?"

"The boat," he says, his eyes locked on the ferry as it draws closer.

"What?"

"I made him my partner. It would have been easy to repay him out of my half once the ship was back on the water, but then it needed the repairs and everything went to shit."

"Is he on the loan with the bank?" I ask.

He shakes his head. "It's off the books."

"Can he not pay for the loan, then?"

"The loan I have to repay isn't with the bank, it's with him," Garrett mumbles. "And he is not a forgiving kind of person."

I drop my head into my hands, my mind reeling.

"So you see why I didn't want to tell Leon about this," he says.

I stare at the waves the ferry has kicked up, crashing against the rocks at the end of the jetty. "What will happen if you don't pay?" I ask, though I'm afraid I know.

"I won't be safe," he says quietly. "We won't be safe."

"Fuck, Garrett."

Finally, he turns to face me. "I'm sorry," he says. "I'm so sorry. I just need to get out of this situation, and then—"

"And then you can sell your interest in the boat you share with this person," I say hotly.

"It's not that simple—"

"I won't live in fear," I warn, anger simmering inside me. "We're about to make fifteen million on the sale of the house. You can buy him out. We can live more simply—"

"We'll cross that bridge when we come to it," he says. "For now, I need your help getting the money to pay tomorrow. Please." The fear in his clear blue eyes sends a shard of ice into my heart.

I jump as the ferry's gangplank is lowered with a clank. "I'll figure something out."

"Please don't tell your brother," Garrett begs.

I scan the ship and find Benny waving at me from the railing, grinning, his dark hair windblown. "Okay."

BENNY IS ONE OF THE first off the ferry, wrapping me up in his strong arms and nuzzling his rough chin into the top of my head.

It's still strange to me that my baby brother is so much bigger than me, no longer the shrimpy bookworm but a handsome, confident, successful Hollywood writer thirsted after by women everywhere he goes. Never pretentious, he's dressed now in a white T-shirt and rumpled linen shorts paired with worn-out boat shoes, a duffel bag thrown over his shoulder. The girl behind him, however, is a different story.

I recognize Camila Delgado immediately, despite the giant black sunglasses and wide-brimmed sunhat, paired with a flowing maxidress and jewel-encrusted sandals. She's shorter than I'd realized, her dark waves honey-kissed to match her flawless caramel skin, her luscious lips painted red, and I know that when she takes off her sunglasses she'll reveal the sea-green eyes that shot her to stardom when she played the sex robot with a soul in the movie that won her an Oscar nom two years ago.

"Hi, I'm Gia," I say, extending my hand to her. "And this is my husband, Garrett."

"So nice to meet you," Camila says, her scent light and floral as she air-kisses me on each cheek. She speaks with a softly Colombian accent and doesn't bother to introduce herself, I guess because she assumes we know who she is. I notice the kisses she gives Garrett are not of the air variety, leaving a red lipstick stain on each of his cheeks. She lowers her glasses to size him up with those famously hypnotizing eyes, squeezing his biceps playfully. "What a beautiful couple," she says without so much as a glance in my direction.

I shoot Benny a look. *Who does this bitch think she is?* He shrugs as if to say I shouldn't take it personally.

Once her giant Hermès roller bag is loaded onto the luggage rack, I toss Benny the keys to the ATV. "You can drive, I'll ride with Garrett."

"Take your sister," Camila says as though she's doing us a favor. "I'm sure you want to catch up. I'll ride with Garrett."

Unsure how to tell her to fuck off without telling her to fuck off, I straddle the four-wheeler carrying her suitcase while she wraps her arms around my husband's chest, her long red nails like streaks of blood on his white shirt.

"You wanna drive?" Benny asks.

"I'm good," I say, eyeing the strap holding Camila's twelve-thousand-dollar suitcase in place. I scoot back so Benny can get in front of me. "Let them go first."

"What's her deal?" I shout over the motor as we speed up the hill.

"She's an actress," he says, as if that explains it. "She needs attention."

"She must be great in bed," I goad, "because it can't be her personality you like."

He laughs. "Guilty as charged."

"Why did you bring her here?" I ask, fiddling blindly behind me with the strap securing her suitcase as we climb higher above the town.

"I can't say no to her, G, she's nuts. Guys on the crew tried to warn me, but I didn't listen. I never should have started things with her, but I'm in now. Stuck with her at least until we wrap."

"Jesus." I feel the belt behind me snap, and her suitcase thunks to the road behind us with a satisfying crack.

Benny slams on the brakes. "What was that?"

I look back to see Camila's suitcase split open, her clothes strewn across the dusty road. "Looks like the strap popped," I say innocently.

But Benny knows me. "Jesus, Gia," he mutters. "You know I'm going to be the one who bears the brunt of this."

I hold my hands up. "Sorry. I didn't think."

Garrett must have noticed we dropped back, because I see him turning his quad around up ahead, Camila peering out from behind him, concerned.

I pick up a white Dior dress crumpled on the road, knocking the dirt off the silk. Her fault for bringing a silk Dior dress to a rural island. And for laying her hands on my husband.

Garrett pulls up and Camila flies off the back, snatching the dress from my hand. "My clothes are all over the road!" she cries, her accent suddenly more American than Colombian. "What the fuck happened?"

"The strap popped," I say sympathetically, picking up a lacy bra and shaking it off.

She doesn't reply, but I can sense her suspicions as we retrieve her clothes from the roadway. I feel a little guilty, now that I see how poorly the suitcase held up. You'd expect something so expensive to be more durable, but the silver is scuffed, the leather scratched, one of the latches broken.

"I'm sure you can send it in, and they'll repair it," I say as Benny fits it back together and straps it once more to the back of the ATV. "You may want to hold it so it doesn't happen again on the way up to the house. It's a bumpy road."

I straddle the other ATV and Garrett hops on the back. "What did you do?" he asks as we hurtle up the mountain toward the house.

"Nothing," I say, hiding a smile. "Just bad luck."

ABBY

CHAPTER 6

I WAS AWAKENED BY THE CLANG OF A SINGLE BELL, ITS SOUND REVER-berating around the glass walls of our igloo. My body was so tired it felt drunk with sleep. I didn't open my eyes, willing the sound to go away.

I was so jet-lagged that I'd turned in soon after Benny and I returned from the restaurant, curling up on my throne of furs and feathers, my head swimming with images from the hours we'd spent together. The warmth of his smile when he first saw me, his eyes holding mine a moment too long in the flickering candlelight of the restaurant, the brush of his lips against my cheek when we said good night.

It was overwhelming, the affection I felt for him. The camaraderie and understanding we'd always shared, shot through with a current of desire so strong it left me breathless. I was high from the contact with him, my brain awash in enough chemicals to overpower the unease that had been lurking at the periphery of my subconscious ever since I received the first email—at least temporarily.

He felt the attraction too, didn't he?

But it didn't matter; we couldn't act on it. Our lives were far too enmeshed, and he was far too important to me to risk an ill-fated romantic entanglement. I needed to be careful. I needed to get hold of my feelings before Gia got here. She'd see through me the moment she arrived, and . . . what? She'd teased Benny mercilessly about his crush on me when we were younger, jokingly pleaded with us to get married so I could finally be her real sister. But did she mean it?

Maybe she intentionally hadn't shown up to give us the night alone. I hoped that that was the case.

"Abby, wake up," Benny said.

I wrenched myself from the clutches of slumber, forcing my eyes open to see him in the doorway of my room, shirtless in pajama pants. For fuck's sake, he looked like he belonged on one of those sexy man calendars.

"That was the aurora alarm," he said. "The lights are here."

He approached the bed, grinning down at me, his face awash in soft green light as I sat up, rubbing the sleep from my eyes. Above us, wispy threads of lime-green danced zephyr-like across the heavens, illuminating our igloo with an otherworldly glow.

"Beautiful," I breathed, gazing up at the sky.

He wrapped his arms around his bare chest as though suddenly realizing he'd neglected to put on a shirt, rubbing his hands over his biceps for warmth. Our eyes caught for a moment before he looked back up through the glass ceiling, and my heart rate sped up.

"You look cold," I said.

He smiled sheepishly. "I was so excited I ran in here without a shirt."

I scooted over and patted the bed next to me. "Have a fur."

"Thanks," he said. He sat on top of the covers, pulling one of the furs up over his chest. "That's better."

I smiled, fighting the urge to curl up next to him and lay my head on his shoulder the way we used to do when we were teenagers, and looked up at the billowing lights instead. The videos I'd seen of the aurora borealis must have been time-lapse, because the strands were more languid than I'd imagined, like thick tendrils of smoke unfurling across the star-laden sky. We watched in awe as the auroras caressed the heavens, both of us stunned to silence by the flares of flickering light. After a while a band of pink developed at the far edge, darkening to a deep magenta as it undulated, and I grabbed Benny's hand in excitement before I remembered I shouldn't do that. But he didn't seem to remember either, lacing his fingers through mine and turning to me with a smile.

I flushed as he stroked the inside of my wrist with his thumb. "So I guess you can strike the northern lights off your bucket list," he said.

I nodded, daring a glance over at him. His eyes were warm, inviting, his lips curled into a smile. "Is it everything you imagined?"

"Better," I whispered.

My breath was shallow, my skin hot where it touched his.

I wrenched my gaze away to watch the swirling lights overhead, the magnetic pull of him so strong I could hardly think. I didn't dare glance over again for fear the tenuous control I maintained over my desire would fall apart the moment our eyes met. But I also didn't withdraw my hand, and he didn't withdraw his. Our fingers remained entwined until the light show was over, the longest and yet briefest twenty minutes of my life.

When the sky darkened, he rose from the bed quietly. "Sweet dreams," he said before returning to his room.

But my dreams that night weren't sweet, they were downright steamy.

GIA'S MANUSCRIPT

CHAPTER 10

WHEN BENNY, CAMILA, GARRETT, AND I RETURN HOME FROM THE ferry, I excuse myself, closing the door of the dusky library behind me and settling into the cool leather couch with my laptop. I stare at the revolver in its glass case as I listen to Leon's voicemail asking me to ring him at my earliest convenience, but I'm unsure what to say to him yet, so I don't return his call. Instead, I log in to the bank account I'd set up to handle the repairs for the house.

Not wanting to have to involve Leon every time the contractor needed to be paid, I'd opened an account with both Garrett's and my name on it at a Greek bank with the amount of the contractor's budget plus the twenty percent everyone said I would need for in-evitable overages. I don't even have a bank card for the account, only the checks we use to pay the contractor's invoices, which I normally keep in a neat stack inside the desk at the end of the hall, though I've moved them into the top drawer of the master bedroom dresser since Timeo and Emelia came to stay.

I figure I can spare the extra twenty percent I put in the account to pay whatever shady character Garrett's gotten involved with. If I have to go to Leon for more cash to finish the house repairs later, so be it. Once the sale to Melodie goes through, this will all be in the rearview mirror.

The estimate for the repairs was right around a million euros, so the account started out with one point two million in it, and I've paid out about two hundred thousand so far, so there should be a million left. However, when I complete the double verification, I'm surprised to find I have only about nine hundred thousand. Admittedly, I'm not very diligent about balancing the account—in fact, this is only the second time I've logged in to it, the first being when Garrett helped me set it up—but I have kept track of the contractor's invoices, and I know there should be more money.

My pulse racing, I go through the withdrawals, recognizing the checks made out to D&D Construction. But a week back, I come across a ten-thousand-euro check made out to cash, in Garrett's handwriting and bearing his signature. *What the hell?*

There are a number of these "to cash" checks, nine to be exact, totaling ninety thousand euros. Breathing through my nose to stop myself from screaming obscenities, I leave the laptop open on the couch and march across the hall to the master suite, where I find Garrett reposed on the couch with his computer in his lap, happily typing away.

"Working?" I ask tensely.

He nods. "What's up?"

"Can we talk?"

"Sure."

"In the library? I need to show you something."

He follows me into the library, where I thrust my laptop into his hands. "What am I looking at?" he asks.

"In the past six weeks, you've withdrawn ninety thousand euros from the house repair account," I say, my voice quivering.

He nods. "For raw materials."

"What?"

"The builder needed cash for wood, concrete, marble, things like that."

I squint at him. "And he asked you for it without mentioning it to me."

He shrugs. "I'm the man of the house. This is Greece, you know how these guys can be."

"Why didn't you tell me?" I ask. "I have a budget—"

He snickers, evidently amused. "A budget."

"Don't mock me."

"It's just, you've never made a budget in your life, that I'm aware of."

I cross my arms, annoyed. "I'm keeping up with everything that's spent and sending all the receipts and invoices to Leon."

"So Leon has a budget."

"Stop it," I snap. "Budget or no budget, you can't be writing ninety thousand euros' worth of checks without even telling me. It's not okay."

He throws his hands up. "You're impossible. I'm trying to help you, and you act like I'm trying to steal from you. I'm your husband, for fuck's sake."

"If you're trying to help me, you have to keep me informed—"

"You don't listen!" he barks. "Every time we talk about money, you get like this—defensive, accusatory, refusing to see reason. You won't even put me on your other bank accounts—"

"That's not my choice!" I retort. "Leon sets up my accounts."

He hovers close to me, his stare icy cold. "And you buy into all his bullshit because you're paranoid, just like your mother."

It takes all my willpower not to slap him for a second time in one day, instead balling my fists at my sides. "You know why I was even in this account?" I say through gritted teeth. "I was trying to transfer the money you needed to pay off whatever dirtbag you've gotten involved with. But you don't even need me, do you? You can just write a check to yourself."

"You know I would never do that," he says.

I grab my checkbook and slam the laptop shut, using the hard surface to write out a check for a hundred fifty thousand euros to

Garrett. A tear splashes onto the amount line, blurring the ink as I sign it. I tear it out of the checkbook and hold it out to him. "You know, I always thought my father was such an idiot for the amount of money he spent on his wives and mistresses. But you're turning out to be more expensive than any of his whores."

He snatches the check from my hand, his eyes burning with anger. "Fuck you, Gia."

"You're welcome," I shout at his back as he marches from the room.

GARRETT DOESN'T COME TO DINNER that night. I don't know where he's gone, roaring into the dusk on the ATV, and I don't care. I clean myself up and down a Xanax to help me relax before I join the others on the outdoor terrace, making excuses for Garrett that he had a prior commitment he couldn't reschedule. If anyone senses anything, they don't let on.

I make a round of Aperol Spritzes and pass them around, but Camila demurs. "I'm sober," she says.

I raise my brows. "Good for you."

"My mom was in AA," Emelia volunteers. "Well, in and out."

"Oh, I'm not an alcoholic," Camila says. "I just prefer to feel my feelings. Alcohol is a crutch I don't need."

"I love that journey for you," I say, taking a long draw of my Aperol Spritz.

The sun has finally loosened its grip on the day, trailing rays along the sky like fingers over glass. The moon rises and the outdoor lights come on, the pool a luminescent blue, the village glowing beyond the mountain to the north.

Camila is just as flirtatious with Timeo as she was with Garrett earlier, and I can tell it gets under Emelia's skin as much as it did mine. Benny, on the other hand, seems relieved that her attention is elsewhere, excusing himself after we eat the simple dinner of orzo and vegetables Aristea prepared in deference to Camila's vegan diet to take a conference call with Los Angeles. I'm tired as hell after the emotional day I've had, and I consider turning in early, but I feel bad leaving Emelia alone to watch Camila flirt with her husband, so I stay.

"What do you do for work?" Camila asks Timeo, adjusting her sizable boobs inside the halter top of her flimsy red dress.

"Real estate," Timeo answers, though this is the first I've heard of it, outside of his offhand comment about buying the Palaces at Kampos. He doesn't elaborate.

"Do you love it?" she asks.

He shrugs. "It's profitable. Not as much fun as what you do, I'm sure. Do you love acting?"

"So much." She smiles. "It's transformative, it gives me purpose. I feel so fortunate to get to do what I love every day, to work with so many creative people. Your work is so much of your life. If you don't absolutely love it, you're wasting your time."

I can tell this doesn't sit well with Emelia. "You never had to work a job you didn't love so you could pay your bills?" she asks.

"It's true, modeling wasn't my dream job," Camila says. "But I knew if I kept working hard, it would lead to the career I wanted. And it did. If you truly believe in yourself, you can have whatever life you desire."

"I think it's a really profound way of looking at it," Timeo says, encouraging her.

Profound. I manage not to laugh. "I don't know that that's true for everyone," I say.

"Not everyone is willing to sacrifice to attain their goals," Camila expounds. "But that's largely because of attachment. People have attachments to other people, places, ideas, money. So many attachments that get in the way of becoming your most authentic self."

"Fascinating," I say.

But she doesn't notice the dry tone to my voice, and Timeo, apparently, is actually fascinated, encouraging Camila to continue enlightening us with her skin-deep, tone-deaf philosophy. I tune out, wondering if she was always this self-absorbed or if fame made her this way. Not all the actresses Benny's brought around have been this awful. Most of them have been fun, actually. But none have been quite this famous.

I've just brought out lemon gelato when Benny thankfully returns from his phone call.

"All good?" I ask him.

He nods, pouring everyone but Camila a round of ouzo.

Once we've all downed our shots, Benny aims his gaze at Emelia and Timeo, turning on the charm. "So, my sister tells me you two are interested in purchasing the place."

Emelia looks to Timeo, who nods. "I know you're already under contract, but you never know. We wanted to see it, just in case. Garrett and I walked the property and talked through the details of the renovation today."

"You know, if you really want to know about the property, it's Gia you should be talking to," Benny says lightly. "She and I grew up here."

Timeo nods. "She mentioned."

"Summers here were the best," Benny says wistfully, shooting me a sideways glance. "We ran this island, didn't we, Gia?"

I laugh and clink my glass to his. "We certainly did."

"My summers in Colombia were like that," Camila chimes in. "My abuela's farm was a paradise."

"As was your family's place in Nantucket, I'm sure," Benny comments. "Her parents have the most incredible beach house," he explains to the rest of us before focusing on me. "She grew up spending summers with the Wheelers—you know, Katherine and Johnny, they were a few years older than us?"

I nod, fully aware he's dispelling the myth Camila's fed the press of her humble upbringing in Colombia. "You know Johnny's a CNN anchor now," I say.

Camila, for once, doesn't quite know what to say.

"Anyway, it's too bad about your boat," Benny says, turning his attention to Timeo and Emelia. "But it certainly seems like kismet that it happened here."

"It's crazy the way fate works, isn't it?" Emelia agrees.

"And Gia tells me you went to Harrow," Benny says to Timeo.

Timeo nods.

"What year did you finish?" Benny asks.

"Ten years ago next spring," Timeo says. "Can't believe it's been that long."

"So you must know Buster Haxton-Smith," Benny says, grinning. "He would have been your year, I think. I was best friends with his brother George, who went to school with me in California. Both of them have come here to visit."

Timeo nods, but without Benny's enthusiasm. "I remember Buster."

"And his sidekick, Denton Knox," Benny continues. "You remember Denton?"

Timeo's jaw clenches as he nods again. "Yes, of course."

"Such a small world," Benny laughs. "Those two are a riot. Do you keep in touch with them?"

Timeo shakes his head. "Can't say I do."

"We should text them," Benny says, taking out his cellphone. "Tell them we've found their old classmate."

"That's really not necessary," Timeo says tersely. "We weren't close."

Benny scrolls through his contacts, landing on Buster Haxton-Smith, and shows Timeo before he begins typing. "What's your last name, mate?" he asks Timeo.

"Really, I don't know that he would even remember me," Timeo protests.

"With class sizes that small? He has to," Benny says, continuing to type.

"Please," Timeo says, laying a hand on Benny's arm. "Don't."

Benny looks up at him, surprised.

"We had a falling-out," Timeo says, clearing his throat. "I'd rather not reopen that door."

No one speaks for an awkward moment, before Benny nods. "Got it," he says. "Deleted, see?" He holds up the phone to show Timeo, then sets it on the table. "No harm done."

But that's not entirely true. Timeo and Emelia are both clearly uncomfortable, Benny is dubious, and I'm annoyed with my brother for ruining my dinner party. I stand with an apologetic smile. "I'm sorry to be the party pooper, but I'm beat," I say, faking a yawn. "I'll see you all in the morning."

I blow kisses as I make my exit, hoping there's a plausible reason for Timeo's reticence. Who knows. Perhaps he was bullied, or expelled for cheating. Maybe he slept with Buster's girlfriend, or sister . . . or Buster himself. It's not the first time Benny's poked holes in my relationships, and after what Emelia has shared with me, there could be many explanations that don't necessarily mean Timeo's lying.

Still, I have to admit, it was strange.

ABBY

CHAPTER 7

GIA COULDN'T HAVE TIMED OUR TRIP BETTER; THE SKY IN SWEDEN was a deep blue, the leaves on fire, the temperature a brisk but invigorating fifty degrees. The smell of woodsmoke hung in the air as Benny and I trekked back up the steep path from the lake to the hotel, leaves crunching underfoot. It was the perfect day, except for the fact that we'd had no updates from Gia after her text message last night and hadn't been able to reach her since, leaving us both uneasy.

Over breakfast on the observation deck this morning, we'd debated whether we were overreacting. Maybe Gia had hopped on a plane with Garrett at the last minute, gone to Dubai or Ibiza or some other place rich people went when they got bored. As much as we wanted to convince ourselves that could be what had happened, neither of us really thought she was that flaky. Not with us, anyway. Not on her birthday, when she'd been so excited about the trip.

Benny had gotten in touch with their stablemaster in Miteras, who'd agreed to go by the house to check on her, so we'd hiked down to the lake in hopes of distracting ourselves while we waited for him to get back to us. But it was hard to enjoy the scenery with all the alarm bells ringing in my mind.

"This landscape reminds me a lot of that school you guys went to in Vermont," Benny said.

An obvious attempt at counterfeit normalcy, but I'd take it. "You came to visit for Halloween."

"And you made me be Cousin Itt to complete your Addams Family costume."

I snorted, thinking about it. "We put those two witches' wigs on you, one backward and one forward—"

"And made me walk around on my knees all night!"

Our eyes caught as we laughed, and I quickly looked away. "Do you remember the blue girl? The one dressed as a character from *Avatar*?"

He closed his eyes, trying to recall. "Not really. But it was hard to see through all that hair."

"I was dating this guy who dumped me for her right before Halloween, and I was heartbroken. So Gia befriended the girl and planted the idea for her to go as one of the Na'vi."

"I have an idea where this is going," he said, wincing.

"Gia told her she'd help her find blue makeup that wouldn't clog her pores, but she gave her some kind of permanent dye. The poor girl was on the homecoming court the following weekend looking like a damn Smurf."

Benny shook his head. "Why does that not surprise me?"

"She's a loyal friend." I gave him a wry smile. "Has your back whether you want her to or not." I paused to take a sip of water, looking back at the peekaboo view of the sparkling water and the ridged mountains beyond.

"Did I ever tell you what she did for me when I ran for class president in high school?" he asked as we continued up the slope.

"I'm afraid to ask."

"The guy I was running against was this entitled ass who was playing dirty, spreading lies about me—but the day of the election, these flyers appeared all over the school with his class picture and a dick pic."

"Wait, what?" My head snapped toward him. "You never told me this."

"He swore it wasn't his, but what was he gonna do, whip it out and show everybody?"

"Lemme guess, Gia left the flyers."

He pointed at me. "She admitted it to me a few weeks later, though she wouldn't ever say how she came by the dick pic, or how she got into the school."

I bit my lip, realizing. "You wanna know what's really crazy? That same thing happened our junior year. This guy was an asshole after Gia turned him down for prom, then boom. Dick pics with his class picture plastered all over the school."

Our eyes caught. "Damn," he said.

"Yeah," I agreed. "I'd never thought about the possibility it could be fake, but . . ."

"That kind of picture is a hard thing to disprove," he finished.

"To be fair, the guy at our school deserved it."

"The one at mine too," he agreed.

"I hope she's okay," I finally said. "To not even respond to our text messages . . . she must be really sick."

"Yeah," Benny said, his brow furrowed. "Or something."

"It's weird Garrett's not answering either." His phone had gone straight to voicemail the handful of times we'd called, just like Gia's.

"I'm getting a bad vibe. It's not like her not to respond at all. Especially knowing we came all this way." We picked up our pace as he checked his phone. "The stablemaster should have had time to get over to the house and check on her by now, but I still don't have any service."

The trees opened up to reveal the futuristic satellite suites jutting off the hill ahead of us, the hotel rising behind to reflect the blue sky. I was warm from our hike and unwound my scarf, allowing the breeze to cool my neck as we followed the narrow footpath that led to the steps up to our rooms.

Before our trek this morning, I hadn't realized the trails were so close to our suite, and while the windows were dark in the day, now I wondered whether hikers could see into our rooms at night. The walls were glass, after all, and we'd learned from the concierge this morning that while the front of the resort was gated, the property backed up to National Park land, usable by anyone and everyone.

When he reached the deck off our room, Benny held his phone to the sky. "Still no service," he groaned.

I checked my screen. "Same."

Inside, neither of our computers could reach the internet either.

"Go up to the lobby to check your messages," I suggested. "I'll call the front desk and get them to send somebody to fix the Wi-Fi."

ONCE BENNY HAD LEFT AND the front desk had assured me someone was on the way, I took a cup of hot tea out onto the deck and settled into one of the loungers facing the view, hoping against hope that once our service was restored, we'd find Gia had texted to say she was on her way. It was entirely possible. But I had a sinking feeling it wouldn't be the case.

Again, my mind turned to the emails. I'd managed to keep quiet about them for twenty-four hours now, but the secret was burning inside me.

You're a liar.

The truth will out.

I wondered for the millionth time today whether the timing of the messages was coincidence or was somehow linked to the fact that Gia wasn't here. It had seemed plausible last night that she really was sick. But the longer she remained unreachable today, the more convinced I became that something bad had happened to her. Had she been kidnapped? Were the emails a precursor to a ransom note? They wanted money, or—or what? My heart raced, thinking about the possibilities. I wished more than ever that I could talk to Benny about it, but he might never speak to me again if I told him the truth.

The wind rustled the branches of the trees, sending rust-colored leaves twirling to the ground. At the edge of the forest, a man emerged from the woods on the trail and stopped, looking up at the suites. He was dressed all in black—combat boots, jeans, fleece, baseball hat—with mirrored aviator glasses that glinted as he turned his head toward me.

A current of fear ran through me. But that was silly, I assured myself. I was just jumpy due to the circumstances. Regardless, I hid behind my own sunglasses, pretending not to see him while I contemplated going inside.

Out of the corner of my eye, I watched as he started up the path, relieved for a moment, until he stopped in front of my suite. The deck was about twelve feet off the ground, so he was below me, perhaps another twelve feet from the edge of my deck. He waved. "Hello, there," he called.

His accent was British, which irrationally calmed me for just a moment, before he started for the bottom of my stairs.

I stood. "Can I help you?"

"I'm a bit lost," he said with a smile as he began to climb the stairs.

I edged closer to the door. "I'm afraid I won't be any help."

As he drew closer, I could see he was handsome, about my age, with caramel skin, jet-black hair, and a prominent nose. "Is this satellite seven?" he asked.

I hesitated. He was halfway up the stairs now. "I'm sorry," I said, backing toward the door. "I can't help you."

"Are you Abby?" he asked.

Icy fear shot through me, rooting me to the spot for a split second until my fight-or-flight response kicked in and I darted into the suite, locking the deadbolt behind me. And just in time. The man was on the deck now, knocking on the door. "I just want to talk," he called through the glass.

I instinctually lifted my phone to call Benny before I remembered the Wi-Fi was out and rushed across the room to grab the house phone from its cradle on the hall table. I hit the button for the front desk with shaking fingers. "There's a man here," I cried into the phone.

Outside, the man cupped his hands to peer through the door, jostling the handle. "I'm not going to hurt you. We need to talk!"

"Please send security," I said into the phone as I ran to the back door and bolted it, my pulse pounding. "There's a man outside on my deck, trying to get in. I don't know him."

I could see him outside, knocking on the glass now. "Abby, I need to talk to you," he said. "It's important! Please, let me in."

"Go away!" I shouted.

"Security is on the way now," said the voice on the other end of the phone, just as a knock sounded on my back door.

"Now there's someone at the other door," I said into the phone.

I peered through the peephole to see a burly blond man in a hotel uniform.

"That should be the tech about your Wi-Fi issue," the concierge said. "His name should be Paul."

I clocked his name tag, then unfastened the lock and ushered him in, quickly bolting it behind him as I hung up the phone.

"Ma'am, are you okay?" Paul asked, taking in my wide eyes, my trembling hands.

I shook my head, my teeth chattering. Suddenly I was eighteen again, shaking violently as blood pooled at my feet. It was still warm when it reached my toes, sending me crashing backward.

"Ma'am?"

I blinked at the powerfully built man before me, jerked into the present by his voice.

"There's someone out there." I pointed toward the front windows, where the guy outside had stopped banging and was peering at us through the glass.

"You don't know him?"

I shook my head. "But he knows my name. He's trying to get in."

"Go to the lobby," Paul instructed, taking the walkie from his belt.

The man on the porch bolted as Paul started toward him with squared shoulders, and I dashed for the other door with quaking knees, my heart in my throat. Time folded in on itself as I sprinted blindly up the corridor fighting dizziness, the images I'd worked so hard to forget flashing before my eyes.

Noah on top of me, his blond hair backlit as he turned toward the door. A rush of movement as the heavy lamp base connected with his skull. Gia's terrified face as he fell to the floor with a sickening smack. His fingers twitching on the tile floor.

And the blood, darker than I would have imagined, and thicker.

GIA'S MANUSCRIPT

CHAPTER 11

IN THE MORNING, I WAKE TO FIND I'M ALONE, GARRETT'S SIDE OF THE bed untouched. Outside I hear laughter and the sound of someone splashing into the pool. Tension creeps into my shoulders as I remember Camila's presence. I shudder, trying to shake it off, but I just don't like her. She's a phony and a narcissist, and she brings out a nastiness in me that I haven't felt in a long time. It's unfortunate, because I haven't seen my brother in months and I'd like to spend some quality time with him, but not if it means spending time with her. Or even worse, leaving her alone with Garrett.

Though perhaps she'd be doing me a favor, taking him off my hands.

I don't mean that. But after yesterday, I think it's safe to say the honeymoon is over, and I wonder if I made the right choice in marrying him. I wanted passion and excitement and unpredictability, but maybe those aren't the right ingredients for a marriage. Maybe Abby was right.

Shaky and in need of caffeine, I slip into a sundress and emerge from the master into the deserted great room. Outside, the pool sparkles in the sunlight as Timeo swims laps, throwing liquid reflections through the wall of glass that shift and shimmer on the wood-paneled ceiling. I can make out Garrett in one of the lounge chairs on the opposite side of the pool, dressed in the same outfit he was wearing when he roared off on the ATV last night.

A hot wind lifts my skirt as I slide open the door and step into the blazing day, raising my arm to shield my eyes from the sun. As I cross the terrace, I notice Camila in the lounger next to Garrett. She's wet from the pool, her dark hair slicked back from her forehead—and topless, her tits resting on her chest like two perfectly formed sunny-side-up eggs.

A lightning bolt of spite shoots through me.

It's no big deal, I remind myself, *I sunbathe nude all the time.* The beaches of Europe are full of topless sun worshippers, and I am often among them. I don't care if Garrett looks at other women's chests—in fact I like the lust it spikes in him, which he takes out on me—but Camila is a different story. She's not European, she's American, and she's out here alone with my clearly untrustworthy husband, first thing in the morning. Isn't it a bit early for nudity, anyway?

Timeo emerges at the end of the swimming pool and I remember they're not alone. But the fact that she's topless with both Garrett and Timeo does little to quell my indignation. Timeo waves as he dives back under, continuing his laps, but Garrett and Camila are so deep in conversation—him on his stomach, his face angled to her, and her on her back, her face angled to him—that neither of them notices me until my shadow falls over them.

"Good morning," I say. I'm trying to sound friendly, but it comes out combative.

"Morning," Camila says lazily. "It feels like afternoon, we've been out here for hours."

"Have you?"

"I'm an early riser from years of having to be up early to be on set," she says. "I found him sleeping out here."

"Garrett, I need to talk to you," I say.

Garrett remains on his stomach, unmoving. A bead of sweat trickles down my chest, absorbed by the fabric of my dress.

"Garrett," I repeat.

He grunts. "Give me a minute."

"Where's my brother?" I ask.

"Sleeping," Camila says. "He was up late working on a rewrite for the film we're shooting."

I see Aristea removing empty coffee cups from the outdoor dining table and signal her that I'd like an espresso. She's not crying this morning, but she's moving slowly, with dark circles beneath her eyes. Down below, the guesthouse appears to be empty.

"Where are the workers?" I ask Garrett.

"Your boyfriend isn't here today," he answers. Camila looks at me with interest. "The others are working on the irrigation system in the olive grove." He rolls onto his back with a groan, then pushes himself up to sitting. "I need a shower."

He rises without looking at me and trudges across the pool deck into the house. I stare after him, weighing my options.

"Boyfriend?" Camila asks, one brow arched.

"Inside joke," I say flatly, before turning on my heel and following Garrett into the house.

I find him in our white marble shower, the V of his stomach muscles flexing as he tilts his head back under the stream of water, a sight that until a few days ago would have prompted me to shed my clothes immediately and get into the shower with him. Now all I feel is resentment.

"Where did you go last night?" I ask, crossing my arms.

"I'm trying to shower, can we do this later?"

"It's a simple question," I say evenly. "Where did you go?"

"Out," he says.

"To the disco?" I ask. It's a small island and all the bars shut by eleven; unless he was at someone's home, he could only have been at the disco.

"I needed to get out of here, away from this toxic energy."

"Yeah, it's so toxic when your wife gives you a hundred fifty K to save your ass," I say bitterly.

He cuts the water, his face dark as he reaches for a towel. "Look, I'm having a shit time right now. My dad's on my ass even worse than you are. So can we just cool it for now?"

In the interest of keeping the peace, I nod.

Garrett's relationship with his father, Nick, is a mystery to me. My family hasn't ever been the most healthy or traditional, but there was never any outright strife. I might not know my half-siblings well, but we've always been mostly civil, and there have never been any disagreements over money, not even among all Dad's wives.

Though it strikes me now that perhaps that was only because there was always enough to go around.

But despite building a successful business together, Garrett and his dad clashed all the time. Nick was a bulldog—blue-collar, stubborn, and liable to get into fights—while Garrett was sophisticated, erudite, and able to charm the socks off anyone, thanks to his poet mother's emphasis on education and culture. Garrett, who liked the thrill of the gamble and the satisfaction of winning, wanted to keep expanding, while Nick was more conservative and inclined to leave well enough alone.

I was surprised, when Garrett introduced me to Nick—at a dusky, deserted pub on a Tuesday afternoon in Camden Town—to find that while he was more weathered and less polished than his son, he was just as good-looking and magnetic, his blue eyes crinkling as he greeted me with a firm handshake and a lopsided grin. We sat in a green leather booth and drank pints while he told stories featuring pickpockets he'd punched out, brushes with death while fighting as a mercenary, and beautiful women he'd seduced across the world. Garrett had warned me not to bring up work in the interest of preserving the peace, and in the three hours we spent together, we never spoke of it.

I haven't seen him since, though Garrett has gone to meet him various places a few times, most recently at a port near Athens, where the *Suezmax* is being repaired.

Now I look over at Garrett as he pulls on a pair of linen shorts. "You'll use the money I gave you to pay what you owe?"

"Yeah."

"And that's it?" I ask. "You won't need any more?"

"I don't know, Gia. I can't predict the future."

I cross my arms as he pulls on a T-shirt. The blows we've dealt each other this week are the kind that leave scars, and this heavy bitterness between us is new territory.

"They all want to go into town," he says, waving his hand in the direction of the pool. "Do you want to come?"

I shake my head. "I'll stay. I want to spend some time with my brother."

A DELICIOUS QUIET DESCENDS AS the sound of the ATV motors fades away. I go upstairs, where I sit at the typewriter and pick up where I left off yesterday, losing myself as I lay my hands on the keys and the present folds in on itself to become a window into the past.

After a few hours I'm ready for a break and Benny still hasn't appeared, so I grab a towel and head down the packed dirt path to the beach, my flip-flops clopping as I walk. When I reach the sand, I drop my towel and run into the sea, wearing my swimsuit this time out of respect for my brother. I dive beneath the surface, my hair swirling as I spiral downward, then back up, the water growing warm with sunlight as I reach the surface. I do some of my best thinking when I'm swimming, so I aim for the jetty at the end of the cove, savoring the feel of the smooth water against my skin as my muscles fire.

What will I do when I've sold this place? I'll have fifteen million and change, enough to live off for a very long time, if I play my cards right. We, that is. Garrett and me.

If he doesn't spend it all or get us killed by one of his unscrupulous business partners.

I've thought it before I can stop myself.

What is wrong with me? This is my husband I'm talking about. We've had a rough couple of days, but we made a vow to love each other till death do us part.

I'd thought that once we sold, Garrett and I would travel together, go skiing in Chile and dancing in Rio, fishing in the Caribbean and biking in France. But now I'm not so sure I want to do any of those things with him. I'm not so sure I know him at all. Besides the sketchy business partner he's taken on, and the ninety thousand euros in checks he's written himself, he's shown himself to be very nasty when he doesn't get his way.

Also, there's the question of his relationship with Aristea. And if he's screwing the housekeeper right under my nose, chances are it's not the first time he's strayed. I'd always imagined I'd be fine with an open relationship, but now that I'm married, I don't like the idea at all. When I think about the man in the bar in Paris and the girl in Ibiza, I feel queasy.

At the sudden sound of a motor nearby, I swivel to see *Icarus Flies* skating over the water, headed straight for me. I gasp and throw my arms overhead, adrenaline flooding my veins as I wave and splash to draw attention to myself.

The boat cuts engine abruptly, sending waves rippling toward me as it comes to a stop twenty yards out from where I'm treading water. Benny appears over the side of the boat, grinning.

"Fuck you, Benny, you scared the shit out of me," I cry.

He laughs. "I'm picking you up."

I swim for the boat and climb aboard using the ladder at the back. Benny tosses me a towel and I wrap it around myself. "Thought you might want those too." He points to the sundress I'd worn down to the sand, my flip-flops and sunglasses.

I dry my face and put on my sunglasses. "Aren't you considerate?"

"We're taking a picnic to Kampos Bay," he says, throwing the boat into gear. "I had Aristea pack us lunch."

I drop to the seat beside my belongings. "Genius."

"A considerate genius, that's me!" Benny yells over the wind and the motor.

My wet hair whips around my face as we fly over the sparkling turquoise water between the islands. I'm at home on a boat; I love the vibration of the deck, the slapping of the sea against the hull, the spray of salt water on my skin.

Kampos Bay is, in my humble opinion, the most beautiful beach in Greece. Situated beneath the Palaces at Kampos, the crescent of golden sand rims the clear water, the spires of the palaces hidden by majestic cliffs that part naturally in the center, where a trail leads up the hill to the abandoned development. Though the beach is no secret to locals on the neighboring islands, Benny and I have always thought of Kampos Bay as our place. It's not far, and within ten wind-blown minutes Benny is dropping anchor.

We stuff the things we don't want to get wet into the waterproof backpack we keep on board and plunge into the sea. On the shore, I trail Benny to a thatched sun shelter that provides the only patch of shade on the bright beach. He sets the backpack on a picnic table painted in shades of faded teal, white, and blue that mimic the water and takes out two cold beers.

"Have you been here yet this summer?" Benny asks as we crack them open.

I shake my head. "Garrett doesn't actually swim much. He's more of a city person than a beach person."

"Fool. I don't think I could ever live in a city that didn't have a beach."

We clink our longnecks together and I take a long swig of my ice-cold beer, glad for the time with my brother. Glad for the time away from Garrett. *It doesn't have to mean anything,* I tell myself. Everyone needs a break.

"What did Aristea pack us?" I ask.

He extracts three glass containers from the backpack and opens the lids one by one, revealing orzo, a Greek salad, and freshly grilled octopus, still warm enough that it's fogged the glass of its container.

"It's good to see you, Sis," Benny says, spooning food onto our plates. "It's been too long."

"I was just thinking the same thing," I agree, fingering the label on my beer. It's been two months since we last saw each other, when I introduced him to Garrett, five since the time before that, at Dad's funeral. I'd planned to visit him in L.A. before we came down here, but it didn't happen.

"How's married life?" he asks.

I look up to see him studying me. I've never been able to lie to Benny, he knows me too well. I sigh. "If you asked me a week ago, I would have said it's fine."

"What's happened since?"

Benny hands me a plate and sits opposite me. I toy with my fork for a minute before setting it down, my appetite stolen by my anxiety about sharing the truth.

"His business isn't doing well," I admit, tamping down the twinge of guilt I feel for spilling my husband's secret.

Benny waits, listening. This is one of the things I love about my brother. He doesn't pepper you with too many questions or jump in with assumptions. He allows you to talk at your own pace, nudging gently only when necessary.

I focus on peeling the label off my sweating beer as I talk, afraid to see the reaction on his face as I explain the situation with the *Suezmax*, the loans, and the shady business partner.

"What did Leon say about all this?" he asks.

"He wanted Garrett to call him, but Garrett wouldn't do it."

"So how did you get the money?"

I fold the wet Mythos label into ever smaller rectangles. "I took it out of the account with the money for the house repairs," I say feebly, neglecting to mention the ninety thousand that Garrett withdrew. I look up with a wince to see the unmistakable disappointment in his dark eyes, so similar to mine. "I know I shouldn't have," I admit. "But he said if we didn't pay the guy, we wouldn't be safe."

"How much do you know about Garrett's business?" Benny asks thoughtfully.

I snort. "Not enough, obviously. But I'm sure Leon's doing his research with the information I gave him." Information I know we both wish I'd given him before.

He nods. "Whatever he says, listen to him, please."

"Of course."

Benny stabs a piece of perfectly charred octopus and pops it in his mouth, groaning as he chews. "You have to try this," he says when he swallows.

I'm glad to find that now that I've unburdened myself, my appetite has returned, and my mouth waters as I squeeze a lemon slice over the tendrils on my plate. I always feel a little guilty eating octopus because of how smart they are, but as I take my first bite, the smooth, nutty flavor combined with the tang of the lemon displaces my remorse.

"You know female octopuses self-destruct after they lay eggs?" I ask.

"I was not aware."

"They only reproduce once before they die," I say. "I saw a documentary about it. Also, they can be cannibalistic. The babies sometimes kill each other, and the females often kill the males after mating. But even if they don't, the males stop eating and die of starvation. It's something to do with the optic gland."

Benny looks down at his plate. "Thank you for that."

"It makes me feel better about eating them, knowing they eat each other."

He laughs and I take a swig of my beer, enjoying the buzz creeping in at the edges of my consciousness.

"How well do you know Timeo?" he asks.

"I know he doesn't fuck his wife."

"Of course you do. What else?"

"His money is all his parents'. He does whatever they ask of him. He says he's in real estate, but I think it's really his father that's in real estate. He doesn't seem to actually work."

He rubs the scruff along his sharp jaw, then takes a swig of his beer.

"I can see you know something you're dying to tell me," I say.

"He didn't go to Harrow," he says finally. "Or at least he didn't graduate. I looked it up."

I furrow my brow. "But why lie about that? It's so easy to trace."

He shrugs. "Most people don't check."

"Fuck," I say, a knot of apprehension beginning to form in my stomach.

"Be careful with them," he says.

"But they want to buy the property—for cash," I specify. "How could they exploit us by giving us money?"

"I don't know," he says. "Just let Leon handle everything. You and I are—"

"Idiots," I fill in the blank.

"I wasn't going to say that. We just don't have the experience with money that most people in our position do."

"I wish Dad was still here," I muse. "I feel like a kid at the adults' table, trying to figure out which fork to use. You're better at it than I am."

"I feel that way too, a lot of the time," he says. "I mean hell, look at who I chose to date."

I chortle. "That woman's a piece of work."

"Watch out," he warns. "Camila doesn't believe in monogamy and relishes proving it's a faulty concept."

I stare at him, agape. "And here I was, feeling stupid for having married Garrett."

"I haven't married Camila."

"Touché, brother dearest. Touché."

We clink our beers and drink, and in this moment, I don't feel quite so alone.

GIA'S MANUSCRIPT

CHAPTER 12

IT'S *SURVIVAL OF THE FITTEST,*" CAMILA SAYS BREEZILY.

The wind has died down, leaving the night warm, and the dark sky glitters with stars. We're all seated around the outdoor dining table again, scooping lemon gelato out of palm-size bowls, the delicious vegan stew Aristea made long devoured. She may be screwing my husband, but at least the girl can cook.

I've set the pool light to red tonight, which seems to have charged the mood for the evening. Or perhaps it's the shifting alliances among the three couples seated at the table.

"So where are you on the food chain, Camila?" Timeo asks, taking a drag of the joint Benny passes to him.

"I'm a tiger."

Of course she is.

"What are you, Timmy?" she asks.

"Timeo's a swan," Emelia cries with a giggle.

He gives her a dirty look as he passes the joint to me.

"What?" she teases. "He was such a nerd when he was young, but look at him now!" She grabs his face and presses her lips to his.

"So gorgeous. And swans mate for life, so I guess that makes me a swan, too."

I lean past Camila to hand the joint to Garrett, who sits on the other side of her, but Camila plucks it from my fingers, putting it to her lips.

"I thought you were sober," I say.

"I don't consume alcohol," she confirms, blowing a straight line of smoke that hangs in the night air.

"She's *L.A.* sober," Benny specifies.

"What the fuck does that mean?" I ask.

Benny's eyes glitter. "It means she doesn't drink, she only does drugs."

"I choose to alter my mindset only in ways that will raise my vibration," Camila clarifies, taking another drag.

"Oh?" I ask, fully aware I'm smirking. "So, what other drugs do you do?"

"It's not about *doing drugs,*" she says. "It's about shifting perspective."

"So, marijuana," I say. "Mushrooms, I'm guessing?"

Camila nods as Garrett takes the joint from her.

"What about painkillers?" Emelia asks.

"Never painkillers," Camila says earnestly. "Pain is part of the human condition. It's important to feel your pain."

"LSD, perhaps?" Garrett throws out.

"Molly?" Emelia asks.

Camila shrugs in acquiescence.

"Damn, maybe I should get sober too," Garrett says, rattling the ice in his drink.

"I'll show you the ropes," Camila returns playfully. "What animal would you be, Garrett?"

"I think I'd be a wolf," he says.

"I like it, a fellow predator," she says, smiling.

I want to strangle her.

"You know, survival of the fittest isn't really a reference to the food chain," Benny pipes up. "Darwin actually suggested that organisms best adapted to their environment are the most successful. Sometimes those are smaller organisms. Cockroaches are actually one of the most successful species."

"Leave it up to my baby brother to turn it into a debate about *The Origin of Species,*" I say, laughing. "He was obsessed with that book as a kid."

"I'm just saying, it's completely natural that when pressed, we all choose ourselves," Camila continues her line of thought, surveying our faces to see who will take the bait. This isn't about evolution to her, it's about provocation.

Emelia speaks up, raising her voice over the chill trance music that thrums from the outdoor sound system. "I guess in some ways," she says, reaching out to take the joint. "But when you love someone, you often put their needs first."

"Says the swan," Garrett interjects.

"Because it suits you to do so," Camila specifies. "You're in a relationship with that person, so you are tied to them. If your partner's not happy, they will make sure you're not happy."

Garrett raises his glass. "Hear, hear."

"Zeus's affairs made Hera unhappy," I say, fixing my eyes on Garrett, "so she slaughtered his mistresses. Then he was unhappy, too."

"Humans are meant to be more evolved than the gods," Benny says, rising to go to the bar cart, where he pours himself a bourbon on the rocks.

Camila shrugs. "It's self-preservation. We're animals, wired to protect ourselves."

"And procreate," Garrett pipes up.

"Ah yes, it always comes back to procreation," Timeo says.

"Zeus was only doing his job as king of the gods, sowing his immortal oats," Garrett agrees.

"And poor Io paid the price," Emelia chimes in.

I snatch the joint, inhaling to blunt my annoyance with Garrett as Camila looks directly at him, smiling. "Think about how easy it makes the world if we know that everyone is out for themselves."

"At least we now know that to be true of you, Camila," I say, blowing a line of smoke in her direction. "So, thank you for that."

"If we could all stop pretending to care about other people's feelings, we could live so much more simply," Camila says. "Without attachment or guilt."

"Yes, look how that turned out for the gods," Benny counters, amused. "It's our empathy that makes us human."

"Oh, I'm not saying we don't have empathy," Camila says, taking the last puff before depositing the expired joint into the ashtray. "Just that it's not what drives our decision-making processes."

I don't like the sound of what she's saying, but is she right? I've been thinking all day about what's right for me, not what's right for Garrett, whom I claim to love. True, I've given him four hundred fifty thousand euros over the past three months, but it wasn't exactly selfless. I want his business to succeed because his success is my success.

The music changes to something with a dark beat as Camila stands and goes to the edge of the pool, her skin lit scarlet by its ruby glow, and dips her toe in the water. "The water's warm," she says, glancing over her shoulder at us with an enticing smile, obviously enjoying our attention. "We should go for a swim."

"I'm always up for a swim," Timeo says.

Emelia pushes her chair back, not to be left out. "I'll grab my suit."

Camila laughs. "Who needs a suit?"

I look over at Garrett to see him watching me, gauging my reaction. I'm careful to keep my face neutral as I take another sip of my drink.

"Oh, come on," she taunts. "We're all friends here."

Timeo puts down his drink and stands, pulling off his shirt. He shucks his shorts with a whoop and cannonballs into the pool. Camila claps heartily. "That's the spirit!"

Emelia rolls her eyes. "I'm in," she says, approaching Benny. "Unzip me, will you?"

Camila whistles as Benny unzips the back of Emelia's dress. "Bravo!"

Emelia's expression grows darker as she shimmies out of her dress while Camila eyes her like a cat licking its paws. "Beautiful," Camila says appreciatively as Emelia strips down to her lacy bra and thong. "Get me, will you?"

She turns her back to Emelia and lifts her hair so that Emelia can untie the knot of her halter top. Of course Camila's naked beneath, her famous curves backlit by the red glow of the pool as she saunters toward the water like some kind of Siren risen from the gates of hell. She steps into the water and shamelessly turns to face us, pointing at Emelia. "Come on, take it all off."

Emelia grabs Timeo's glass and downs the end of his drink, then unclasps her bra and throws it at me. "You're next," she says, sliding her thong over her hips before scampering into the pool with a splash.

"Go on then, Gia," Garrett goads, his eyes lighting on me. "You have no problem skinny-dipping in front of the help, there's no reason you shouldn't do it now."

I have no problem skinny-dipping in general, but Camila's turned this into some kind of weird sex power play, and I don't like it. "My brother's here," I say, shooting Benny a displeased look.

"I'm going to bed," he says, rising.

I think perhaps he misinterpreted my look, assuming I wanted him to leave, when in fact it's his psychotic girlfriend I want to leave.

"Square!" Camila taunts, splashing him as he walks by the pool.

Benny smiles, unfazed. "I'll sleep in another room so you don't wake me when you come in." He turns and salutes the rest of us before going inside.

"And what about you two?" Camila asks, turning to Garrett and me.

He raises his brows at me and begins unbuttoning his shirt. "Come on, love. Everybody's doing it."

I'd be the first to strip down if Camila weren't here pulling our strings like a bunch of puppets, but as it is, I'm torn between shucking my clothes just to show her she doesn't intimidate me and withdrawing to let them all have at it. I don't want to be a part of her game, and if there's any hope of our staying together, I don't want my husband to, either.

I rise and go into the deserted kitchen, where I grab a lime from the center of the island and slice it in half, using the sharpest knife I can find.

I am not about to let this bitch win.

I take a deep breath and draw the blade quickly and precisely across the pad of my middle finger.

Scarlet blood blooms from the gash. "Fuck!" I scream.

I run to the sliding glass door and hold up my bloody hand to Garrett, who is in the midst of unzipping his pants. "I've sliced my finger!" I cry.

The finger stings as blood oozes over my hand. Camila backs into the pool. "The sight of blood makes me ill," she says.

"What happened?" Garrett asks.

"I was trying to slice a lime for our drinks, but I'm a bit drunk and it slipped." The blood drips from my hand to the stones. "It's really deep, I think I may need stitches."

Garrett looks more annoyed than worried, but Emelia pushes out of the pool and runs over, dripping wet. "Are you okay?" she asks, taking my hand in hers, concerned. "I can take you to Urgent Care."

"No, I want Garrett to take me," I say. "But thank you."

Garrett snatches his shirt off the back of his chair and forces his arms into the sleeves. "Okay," he says with a strained smile. "Let's go."

"Thank you, darling," I say sweetly. "I feel so stupid."

But I don't. I feel as sharp as the knife that sliced my skin. As we wave goodbye to the others, I think perhaps I may have more in common with Camila than I'd thought. I might not be able to turn her into a cow and send a gadfly to chase her across Greece, but I'm not afraid to spill a little blood to protect my interests. Even if it's my own.

ABBY

CHAPTER 8

I AWOKE WITH A START TO AN ACRID SMELL AND BLURRY FACES. I WAS on the floor, a woman in a blue uniform waving something beneath my nose while two other hotel employees hovered behind her. I blinked, willing my eyes to focus.

"There you are," the woman said. The men behind her drew closer, but she raised a hand, holding them back. "Give her some space."

What was I doing on the floor?

"Ms. Corman?" she asked gently. Her face was coming into focus, her blue eyes concerned. "Do you know where you are?"

"Sweden. The Two Pines Arctic Hotel. How did I—?"

"You fainted. Our security officers found you here."

"Abby!" I turned to see Benny running down the hallway from the main building, his face frantic.

"Give her room," the woman said, sitting back on her heels as he crashed to his knees beside me.

He wrapped me in his arms, ignoring her. "Are you okay?"

I nodded. "A little woozy. I fainted, apparently."

"They just told me about the man."

It all came rushing back to me. "Where is he?" I sat up, panic-stricken. "Did they catch him?"

"They're looking for him now," the woman said calmly. "You're safe. Do you want a doctor, or would you like to go back to your room to rest?"

My pulse raced as I shook my head. "I'm not going back in there."

"We're gonna need a different room," Benny told her. "In the main hotel. On an upper floor."

She nodded. "I'll see to it. Do you think you can stand?"

I clung to Benny as I struggled to rise, but I still felt faint. "She's gonna need a minute," Benny said. "Can we get her some water? Something to eat?"

She rose to speak to the other two employees in Swedish and one of them scuttled off toward the hotel.

"What happened?" Benny asked.

I closed my eyes, resting my head against his chest as I related all that had happened in the short time since he went up to the lobby.

"What did the guy look like?" Benny asked when I'd finished.

"He was about our age, dressed all in black. Thin, dark hair, big nose—"

Benny pulled back to stare at me, his brow furrowed. "Did he have a British accent?"

"Yes!" I said, dumbfounded. "Do you know him?"

But Benny was already fishing in his pants for his phone. He opened the photos app and scrolled through pictures until he landed on the one he wanted and showed me the screen. "Is that him?"

Adrenaline shot through me as I recognized the guy, pictured next to none other than Gia at the table by the pool in Miteras. "That's him," I said, my voice catching in my throat. "Who is he?"

"That's Timeo. Of the couple I told you about."

The woman leaned forward from where she stood against the window. "You know this man?"

"I do," Benny said, showing her the phone. "His name's Timeo

Khan. He and his wife, Emelia, were staying with my sister in Greece when I was there last month. Though what the hell he's doing here in Sweden, scaring Abby to death, I have no idea."

"Maybe he knows something about Gia," I suggested.

"Then why not message me?" Benny mused, the corner of his mouth twisting down. "He follows me on social media."

"Do you think he means you harm?" she asked.

My heart raced as Benny glanced at me. "I don't think so." He looked back up at the woman. "But I can't be sure. Please, let me know when you find him. I want to talk to him."

ONCE I WAS FEELING BETTER, Benny and I holed up on a soft leather loveseat in front of one of the giant stone fireplaces in the hotel lobby while the concierge took care of moving our things from our satellite suite to a room on the top floor. Benny hadn't left my side since he found me in the hallway, going so far as to stand outside the bathroom while I used the facilities.

Now he sat beside me, calling anyone he could think of who might know anything of Gia's whereabouts while I sipped a hot toddy, staring into the crackling flames. My nerves were shot; I was emotionally spent and shaky, filled with apprehension about what might have happened to Gia, the dregs of adrenaline swirling through my veins.

Looking around, I couldn't help but feel a stab of jealousy for the other guests, so obviously relaxed and enjoying their exorbitantly expensive vacations. That was supposed to be the three of us, reconnecting beneath the otherworldly aurora borealis on a holiday I never would have been able to pay for on my own.

Now Gia was MIA while I was getting threatening emails and this Timeo person had clearly followed us here.

He'd somehow evaded capture by security, and while the hotel staff assured us that we were safe here, with guards at the gate on the lookout for anyone matching his description, I was still jumpy.

How had he found me to begin with? Just thinking of it sent an icy shard of fear through my heart.

"Debby said Leon had gone for the day but would call us in the morning," Benny said as he hung up with their accountant's office. "I don't know that he'll know anything, but it's worth a shot. Anyway, we need to tell him what's going on. If something has happened . . . he'll be helpful."

While we waited on word from the stablemaster, who hadn't yet made it to check on Gia because he'd been held up by a mare in labor on another property, I pulled up Gia's social media account and perused her most recent pictures, looking for clues. Her last post was from a week ago and featured a picture of the typewriter at the end of the upstairs hallway in the Miteras house, the sea visible through the window above, with the caption "Back at it."

"Did you know Gia was writing another book?" I asked, displaying the picture on my screen.

"She mentioned she was working on something new," he said.

I clicked on a picture I recognized as the Swiss Alps. "It looks like she went to visit your mom about a month ago."

He took the phone from my hand. "Yeah, that's definitely taken in the garden at Vue sur la Montagne."

"She didn't say anything to you about going?"

He shook his head. "We texted some but haven't spoken since I left Greece a month or so ago. I did talk to my mom about two weeks ago, but she wasn't totally coherent and didn't mention anything about Gia visiting. I left a message for her earlier."

He pulled up Instagram on his own phone and typed in Timeo's name. "That's weird," he said, his brow furrowed. "I know it was here."

"What?" I asked.

"Timeo's Instagram. It's gone."

He typed in Emelia's name and scrolled through the list of accounts that popped up. "Emelia's is gone too."

Before we had time to contemplate what that might mean, our

phones dinged simultaneously, and we both lifted them to see Gia's name on our screens. My stomach dropped.

> Ugh I'm still feeling like shit. This really sux but I don't think I can leave the house, much less make it to Sweden. U guys enjoy. We'll plan a raincheck soon! Love, G

Rattled, I immediately hit Dial on her number. It rang twice before going to voicemail. Without leaving a message, I quickly typed out a text, hoping her phone was still on.

> Please answer your phone. We're very worried about you.

Benny's jaw tensed. "This is so fucked up."

"These texts are bullshit, right?" He looked up from his phone and I held his gaze. "She's not sick."

"Right."

The text had snapped me out of my shock over Timeo, sharpening my mind. "It may not even be her."

He nodded slowly. "I wrote on a series last year where a guy killed his wife and no one knew for a week that anything was wrong because he was replying to all her messages as her."

A wave of nausea rolled through me. "I hope that's not the case, but I think at this point we have to consider it. Is there anything you know that you're not telling me?"

He bit his lip, thinking. "No, nothing," he said after a moment. "I don't know what the fuck Timeo was doing here. He must want something."

"Do you think he could have kidnapped Gia?" I asked.

"He didn't seem like the type, but after the way he showed up here—obviously I don't know him that well."

"It's too much to be a coincidence," I mused. *Especially combined with the emails I couldn't tell Benny about.*

He stared into the fire, popping his knuckles. "I keep thinking of

Garrett's money troubles. Gia made it sound like he'd gotten into bed with some shady characters."

"And these shady characters what, kidnapped them? And pretended to be her, texting us from her phone?"

"It's not impossible."

"But if they wanted money, wouldn't there be a demand?" I asked.

"Maybe that's what Timeo's here for."

I downed the rest of my hot toddy, but it did nothing to erase the sinking sensation inside me. "That makes sense."

His phone began to vibrate. "It's the stablemaster," he said.

"Finally."

He put the phone to his ear. "Hi, Christos. Any luck?" Benny's face grew grim as he listened. "Are you sure? Okay. I know she had a woman there cooking and cleaning. Aristea. Can you possibly get me her number? Thank you."

"What is it?" I asked as he hung up.

"He wasn't able to get inside because the locks had been changed, but he knocked and looked through the windows."

"And?"

"No one was there." A current of foreboding shot through me as our eyes met. "The house was empty."

GIA'S MANUSCRIPT

CHAPTER 13

IN THE MORNING, I'M AWAKENED BY A TAPPING ON THE DOOR TO THE master suite. I lie still for a moment, hoping the tapping will stop, but whoever it is must really want to come in because it only grows louder.

"One second," I call, glancing over at Garrett, who continues sleeping. The man could sleep through an earthquake.

I trudge over to the dresser and grab the first clothes I see, the thick bandage around my middle finger catching in the fabric as I clumsily pull on a pair of jean cutoffs and a sleeveless shirt. I didn't need stitches after all, but the attendant at the urgent care center closed the wound with surgical tape and wrapped it up.

I gently close the door to my bedroom behind me as I exit, then open the door to the suite to find Benny standing there. He's freshly showered, his duffel bag slung over his shoulder.

"They need me back in Rome," he says. "The director wants to work with me on some script changes before we start shooting again next week." He grabs my injured hand. "What the hell happened to your finger?"

"You didn't hear?" I hold the bandage up for him to inspect. "I sliced my finger. Garrett took me to the care center in town. I'm not entirely sure the attendant was sober."

He evaluates me, concerned. "I'm not entirely sure I should be leaving you alone with these animals."

"Then stay."

"I wish I could. But I'll see you in a month in Sweden."

"I forgot to tell you, I got a text from Abby yesterday. She's coming."

He smiles. "Great."

I look past him into the quiet house. Not even Aristea is here yet. "You're taking Camila with you, right?"

He sighs, his face a mask of apology.

"No," I protest, shaking my head vehemently. "You can't leave her here. Please."

"She refused to come."

"No, Benny. Please, let me talk to her—"

"The ferry I need to catch to make my flight leaves at eight," he says, checking his watch. "That's in thirty minutes. Even if she agreed, there wouldn't be time now. She's in bed with Timeo and Emelia, and her shit is all over our room."

I raise my brows. "So that happened."

"Evidently."

I sigh. "Okay. I'll drive you into town."

AFTER I DROP BENNY AT the ferry, I linger over an espresso beneath the flowering trellis at my favorite café. A black cat crosses the white-washed alley to rub against my legs, allowing me to twirl her tail through my fingers. I'm in no hurry to get back to the house; I don't especially want to see any of them, other than Emelia. I feel bad for her, allowing a woman she can't stand into bed with her and her husband in an effort to preserve her marriage. It can't have been easy, and I'm nearly certain it won't have had the effect she desired.

I bit the bullet with my husband too last night, though in a much less steamy fashion. A teary apology while we waited at Urgent Care. I was stressed about having to sell, I said, and missed my dad. It was true, but it wasn't genuine. I have nothing to be sorry for; he's the one who should be apologizing. Inspired by Camila's argument for egotism, I did it in the interest of self-preservation, because softening the antagonism between us was better for me. As she predicted, it was empowering to feel no guilt for thinking only of my own interests for once.

I take a sip of espresso, fingering the flyer that was left on the table for tonight's full moon party on the beach. A list of DJs spinning electronic music, specialty drinks, lights, a bonfire. *Bacchanalia*. The same as it ever was. As a provocative teen, Bacchanalia—plenty of drugs and alcohol, no ID required—was my favorite night of the summer. But I haven't been back since the terrible night I came home to find Noah assaulting Abby in the guesthouse, and I swore I'd never return.

The sound of a broom scratching over the stone draws my eye to a storefront near the bottom of the sloping hill, and I'm surprised to see the man holding the broom looks exactly like Dimitrios, tall and broad-shouldered, with thick dark hair tucked behind his ears. Curious, I slip the party flyer into my back pocket and saunter down the lane toward him.

He turns as I draw near, and I grin. "Dimitrios," I call.

He looks surprised, but not excited, to see me, and I immediately worry that Emelia and I took it too far on the beach the other day.

"What are you doing here?" I ask lightly.

"My mother's shop," he says, gesturing to the dress shop.

"Oh, she's a dressmaker?"

"She make some dress you wear," he says, and looking through the window I see he's right. She makes a lot of the dresses they sell at the little store down the hill that I took Emelia to the other day.

"I love those dresses."

He nods, returning to sweeping.

"We missed you at the house yesterday," I say, watching as he continues to push the broom rhythmically without meeting my eye. "Will you be back today?"

Sweep. Sweep. Sweep. Finally he glances up at me and shakes his head.

"Why not?" I ask.

His powerful shoulders tense. "I not say," he says.

"I hope Emelia and I didn't offend you the other day," I apologize. "We shouldn't have done that. We didn't mean to put you in a bad position."

He stops sweeping and looks up at me, a flicker of something suggestive behind his dark eyes. "Is not that. That was . . . nice. Sorry, my English." I can tell he wishes he had better words to convey his feelings. "Is not you."

The way he says it makes me think it is someone, though, not something. "My husband?" I ask.

"Please," he says, his face strained. "They send other worker."

I nod. "Okay."

Once he sees I'm not going to push for answers, he relaxes a little, his lips parting slightly as he looks at me.

"I'll miss having you around," I say.

He holds my gaze with a slight smile, sending a shiver through me. "You want, you find me here. I open and close."

Impulsively, I hug him, my arms around his thick neck, his body firm against mine. There is nothing manufactured about him; his muscles are hardened by manual labor, his scent that of skin warmed by the sun. I imagine he would taste slightly salty, that he would lift me easily.

Flushed, I release him, squeezing his large hand. "I'll see you around," I say. And I force myself to walk away.

BACK AT THE HOUSE, I find Camila and Emelia sunbathing by the pool. Shockingly, both of them are actually wearing their swimsuits—in deference, I suppose, to the workers who are toiling in and out of the guesthouse again today. Emelia sits up when she sees me come out of the living room, shading her eyes against the sun.

"How's your hand?" she calls, getting up to meet me.

"Okay," I answer, showing her my bandage. Across the pool, Camila doesn't budge. "I feel a little silly, actually, it wasn't as bad as I thought it would be."

"Better safe than sorry," Emelia says, tucking a wisp of flaxen hair behind her ear.

"Benny went back to Rome this morning," I say.

"I wondered where he was," Emelia says. Camila remains unmoving. Emelia sees me looking at her and taps her ear. "She's meditating with earbuds."

I lower my voice. "I wish he'd taken her with him."

"Why didn't he?"

"She didn't want to go." I eye her. "I hear she was in bed with you and Timmy this morning."

Emelia blushes.

"What happened?" I ask.

"I was very drunk," she says, embarrassed. "One thing led to another."

"And? Come on, I want details," I press, grabbing her hand and pulling her to sit with me on the couch in the shade of the portico. "You slept with the enemy. How did it happen?"

"We were in the pool and she was— Well, you saw the way she was," she whispers. "There was a lot of . . . provocation. At first I was just going along to prove something—to her, to Timmy, to me, I don't know, but then it changed. Like a different person took over my body. I felt sexy and naughty. And Timmy was enjoying it so much. He hasn't looked at me like that in a long time."

"And her?" I ask.

"She was at the center of it."

I laugh. "Right where she likes to be. And you were okay with that?"

"I knew it was dangerous, but in the moment . . ." She shrugs. "We went upstairs when things started getting . . . you know."

"And you all—?" I ask.

She nods. "No one was left out. But this morning when I woke up, they were fucking in the bed beside me."

"Oh." I involuntarily wince. "What did you do?"

"I tried to touch him, but he told me he just wanted me to watch. I tried. But it was like I wasn't even there. They were just staring into each other's eyes. I couldn't take it anymore, so I left. Went downstairs, had breakfast. Then she came out like nothing had happened and said she was going to meditate."

"Should I ask her to leave?" I ask, gazing across the pool at her.

She shakes her head. "That'll only make things worse between Timeo and me. At least this way . . ." She shrugs. "I'm trying everything I can to stay married right now."

"I know," I say. "I just wish you didn't have to." In my pocket, my cellphone begins to ring, and I read Leon's number on the screen. "Hi," I answer.

"I have Leon for you," his secretary, Debby, says.

"Give me one second," I reply. "Sorry," I tell Emelia, putting the call on mute. "I have to take this."

In search of privacy, I ascend the stairs quietly and steal down the second-floor hallway. I'm feeling more and more like Leon is the only one—besides Benny, of course—with my best interests at heart, and I don't want Garrett listening in on our phone call.

I enter the unused guest room at the far end of the house over the kitchen, softly closing the door behind me, and sit on the plush white bed. "I'm back."

"Gia, I've been trying to reach you," Leon says.

"I know," I say. "Things have been a bit hectic around here. What's up?"

"It's a somewhat delicate matter," he says deferentially. "Concerning your husband. Are you alone?"

Apprehension speeds my heart, driving me to my feet. "Yes."

"His company, Hoegg Worldwide—they've paid no taxes the past two years."

"What does that mean? Is he in trouble?"

"It could mean any number of things, but in this case it most likely means the business has closed, though no paperwork was filed to close it properly."

Suddenly woozy, I go to the window and lean my head against the warm glass, staring across the channel at the hills of Kampos shimmering in the heat. If the company's closed, then where has all my money gone?

"Maybe they couldn't pay taxes?" I ask hopefully, fully aware of the irony that I'm hoping my husband is a tax evader.

"Possibly," he says. "His business partner, Nicholas Hoegg, the man he claims is his father—"

"He claims?" I ask. "Is that in question?"

"I'll get to that. Regardless, Nicholas Hoegg was incarcerated in the Netherlands for three years recently for embezzlement."

Embezzlement. I shudder. "When did he get out?"

"About three months ago, but just last week he was taken back in for violating his parole."

So that was the real reason why Garrett had asked me not to talk about the company with Leon. I wonder now whether he and his father had ever really run it together. Whether it was real, or a front for something else.

"Did you learn anything else about the company?" I ask.

"Very little, which is never a good sign," he says. "I'll have my people continue to investigate. However, I'm concerned about the money you've given him."

"Loaned," I say, unconvincingly.

"Right," he says. "The two six-figure sums of money you asked me to transfer earlier this year are likely gone by now, but you also wrote a check to him personally this week, out of the account we created to manage the repairs on the house."

I'd forgotten he could access all my accounts. "That's right."

"He tried to deposit it day before yesterday, but we put a stop order on it."

My breath catches in my throat. "You what?"

"We caught it before it went through."

Out on the sea, the speedboat cutting a straight line toward the horizon looks like a toy. "Why did you do that?"

"It was suspicious activity, outside the proposed budget for repairs, and when I looked through the account with a more detailed eye, I noticed the checks written to cash were signed by him."

I sink to the floor, cradling my head in my hands. Clearly Garrett doesn't know about the stop order yet, but he will soon.

"Any time there's a red flag like this," Leon continues, "we lock down accounts until we can talk to the client to ensure the charges are legitimate."

"I told you he needed the money," I say.

"Yes, and you also promised he was going to ring me before you gave it to him. Can you confirm where the ninety thousand euros he wrote checks to cash for went?"

I feel like I'm at school again, being reprimanded for doing something stupid. "They were for raw materials."

"The price of raw materials is built into the contract."

My husband is stealing from me. The words he won't say. The line is silent, my head heavy with too many treacherous thoughts to speak.

"Gia," he says gently. "Your marriage is not my business, but your money is."

"So why didn't you stop the checks to cash?" I ask desperately. "Why didn't you stop me giving him the three hundred thousand I already gave him?"

"Your father asked me to give you some autonomy with your money," he says. "It has not been uncommon for you to take out six-figure amounts for various business ventures, or to write large checks to cash. But there's a limit to what is normal behavior, and that line has been crossed."

I sigh. "Garrett took a loan from a shady guy and made him his business partner." Saying it out loud, I realize how terrible it sounds.

"He just told me, before I wrote him that last check. He needed it to pay the guy back, or he said we could both be in danger."

"Gia . . ." I can hear the frustration and disappointment in his voice.

Suddenly my mother's words come back to me. *He's a fraud. He tried to steal from me.*

"Did my mom say anything to you about him?" I ask.

"She called here after your visit, very upset. She swore he'd posed as a philanthropist interested in her art for a charity auction." He sighed. "It wasn't the first time she'd accused someone of something like that, and I had no way of proving one way or another whether Garrett had ever met her before, which was why I didn't say anything to you, but I've had someone looking into him since you married. Whoever he is, he's slick—"

"Whoever he is?" I echo.

"Gia . . ." He pauses. "I'm afraid you may need to consider that Garrett might not be who he says he is. His LLC is a shield and there's no trace of him online that my guy could find, other than his profile on his company's website, and a few business networking accounts that could easily be fabricated. Your mom could be right about him."

I stare at the floorboards, at a loss for words. I feel as though I've just been pushed out a window, the ground rushing up at me.

"What would be the financial ramifications of a divorce?" I ask in a small voice.

"Your prenup stipulates he gets a million unless he cheats," he says.

"I know." He doesn't need to remind me he'd advised that I tie the amount to the length of our marriage and how much I had in the bank.

"So." He clears his throat. "Let's hope he cheats."

I can't help but think of Garrett and Aristea in the kitchen, the sharp knife between them as she sensuously ran her finger down the blade. I picture Camila in the pool last night, her ample breasts like ripe fruit as she enticed him to take his clothes off. He might well have ended up in bed with her if I hadn't dragged him away to Urgent Care.

If he hasn't strayed yet, I think it's safe to say he will, and there's a woman under my roof who would love nothing more than to lure him in. Perhaps I should let her.

GIA'S MANUSCRIPT

CHAPTER 14

L UNCH ON THE OUTDOOR TERRACE IS SURREAL, THE KNOWLEDGE
I've just acquired like a wrecking ball swinging around my brain,
smashing everything I thought I knew into a fine dust that coats the
gears of my mind, making it hard to think. I cringe to recall how will-
ingly I'd handed over the first two chunks of cash to Garrett, feeling
so pleased with myself for being able to help my husband. If the
money hasn't gone to his business, where *has* it gone? And what will
he do when he finds out the latest check has been canceled?

What's his end game?

I don't know that I want to find out.

The day is still and clear, the heat pressing down like a weighted
blanket. I observe Aristea as she sets platters of steaming chicken
souvlaki in the center of the table, her eyes lowered, long black
lashes resting on full cheeks. She's always been demure, but she
seems especially so today, beads of perspiration glistening on her
upper lip as she places individual bowls of homemade tzatziki before
each of us, and I wonder whether my husband has done something
to make her uncomfortable.

Emelia exclaims over the orzo salad, punctuated by chunks of cool green Persian cucumber and cherry-red grape tomatoes that explode with flavor when you bite into them, but the tzatziki is my favorite, tangy and fresh, the dill rough on my tongue. A thrill of nasty pleasure vibrates in me as I see Camila wrinkle her nose at the chicken. I wanted so badly to ask Aristea to sprinkle bacon on everything but as much as I'd love to go full carnivore on Camila, she may prove of use to me yet, so I exercised restraint.

"The olive oil is pressed from the olives in our grove," I say, striving to keep my voice light.

Having already achieved whatever she wanted with Timeo, Camila is more focused on Garrett today, impressing him with her knowledge of the Greek playwrights. Between the two years she attended Yale drama school (before leaving to film a Marvel movie, she's sure to tell us) and his recent time spent in the library here, they have much to banter about. The rest of us have little to add as they discuss the differences between the Sophocles and Euripides versions of *Electra*, obviously pleased with themselves and each other.

My crisp, dry sauvignon blanc goes down ice cold, their voices fading to background noise as I silently lay the groundwork for my scheme.

Emelia mentions it might be fun to go out tonight, and, feeling out-of-body, I show them the flyer for Bacchanalia. The timing is almost too perfect. The knot of apprehension that forms in the pit of my stomach when I suggest we go grows only tighter when they respond enthusiastically. It's all happening so fast. Timeo has molly, of course he does. And it's on Camila's list of vibration-raising drugs. So it's decided, we will have a light supper and leave around eleven tonight. Seeing as there are no taxis on the island, they debate how we should travel, given the plan to get high.

"The horses," I tell them. "We always take the horses. You can trust them not to get too plastered."

They laugh, thrilled by the prospect of riding to the party.

"Bacchanalia," Emelia reads, looking at the flyer. "What does it mean?"

"It's a festival to honor Bacchus, the god of wine and ecstasy," I answer.

"Appropriate," Timeo says with a smirk.

We don't finish lunch until late afternoon, at which time everyone falls into a drowsy torpor by the pool, too dazed to notice when I slip out the front door and fire up one of the ATVs. The pleather seat burns my thighs as I cruise down the hill toward the town, the hot wind tossing my tangled hair.

I park the quad on the street in a patch of shade cast by a scraggly tree and tread slowly up the whitewashed lane that leads to Dimitrios's mother's shop. It's not quite five, so I purchase a cold Perrier at the empty café and sit in the shade beneath the blooming bougainvilleas that crawl the trellis, watching the black cat I saw earlier toy with a nearly dead lizard in the alley.

I'm facing downhill toward the shop when he approaches from behind me, and I nearly miss him, calling out as I recognize his broad shoulders and loping gate. He turns, his expression quizzical. "Gia," he says. "I see you two today."

"Twice, yes," I say. "I'm sorry, I promise I'm not stalking you, but I needed to talk to you."

He casts a glance down the hill toward his mother's shop, then takes the seat opposite me.

"I'm sorry," I repeat. "I know you don't want to talk about this, but it's important that I know—"

"Okay," he says, resting his clasped hands on the table, his dark eyes unsettled. "I see you are upset."

"Yes," I say. "I need to know if you . . . Do you know whether my husband might have had—or might be having—an affair?"

"More slow," he says with an apologetic smile.

"Do you know if Garrett has cheated on me? Had sex with another woman," I translate bluntly.

His face changes as he understands, the words hanging between us. "I . . ." He bites his lip, studying his hands.

"Please, Dimitrios," I say, reaching across the table to place my hands over his. I wait until he looks at me. "I won't tell him you told me, I won't even tell him I know. I just need to know for myself."

His eyes search mine, his expression sympathetic.

"I will not tell anyone," I repeat. "I need to know."

He closes his eyes and nods ever so slightly. I let the breath I didn't realize I was holding out through pursed lips. "Aristea?" I whisper.

Again, he nods.

"Is it still going on?" I ask.

He opens his deep-set eyes and leans across the table, lowering his voice. "It was before Aristea and me, we were . . ."

I nod, acknowledging that this is not news to me.

"But this week, I see them again. It is why I leave work."

"A few nights ago?" I ask, thinking of the day Benny and Camila arrived, when Garrett hurtled into the night on the ATV, the check I wrote him burning a hole in his pocket.

He nods.

"Okay," I say. "I won't tell." I press my thumb and forefinger together and draw them across my mouth as though zipping and locking it. "Thank you."

He glances down the hill toward his mother's shop, where I see a woman in her fifties standing with her hands on her hips, looking up and down the alley. Her hair is shot through with gray and her face is lined from the sun, but she's still beautiful, like her son. Dimitrios grabs a pen and scribbles a number on a cocktail napkin. "My number. If you need."

"Thank you."

He rises, casting an ambiguous glimmer of a smile over his shoulder as he walks away. I see his mother's face light up when she spies him, notice the familial ease between them as they go inside her shop. Sudden longing squeezes my heart. My parents loved us, of course, but never in the effortless, uncomplicated way that Dimitrios's mother obviously loves him.

I appreciate that I've led a charmed life, that my father's fortune has afforded me opportunities and freedom few others will ever experience. But sometimes I wonder what it would have been like if I'd had a simpler childhood, with parents who kissed us good night and bandaged our skinned knees, who laughed together and came to our school plays. Perhaps if they'd known how to be happy, I would have learned it too.

Of course I'm feeling sorry for myself, though; in a matter of hours I've learned my husband is both stealing from me and cheating on me. That news would turn even someone with the rosiest childhood morose. I just feel so fucking stupid.

But I won't wallow. I can't. I have to fix this.

ABBY

CHAPTER 9

I NEED TO GO TO GREECE," BENNY SAID, HIS GAZE FIXED ON THE VIEW. The morning was cold and gray, the lake at the bottom of the hill a dark stain beneath leaden skies.

I took a sip of my espresso, joining him at the floor-to-ceiling window. "I'll go with you."

He turned, his eyes rimmed with dark circles but lit by surprise. Pleasant surprise, I thought. "You could stay here if you wanted, we have the suite until Friday."

Like our previous suite, this one boasted two luxurious bedrooms flanking a living room, and while there was no glass ceiling, it had the advantage of being on the top floor with only one door. But there was no way I was staying here.

"I want to go," I said. "Did you sleep last night?"

He shook his head. "You?"

"Not well." I'd tossed and turned for hours, finally drifting off to be tortured by nightmares that Gia was dead and I was the one who'd killed her. "I keep wondering if we need to get the police involved."

He met my eye, the past hovering in the space between us.

The events of that terrible night were etched indelibly into my brain, even after twelve long years.

IT WAS DARK IN THE guesthouse when Gia swung the heavy lamp into Noah's head from behind, knocking him off me with one hard blow. The rug that was usually beneath the couch had been sent out for cleaning, and his skull smacked the tile with a sickening thunk as he fell to the floor, revealing Gia, backlit by the light through the door, her hair wild. The lamp dangled from her hand, shade askew, the metal sailboat base dented and smeared with blood.

I didn't realize I was screaming until she dropped the lamp and rushed to me, her face a mask of shock and horror. "Abby," she kept repeating as she grabbed my shoulders. "Abby. Abby. Abby." She pulled me up to sitting, wrapping her arms around me, smoothing my hair. "It's okay," she said. "You're okay now."

My teeth chattered in shock as I looked down at Noah's form, unmoving on the floor.

"It's okay, he's out cold," Gia said.

"It's not okay, look at him." Even in the shadowy room, I could tell his body was crumpled on the floor in an unnatural way. "You probably gave him a concussion—"

She pushed back, her eyes flashing. "He was fucking attacking you, what was I supposed to do?"

"I don't know!" I said, my head spinning so fast I could hardly process what was happening. My hands shook violently as I reached around her to grab my underwear from where it was bunched in the cushions of the couch.

In a panic, Gia and I tried to figure out what to do next, deciding finally to wake up Benny and get his opinion, which was that we should immediately call the police. By the time the three of us returned to the guesthouse, thick, dark blood was seeping from beneath Noah's skull, and we couldn't find a pulse.

What didn't make it into Gia's book was the frenzied, near-hysterical debate we had about whether to hide the body in the old well or call the authorities. In the end, we came to our senses and called Papa Hugo, who advised us to sit tight while he rang his fishing buddy on the island police force, then found us a lawyer.

Unfortunately, his fishing buddy was vacationing on another island and the lawyer had to fly in from Athens, so neither would be able to make it for hours. In the interim, two other officers were sent to deal with the scene.

The sun was coming up by the time the cops arrived, one who couldn't have been more than a few years older than us, the other with one foot in the grave. While the old one secured the crime scene, the young one handcuffed all three of us and threw us in the back of an old pickup truck to take us down to the police station, where they chucked us into the holding cell on the basement level.

We'd seen enough crime procedurals to know not to say anything until we'd spoken to a lawyer, so after providing the basic details of what had happened, we kept our mouths shut while they peppered us with questions. They were clearly skeptical of our account, dubious both of whether Noah was truly assaulting me and whether Gia had genuinely not meant to kill him. Since there was no hospital on the island, a nurse who was as nervous as I was, neither of us ever having completed a rape kit before, performed the collection on a plastic folding table in one of the offices, with a newspaper covering the window in the door. It came as no surprise to me when we later learned the sample was contaminated so badly as to be unusable.

Officer Theodoropoulos finally turned up around noon. As a family friend, he was far more inclined to believe our story than the other officers were. Our lawyer arrived on a helicopter from Athens not long after, and over the protests of the other officers, Theodoropoulos allowed us to go back to the house with our new attorney and get a good night's rest before we returned for questioning the next day.

We had no way of knowing that that wasn't standard procedure, but much was made of it in the press afterward, and while Noah's death was ruled a justifiable homicide and no charges were ever pressed against any of us, the other police officers made it known they were doubtful of our story. In an echo of the Amanda Knox debacle, rumors swirled that we'd been involved in some kind of satanic sex ceremony, or that Gia had killed Noah in a fit of jealousy when she found him in bed with me.

In the end, talk is just talk, and Gia's memoir drowned out the other voices in the conversation, casting her as the hero.

But even all these years later, I was wary of asking the island police to look for her.

"IT'S HARD TO WANT TO get them involved unless we absolutely have to," Benny said now, echoing my own thoughts.

"Agreed."

"There's a flight from Kiruna at eleven," Benny noted, looking at his phone. "It goes through Stockholm, then Frankfurt, to land in Athens tonight. We'll have to stay the night but can take the first ferry out tomorrow and be to Miteras by noon."

I closed my eyes, mentally preparing for the journey. "Okay," I said. "Let's do it."

While Benny spoke to his assistant to book our travel, I called Gia again, but her line continued to go straight to voicemail. I refreshed my email for the millionth time, adrenaline shooting through me as the name Gia Highsmith Torres appeared at the top.

"She emailed!" I cried, showing Benny the phone.

He looked over my shoulder as I opened the untitled email.

Feeling much better today but I've lost my voice! Think I may actually venture out of the house this morning to hit the store. I got your messages. Please don't worry about me. I'll call as soon as I get my voice back! Love you! G

"Venture out of the house," he said. "But she's not in the house."

His face was as grave as mine as we locked eyes. "It's not her," I said. "Someone has her phone."

"Fuck." My heart sank as we stared at each other, processing.

Again it was on the tip of my tongue to tell Benny about the emails, but what good would it do, when I didn't know who'd sent them or what they wanted?

We were going to Greece. I had a feeling I'd find my answers there.

GIA'S MANUSCRIPT

CHAPTER 15

T HE NIGHT IS QUIET SAVE FOR THE CLOPPING OF THE HORSES'
hooves on the road, the moon above full and bright, casting the
rolling hills in a silvery sheen that turns the landscape of the island
mysterious and foreign. Timeo, Garrett, and I are the most expe-
rienced riders, so we're the ones at the reins, with Emelia behind
Timeo on Duke, the large gray stallion, and Camila behind Garrett
on Sandstorm, the palomino. I'm alone in the lead on Athena, the
formidable black alpha mare. Horses maintain a strict herd hierar-
chy, jockeying for position any time a new horse is introduced, but
Athena has maintained her position as leader since she joined the
pack.

Camila hasn't realized yet that I'm the alpha mare of my herd.
But she will. I'm the one who suggested she ride with Garrett; it took
no convincing for her to take the bait. I don't need to turn around to
know she's pressing her ample breasts into his back.

The road is white in the moonlight, our shadows tall and thin.
All day I've successfully hidden the loathing for my husband that's
spread through me like wildfire, charring the last remaining scraps of

love; if I can just keep up the charade a while longer, I'll be able to walk away without having to pay him for the privilege.

I'm heartbroken, though I doubt now that the man I loved ever really existed. I should have been more wary of the miraculous way we fitted together, how he always knew just what to say to me, just what to do.

Someone once told me that if you listen, in the beginning of a relationship, a person will tell you everything you need to know about them, both positive and negative. The problem is that most of the time we're so blinded by infatuation that we don't listen.

Garrett told me he'd never met a woman capable of holding his attention, and I felt special, believing I was the woman who could. He told me that he was good at reading people and seeing opportunities where others failed to, and that he played the long game, unafraid to hold out for the win. Never did I think the long game would be me.

Meanwhile, encouraged by a man who challenged me, who regularly gave me multiple orgasms and seemed to understand me in a way others didn't, I told him everything. He knew how badly I wanted the love I'd never felt as a child, that I was impulsive and rebellious enough to marry quickly and without the approval of my family. He was well aware that I was bad with money and overly generous because I felt guilty for being rich, that I was loyal to a fault to those closest to me, and that when I loved someone, I trusted them fully. He knew I loved him. He saw the opportunity and held out for the win.

I realize now that luck likely had no hand in our meeting that day on the beach. I thought he believed my charade, but he must have known all along that I was the late Hugo Torres's daughter.

In our marriage vows, we swore that we would sharpen and strengthen each other, that our love would never make us soft. That was one promise he kept. His love was hard and brittle, and now it's broken and jagged, with dangerous edges. If it was ever love at all.

I did soften, though, didn't I? I gave him money when he needed it, stood by him when he made poor decisions, took his word as truth. My love, it turned out, was malleable and compliant, just like all those contented couples we mocked. After everything, I was just a normal girl who wanted to love and be loved, like Emelia.

Ahead on the beach at the bottom of the road, I can see the colored lights of Bacchanalia, feel the bass booming. The party here is a tamer version of the famously wild full moon celebration on Koh Phangan, with its thousands of pleasure seekers, and I much prefer this celebration to that. This gathering is built around a lone beach club centered on a perfect crescent beach and numbers perhaps two or three hundred revelers, a mix of tourists and young locals from the neighboring islands.

We dismount and tether the horses behind the berm at the edge of the dirt parking lot, and I tip one of the parking attendants to keep an eye on them. We're all adorned with face paint, Emelia and I in bikini tops and shorts while Camila wears glow-in-the-dark pasties beneath her white mesh shirt—an outfit it strikes me that she chose to pack into her suitcase before she came here, unaware we would go to this party.

Inside the beach club, the crowd is not yet thick, but the vibe is celebratory. At the turntables perched above the sandy dance floor, a sweating DJ wearing a toga revs up the crowd with bass-heavy music that rattles my bones, while red, blue, purple, and green lights slide over gyrating bodies.

A waitress appears with a bottle of gin and a bucket of tonic and water, and I pretend to down my molly with the group, smiling and shaking my hips as if I don't have a care in the world. We move to the sandy disco floor where I dance wildly and drink slowly, just enough gin to take the edge off without making me sloppy or sleepy. The pills hit the others fast, slurring their speech and taking over their bodies, their eyes rolling back in their heads as they caress themselves and one another.

I pretend not to care when Camila places Garrett's hands on her nearly bare breasts, rubbing against him with her eyes closed, but I'm gruesomely thrilled. I watch as Timeo nuzzles into her back and she places his hands on her stomach, just beneath Garrett's, their arms brushing against each other as they grind on her.

Fucking perfect.

I locate Emelia, too out of her head to notice or care what her husband is doing, dancing by herself so close to a giant speaker that I worry she might blow her ears out. She grins when she sees me and gives me a bear hug, squeezing me so tight I can hardly breathe.

"I'm so glad I met you, Gia," she says, grinding her jaw. "I'm so happy you're my friend. I wish . . ." She stares into my eyes, unable to focus at close range.

"What?" I ask.

She looks up at the stars and lets out a giant sigh. "I wish I were a better person."

"You're a great person," I assure her.

"But I'm not," she says, pushing the heels of her palms into her eyes. "I'm not."

"Come with me," I say, squeezing her hand as I pull her away from the crowd, past the bonfire and down to the beach.

"Where are we going?" she asks, skipping along beside me.

"I wanted to talk to you away from the others," I say.

"Ooh, secrets," she enthuses, and I worry that perhaps I shouldn't tell her what I'm about to. Then again, she probably won't remember any of this in the morning.

We reach the shore and the sun-warmed water laps over our bare feet. Emelia bends down and splashes it on her face, smearing her makeup, and on her arms and legs. "Feels so good," she murmurs, rubbing her own shoulders.

"Here," I say, grabbing an errant plastic beach chair and placing it where the water meets the sand. "Sit down. I'll give you a massage."

"You're the best!" Her eyes go wide with pleasure, and I see in the lights from the dance floor that her pupils are the size of bowling balls, the blue of her irises just a thin rim around the black. "But what about your finger?" she asks, grabbing my injured hand.

"I've got nine more," I say.

She gamely sits in the chair and I tie her long hair up with the ponytail holder from around my wrist and begin kneading her delicate neck. Her body feels birdlike in my hands, soft and bony and vulnerable, as though with one quick move I could snap her in two.

"God, that feels good," she says, relaxing her head against my chest. "You're so nice. Not like I thought you would be."

"Like you thought I would be?"

She turns her face, resting her cheek on my boob. "And your boobs are so soft."

I laugh. "I bet Camila's are softer."

"But you're nicer."

"I want to play a little game," I say, staring out at the moonlight shimmering on the ocean.

"I like games," she murmurs.

"This is the *what if* game." I slide my thumbs up and down her neck. "*What if* you could live anywhere in the world, where would it be?"

"That's easy," she answers with a laugh. "Right here in this chair on the beach with you rubbing my shoulders."

"And *what if* you could be anything you wanted to be? What would you be?"

"Also easy," she says. "I'd be a mom. A good mom, with so many children I couldn't hold them in my lap all at once."

My heart breaks a little for her as I ask the next question.

"What if you could leave Timeo and still have plenty of money? Would you?"

She quiets, watching the waves lap over her pink toenails. "Would I find someone else to love?"

"Of course you would," I say, rubbing my thumbs between her shoulder blades.

"Then yes," she whispers. "I would leave him, and I would find someone else to love."

THE PARTY IS STILL RAGING when I suggest we leave. Only I know what time it is, the rest of them rolling their faces off, their brains flooded with serotonin. I want to keep it that way, to make sure they're all sexed up and not thinking clearly when we return to the house. I put Emelia on the horse behind me and she holds on so tightly that I have to gently loosen her grip to breathe. Garrett rides alone, with Camila—who wanted to "straddle the big stallion"—behind Timeo this time. We canter up the hill three abreast with me in the center, watching to make sure none of them fall off.

At the house, I lead the group to the living room, where I put on sexy chill trance music and pour everyone another stiff drink, lighting the array of candles in the fireplace to set the mood. It works almost too well. Camila suggests the girls dance for the boys, a performance she quickly turns into a strip tease. I'm grateful for her now, I remind myself as she runs her hands over my body, pulling my triangle top aside to palm my breast. It's kismet that she turned up when she did, that she's a nymphomaniac exhibitionist who gets off on coming between couples.

She's perfect, I think, as she kisses Emelia and strips off her mesh shirt so that she's only in her daisy pasties. She releases Emelia to throw her shirt at the boys and I wrap my arms around Emelia and whisper in her ear, "Now."

Emelia sways. "I don't feel so good," she announces. "I think I need to lie down."

Timeo looks up, annoyed, but I smile at him.

"I'll go with her," I say. "Don't worry. Enjoy yourselves." For good measure, I saunter over and kiss Garrett, unzipping his pants to fondle him before I stand, smiling seductively, then plant a kiss on Camila's mouth.

I slap her ass as I walk away, grabbing my phone before I follow Emelia up the stairs.

When we reach the top of the stairwell, Emelia turns to me, her face creased with worry in the shadowy hallway, and I'm afraid she's going to back out and return downstairs, ruin things for herself.

"All you have to do is go to sleep," I say. "I'll take care of everything else. In the end, it's up to you whether you want to use it or not. I'm just giving you an option."

She nods. "Okay."

I walk her to her bathroom and help her clean the smeared paint off her face, then wait as she sloppily showers off the sweat and salt water and changes into one of Timeo's T-shirts. As I'm tucking her into bed, I pause.

"What did you mean earlier tonight when you said I was nicer than you thought I would be?"

"Oh," she murmurs, settling into the pillow. "Just when we met, I thought you'd be like the girls Timmy went to school with. They always looked down on me because I didn't come from money. But you're not like that."

Once I've turned off the light, I hasten to the opposite end of the hall, where I quietly open the door to the roof deck above the kitchen, then steal down the outside stairs in the dark, careful not to make any noise as I linger in the shadows on the pool deck.

The bacchanalian tableau inside is bright through the windows, Camila, Timeo, and Garrett the players on a candlelit stage, the three of them moving together in time to the music, caressing one another sensuously. I raise my phone and press Record as Camila kisses first Timeo and then Garrett, without a hint of awkwardness or guilt, her red talons buried in their hair. I watch as the clothes come off and the carnal scene becomes a pornographic blur that would make a whore blush. I watch it all as the flames of bitterness rage inside me, blackening my soul.

They're still at it when I go to bed upstairs in the guestroom where I spoke to Leon earlier today. I'm tired, empty, and nauseated, my heart charred to a crisp. I set this up, suggested the full moon party, pushed the drugs, encouraged their lust, knowing exactly where it was headed. But watching it happen was a different thing. Watching, I realized I hadn't need to do any of that. What happened tonight was going to happen whether I wanted it to or not.

ABBY

CHAPTER 10

WITHIN AN HOUR OF MAKING THE DECISION TO LEAVE, BENNY AND I were on our way, the trunk of our rental loaded with our bags as we retraced our steps from two days ago, down the mountain, around the lake, and back to the Kiruna airport. The situation felt surreal, similar to the days following Noah's death. Only this time it wasn't the past that loomed specter-like, but the future.

As we drove along the winding road, Benny's cellphone began to vibrate and he lifted it from the center console, checking the number. "It's our accountant." He accepted the call. "Leon. You're on speakerphone with Abby. Did you get my email?"

"I did," Leon said. "I understand why you're concerned and I'm glad you called me." He paused. "Something a bit peculiar did happen yesterday. I don't normally share these kinds of details about my clients, but seeing as you're her brother and I know how close you are . . ."

"What is it?"

"The money from the sale of the property to Melodie went into Gia's account on Friday, and yesterday morning she tried to transfer it out, but the deposit was still pending, so the transfer didn't go through."

Benny's eyes met mine, his brow creased. "How long will the deposit take to post?"

"For an amount this large, it can take a few days. It just went in on Friday, and Saturday and Sunday aren't bank days, so it's unlikely it will be available in full before Wednesday."

"Can you put some kind of lock on the account so she can't do anything?" I asked. "We're afraid someone may have logged in to her accounts and be posing as her."

"The best I can do is a fraud alert, which will delay any transfers. To lock it, we'll need to get the police involved."

"Okay, it's a start," Benny said. "Can you tell where she was trying to transfer the money to?"

"Yes, to a numbered account I don't have access to. I did some digging and it's owned by an LLC called Hoegg Holdings. Garrett's business is Hoegg Worldwide, so one can assume it's one of his accounts."

Benny's jaw dropped. "She tried to transfer fifteen million to her husband's business? Why would she do that?"

"The agreed upon price was actually fourteen, as she elected not to finish repairs," Leon said. "And I don't know. What makes it stranger is that, as I'm sure you know, she's been unable to locate him to serve him divorce papers."

Benny and I looked at each other, thrown. "Divorce papers?" Benny asked.

Leon paused. "My apologies, I could've sworn she told me she'd talked to you about it."

"No," Benny said, swerving to avoid the bloated carcass of a deer. "I wasn't aware they were divorcing. Did something else happen?"

"I shouldn't—"

"I know this isn't information you would normally give out," I said, "but we are seriously worried something may have happened to Gia."

"We're on our way to Greece now to look for her," Benny added.

Leon sighed. "There was a video . . . of Garrett with another woman. I gave her the number for your father's divorce attorney."

"When was this?" Benny asked.

"About a month ago."

"That was right after I left," Benny said. "Did she mention who the other woman was?"

"I'm sorry, I can't—"

"Was she by any chance Camila Delgado?"

The line was silent as I raised my brows at Benny, recognizing the name of the famous actress. He shrugged sheepishly, and I understood Camila was the girl he'd mentioned bringing with him to Greece.

Suddenly I felt very stupid for thinking he might still harbor feelings for me.

"I'm sorry, I can't answer that," Leon said.

I cleared my throat. "Can you tell us it wasn't Camila Delgado?"

Again, the line was silent. Benny and I looked at each other in comprehension.

"Regardless," Leon said after a moment, "cheating negates the prenuptial agreement of a million-dollar payment."

"Okay," Benny said. "I hate to ask this, and it's probably unnecessary to even think about, but did Gia have a will in place? I'm just thinking—"

"I understand," Leon said. "Fortunately, she changed her will at the same time she filed for divorce. Her entire estate, in fact, goes to you, Benecio."

"Does Garrett know that?" I asked.

"Again," Leon said, "I don't know."

"Okay." Benny looked over at me and shook his head, his jaw clenched. "We'll be there tomorrow, I'll let you know what we find."

"I'll do the same," Leon said.

Pine trees blurred past as Benny hung up the phone and looked at me, resigned.

"It seems like we know who's in her accounts," I said.

"Fucking Garrett," he muttered. "I knew I didn't like that guy."

"She didn't mention the divorce to me. But that's not surprising, considering the fight we got into when I told her not to marry him."

"She probably wanted to tell us in person," Benny said.

We came around a bend and the airport loomed on the horizon. I sighed, thinking of the time it would take us to reach Miteras. "Do they do welfare checks in Greece?" I asked.

"I don't know," he said. "Probably."

"I think it's time to call the police. It's been twelve years, the guys we dealt with probably aren't even there anymore."

"That's true." He glanced at me. "Are you sure about going back there with me, dealing with the police again? I know how traumatic it was for you last time."

I nodded. "This isn't about me."

At least I hoped it wasn't.

GIA'S MANUSCRIPT

CHAPTER 16

UNSURPRISINGLY, I'M THE FIRST TO WAKE IN THE MORNING. THE guest room is too bright; the sun floods through the gauzy curtains, chasing hazy, grasping nightmares to the shadowy fringes of my troubled mind. My brain feels like it's been put through a meat grinder, my mouth dry as a bone, my insides scorched earth. I lie there for a moment plotting out my day before I rise to throw the curtains open, squinting out at the glassy azure sea. The ridges of the hills and spires of Kampos are sharp against the powder-blue sky, the view through the windows ever the same, despite what happens in the house.

After showering in the attached bathroom, I put on an old dress of my mother's I find in the closet, a long black halter dress with gashes of red flowers on it that look more like blood than blooms. I peek into Emelia's room to see she's alone in bed, sleeping soundly, then steal down the stairs to find Timeo and Camila asleep on the couch among the scattered cushions. He's had the decency to put on underwear, at least, but she is naked. Garrett, I assume, is still keeping up appearances, sleeping in our bed like a faithful husband. The louse.

I swim up through the wave of anger that crashes over me, gasping for air at the surface. I can't let my emotions get the better of me today. One foot in front of the other.

When I see the countertops in the kitchen crowded with empty glasses and water bottles, I realize it's Sunday, which means Aristea and the workers have the day off. I down two headache pills and drink two espressos in rapid succession, sharpening my mind like a knife, then shut myself in the library, taking a seat at the secretarial desk with my laptop. The gun in the glass case at eye level as I execute my to-do list feels somehow symbolic.

It's a good thing it doesn't have bullets.

First, I check the Cloud to ensure all the videos I shot last night are safely uploaded and duplicate them to a second account. Next, I transfer all the money out of the house checking account that Garrett has access to and into a personal savings account he won't be able to touch. Then I compose an email to my father's divorce attorney, attaching my prenup agreement and an especially damning still frame from one of the videos I shot last night. Finally, I check the ferry schedule, confirming the departure times for the day.

When I'm finished with all that, I stalk into the living room, where I roughly shake Camila's shoulder until she awakens, groggy and confused. "Get up," I snap.

She frowns at me. "It's too early."

"I have something you'll want to see."

It gives me pleasure to see she's a mess, her hair matted, her makeup smeared. "Can't it wait?"

"No." I grab her arm just above the elbow, jerking her up to sitting, then toss a throw blanket into her lap. "Cover yourself."

She clumsily swaddles herself with the blanket and gets unsteadily to her feet, following me into the library, where she immediately drops to the couch, curling up in her blanket. I sit next to her and open my laptop, then press Play on one of the more explicit videos of her with my husband and Timeo. She bolts upright, suddenly awake. "What's this?" Her voice cracks.

"This is a very graphic video of you fucking two married men."

She looks at me, bewildered, as the screen version of her straddles my husband's face. "We were just having fun."

"I can see that," I say.

Her eyes are still dilated. "Why are you showing me this?"

"I thought you'd be interested to see a preview of what I'll be sending to TMZ if you aren't on the next ferry out of here. Do you think your fans will like it?"

She looks at me in shock, her mouth opening and closing like a fish flopping around on the bottom of a boat.

"I mean, really, it's so much smuttier than Kim or Paris's videos. And so much clearer. Look there, I can see your labia."

She blinks, unable to speak.

I smile. "No? Well, then, you should probably start getting your things together. We need to leave in fifteen minutes."

She rises, swaying. "You're fucking crazy," she hurls as she totters toward the door.

"That makes two of us," I say. "Oh, and Camila? Leave my brother alone."

She glares at me before turning on her heel and lurching out of the room, and I feel a surge of power as control slips from her hands to mine.

WHEN I RETURN FROM DROPPING her at the ferry, the villa is as still as it was when I left, the only sound that of the whirring air conditioner, fighting valiantly against the heat of the day. I let myself into the master suite, locking the door behind me, then take a moment to focus on what I want to say before I open the door to the bedroom.

The bed is slept in but empty, the curtains open to the day, allowing beams of sunlight to bounce around the white space. I hear the water running in the bathroom and sit in the wicker chair by the window to wait, angling it toward the glass so I can gaze out at the boats on the sea below. I wish I were on one of them, sailing away.

Garrett emerges fresh from the shower with a towel around his waist, stopping halfway to his dresser when he notices me in the chair. "Morning," he says with a tinge of surprise.

"How was the rest of your evening?" I ask evenly.

He pulls on a pair of shorts, ignoring my tone. "I turned in not long after you."

"Did you?"

He comes to sit on the bench at the end of the bed, leaning on his forearms as he faces me, assessing. "What is it now?"

"Have you checked your account lately?"

"Not since yesterday morning," he says warily.

"You'll find that the check I gave you has been pulled back."

His face darkens. "What?"

"Leon thought it was fraudulent activity and flagged it."

He shoots to his feet. "You have to reinstate it. This is bad, Gia. This is really bad. These men are mafia. They don't ask twice."

"Really?" I ask dryly.

My tone stops him in his tracks. He narrows his eyes at me, suddenly suspicious. "What are you trying to say?"

"Where's the money going, Garrett?"

His muscles tense. "I told you."

My heart is speeding ninety miles an hour, but I keep my voice steady. "I need the truth."

"Are you accusing me of lying?"

"Are you lying?"

"I'm not even going to—"

"Why hasn't your company paid taxes the past two years?"

He clenches his fists, his veins popping out of his biceps, then swallows and sits on the bench, changing tactic. "Who told you that?" he asks in a controlled voice.

"Leon," I say. "He also mentioned that your dad was in jail for embezzlement."

"He's lying to you." He sighs and shakes his head, as though he feels sorry for me. "I'm your husband, don't you think I would have told you if any of that was true? He's trying to come between us because he doesn't want you giving me money." He focuses his captivating blue eyes on me as he has so many times before, but this time the spell doesn't work. "He's probably stealing from you, sweetheart."

I struggle to maintain my composure. "Like you?"

His jaw tenses as he shakes his head again. "I'm trying to help you." He approaches my chair and places a hand on each of its arms, effectively locking me in place, his face inches from mine. "I'm the one working my ass off to get my ships back on the sea so that I can make money to support you—"

"What ships?" I ask. "I don't even know if you have ships. You've lived off me since we got together—"

He grips the arms of the chair, his eyes hardening. "So I'm not rich enough for you, is that it?"

"I just want you to tell me the truth."

He grabs hold of my arms hard, pulling me up to standing. "Don't patronize me," he growls.

"Let go," I cry, sudden fear coursing through me.

He forcibly releases his grip, throwing me off balance. "You're a selfish bitch who wouldn't recognize a good thing if it slapped her in the face."

"I want a divorce."

He turns, his fists balled. "What did you say?"

"I want a divorce," I repeat more loudly this time.

His face is twisted with anger, all the beauty gone out of it. "If you divorce me, you'll never see the money you gave me again. And don't forget, you'll have to pay me a million dollars. A million dollars you can't afford until you sell this place."

My hands shake as I open my phone and pull up one of the many videos I filmed through the window last night. He roughly grabs it out of my hand, watching for only a moment before he deletes it.

"It's backed up multiple times," I say. "I don't owe you anything."

"You set me up," he seethes.

I'm about to tell him that I know about Aristea too, but he slams my phone into the tile floor, cracking the screen. I jump back as he slams it again and again until the screen goes dead, then tosses it aside, glaring up at me with bloodshot eyes.

"I want a divorce," I say again.

"I'll kill you first," he whispers.

A bolt of terror shoots through me and I step backward.

He sniggers, pleased with himself. "That's right, you should be afraid," he says. "You don't know what I'm capable of."

"You don't mean it," I say.

"Test me."

In my mind's eye I sweep the house for weapons. Hammers, shovels, rope, knives, gardening shears . . . and one very old revolver.

Does it even work? And where would I find bullets?

"If you kill me before the sale goes through, the property reverts to my family," I say, my heart beating so fast I'm breathless.

"Then perhaps I'll let you live that long." He says it like it's a joke, but neither of us is laughing.

"I'll go to the police, take out a restraining order."

"Ooh, I'm so scared," he mocks me.

"I want you out," I say. "Now. This is over."

"Oh no, this is just beginning, *love*." He flashes his winning smile. "This is the part where we really get to know each other."

"Out," I repeat. "By tomorrow morning. My attorney will be in touch."

"Good luck with that." His laugh sends chills down my spine. "Poor little rich girl. You were so desperate to be loved that you bought it all, hook, line, and sinker. Believed every word I said."

"Fuck you, Garrett."

Seething and scared, I rush into the closet, blindly throwing clothes into an overnight bag with violently shaking hands while he watches, amused.

"Where are you going?" he asks when I emerge with the stuffed bag.

"I need you out by tomorrow," I repeat, feigning a bravado I'm sure he can see straight through.

With wobbling legs, I rush from the room, quickly collecting my computer from the library and my cross-body purse from the end table next to the couch where Timeo is still sleeping. I shove the computer into the purse and hurtle into the torrid day, slamming the front door behind me with a silent prayer that he doesn't follow.

ABBY

CHAPTER 11

Day turned to night in a blur of airports and countries and phone calls as we inched toward Greece, trying in vain to obtain any information about Gia's whereabouts. On the phone, the island police didn't seem worried and assured us everything would be fine. With the door locked, they wouldn't be able to see any more than the stablemaster could, and without reasonable cause, we couldn't demand the door be broken down. It was clear nothing was going to be done until we arrived, and we couldn't get there any faster than we were going.

By the time we reached Athens, we were wiped out, both physically and mentally. The first ferry wasn't until the next morning, so we checked in to a small hotel near the port and grabbed a quiet dinner in the hotel bar, though neither of us had much of an appetite.

"Have you been back to Miteras since that summer?" Benny asked as we picked at our food.

I nodded. "I went with Gia when she returned two summers later, right before her book came out."

"Was it strange, being back?"

"At first. But Gia and I both had so many other memories there that it also felt oddly comfortable. And it helped that the guesthouse had been renovated."

"It's bittersweet, selling the place."

"Melodie would be thrilled to host you, I'm sure," I insinuated.

He laughed. "She does have a soft spot for me. And I want to be a brother to Hugo Junior."

"It always seemed strange to me that your dad married her. He was so warm, and she's so cold."

"She's really not as bad as Gia makes her out to be," he said. "When you get to know her, she actually has a lot of depth."

I paused, feeling guilty for having been so quick to judge her. "Why does Gia hate her so much?"

"Gia was wary of their age difference from the start, though Melodie wasn't in it for the money—she has her own. Then, after Hugo Junior was born, Dad tightened the purse strings on Gia, told her she was an adult and needed to start acting like one. He claimed it wasn't Melodie's influence, but Gia blamed her anyway."

"Ah," I said. "I didn't know that."

He stared into his wine for a moment, thoughtful. "I think our mom's illness took more of a toll on Gia than it did on me. By the time she was in middle school, Mom had become so depressed and paranoid she seldom got out of bed unless Dad was there—which was rarely. Gia stepped into the maternal role for me, but she didn't have anyone to do that for her."

It's funny, when I'd met Gia at thirteen, I'd thought it was so cool that she had no rules. As an adult I realized how sad that was. "Gia had to be so responsible early on that she did a one-eighty as soon as she was out of that house," I mused.

"It's why I have so much empathy for her, even when she drives me nuts." He checked his watch. "We should probably get out of here if we want to catch the seven A.M. ferry."

WHEN WE PARTED IN THE hotel hallway in front of our rooms, I went to kiss him on the cheek and he wrapped me in a hug. I laid my head on his chest, taking refuge in his strong arms.

"I'm glad you came," he said.

"I wasn't going to let you do this alone."

I looked up at him, our faces so close I could see the stubble on his chin, the nearly black rings around the irises of his brown eyes. I didn't want to let go. His eyes searched mine, and my breath grew shallow as we stood there like that, neither of us moving. His gaze dropped to my lips, sending a tremor through my body.

This was wrong. Gia was missing. I should be out looking for her, not tumbling into bed with her brother. But the longer we stood here, the warmth of his skin beckoning to me through his shirt, the hint of aftershave on his neck making me dizzy, the weaker my resolve was becoming.

"Abby . . ."

"We should go to bed," I murmured into his shirt.

"Yeah." But he didn't move.

We weren't thinking clearly. We needed to rest, to focus on finding Gia.

I took a deep breath and pulled away, avoiding his gaze as I inserted my key card into the lock of my door. "I'll see you bright and early," I said.

I pushed the door open, finally meeting his eye.

"Good night," he said without moving.

"Good night."

I closed the door behind me and leaned against the wall on the other side of it, my heart beating fast, until I heard the door to his room open and close.

THE SEA WAS CALM FOR our early morning ferry, the golden sunlight sparkling on the deep blue water. The salted breeze cooled my skin as we shuttled from island to island, dropping off and picking up a mix of locals and tourists. But the closer we drew to Miteras, the heavier the dread inside me became.

"What is it?" Benny asked, studying me.

"I just— Gia invited me to visit, earlier this summer, and I blew her off. I can't help but think if I'd—"

"Don't do that." He caught my eye. "It wouldn't have made any difference. Gia's gonna do what Gia's gonna do. There's nothing we've ever been able to do to influence her decisions. You can't change people."

"Why are you so damn wise?"

"I'm not." The wind lifted his hair as he pushed his sunglasses up on his nose. "But—you gotta understand people to write about them. After a while, you start to notice the patterns."

I looked over at him. "What are my patterns?"

"You sometimes find it difficult to say or do what you really want for fear of disappointing others," he said gently.

I opened my mouth to protest, but he was right. "You think I'm a people pleaser?"

"It's not a bad thing to care about people, as long as you're true to yourself. And it's common for only children."

"And girls whose best friend's dads pay for their education?"

He shrugged. "That might contribute. But like I said, it's not a bad thing. As long as you're looking out for your own interests as well."

He pointed as Miteras came into view on the horizon. The name means "mother" in Greek, and from this vantage point, the island looked like a woman lying on her side, her head the rounded hill that protected the house from the famous Aegean wind, the port where her torso met her legs.

"I stayed in my last relationship about a year too long because I didn't want to hurt him by breaking up with him," I admitted.

"But you did leave?"

I nodded, and a half-smile crept across his face. "What?" I asked.

"This is good news."

"Why's that?"

"Because it means I stand a chance."

I laughed, grateful for his attempt at levity, though I knew he didn't mean it. "Mm-hmm, yeah," I said, playing along. "From Camila Delgado to me. Sounds like a logical progression."

He bumped me with his shoulder. "I was only dating Camila Delgado because you weren't available."

I laughed it off, but the glimmer in his eye as he held my gaze sent a flutter through my chest, and suddenly I didn't know where to look.

By the time we'd disembarked and found our ATVs waiting for us on the jetty, my anxiety had returned with a vengeance, tightening into a knot so tight I felt physically ill.

When Benny had successfully strapped our suitcases to the luggage rack, he straightened up and pointed at a cluster of red umbrellas facing the port. "I'm gonna run into Aíolos and grab us gyros to go. That sound good to you?"

"Incredible," I said. "I'm starving."

While he was gone, I sat on a nearby bench overlooking the clear water and checked my email on my phone. The connection was slow, but one by one, the emails popped up in my inbox, though none of them were from Gia's account. I scrolled through the junk until I landed on the one I'd been dreading. I felt the blood drain from my face. The subject line again read simply URGENT, the email just one line:

An eye for an eye.

A bolt of fear shot through me.

"What is it?" Benny asked as he approached, a full paper bag in hand. "You look like you just saw a ghost."

Tears sprang to my eyes as I looked up at him, and I blinked quickly to keep them from spilling down my cheeks. "I don't want to talk about it here. Let's get up to the house."

It was time to tell the truth.

GIA'S MANUSCRIPT

CHAPTER 17

THE SEAT OF THE ATV BURNS THROUGH THE FABRIC OF MY DRESS, the bumpy road vibrating my joints as I fly up the driveway and over the top of the hill in the blazing sun, swerving to avoid a snake that slithers across the road. I don't know where I'm going, and it doesn't strike me until I'm halfway to town that I should have taken the boat instead. What if Garrett steals it? But I don't want to go back now and risk running into him again.

I park beneath the scraggly trees near the water and walk up the narrow cobblestoned alleyway into town. It's Sunday, and most of the shops are closed. The midday sun is high in the sky; not even the alley is safe from her wrath. I walk up the stone path to the café, where I take a seat inside and sit staring out the window at the blue door of the closed jewelry shop across the way. There's no air-conditioning, but the windows are open and the fans move the air around enough that it's not unbearable inside.

I'm amped up, my heart racing, thoughts buzzing around my brain so that I can hardly keep a line of thought pointed in one direction.

I should probably go away for a while, somewhere Garrett can't find me, just until the divorce is finalized. It won't be easy to manage the house repairs from afar, but maybe I could get someone to help me—Benny, perhaps, or Abby. God, I wish I'd listened to her when she told me to take my time with Garrett.

I wish I'd listened to my mother when she tried to warn me about him. She still hasn't returned my call. I'll have to try her again. Maybe I should go to Switzerland to see her. There's a direct flight from Mykonos to Zurich every day this time of year.

Kicking myself again for not taking the boat, I open my purse to take out my phone to check the ferry schedule, and remember that Garrett smashed it. Perhaps I should go back and get the boat now. But the key is in the house. As are Timeo and Emelia. Surely Garrett wouldn't do anything to me in front of them?

After the things he said just now, I'm not so sure.

In my purse I spot the folded cocktail napkin Dimitrios wrote his number on yesterday. I spread it on the table before me, straightening the creases. I think of the concern in his dark eyes when he spoke to me yesterday, and before I know it, I'm at the counter of the café asking to use the phone.

I'm about to hang up by the time he answers. "Hi," I say. I can hear the blasting of a radio in the background, and the clanging of metal. "Where are you?"

"I am working."

"On a Sunday?" No one in Greece works on a Sunday.

"I have to fix a boat to go the day after tomorrow."

"Ah," I say, disappointed. "Sorry to interrupt."

"Are you okay?" he asks. "Your voice . . ."

"I'm . . . no," I admit, my voice cracking. "It's—"

"What is happening?"

"It's too much to get into over the phone. I—"

"You want, you come here. We can talk."

"Okay," I say. "You're at the boat repair mechanic's?"

"Yes. I am here."

I thank the girl behind the counter for letting me use the phone and sling my bag over my shoulder as I emerge into the scorching day, warily scanning the crowd of tourists and day-trippers strolling along the promenade for Garrett's face. When I reach the ATV, I fire up the engine and bump along the road that curves around the recreational harbor, casting furtive glances over my shoulder, but I never see him.

The boat mechanic's shop is a corrugated steel warehouse on the other side of the jetty where the ferry lets out, past the commercial ship docks. The asphalt outside is littered with parts and machinery, some of which look like they've been there since before I was born, and the stench of fish unloaded from the trawlers next door permeates the air. I park my quad in the shade of a sailboat elevated on rickety-looking sticks and enter the building through the nearest of a row of open garage doors, scanning for Dimitrios.

Inside, giant fans alleviate the fish smell but do little to cool the cavernous space, and a boom box blares Greek rock music. I spot a shirtless Dimitrios bent over the hull of a speedboat partially hidden by the large fishing boat at the center of the warehouse, where two other men are working. They watch with curiosity as I approach Dimitrios, who smiles when he sees me, wiping his hands on a rag.

An unexpected flood of relief washes over me at the sight of him. To have a friend, after the things that Garrett said to me this morning—and not just any friend, but a large, powerfully built friend—alleviates my dread, if only temporarily.

His brow creases with concern as he takes me in. "Are you okay?"

I shrug clumsily. "Not really."

"Come," he says, beckoning me to follow him past the hulking boats, through a side door to a shaded portico overlooking the water. The smell of fish isn't so bad over on this side of the building, with the breeze off the sea.

He sits in a plastic chair at one of the two round tables, and I take the seat across from him. "Tell me what is happening."

No one is around, but still I lower my voice so far he has to lean across the table to hear as I relate the events of the past few days in hushed tones. He listens quietly, stopping me every so often when I start talking too fast or I use a word he doesn't know.

When I'm finished, he takes a key ring from his pocket and unwinds one of the keys from it, sliding it across the table to me.

"Go to my house," he says. "You are safe there. I am home in three, four hours. Then we talk more, make a plan."

I realize, as he offers it, that it's what I've wanted all along, and I accept gratefully. Once he's given me directions, I start to rise, then remember I need to call my mom.

"Could I possibly use your phone?" I ask. "I need to call my mom. She's in Switzerland, but I'll make it fast."

"Is okay." He hands me the phone. "I give you . . . time," he says, standing. "I am inside when you finish."

But it turns out I don't need much time. The receptionist at Vue sur la Montagne tells me my mom's not in her room and takes down Dimitrios's number, promising to have her return my call.

Back inside, I examine the boats in the shop as I thread my way through their shadows toward Dimitrios, looking for the yacht that might be Emelia and Timeo's. Catamarans, sailboats, sport fishing boats, and all kinds of other boats I can't name stand on sticks mid-repair, but none of them fit the pictures Emelia showed me of their boat.

As I approach, Dimitrios looks up from beneath the boat he's repairing, a wrench in his hand. "Did you reach her?" he asks.

I shake my head, returning his phone to him. "I gave her your number since my phone is broken. If she calls, will you please ask her a good time for me to call back?"

"Yes," he says.

"Do you have any yachts here?" I ask.

"What kind?"

"I don't know. White. Not huge. I'm guessing seventy, eighty feet? So, what, twenty-five meters?"

He shakes his head. "No. Why?"

I frown. "My friends—you know, Timeo and Emelia—their boat is being repaired here."

He rises to his feet, doubt written across his face. "Here? Are you sure?"

"This is the only repair shop on the island, isn't it?"

He nods. "We don't fix boats so big."

I raise my brows, unsettled. Could Timeo be mistaken about where their boat is being repaired? But he specifically said it was being repaired here on the island. Didn't he?

"I take you to ask George," Dimitrios says. "He is owner. He knows all boats come here."

I nod, and he leads me to the back of the warehouse, up a set of concrete steps to an open office door. "George," he calls, knocking on the metal doorframe.

A sweating older man with patchy gray hair and a stomach like a drum looks up from the cluttered desk, setting his smudged glasses down on the pile of papers before him.

"Sorry to disturb you," I say. "I'm looking for a boat belonging to a friend of mine. He told me it was being repaired here. It's a yacht, probably twenty-five meters, belonging to Timeo Khan. Though it may be under his father's name, or an LLC."

He clears his throat. "And this boat, you say was towed here?"

I nod. "About a week ago."

He shakes his head. "The only boats come here last week, you see on the floor. Last pleasure boat was, let me see—" He flips through a binder, sliding his finger down a roster until he comes to the entry he's looking for. "May twenty-six. Returned to owner June thirteen. But that was catamaran. We don't take boat so big. The big ones go to Naxos."

I absorb this new information, my chest growing tighter with worry by the second.

"Okay," I say. "Thank you."

I follow Dimitrios out of the office, my head spinning.

I guess I should have thought to verify the boat was in the shop myself, but why would I? I had no reason to believe they were lying; I saw pictures of them on the boat. A boat. Of course, I now realize it could have been anyone's.

I remember what Benny said about how Timeo lied about attending Harrow, and a picture begins to form. If Timeo didn't go to Harrow and doesn't have a boat, it's likely everything else he's told me is a lie as well. So, what are he and Emelia really doing here? And why are they lying?

Dimitrios walks me back to my ATV, waiting until we're outside to speak, his voice lowered. "Timeo lied to you."

I nod. Though for some reason, all the anger I feel is directed at Emelia. Timeo was always slippery, but I liked her, and thought she liked me. Were all the secrets she told me lies? Are she and Timeo even really a couple, or are they just a team of con artists out to defraud rich fools like me?

It seems awfully coincidental, learning this after what I've just learned about Garrett. Could they have known each other before? It's far-fetched, but not impossible.

"I'm an idiot," I say, pulling my sunglasses down to cover the tears welling in my eyes. "All any of them wanted was my money."

"No," he says. "You are not idiot. Is not your fault."

"The funny thing is," I say, catching a tear beneath my glasses with my fingertips, "I don't even have any money anymore. Not until I sell the property. I barely have enough to pay for the repairs. They're fighting for scraps."

"Is better, maybe." He smiles. "You have no money, nobody can take."

"That's true," I say. "What a fucking nightmare. I'm sorry to drag you into this."

"Is fine," he says. "Go to my house. I see you there."

I straddle my ATV and gun it past the jumbled buildings of town, up the hill to Dimitrios's neighborhood on the west side of the island, mercifully as far from the villa as you can get on this mound of land in the middle of the Aegean Sea. Off the paved street, a dirt road leads to a cluster of square white houses, each with its own balcony and patio.

Dimitrios's house is on the end facing the sea, with herbs spilling out of a window box and a freshly planted lemon tree to the side of his blue door. I park my ATV out front and use his key to open the door, breathing a sigh of relief as I lock it behind me.

Inside, the floor is flagstone and the walls are all white, with sliding glass doors that open onto a patio facing the sea, flooding the space with light. The kitchen is to my left, small and neat, painted the same blue as the door and open to the living room, where a comfortable-looking gray couch faces a television mounted above the fireplace. To my right is a stunning live-edge dining table that appears to be made from one wide tree, and past that a hallway with a bedroom and bathroom.

A black-and-white cat yowls as she skulks out of the bedroom and over to me, sniffing at my ankles, and I bend down to stroke her head, leaving my bag on the floor.

It's strange to be in Dimitrios's home with his things, looking at pictures of his family, petting his cat, when I've fantasized about him all summer, not taking into account that he's a real person. I'm embarrassed to think of how brazenly I acted around him, making him an unwitting pawn in the games Garrett and I played with each other. What must he think of me, an heiress with an extravagant villa, prancing around naked to make her lying cheat of a husband jealous?

Standing here in his cozy home, I see myself through his eyes, and I'm ashamed.

FOR A BRIEF MOMENT WHEN I wake, my mind is wiped clean with sleep. I'm free of apprehension, unsure where I am. And then it all comes rushing back, crushing me under its weight.

Dimitrios smiles at me from the kitchen as I sit up on the couch, rubbing my eyes. "Have a nice nap?"

"I didn't realize how tired I was," I say. "What time is it?"

"Nearly five."

I stretch as I rise to see he's preparing a tray of pita, hummus, and tzatziki. "Are you hungry?" he asks, placing a bowl of olive oil and a cold bottle of pinot grigio on the tray.

"I am, thank you." I run my finger along the rough edge of the dining table. "This table is beautiful."

He doesn't look up from slicing the cucumber before him. "Thank you. I make."

"You made this?" I inspect the table more closely. It's remarkable, the craftsmanship on par with what you might find in a fancy design store in a big city. "Incredible."

"I like work with wood," he says. "The nurse of your mother call."

I point to his phone. "Can I?"

He hands it to me and I hit the number for Vue sur la Montagne, but when the receptionist answers, he refuses to put me through to my mother's room. "She asked to see you in person," he says. "As soon as possible."

"Okay," I acquiesce, mentally running through the steps I'll need to take to get myself to Switzerland. It wasn't my plan, of course, but I do have my passport in my purse and enough clothes in my overnight bag to make the trip. "Please tell her I'll take the afternoon flight tomorrow. It doesn't get in until the evening, so I'll have to spend the night in Zurich, but I can be there the following morning."

"All okay?" Dimitrios asks as I hang up.

I return his phone, shaking my head. "I have to go to Switzerland."

"Now?"

"Tomorrow. My mom . . . isn't well."

"I'm sorry." He places the sliced cucumber on the tray and hands me two rocks glasses to carry. "On the patio there is—what is it called—" He fans himself.

"Fan?" I ask.

He shakes his head.

"Wind? A breeze?"

He points at me with a grin. "Yes, a *breeze*. And shadow."

"Shade?"

"Yes." He points to a thick *English as a Second Language* book resting on the heavy wooden coffee table, which I now notice is also live-edge, and I assume also crafted by him. "I practice. You help me learn."

"Okay," I say gamely as he opens the sliding glass door.

On the patio there is indeed a breeze, and shade cast by an olive tree. Flowers spill out of planters, and a small lion's head fountain gurgles. Dimitrios sets the tray on the bistro table, and we take the two chairs facing the sea.

"This is lovely," I say as he pours me a glass of wine. It's refreshing, cold and light. "I like the wine."

"A friend bring from Italy," he says.

We sit in silence for a moment, and though the setting is delightful, foreboding hovers at my periphery like thunderheads on the horizon, warning me to take shelter. I feel Dimitrios looking at me and give him a half-hearted smile.

"Do you want to talk about it?" he asks.

I shake my head. "Can you tell me about your family?"

He obliges, relating colorful tales about each of the members of his family with the aid of a translation app that gets the words right about half the time. But unlike my husband, Dimitrios has a sense of humor about himself, and he laughs harder than I do when I explain the mistakes to him, jotting down the right words in the notes app on his phone.

The sunset on his side of the island is even more spectacular than it is on mine, the sky awash in the colors of a fruit bowl as we sit side by side watching the sun melt toward the horizon.

I realize I may have disrupted his plans this afternoon, that he's probably wondering when I'll leave, and I feel compelled to let him know I don't mean to make a nuisance of myself.

"You will stay tonight," he says before I can open my mouth, as though he can read my mind.

I should protest, but as I turn to look at him, I find I can't.

"I sleep on the couch," he says. "You have my bed."

I don't want him to sleep on the couch; I don't want him to sleep at all until I've had my way with him so many times that neither of us is able to keep our eyes open any longer, and then I want to sleep in his powerful arms, his thumb tracing my bare skin gently as he dreams.

Stop it, Gia.

I rip a piece of soft pita and dip it in the tzatziki, focusing on the taste of it to draw my attention away from the lust coiled heavily between my legs.

I don't want to be this way anymore. I don't want to seduce and destroy, to light the fuse and brace for the explosion over and over again. I don't want to be like Garrett.

"Thank you," I say once we've placed all the dishes in the sink. "For everything. I'm really hoping Garrett's gone once I get back from Switzerland."

"You must stay away from him," he says emphatically. "Is not safe."

"I don't think he'd actually—"

"A man who threaten a woman is not a good man," he says, the sharp simplicity of his logic landing hard on my heart.

"Timeo and Emelia are still there," I say weakly.

He gives me a look.

"You're right," I say.

"You can stay here as long as you want," he offers.

I look up at him, imagining living here with him, having wine on the patio in the evening. It seems like a fairy tale, like someone else's life.

"I won't be here," he goes on, shattering my fantasy. "The boat I am repairing, I sail to Spain the day after tomorrow, for a month, maybe two. But you can stay if you like."

"I'll think about it, thank you. Two months, huh?" I look up at him with a sad smile. "Will I see you again?"

"You know where I am."

I still as he leans in and plants a soft kiss on my forehead. I could tilt my head up now, could let our lips meet, could let him take away all my pain, if only temporarily. But I don't.

Instead, I climb into his bed alone, where cocooned in sheets that hold his scent I drift off to nightmares of Garrett pushing me down the well, my screams echoing off the damp walls as I tumble down the shaft to be swallowed up by the darkness.

ABBY

CHAPTER 12

THE DEEP BLUE SEA GLITTERED IN THE MIDDAY SUN AS BENNY AND I crested the hill on our ATVs and the house came into view, the bright day turning its white walls reflective. Everything was just as I remembered it, the wild garden of succulents spilling onto the flagstone walkway, the fountain trickling in front of the heavy front door, the dirt path winding down the hill to the sea. No other vehicles were parked in the pea gravel, and I couldn't see any lights on inside.

"I'll come back for the bags," Benny said once we'd cut our engines.

He grabbed the food as I shouldered my purse and followed him up the walkway, foreboding slowing my feet the closer to the door we came. I waited as he jiggled his key in the lock, but the bolt wouldn't budge.

"Didn't the stablemaster say the locks had been changed?" I asked.

"Shit, you're right."

"The extra key," I said, cutting through the shrubbery along the front of the house. "We always kept it under that rock."

I lifted the heart-shaped rock and sure enough, beneath it was a shiny silver key, larger than the original.

"Wish we'd thought of it yesterday," he muttered as we tromped back through the bushes. He fitted the key into the lock, turning the bolt easily this time.

"Hello?" he called as we stepped over the threshold into the dark foyer. "Gia?"

The house was silent and clean, smelling of lemon verbena as it always had.

"Gia," I yelled. "Are you here?"

We went around the fireplace and into the sunken living room, illuminated by the dying daylight through the wall of glass that looked out over the pool to the sea. The white sectional couch was new, bigger and more modern-looking than what had been there last time I visited, and a wheel-shaped iron light fixture had replaced the chandelier that had once hung overhead. But everything was orderly, not a cushion out of place.

I dropped my purse on the couch as Benny headed into the kitchen, where I could hear him opening the refrigerator. "Good thing we brought food," he called. "There's nothing here but condiments."

Nervous about what might lie behind closed doors, I waited until he had rejoined me to start for the primary suite, where we found the attached sitting room tidy, a small vase of withered flowers on the end table.

I followed Benny into the bedroom, where the heavy wood-framed bed was freshly made with white bed linens, and watched as he opened the top dresser drawer. It was full of Gia's underwear. Our eyes caught and my heart plummeted. "Her stuff is still here," he said, opening the next drawer down to reveal her swimsuits.

I flung open the door to the walk-in closet to find her dresses hanging on the rack, shorts and T-shirts folded on the shelves at the far end, and two roller suitcases stowed behind the door next to a stack of extra pillows.

In the spotless bathroom, the medicine cabinets were also full of Gia's things: a bottle of her signature scent, her expensive face creams, bottles of Ambien and Xanax bearing her name.

True, there were no signs of a struggle, but I'd also read enough thrillers to realize that it wasn't unusual for a criminal to clean up a crime scene afterward. In most circumstances, a clean house like this could be more of a red flag than a dirty house. But most people didn't have a daily housekeeper.

I opened a cabinet that contained sunscreen, shampoo, and towels. The silver tray that held her jewelry, however, was conspicuously missing the items I knew she loved most: her wedding ring, her vintage Rolex, the diamond key necklace she'd sent me pictures of after Garrett gave it to her on their honeymoon.

"Some of her jewelry is gone," I said. "But I don't think there was a robbery because there's plenty of expensive stuff here." I held up a Cartier watch and a pair of diamond earrings. "I also haven't seen her computer or purse anywhere."

Benny seemed to think of something and started for the door. "I'm gonna check the library."

I followed him out of the master suite to the library, where we both paused in the doorway, looking from shelf to shelf. The library looked like a first grader's mouth, full of holes. It was jarring to see the shelves so bare.

"Someone took the books," he said, bereft.

"Garrett?"

I ran my fingers over the remaining books, scanning the shelves as I always did for the annotated copy of *The Odyssey* I'd lost somewhere in this house the summer we were eighteen. But as always, there were no paperbacks in this library.

"Looks like he knew which ones to take," he said, inspecting the shelves. "Hundreds of thousands of dollars' worth of books, I'd guess."

"He had the time to get to know the library."

I glanced up at the glass case where the revolver was normally displayed to find it empty. My skin prickled. "The gun is gone."

AFTER WE DID A SWEEP of the immaculate upstairs, Benny and I took our gyros out to the dining table on the patio by the pool. The trellis cut the glare of the sun, and a wind chime tinkled in the gentle breeze.

"Are you ready to talk now?" he asked as soon as we'd sat down.

"About what?" I asked, though I knew.

He leveled his gaze at me.

I wasn't, and I'd never be, but I nodded, setting my untouched gyro on my plate. "I've been getting threatening emails," I confessed.

He leaned forward on his elbows, concerned. "What do you mean? How many?"

"Three. I got the first one the day I left Atlanta, and the second one arrived right after I landed in Kiruna. The last one came today when you were picking up our lunch."

"Why didn't you tell me?"

"We've had other stuff going on."

I could tell he didn't buy my flimsy excuse. "What do they say?"

I took a deep breath. "The first one said *You're a liar,* the second one said *The truth will out,* and the third one *An eye for an eye.*"

He furrowed his brow. "But what does that mean?"

"I'm not entirely sure." That, at least, was true. I wasn't *entirely* sure. "I thought at first it was just some kind of phishing scam or something. But now that Gia's disappeared, it seems like they could be connected somehow."

He bit his lip, thinking. "But how? What could you possibly have to do with any of this? You only met Garrett, what, once?"

I nodded. I'd leave it there for now; I'd told him the immediate truth. I knew eventually this disclosure would lead to the whole truth, but I wasn't ready for that.

"Maybe Leon can help," Benny mused.

"Your accountant?"

"We call him that for simplicity's sake, but he's more than that."

"Like a fixer."

"I mean, we're not exactly hiding bodies, but yeah, I guess that's pretty accurate." He took out his phone and started typing. "I'm writing an email to both of you so you can forward the emails to him, then we'll go down to the police station to file a report for Gia."

I nodded, torn between hope and fear that Leon could find out who had been threatening me. More than anything, I wished I could tell Benny everything. But for now the important thing was not the past, but the present. Once we'd found Gia, I would tell Benny the whole truth and bid him farewell for good.

GIA'S MANUSCRIPT

CHAPTER 18

IN THE MORNING, I WAKE FROM FITFUL SLEEP BUZZING WITH ANXIETY to find Dimitrios is gone.

The knot of dread in my stomach only grows tighter as I shower then slip into a loose dress from my overnight bag. In the kitchen, sunlight pours through the window over the sink and reflects off the cobalt cabinets, tinting everything blue, like I'm underwater. I make myself an espresso and sit at the breakfast bar with my computer to DM Emelia on Instagram, asking her to meet me for breakfast alone at the café. I think she's going to laugh when she finds out I slept in Dimitrios's bed without Dimitrios, then I remember we're not friends anymore, that we were never really friends to begin with, and it's none of Emelia's business what I did or didn't do with anyone.

Emelia agrees almost immediately to meet me at noon at the café. She writes that she hopes I'm okay, that Garrett told them I was visiting a cousin but she didn't believe it. She doesn't mention whether Garrett has left, which I assume means he hasn't.

A blinding flash of rage flares inside me. I could have him removed, I suppose, though the island police force had four officers last time I checked, whose main duties included breaking up bar fights and ensuring that known pickpockets didn't get off the ferry. Anyway, fights between married couples are seen as domestic, the resolution left up to the couple unless violence is confirmed—meaning basically that the officers have to witness it.

I wonder if any of the officers are the same as last time I dealt with the police on the island? It likely wouldn't help my case if they were.

The thing that's most evident to me is the need to put distance between Garrett and me. And to do that, I must get rid of the house. Struck by a bolt of inspiration, I open my email and compose a message to Leon:

Hi Leon,

I want to expedite the sale of the house and close without completing repairs. I know this will lower the price, I don't care. I just want out. Please email your thoughts instead of calling, my cell is dead and Garrett is at the house without me.

Thanks,
Gia

I press Send, suddenly desperate to be back in New York surrounded by the crush of humanity, safe on the twentieth floor of a doorman building.

AT THE CAFÉ, THE LINE to order nearly reaches the door. I don't spot Emelia among the vacationers seated inside, so I head to the patio, where I thread my way past a couple canoodling as their eggs congeal and a table of six hungover-looking Brits who all unabashedly check me out as I pass.

I take a seat at a corner table in the shade of the bougainvillea-covered trellis and pull out my computer, hooking up to the café Wi-Fi to check my email. I'm surprised to see Leon has already replied to the message I sent him this morning.

Gia,

I've spoken to Melodie and she is amenable to the change, willing to set the price at $14M including furniture and taking into account the repairs you've already done. Closing will take thirty days, and she'll give you another week or two to clear out if you need it, so please start thinking about packing. I'll be in touch with the lawyer to start prepping the paperwork.

Sincerely,
Leon

A mix of relief and regret washes over me. I've loved that house, but I'm ready to be free of it, to be able to use the money from the sale to construct my life the way I want to. I write him a quick thank-you, hitting Send just as another email comes in.

A jolt of alarm shoots through me as I recognize Garrett's email address. The subject line reads I'M SORRY.

Blood rushes in my ears as I click on the email.

I'm so sorry for the way I behaved yesterday. I was upset and I took it out on you. I should never have said those things. I didn't mean any of them and I feel like shit for treating you like that. I'll do whatever it takes to make it up to you.

Please come home so we can talk.

I love you.

I stare at the computer screen, agape. He's *sorry*? He threatened to kill me, surely he knows *sorry* isn't going to cut it.

It's true I've accepted his apologies in the past, but this was different. There's no way in hell I'm going back to him. Still, I realize it's probably best to placate him while I work out the best way to divorce him.

"Hey."

I look up to see Emelia hovering over my table, smiling tentatively. I close my laptop as she tucks her baby blond hair behind her ear and leans down to kiss me on each cheek.

"Are you okay?" she asks. "Where have you been?"

As tempting as it is to tell her I've been at Dimitrios's house, I decide not to. I haven't completely ruled out returning there, and if this meeting doesn't go well, it might be better if she can't find me.

Instead, I gesture for her to sit in the turquoise wooden chair across from me. "I've been to the boat repair mechanic's."

"Why?" she asks, her smile slipping.

"To inquire after your boat."

She drops her gaze to her pale pink nails, picking at the cuticles. "And?"

"I think you know the answer to that."

"It's not the way it seems." She looks up at me, her blue eyes apprehensive. "I can explain."

"Go on."

She toys with the strap of the dress I bought her the other day. "It's complicated." A small plane buzzes overhead and she looks up, though it's not visible through the trellis. "I wanted to tell you."

"But you didn't," I say evenly, not taking my eyes off her. "Has anything you've told me been true?"

She nods, shamefaced.

"I know that Timeo didn't go to Harrow," I say.

"He did go," she protests weakly.

"Benny looked him up. He wasn't in any of the graduating classes."

"He went for a year," she says.

"Are you even married?" I ask.

She nods, twisting her engagement ring on her finger.

"And the problems you told me about?"

"They're real, I swear."

I take off my sunglasses and hold her eye. "I need you to back up and tell me what's going on."

She bites her lip, looks up at the bougainvillea above us. "I wish I could. I really do."

I snort, rising. "And you called yourself my friend."

She grabs my arm, stopping me. "I *am* your friend."

"Then fucking spill it."

She glances over her shoulder and scans the street and restaurant, then lowers her voice. "You can't let him know I told you. Please. I don't know what he'd do to me."

I nod, sitting back down. "If you tell me the truth, I won't let him know you told me."

She closes her eyes and takes a shaking breath. "I was nineteen and working in a bar when we met. He swept me off my feet—picked me up for our first date in a Ferrari, took me to the fanciest restaurant I'd ever been to. It was true he'd grown up rich—not as rich as he makes out, but well off—but they lost all their money when he was a teenager, which is why he only went to Harrow for one year."

"So how did he have the money for Ferraris and things?" I ask.

"He'd been with a wealthy woman before me." She sweeps her hair over her shoulder. "Older. But he burned through that money pretty fast. He always goes through it fast—he says it's an investment, spending to impress. Rich people trust other rich people. Once they assume you're one of them, they don't second-guess it."

"So this is what you do? You scam people?"

She nods. "But we only take from people that have enough so it doesn't matter."

"Like Robin Hood," I say caustically, shaking my head.

"That's what he says."

"Only you're not exactly using the money to support starving children, are you?" I look pointedly at her Cartier bracelets.

I see her hand is shaking as she takes a sip of her Perrier. "I didn't mean to get into this lifestyle," she says. "I didn't even know about it for a long time, and by then I was in deep. I'd already unknowingly been part of multiple scams he'd pulled. He's good at it, coming up with schemes, making people like him, and . . ." She peels the label from her water bottle, embarrassed. "I'd never been good at anything, but it turned out I was good at it too. Most of the people we took from were pretty terrible anyway, and the amount we took made no dent in their wealth."

"Like me?"

"No! You're different. That's why we decided not to take anything from you."

I eye her skeptically. "Or so you say."

"I swear!"

I cross my arms. "Why did he marry you? Why not just go on swindling rich women?"

She hesitates, watching a couple a few tables over calm their crying baby. "He loved me, I think—at first, anyway. And we do better as a couple than he did alone. People trust a couple more than they do a single man, and I was in love with him, so I married him." She shifts her gaze back to me, her shoulders slumping. "But then all the problems I told you about started. I didn't know what marriage was supposed to be like, I'd never even had a boyfriend before. So I went along for too long, and now I can't leave because he has so much dirt on me. If I divorce him he'll turn me in and I'll go to jail for the rest of my life."

I frown. "But wouldn't he as well?"

"Oh, he's been careful to collect evidence on me alone just to keep me in place. And he's so good at disappearing that if I flipped on him, he'd be long gone before they ever even started looking for him. He has the resources, it's a lot easier for him than it is for me to start over."

I can tell she's nervous, constantly fiddling with this and that as she talks, her eyes anxious and clear, which I take to mean she's telling the truth, or at least part of it.

"So, what did you want with us?" I ask.

"He never knows at first. He's an opportunist. He decides his angle after he's acquainted with people. He saw that article in the magazine about you, and then there you were at the restaurant. He knew he could figure something out around the sale of your property."

"And?"

She twists her napkin around her finger. "Once I got to know you, I begged him to move on. He agreed yesterday. Said you were too difficult of a target until you sold your property. He knew he'd overreached with the offer to buy it, and I think he also realized your brother caught the Harrow thing." Tears well in her blue eyes as they meet mine. "I'm sorry, Gia. I really do like you."

I tilt my head, evaluating her. I did enjoy her company, and I'd like to believe her, but she's just admitted she's a professional liar, so I recognize it would be against my better judgment to do so.

"Did you know Garrett before we all met at Ammos?"

She shakes her head. "No. Why?"

But it doesn't seem prudent to tell her my husband is as big a liar as she is. "Just curious."

I open my laptop, then pull up one of the videos I shot of Garrett, Timeo, and Camila the other night. I make sure the sound is off before I press Play and spin the computer to face her.

She raises her hand to her mouth as she watches, wide-eyed.

"I'll send it to you," I say. "Though I don't know anymore that it'll do you any good." I close the laptop and catch her eye. "I want you out of my house."

She nods, contrite. "What will I tell Timeo?"

"Whatever the fuck you want, I don't care."

"Okay." She stands. "I'm really sorry, Gia."

"I hope you figure your life out, Emelia. Or whatever your name is."

"It's Anna," she says, wiping her eyes. "Anna Huber."

"There's a two o'clock ferry," I say. "You can park the ATV under the trees at the base of the jetty. Just leave the key in it, no one will take it."

She lunges forward and wraps me in a hug. "I appreciated your friendship," she whispers into my hair.

I don't hug her back, but I meet her eye with a nod when she stands. "Take care."

It's hard to put a finger on what I feel as I watch her walk away, the white sundress I bought her swinging, her blond hair glowing in the sun. Pity is part of it, indignation at how she played me, and perhaps a bit of wistfulness for the friendship that could have been, had she been real. Mostly, I think, I just feel empty.

ABBY

CHAPTER 13

THE SUN BEAT DOWN, BAKING OUR EXPOSED SKIN AS BENNY AND I rode into town on the ATV. We parked on the street in front of the police station, exactly where it had always been at the edge of town in a squat white building. Walking into the small waiting room was like walking back in time. Suddenly my palms began to sweat as I took in the metal folding chairs, the chipped tile floor, the un-manned front desk. My breathing grew fast, the room began to swim. I grabbed Benny's arm. "I don't know if I can do this."

His eyes locked on mine. "Breathe."

I took a deep breath.

"I can talk to the police alone but it's hot outside," he said calmly, his eyes never leaving mine. "Let's sit down here for a minute, okay?"

I nodded, allowing him to guide me to the nearest chair. The metal was cold against my legs as I rested my head in my hands.

"Keep breathing," Benny said, placing a reassuring hand on my back. "It's okay."

"Hello?" came an uncertain voice.

I looked up to see a guy in a short-sleeved police uniform, the door beyond the desk swinging behind him. He looked like he couldn't be more than twenty, dark-haired and small with no facial hair to conceal the acne sprayed across his cheeks, just like the young cop who had taken us down to the station the night Gia killed Noah. *But it wasn't the same person,* I rationalized. This guy would have been a child twelve years ago.

"Hi," Benny said. "Could we get some water? She's feeling faint."

"One moment."

Benny rubbed my back gently as the cop disappeared through the door, returning with a bottle of water.

"Thank you," I said, taking it from him.

The young man shifted his weight from foot to foot, watching as I drank the water. The fact that he looked as nervous as I was made me feel somewhat better. "Can I help you?" he asked finally.

"My sister's missing," Benny started.

The guy glanced out the windows behind us as though hoping someone else would show up to handle whatever we wanted. "For how long?"

My limbs were starting to feel more solid again as the dizziness subsided. I wasn't a scared eighteen-year-old anymore, I was an adult with intimate knowledge of the law. American law, but still, it was something. I took a breath. "Perhaps we could talk somewhere more private?"

He glanced at the empty lobby before shrugging and beckoning us to follow him. Benny looked at me with raised brows, and I nodded, taking another swig of water before I rose. I could do this. I focused on breathing evenly, feeling the floor beneath my sneakers as the young officer led us through the door behind the desk into the office beyond. It was roughly the same size as the waiting room with three large desks, all of them empty.

"Are you the only one on duty today?" I asked. He nodded, and I glanced at his name tag. "Nice to meet you, Officer Primos. I'm Abby and this is Benny."

"Hello." Our names thankfully didn't seem to ring any bells as

Officer Primos took a seat at the desk beneath the window, gesturing for us to pull up chairs identical to those in the waiting room.

As Benny slowly and clearly explained our situation, I watched the police kid's face go from self-conscious to downright uncomfortable. He cleared his throat as he rifled through the drawers of his desk, clearly out of his depth. "We have form."

He came up empty-handed and excused himself to go to the filing cabinet parked against the back wall, where he jerked each drawer out until he finally located the right form. His brow was slick with sweat as he set the Missing Persons form in front of Benny on the desk.

Benny glanced over it, then looked up at the cop. "You know, we used to have a family friend that worked here. Theodoropoulos?"

To our surprise, Primos nodded. "He is director, in Athens."

"Okay, okay," Benny said, encouraged. "Do you know how to get in touch with him?"

Primos looked down at the paper on the desk, hesitant. "He is very powerful man, I do not know if . . ."

"He was a friend of my father's. Tell him Hugo Torres's son wants to talk to him," Benny said. "It's my sister, Gia, we're worried about."

Primos squirmed. "My boss, he is gone for the day but he is in tomorrow, he call for you."

"We'll come by tomorrow morning," Benny replied. "Or you could send your boss up to our house, it's the one on the hill on the east end."

OUTSIDE, THE DAY WAS UNBEARABLY bright after the dark of the police station. As we approached the ATV, a hedgehog scampered out from beneath it, beelining for the shade of the vehicle parked next to it. I pulled on my helmet as I straddled the hot seat behind Benny, but the small visor did little to cut the glare of the low sun.

"Theodoropoulos," I said as we bumped along the cobbled streets of town toward the market. "Your dad's fishing buddy."

He gassed it onto the main road. "Also the one who shut the rumors down and closed the case."

The rumors that we weren't as innocent as we'd claimed.

"I remember."

"He should be sympathetic to us," Benny continued. "I have a feeling that whatever important position he has in Athens now, he owes to my dad."

"What do you mean?" I asked, bracing myself for the answer I'd always assumed but never confirmed.

I could feel his chest rise beneath my hands as he took a deep breath. "Do you really want to know?"

"Maybe not."

"My room was directly over the library, where my dad took all his calls and meetings. I heard a lot through the air vent." He glanced back at me, unsure, as he parked the ATV in front of the market. "I don't want to . . ."

"I'm better now, if that's what you're worried about," I said. "I know I just almost lost it in there, but . . . I've had a lot of therapy. And time. You won't break me."

He evaluated me from behind his sunglasses. "I'm glad to hear that." He shook his head, hanging his helmet on the handlebars. "Abby, I'm sorry I wasn't—I haven't been—more present."

"It's okay. I haven't exactly been either."

"I want you to know I cared, though. I thought about you all the time."

I couldn't help but notice his use of the past tense. "Thank you." I paused in front of the door to the market. It was probably better I didn't know everything he heard through the air vent, but if any of it was pertinent to our situation now, I wanted to be prepared. "Was there anything you heard back then that could affect us now?"

"I don't think so. There was something my dad asked me about— but it was years later."

"What?" I asked, my breath growing shallow.

"Noah's mom and sister tried to get the case reopened. They said they'd received a letter from someone who claimed Noah's death was intentional, but it turned out to be nothing. There was no evidence—the letter wasn't even signed. It was likely a fraud perpetrated by the mom, who'd been in and out of jail in Germany for petty offenses."

I frowned, disturbed. "No one ever told me about that."

"Dad didn't mention it to Gia either. You'd both already been through so much."

Movement in the bushes along the edge of the small parking lot drew my eye, and I saw a long tail slither into the bushes. I shuddered. "But he did tell you?"

He nodded. "He asked me whether I had any reason to believe there was merit to their claim, and I assured him there wasn't. So he made sure Theodoropoulos understood we'd fight it tooth and nail, and it died before it even made it into the press. I don't know how he managed that."

"I could guess."

It did not escape me that had Gia's family not been so powerful, our case might have turned out very differently.

By the time we returned home, the sun was sinking in the sky, sending beams of amber bouncing around the house. I threw together a salad, and Benny poured us each a glass of the Sancerre he'd put in the refrigerator earlier.

My phone dinged with an Instagram message and I opened the app to find a DM from a friend. Instinctively, I navigated to my feed, and there it was again, Gia's snap of the typewriter on the desk at the end of the hallway upstairs.

Of course. Why hadn't I thought of it before? If Gia was writing again, there was a chance her manuscript would be somewhere in this house, and she'd told me she was "putting things down as they happened," so it was likely we'd find some kind of clue in it.

I dropped my phone on the counter and looked up at Benny.

"What?" Benny asked.

"I just thought of something. Be right back." I darted from the kitchen, sprinting across the living room to take the stairs two at a time up to the second level.

At the end of the hallway, the low sun shone through the window like a spotlight, illuminating the black typewriter atop the antique desk. There was no paper in the carriage, but a stockpile of blank sheets sat ready in a basket next to it. I opened the drawer beneath the desk to see a neat stack of typed pages, the top sheet beginning with "Gia's Manuscript: Chapter 1."

GIA'S MANUSCRIPT

CHAPTER 19

V UE SUR LA MONTAGNE STANDS ON A MOUNTAINTOP IN THE ALPS, looking more like the grand hotel it once was than the sanatorium it is today. The temperature is cooler up here, the air thinner, the sky bluer. From my perch on a shaded bench in the garden, I can hear a stream crashing over rocks somewhere far below while jagged snow-capped peaks tower overhead.

The sound of wheels crunching over pebbles draws my eye to the path that connects to the guest apartments, and I see a clean-cut male nurse in white scrubs wheeling my mother toward me. She's dressed in a long tan skirt and a white blouse, her face obscured by a sun hat.

My heart twinges at the sight of her, pale and so thin a strong wind might blow her away. I stand, unsure whether to approach or wait for her to arrive. I don't know what to expect from her. Some days are better than others.

"Hi, Mom," I say as her nurse sets her up in the shade next to the bench.

She looks up at me, her hazel eyes probing. I'm glad to see she's clear today—a shadow of her former self, but at least she's not muddled the way she sometimes is. "Can you give us a moment?" she says to the nurse.

"I'll bring her back when she's ready," I volunteer.

My mother watches the nurse's back as he retreats down the path. When he's out of earshot, she turns back to me, her voice sharp. "You came. I wasn't sure you'd show."

"Of course I came. Did they not tell you I was coming?"

"They said you would try. Where's your husband?" She glances around as though he might be hiding in the bushes.

"I left him. I'm filing for divorce."

She looks at me for a moment before nodding. "Good."

It wasn't worth mentioning that Garrett didn't yet know. Not wanting to risk provoking him further while I planned our divorce, I'd responded to his apology email kindly yesterday, telling him I loved him but wanted some time to think. I requested that he respect my need for space right now and asked him to use the time to work on his anger issues. He agreed, claiming that he needed to handle some business in Athens anyway and would look forward to reuniting with me.

Both of us were lying.

"I want to apologize to you," I say, catching my mom's bony hand in mine. "I didn't listen when you told me he was bad news, but you were right. I was blinded by what I thought was love but . . . I should have listened."

She pats my hand, her sunken eyes glum. "I can understand why you didn't."

"Tell me what happened, from the beginning."

She sighs. "Last spring, just after your father died, the patients here did an art show in the village, at an old church on the square."

I sit on the bench next to her. "I remember. You met a man who wanted you to donate paintings for a charity auction."

She looks over at me, her eyes sad. "I thought I did. But it wasn't true."

"What do you mean?"

"The man I met was Garrett, though he called himself Brian."

I furrowed my brow. "So, Garrett was involved with a charity?"

She shakes her head. "No, he was lying. When he came to visit, he told me the event was to benefit kids struggling with mental illness whose families couldn't pay for the care they needed. He wasn't just looking for art, he wanted the Torres Foundation to get involved as a sponsor. It was right up my alley and his website looked professional, but the more I talked to him, the more I felt like something was off."

"How?"

"It was a number of things—for example, I'm listed on the Foundation website as a founder, but I don't have the authority to write checks—no one does without the board's approval, and anyone who works in philanthropy should know that. But he didn't. He was pushy and said it was a one-time opportunity, that I needed to contribute now, that there weren't many spots left."

I hang my head, realizing where this is going. "What happened?"

"I thanked him, explaining I had no authority, and sent him on his way."

"Then he showed up to the Clean the Beach event a month later, pretending he had no idea who I was."

"I had no way of knowing your Garrett was my Brian—until you showed me your wedding pictures when you came to visit after you got married."

"When he'd conveniently gotten sick that morning." It all made so much sense now. I sigh, taking her hand in mine. "I'm so sorry I didn't listen to you when you tried to tell me."

She smiles sadly. "No one did. Everyone thought I was having a paranoid episode. Which I understand. I even doubted myself."

I shut my eyes against the tears and she squeezes my hand with her cold fingers. "Are you okay?"

I look at her, and the tears spill down my cheeks. "Of course not. I was in love with him. I thought he was in love with me. But he was just using me." I sniff, wiping my eyes on my sleeve. "The man I loved didn't exist."

"How much did he take from you?"

"A couple hundred thousand."

She raises her thin brows. "Better than it could have been, I suppose."

"Thanks, Mom." I take a tissue from my bag and blow my nose, then take a deep breath, forcing a smile. "You seem well today. Clear."

"They've got me on new medication." Her eyes drift to watch a colorful little bird land on the birdbath across the path. "It's great for now. We'll see how long it lasts."

I look up to see the nurse approaching with an apologetic smile, saying he's going to have to take her for a nap.

I lean down to kiss her on both cheeks before I go, and she grabs my face in her hands. "I know I've never been a good mother," she says. "But I love you."

"I love you too, Mom."

I straighten up and turn to go, but she calls out after me. "I forgot to mention," she says, and I turn back to her. "When your husband came to visit, he brought a woman with him."

"He did?"

"She was about your age, I think. Very pretty, blond and blue-eyed."

My heart stops. It couldn't be. I hasten to pull the phone I purchased in Zurich this morning from my bag and load up Instagram, typing Emelia's name into the search bar. I click on a photo of her holding a glass of champagne with the sunset behind her, her flaxen hair blowing in the breeze.

"Is this her?" I ask, showing her the screen.

She nods, frowning. "Yes. You know her?"

"I do, actually."

But I realize as I say it that I clearly don't know Emelia at all.

IN THE BACK OF THE Uber on the drive to the airport in Zurich, I reopen Emelia's social media account and scroll down her page. Her profile is filled with enough pictures of her and Timeo in various glamorous places that no one would ever notice the account was opened only four months ago, unless they had a reason to look for dates, as I do now. As I comb more carefully through the photos, I realize that no one is tagged, and the first hundred or so pictures were uploaded all within a week of one another. As I scroll through her followers, clicking on their accounts, I realize most of them are likely bots.

I click back and forth on the two friends we have in common, neither of whom I've seen in years, then quickly type out identical messages to each of them:

Hey! Long time. Looks like we have a friend in common. Wondering how you know Emelia Khan? X Gia

By the time I'm at the gate, the first has replied:

Hey girl, don't actually know her, just followed her because she requested me recently and I liked her style!

Fucking Emelia. I don't know what's worse, her duplicity or my disappointment in myself for not seeing through her. Even after her admission that she and Timeo were frauds, I wanted to believe she really liked me, that she really wanted to be my friend. When all along she'd been plotting with my husband against me.

Were Emelia and Garrett romantically involved when they targeted my mom, or simply working together? Even with all I now know, the thought of them together makes me sick.

A dizzying cocktail of emotions swirls through me. I'm heartbroken at the realization that the man I loved never existed, ashamed that I was so gullible, furious at all of them for doing this to me and at myself for allowing them to. Garrett played me like a fucking fiddle. He preyed on my vulnerability while I was mourning my father, exploited my weaknesses, love-bombed and gaslighted me.

I've been scammed. Swindled out of hundreds of thousands of dollars by the man I believed was my soulmate. My head understands, but my heart doesn't. I feel claustrophobic, the world closing in on me.

Again I wonder, what was his end game with me? How much more would he have taken before he left me?

Would he have left me alive?

GIA'S MANUSCRIPT

CHAPTER 20

I T'S LATE AFTERNOON BY THE TIME I RIDE MY ATV UP THE DUSTY HILL IN the beating sun, my heart racing faster and faster as I approach the house. I can hear the hammering and sawing of the workers as I cut the engine, but no other vehicles are parked in front of the gurgling fountain.

The front door is unlocked, the house quiet and cool. The cushions on the couch are organized and undented, and all the candles in the fireplace that had melted to nubs have been replaced. I hear footsteps on the stairwell and turn to see Aristea, her arms full of soiled bedsheets. She starts when she sees me.

"Emelia and Timeo left?" I ask.

She nods.

"And Garrett?" I ask.

"He go."

"Did he say where he was going?" I ask.

"No. He say tell you Melodie call."

So he knew about the sale. "Shit."

I move past her, through the door to the master suite, into our room. The door to the closet is open, all of his clothes gone, as is my giant Louis Vuitton suitcase. Of course he took my suitcase. The fucker. After our email exchange, I'd hoped he would want to keep up the charade of repentant husband, but apparently not. I wonder what else he's purloined from this house.

A trip to the library answers that question. The shelves look like a bakery at noon, full of holes with all the good stuff gone. I let out a groan of frustration. My father carefully collected those books over years and years.

Fuming, I glance over at the case containing the antique revolver. But it's not there. I go cold, my heart suddenly in my throat as I spin in a circle, carefully surveying the room. I open each of the drawers of the desk, rifle through the remaining books on the shelves and the pillows on the couch, but I know in my heart my search is futile. Garrett has the gun.

I call Leon from the phone in the kitchen, sitting at the breakfast bar and wrapping my finger in the coil while his secretary fetches him for me.

"Hello, Gia," he says, formal as always.

"I asked Garrett for a divorce."

"Oh," he says, the surprise evident in his voice. I assume most people don't make the decision to divorce as fast as I did. But then, most people's husbands aren't simultaneously stealing from them and cheating on them. "How did that go?" he asks after a beat.

"Not well," I answer. "But he's gone now."

"Gia, are you okay?" Leon asks.

I sigh. I'm not, but there's nothing Leon can do about it. "It is what it is," I say. "He's gone now and I'm going to change the locks. We'll be divorced by the time the sale goes through and I won't owe him a dime."

"You spoke to your dad's divorce attorney?"

"Emailed. We've scheduled a time to talk tomorrow."

"Ah," he says. "Let me know if I can help with anything. In the meantime, I'll send over the contract for the sale and we can review it together. Construction will halt until the sale has gone through, and Melodie will finish it."

"Okay," I say. "I just need to decommission the well first."

"The contractor will roll over everything unfinished to her account, so I'm sure it will be taken care of," he assures me.

"I'll do it," I say.

"She won't do any reaccounting for it—"

"I don't care. It's personal to me."

"Okay," he acquiesces. "As you wish."

After we hang up, I sit there for a long time, watching a fly buzz around the kitchen that will soon no longer belong to me. Outside, the pool shimmers invitingly in the afternoon sunlight, the same as it does every day. I can hear the distant sound of a hammer outside and the whirring of Aristea's vacuum cleaner somewhere upstairs. The fly bounces from surface to surface like the thoughts in my mind until I can't stand it anymore and I throw open the sliding glass door to the patio, shooing it toward freedom. But the fly won't leave.

Thinking back over my relationship with Garrett, the warning signs I'd written off at the time stand out like flashing red lights. The way his temper would flip like a switch, sometimes at the smallest thing. The fights we had this summer, the smashed cocktail glass, my bloody ear. The threats he made.

I wonder if he's with Timeo and Emelia now. And where?

He could be anywhere, with anyone, really. And he has the gun. The thought sends chills up my spine.

It's unlikely he's here in Miteras, I remind myself. The island is too small for him to go unnoticed.

One thing I find odd is that none of the ATVs besides the one Emelia and Timeo borrowed are missing, nor is the boat. It's far too long a walk into town in this heat, especially dragging my giant Louis Vuitton suitcase, so I assume he must have caught a ride with someone—perhaps he piled onto the ATV with Timeo and Emelia? Or maybe he called a water taxi. The service is far from reliable, but sometimes you can get lucky.

"Aristea," I call from the bottom of the stairs. "Can you come here?"

After a moment, she appears at the top of the staircase, holding a broom.

"I know about your affair with my husband."

She freezes, gripping the banister with white knuckles.

Her English isn't as good as Dimitrios's and I don't know how much she understands, but I plow ahead anyway. "Was it consensual?"

She blinks at me like a deer in the headlights, uncomprehending.

I consider whether to attempt to rephrase but decide the better of it. Regardless of the particulars of their affair, Garrett was her boss and clearly held the power. He's to blame, not her. "I'm not angry with you," I say instead. "And I'm sorry if he hurt you. I'm divorcing him. I just need to know where he's gone. Did he mention where he was headed?"

She swallows, her eyes wide. "He say go Athens."

"Okay," I say. "If he comes to you, please tell me. He's a dangerous man. You understand? Garrett is a dangerous man." I lift the sleeves of my shirt and show her the bruises on my arms from where he gripped them the other day. "He did this. And he'll do worse."

She nods, dropping her gaze. "I understand."

"He threatened to kill me."

She looks like she wants to sink through the floor.

"You want I work?"

"Yes," I say with a sigh. "Thank you. You should know I've sold the house, though. I'll be out of here in a month or so. I can give the new owner your information if you like."

"Sorry," she says. I'm not sure whether she's apologizing for screwing my husband or she's sorry I have to sell my house, but either way, I'll take it.

"Thanks. Did you see how Garrett left? Did someone pick him up?"

She shakes her head. "I don't know."

ONCE ARISTEA HAS LEFT FOR the day, I call Dimitrios. He's on the boat already but promises he'll have a friend come around tomorrow to change the locks on the house.

Before I go to bed, I jam the security bars I never use into the sliding glass doors and lock all the windows. Garrett has a key to the front door, so I wedge a chair beneath the knob and drag the heavy entry table in front of it. My improvised security system likely won't keep him out, but at least I'll hear him if he enters and will have time to escape out the bedroom window.

Have I made a terrible mistake in coming back here? But what choice do I have? I need to empty the house of a lifetime's worth of stuff. There's no one else who can do it.

It's unlikely he's still on the island, I remind myself again.

The melatonin I take before bed does nothing to slow my speeding mind, and I don't want anything heavier in case I need to wake up and run in the middle of the night, so I lie awake staring up at the slowly revolving blades of the ceiling fan in the darkened room.

It's funny, I thought I knew my husband so well, but in truth I knew nothing about him. The things he told me were fabricated, engineered to make me love him. I never met his friends or family, other than his father—if that man really was his father. He isn't on social media, and none of our bank accounts outside of the one he swiped ninety thousand from are linked, nor do we share credit cards or even a cellphone plan. I was so blinded by love I'd never thought much about how separate our lives are—until now, when I find I have absolutely no way of tracking him down.

I've gone over our conversations again and again, looking for clues, but he was slick; even our arguments revealed nothing. It strikes me that our last exchange when I asked him for a divorce was likely our most honest, and one thing he said keeps coming back to me. It was after he'd threatened to kill me, and I told him the property would revert to my family if he did so before the sale went through.

"Then perhaps I'll let you live that long," he'd said.

I'd thought at the time he was simply trying to scare me, but now that the sale is going through in a few weeks, I have to wonder whether it wasn't a threat, but a plan.

ABBY

CHAPTER 14

IT WAS MIDNIGHT WHEN BENNY AND I FINISHED READING GIA'S MANU-
script on the plush white couch in the great room.

"Fuck," he said, rubbing his eyes as the final page fluttered to
the floor.

"Yeah," I agreed. "Fuck."

The dread that had come over me about halfway through had
settled into my bones now, cold and heavy. The last events she wrote
about happened over a month ago now, so she must have spent the
past few weeks committing them to paper. But what happened during those weeks? And where was she now?

"We have to show this to the police," I said, closing my eyes as I
leaned my weary head back against the cushions, Gia's last line ringing in my ears. "She disappeared the day after the sale closed. You
think that's a coincidence?"

He shook his head. "This has to be enough to make them start
taking her disappearance more seriously."

He leaned forward and picked up the final page from the floor,
setting it on top of the others on the coffee table in front of us. "She

must have gotten this from Dimitrios," he commented, running his finger along its live edge. "I don't remember seeing it before."

"We need to talk to him."

"And Aristea."

"Do you think . . ." I took a jagged breath. "Do you think Garrett's killed her?"

He shook his head against the idea. "I can't think about that. We have to focus on finding her. Anyway, Leon said the money wouldn't hit the account until Wednesday—"

"That's tomorrow."

"Shit, it is."

"What's your thinking?"

"That he needs her alive long enough to transfer the money to his account."

"Couldn't he just use her passwords?" I asked.

"He may need her fingerprint or her face or her answers for all those confirmation questions banks ask. It seems like a big risk to kill her before he's gotten the money."

"Let's hope." I paused. As unsettled as I was by her account of events, something about it felt off to me. "Was what she wrote about when you were here true?"

He nodded. "Verbatim, as much as I can remember. Why?"

I bit my lip, considering how to reply. "All that stuff about the well. The goats, the curse. I just don't remember it being such a big deal. We did dump flowers and a bottle of wine down it once, but it was a full moon and we'd been drinking and playing with the Ouija board. It was more of a lark than anything serious."

"She didn't mention it to me either, that I remember. But there were summers before you came along when she was here and I wasn't. You know how obsessive she gets about things, and she's always had a tendency to embellish."

"True." Her tendency to embellish often went hand in hand with her obsessions. Though in my experience it was men she was obsessive about, not wells. This time, her obsession seemed to have backfired.

I shuddered, scolding myself for judging her decisions now, of all times. I needed to focus on finding my friend, the friend who had taken me under her wing, defended me, persuaded her father to pay for all the schooling that allowed me to have the life I led now. This was no time to doubt her.

I rose and stretched. "We should get some sleep," I said, though I knew I wouldn't sleep tonight, regardless of how exhausted I was.

"Which bedroom do you want?" he asked.

"Where are you sleeping?"

His eyes caught on mine for just a hair too long and I felt the heat rise in my cheeks. "Where do you want me to sleep?"

When we were younger, I'd often fallen asleep next to him while we read together on his bed, or with our limbs entangled while we watched a movie on this very couch—or rather, its predecessor. Looking back, I realize how cruel it was to tease him with cuddling when I knew he was in love with me, but he had never seemed to mind. These days, though, I didn't turn down the opportunity to sleep on a real mattress, no matter how I hated the idea of being separated from him. "Can we both sleep upstairs?"

He nodded. "I took our bags up earlier. You want to take the big room with the balcony, and I'll take my old room? That way I'll be right next door if you need me."

"Sure."

My limbs were heavy as I trudged up the stairs, Gia's words swirling in my brain. All my pajamas were entirely too warm for Greece and I didn't feel like going back downstairs to borrow something of Gia's, so I went to the bureau beneath the matching mirror and began opening drawers. While the room itself was appointed like a hotel room, with no clutter and a painting of a sailboat over the bed, the dressers in the Torreses' homes were always full of cast-off clothing, and this one was no exception. I took out a man-size crimson Harvard T-shirt and slipped it over my head, then grabbed my phone and charger and crawled into the plush king-size bed, slipping between the cool sheets. As I turned to plug my phone into the base of the lamp on the bedside table, my gaze landed on the book resting there.

I froze, feeling as though I'd stumbled upon a rattlesnake on a narrow hiking trail.

There in the pool of lamplight was a yellowed paperback copy of *The Odyssey*.

I recognized it immediately, this humble paperback in a house of first editions.

Could it possibly be the same copy I'd lost that summer so long ago; that I'd worried about all these years?

It certainly looked the same. I reached for the book, my fingers trembling as I turned it over to find the back cover was missing. I flipped through the pages. There, stashed in the middle of the book, was the note. My hands were clammy as I unfolded the brittle paper and read the faded ink:

A,

I think you'll enjoy this.
    Couldn't find your bikini top, but you look better without it
;) Last weekend was fun. I'll be at Bacchanalia next Saturday,
hope to see you there. Don't worry, I'll totally play it cool, haha.

X,

N

The note quivered as I held it between my fingers, agape. This was it. The missing link. I'd turned the house upside down when the book had gone astray in the days after Noah gave it to me, tormented myself about where it might be and what would happen to me if Gia ever found it. But it had never turned up.

To find it here, now, with Gia unaccounted for . . . The timing and location were too uncanny to be coincidental. It must have been placed on this bedside table intentionally. And the only person who would have done that was nowhere to be found. But how the two could possibly be related was a puzzle with too many missing pieces.

I couldn't go to Benny with this, couldn't go to anyone. The only other person who ever knew about this note had been dead for twelve years.

I rose quietly from the bed and went to the bathroom, where I tore the note into a hundred tiny pieces before I flushed it down the toilet.

ABBY

CHAPTER 15

TWELVE YEARS EARLIER

I SAW HIM FIRST. HE WAS TWENTY-THREE TO MY EIGHTEEN, A NORSE god in a pair of European swim trunks that left a lot less to the imagination than the American board shorts I was used to, swabbing the decks of a catamaran, muscles rippling, sun-bronzed skin glistening with sweat, blond hair falling into his eyes. My cone of gelato dripped over my fingers as I walked up the pier, watching as he tossed a bucket of sudsy water that splashed onto his chest, dripping down his six-pack before being absorbed by the waist of his shorts.

So taken was I by the waist of his shorts that I tripped as I boarded *Icarus Flies,* sending my gelato splashing into the turquoise water.

"Are you okay?"

I looked up from where I'd crumpled in an embarrassed heap on the floor of the boat to see him peering over at me, an impish grin on his face. I nodded, beet red.

"Just tripped." I attempted to rise to standing, but my ankle buckled beneath me and I involuntarily yelped.

"Do you have a medical kit?" he asked.

"I don't know," I said, wincing. "It's my friend's boat."

"Where is your friend?"

Gia was in the back room of a restaurant we liked to frequent, shagging the bartender, but I wasn't about to tell this guy that. "She's shopping," I said instead. "She'll be back soon."

"Hold on," he said, raising a finger before disappearing inside the cabin of his own boat. He emerged with a first aid kit in hand and leaped down from the catamaran to the pier, then onto *Icarus Flies*.

I must have looked surprised because he paused. "Sorry," he said. "I didn't ask. Is it okay if I help you?"

I nodded, happy to shelve my mortification if it meant this hot guy playing doctor.

"I'm Noah," he said.

"Abby. Is that your boat?"

He laughed. "No. I am the first mate on *Amphitrite*." He nodded toward the catamaran. "For Blue Seas charter service. We take groups out for day trips and overnights, up to a week."

"I haven't seen you before," I said.

"I'm new. This is my first week. Is this okay?" he asked, gingerly taking my ankle in his hands.

I gasped. "It hurts."

"It's already swollen." He gently pressed on it. "I think you may have a sprain." He rested my foot on his leg and opened the med kit, taking out a bottle of ibuprofen. "Do you have something to drink?"

I pointed to the small built-in refrigerator behind him and he opened the door and popped the cap of a Mythos, handing it to me. "Take those and drink this, you will feel better."

"Thanks," I said. "Your English is really good."

"I do a lot of charters with British and Americans," he said, taking an Ace bandage from the medical kit.

"Where are you from?" I asked.

"Munich, originally. I live in Crete now."

I took a sip of my beer, trying not to ogle him as he expertly wound the bandage around my ankle. "There," he said when he was finished. "You need to stay off it for a few days, though. Can I help you up?"

I nodded, dizzy with the proximity of him as he wrapped my arm around his shoulders and helped me onto the seat. Our faces were close as he released me, and our eyes caught, making my heart flutter. "You have really pretty eyes," he said.

"Thanks," I said, staring into his baby blues. "You too."

"Do you live here?" he asked.

"I'm here for the summer with my friend."

"I'm around the next few days if you wanna hang out," he said.

I smiled. "I'd like that."

"We could take out the boat—"

"Um, yes, please!" I turned to see Gia, her long hair wild, bikini top askew, jean shorts showing off the perfect crescents of her toned ass. She licked her gelato cone slowly as she looked my new friend up and down. "Who are you?"

NOAH DID TAKE US OUT on the catamaran the next day. I sat on deck with my swollen ankle elevated while Gia jumped off the front, squealing as she lost her bikini top, mixed cocktails so strong I could hardly drink mine, then swam to shore to show Noah a cave we'd discovered last summer. By the time they returned, it was obvious they'd consummated their relationship.

Whatever, I figured. He'd made his choice. It wasn't the first time.

Anyway, it wasn't like he started ignoring me after they hooked up. We all hung out—including Benny—when Noah had time between charters. There was no denying that Noah and I still had chemistry, but I knew better than to lust after the guy Gia was into and was careful never to be alone with him, quick to look away any time I found his gaze lingering. I didn't hold it against him; he was young and hot and working on a boat in the Mediterranean for the summer; why shouldn't he be a player? But Gia didn't see it that way. She was smitten and would hear none of it when I tried to warn her.

ONE NIGHT AFTER ABOUT A month, Gia went to surprise Noah on the catamaran. She'd intended to spend the night, but she returned after a few hours, her face tear-streaked, and told me he was an asshole who had gotten violent with her when they'd had an argument.

I was surprised; I'd never seen any evidence of violence in Noah. He could be dismissive of her when he was drunk, but he was the kind of guy to play peacemaker rather than start a fight. Gia was my best friend, though, so of course I believed her.

A week later, we were at a party on the beach and Noah was there, apparently with another girl. He tried to talk to us, but Gia iced him out. Benny and I went home early, but Gia stayed, and again came home crying, with bruises on her arms this time. Noah had tricked her into having sex with him and been rough with her when she wanted to stop, she said.

I suggested she go to the police, but she blew it off, saying it wasn't a big deal.

OVER THE COURSE OF THE next few weeks, I didn't see Noah. I was working five days a week as a waitress at a restaurant in town where Benny was working as a host—a job he didn't need but had taken "for the experience," which I realized meant he wanted to be close to me.

Gia was left to her own devices most days, and it wasn't long before she found another boyfriend. But she still talked about Noah nonstop—though her praise had turned into complaints about his cheating, how selfish he was in bed, how she always had to pay for everything, and how he wouldn't leave her alone even though she'd told him she didn't want to see him anymore.

He was obsessed with her, she said.

She claimed Noah was stalking her and her new beau, making

threats. Again, I told her to go to the police, and this time she listened. She didn't want to drag her new guy into it, so I went with her, backing up her story when the police dismissed her. Though I hadn't actually seen Noah hurt her, I'd seen the bruises, the tears. That was all I needed.

It didn't matter; the cops didn't do anything, and Noah continued to scare her so badly that she became paranoid, constantly looking over her shoulder, locking doors as soon as we returned home, refusing to be outside after dark.

After about a month of this, Gia and Benny went to visit their mother in Switzerland, leaving me alone in the house for the weekend. They tried to talk me into coming with them, but there was a big party at the restaurant that Friday night, and I knew I'd make a ton of cash. Also, Benny and I had just had our kiss in the library, and I was battling increasingly confusing feelings I knew I shouldn't act on. I was afraid that if Gia spent the night with her mom, as she sometimes did, and Benny and I were left alone in Zurich, I might cross a line with him that would be hard to come back from. So I stayed.

The Saturday morning after the big party at the restaurant, I'd gone into town for coffee when I saw Noah, eating a pastry on the patio of the bakery across the street. He smiled and waved when he saw me, as though nothing was wrong. "Ciao, Abby," he called as I approached.

I frowned at him and hustled into the store, hoping he'd leave me alone. But when I exited the coffee shop, he was leaning against the white wall in the shade of the awning across the way, waiting for me. "Abby," he called, starting toward me as I exited.

I shook my head at him. "Leave me alone."

"Why?" he asked, falling into step with me. "What happened? I thought we were friends."

I spun to face him, anger bubbling inside me. "Friends? You stalked and threatened my best friend, that does not make us friends."

"What?" he asked, his eyes wide. "*Stalked* Gia? No."

"I saw the bruises, you can't bullshit me."

"Bruises? Abby, I would never hurt a woman. I am not like that. I thought you knew—" He seemed so sincere as he said it, his expression pleading with me to believe him. But I wasn't stupid.

"I don't know anything about you, obviously," I said. "You need to leave her alone."

"What has she been saying?"

"You got violent with her when she broke up with you, and you've threatened her—"

"When she broke up with me?" He seemed genuinely confused. "When was this?"

"A month ago, you'd just gotten back from Sifnos and she went down to your boat . . ."

"Ah. Yes, I remember that night." He held up a finger and pulled out his cellphone.

"What are you doing?" I asked.

"I know you're not going to believe me, but maybe you'll believe my captain. Please." He sat on a shaded bench against the wall and patted the seat next to him. "Let Klaus tell you what happened."

He didn't seem dangerous, and we were in public. Maybe I could talk some sense into him, get him to leave Gia alone. I sighed and sat as his captain answered.

"Hey, man, I've got Gia's friend here wanting to know what happened that night she came down a month ago, right after we'd gotten back from Sifnos. Can you tell her, please?"

"The night the girls stayed over?" Klaus asked.

"Yes." Noah turned to me. "We'd had a bachelorette party on board and two of the girls stayed an extra night."

"We were having dinner with them on the boat when Gia showed up," Klaus said. "She had been drinking, and when Noah told her it wasn't a good time, she got very upset and started yelling, making a scene. She wouldn't leave, so we threatened to call port security, then walked her into town."

"You *both* walked her into town?" I asked, dubious.

"We thought it was better," he said. "She was very upset with Noah."

"I'd been clear from the beginning that we weren't exclusive," Noah said. "I thought she was cool with it, but . . ." He shrugged. "Anyway, I told the security guys not to let her back into the port that night and I didn't see her after that until a few weeks later at a party on Kampos beach. She was a little weird, but we . . ."

"You hooked up. She said you were rough with her when she wanted to stop."

He shook his head as Klaus's voice came out of the phone. "The next day, he told me she wanted him to pull her hair and he wouldn't do it."

Noah met my eye. "It was kind of rough, but she was the one driving it, I swear. And she definitely didn't say she wanted to stop."

"Do you need anything else?" Klaus asked. "I'm with a friend."

"That's it, thanks," Noah said, hanging up.

I narrowed my eyes at him. "Have you talked to Gia since?"

"I tried to catch up with her one night when she was walking back from a bar in town, but she sped off on an ATV. I texted her afterward, and she wrote back telling me to fuck off. Same thing happened on the boardwalk a few days later. I was trying to catch up with her to see what the hell I'd done, but she flipped me off and roared away on her ATV."

I thought about this, imagining it from Gia's point of view. She would have been upset when she caught Noah with another woman on the boat, and, especially if she was drunk, she might easily have misconstrued his words and actions. In the wake of this, I could imagine her being aggressive with him on Kampos but not liking what she'd started once she got into it. With that in mind, I could see how she might have been spooked by his chasing her the night she sped off on the ATV, and seen his text message and attempt to flag her down the following weekend as a fixation. She was very proud—so proud, in fact, that her pride could border on delusion—and it might have been easier to create a story in her head that Noah was obsessed with her than to admit he wasn't as into her as she was into him.

The more she repeated her story to me and Benny and whoever else would listen, the more she came to believe it, until she'd worked herself up into a frenzy over nothing. At least that's what it seemed like from this fresh frame of reference.

"Have you seen her since?" I asked.

"Once. At the disco. She was out on the patio smoking when I came out, and we started talking, but she was drunk and started making accusations."

I remembered seeing him across the dance floor that night. Gia had told me he'd intimidated her when she went out to smoke a cigarette. "What kind of accusations was she making?"

He looked at me from beneath his brow. "About you, mostly."

"*Me?*"

"That she'd noticed me flirting with you earlier in the summer and she knew I wanted to—get to know you better."

"Really," I said flatly.

He met my eye and held it. "No, she said she bet I thought of you when I was fucking her."

Involuntarily, a bolt of electricity traveled the length of my torso.

He shrugged, sheepish. "I can't say she was wrong."

I knew then that I should get up and walk away immediately, but I was rooted to the spot, held in place by his magnetic blue eyes.

"What did you tell her?" I asked, my voice barely a whisper.

"That nothing was ever going to happen between us because you were loyal to her."

But his story had to be bullshit, otherwise— "Why did you hook up with her if you were into me?" I asked, narrowing my eyes.

"She told me about your guy back home, so I—"

"My what?"

"Your boyfriend. The guy you're so in love with."

"Wow." I blew out my cheeks, trying to wrap my head around all this. "There is no guy at home. Never was. I was into you, until she swooped in and—"

He stared at me, understanding. "I'm a jackass."

"No," I said. "She's . . . she gets what she wants. You never stood a chance." I pressed the palms of my hands into my eyes, the depth of Gia's duplicity sinking in. "It's better anyway, I'm not really the casual fling type," I muttered.

"Who says it would have been a casual fling?"

I laughed, looking over at him. "No offense, Noah, but you're obviously a player."

He shrugged, not denying it. "Even players fall in love."

"Which is *exactly* what a player would say."

He laughed and bumped my shoulder with his. "Where is Gia now?"

"She's in Switzerland through Monday," I answered.

"I've got the boat today," he said, brightening. "Want to take it out?"

I knew I shouldn't. Gia was my best friend, not to mention her dad was paying for my tuition at Georgetown in the fall. I should walk away, say *No, thank you*. But in that moment, after just having learned how Gia had thrown me under the bus to snake the guy I wanted, I didn't feel much loyalty.

"You can't tell anyone," I said. "It has to be our secret."

He smiled. "I'm very good at keeping secrets."

NOAH TOOK ME OUT ON the catamaran that day and the next, and I did exactly what any other horny eighteen-year-old on a boat in the Mediterranean with a hot guy would have done. I understood afterward why Gia had been so obsessed with him. And after what she'd done to me, I felt no remorse for the illicit things we did behind her back.

In the morning as we were waking up, I noticed a yellowed copy of *The Odyssey* on his bedside table. I picked it up and began thumbing through it.

"Have you read it?" he asked.

I shook my head.

"What? A girl as well read as you, living in Greece, hasn't read *The Odyssey*?" He tickled me, kissing my neck. "That should be a crime."

I knew I couldn't see him after that weekend, and I wasn't upset about it; our fling had been the perfect end to my summer. I was leaving to start school in less than two weeks, where I would meet other boys—boys Gia wouldn't be around to snag. As much as I loved her, I was growing weary of her antics and had a feeling a little distance would do our friendship good.

I realized Monday morning I'd left my watch on Noah's bedside table and, feeling like a criminal, swung by the port to collect it. He was waiting on the deck of the boat for me, his copy of *The Odyssey* in his hand. "My dad gave me this, the last time I ever saw him," he said. "He told me he was going on a great journey, and that I should think of him as Odysseus."

"Where did he go?" I asked.

"Jail." He thrust the book at me. "I want you to have it."

"I don't want to take the copy your dad gave you," I protested.

"I really don't want any part of him in my life anymore."

"What about your little sister?" I asked, recalling the framed picture of the two of them on his bedside table.

"She hates him even more than I do. And you need this book."

"Okay," I said, tucking it into my bag. "Thank you."

While I sat on the bench afterward waiting to meet Benny and Gia's ferry, I thumbed through the pages of *The Odyssey*, still shocked by my own subterfuge, worrying about whether anyone had seen us together. I couldn't help but smile as I read the note Noah had folded inside the front cover. I'd have to be sure to get rid of it later.

When the hydrofoil arrived, I tucked the book back into my bag, zipped it, and rose with a big smile to greet Benny and Gia, as if nothing had ever happened.

But that evening in the safety of my room when I opened my bag to retrieve the book, it wasn't there.

I spent the next week in a cloud of apprehension, searching high and low for the book while pretending everything was fine, terrified that Gia would discover it and my life would be over, my dreams of the future flushed down the toilet by one stupid mistake.

But what happened next was far worse.

ABBY

CHAPTER 16

IN THE MORNING BEFORE WE'D EVEN FINISHED OUR COFFEE, TWO souped-up-looking police ATVs sped up the driveway in a cloud of dust and parked in front of the house.

"Don't mention the emails I got," I whispered as Benny and I approached the door.

He gave me a curious look. "Are you sure? It will be harder to bring them up later."

"Very sure," I said, thinking of the note I'd torn up and flushed down the toilet last night. Its contents were grounds enough to blackmail me, but the only person who could understand what they meant was Gia.

Could she be the person behind the emails?

Was the note the real reason she hadn't shown up in Sweden? Had she recently found the book and engineered some elaborate plan to punish me for my transgression twelve years ago?

No. Surely I was being paranoid. The housekeeper could simply have found the book in the closet or trapped between the bed and the wall and set it on the bedside table, unaware of what it meant. Gia seldom even entered the room where I'd slept.

Gia had believed Noah was a bad guy, a dangerous guy, and I'd never set her straight; she'd believed she was saving me from him when she accidentally killed him with that heavy lamp. And now she was missing, after asking her abusive husband for a divorce. The two facts had nothing to do with each other. I should put my suspicions out of my mind. But that was easier said than done.

"Good morning," Benny said, opening the door to two uniformed cops. "Thanks for coming."

The male officer, who introduced himself as Adrianakis, was burly and short, with a receding hairline and a paunch. "Primos told me your sister is missing. This is Officer Paros."

The female officer gripped each of our hands in turn with a steel handshake, fixing us with inquisitive eyes. She was about my age with a widow's peak, her dark hair pulled back in a ponytail, and she had the physique of a brick house. If it ever came to it, I'd choose her for protection any day over Adrianakis.

"Come in," Benny said, unlocking the door and swinging it wide.

The cops looked around as they entered, scanning the foyer, flanked on one side by the seldom-used dining room, and on the other by the even less often used formal living room. They followed Benny down the steps to the great room and into the kitchen, where he poured them each a glass of water. "Have you spoken to Theodoropoulos yet?" he asked.

"Soon," Adrianakis answered. "Can we sit?"

Benny gestured to the farmhouse dining table, where the officers selected seats with their backs to the window, leaving Benny and me to take the chairs across from them, facing into the sun. I was glad Benny had asked them to come to the house; I was still on edge, but less so than I was in the police station yesterday.

"We have reason to believe the man Gia recently married is violent," I blurted as Paros took out her notebook. "He threatened to kill her, and now she's disappeared, on the day the payment from the sale of her house went through."

The officers exchanged a weighted glance. "How are you knowing he has threatened to kill her?" Adrianakis asked.

I pushed my chair back and grabbed the copy I'd made of Gia's manuscript this morning off the breakfast bar behind me, slapping it on the table between us. "It's all in here."

Paros picked up the top sheet and began reading. "She write this?"

Benny and I nodded.

"We are needing you to start at the beginning," Adrianakis said.

BY THE TIME WE'D FINISHED answering their questions, an hour had passed. While they weren't as worried as we were that something terrible had happened to Gia, they were concerned enough to open an investigation, which meant that the bank agreed to the soft freeze Leon asked to be put on her account, meaning she—or Garrett, posing as her—could log in and initiate a transfer, but the money would never leave the account. This was what we hoped for, as a log-in would ping the server and allow Leon's guys to triangulate the whereabouts of the computer or phone used.

The last email she'd sent us had come from somewhere within a twenty-mile radius, too broad to be of much use in pinpointing her exact location.

We didn't want to upset Caroline by informing her of her daughter's disappearance before we had more information, but Leon was able to confirm that a man calling himself Brian Hunt had visited her at Vue sur la Montagne, bringing along a woman who went by Anna Huber, which we recognized as what Emelia claimed was her real name, though there was no evidence that it was. Leon confirmed that the charity this Brian Hunt supposedly ran didn't exist, but the fact that Garrett had clearly been able to fabricate an ID good enough to pass Vue sur la Montagne security didn't bode well for our search now.

While the police went through the house searching for fingerprints and signs of a struggle, Benny and I sat beneath the trellis out by the pool, poring over Gia's manuscript for clues.

The police attempted to locate Dimitrios, but no one by that name or meeting the description Gia painted of him in her book was recognized by either the contractor or the boat repair shop, and the owner of the boat shop—whose name was not George, but Jerome—swore up and down that none of his men had been hired to sail a boat anywhere, let alone Spain. It wasn't a service they offered.

Furthermore, the woman who owned the dress shop Gia described as Dimitrios's mother's was a Chinese immigrant who had no children.

Had Gia invented Dimitrios out of thin air? Her descriptions of him certainly read more like fantasy than reality.

And what of Aristea, who was another dead end? She, too, seemed drawn with broad strokes in Gia's manuscript, I realized. Though someone matching her description had worked for Gia—after all, Benny had seen her with his own eyes—no one by that name could be located on the island, and Gia had seemingly paid her in cash, which meant there was no paper trail. The simplest answer was that Gia had simply changed her name—though Benny was nearly certain Gia had referred to the girl as Aristea when he visited last month. Which led us to wonder, how many other names had Gia changed?

How much of her manuscript was even real?

The police saw things in black and white, and these fabrications led them to disregard her manuscript entirely. But she'd reported so accurately everything that had happened during the time Benny was here with her that ignoring it felt like throwing the baby out with the bathwater. Gia wasn't a person who lived in black and white; she thrived in full color, and I knew from experience that the truth was hidden between the lines she wrote. I was sure this was true of her latest manuscript as well.

Still, it felt good that the police were on the case and strides were being made, and I was cautiously optimistic—until Adrianakis approached us sometime in the afternoon with a grim look on his face. "Can I show you something?" he asked.

We followed him into the foyer, where Paros was squatting near the front door while a man in plain clothes took pictures of something wedged into the space between the floor and the baseboard. "What is it?" I asked, my heart in my throat.

The photographer checked his camera and nodded to Adrianakis, who inserted his hands into a pair of blue rubber gloves to pull a thin gold chain from the crack. The chain was knotted and broken, the luster of the diamond key dangling from it dulled by something the color of rust.

I gasped, gripping Benny's hand as we stared at the necklace.

"This is Gia's?" Adrianakis asked.

"Yes," I said. "Garrett gave it to her."

"Is that blood?" Benny asked.

"We will see," Adrianakis said.

This was not an elaborate hoax created to punish me for my betrayal. Something terrible had happened to my friend, and I felt doubly guilty for ever thinking she could have been the one behind the threatening emails.

All my hope drained out of me as he dropped the necklace into a plastic bag, saying something about sending it off to a lab to be DNA tested against the strands of long brunette hair they'd collected from the plush white bath mat in Gia's bathroom. I slid down the wall to sit on the flagstone floor of the entry hall, numb with shock. Gia was a victor, not a victim. I refused to believe I'd seen her for the last time. It simply couldn't be.

THAT NIGHT WAS HARD, A chasm of despair opening inside me. At dinner, Benny and I pushed food around on our plates, lost in our thoughts, trying to convince ourselves that it was possible the blood wouldn't be hers, that the necklace had been lost some other day, that the dull red substance wasn't blood at all.

Possible, but not probable.

When I finally crawled into bed for the night, I tossed and turned, unable to stop imagining Gia's violent end at Garrett's hands. The police had found no sign of the missing revolver; had he used it against her? Or slammed something into her skull, the way she'd done to Noah? I pictured the worst, tears soaking my pillow.

I'd given up sleeping and gone to stand at the window, staring out at the moonlit sea, when there was a soft knock on the door.

"Come in," I called.

Benny pushed the door open. He was in boxers and a T-shirt, and I could see in the semidarkness that his eyes were as haunted as my own. "I heard you get up," he said, joining me at the window. "I can't sleep either."

"My imagination is not my friend," I said.

"Mine either."

We stood there shoulder to shoulder for a long time without speaking. Words were unnecessary; our thoughts were the same. When I finally grew tired enough that I thought I could lie down and try to sleep again, he started for the door, but I caught his hand. "Stay," I said.

He nodded and climbed into bed beside me, spooning me gently, his body pressed to mine. My dark thoughts flickered with something else then, and I knew his did too. But we stayed like that, unmoving, our breath shallow, until we finally drifted off just before dawn.

ABBY

CHAPTER 17

WE WERE AWAKENED AT SUNRISE BY THE RINGING OF BENNY'S cell.

He groaned as he rolled over to fumble on the bedside table, knocking the copy of *The Odyssey* to the floor as he grabbed the phone.

"It's Leon," he said, sitting up to rub the sleep from his eyes. It was early in Greece, but Leon was in London, two hours behind us. It was the middle of the night there. "Leon? What's going on?"

"There's been a log-in attempt on Gia's account," he said.

"Were you able to trace it?" Benny asked.

"It's coming from Kampos," he said.

"The Palaces?" Benny sat up straighter. "They're deserted. It would be the perfect place to hide out. I have Adrianakis's personal number here, hold on." He pulled up the number and read it out to Leon. "Keep us in the loop."

His feet had hit the floor before he hung up. "We can take *Icarus Flies*."

Adrenaline swept the cobwebs from my sleep-deprived brain as

I got out of bed and rifled through my suitcase, taking out a pair of jeans and a T-shirt. "You know the cops aren't going to want us to go."

"So we better get out of here before they can stop us."

WE WERE ON THE WATER flying into the rising sun by the time Adrianakis called to tell us they had a team headed over to Kampos.

"Okay," Benny shouted over the sound of the wind and the water. "What? I can't hear you."

He hung up, pocketing his phone. "They don't want us to go."

"I told you."

"Too bad I couldn't hear him." He took his phone from his pocket to show me Adrianakis was calling again, then repocketed it. "Cell service is terrible out here."

"What if Garrett—or Timeo, or whoever it is—is armed?" I asked Benny.

"We'll be careful how we approach. We're not going to let them know we're coming."

"If anyone's looking, it's pretty obvious we're coming," I said.

My ponytail whipped my cheeks as I turned back toward Miteras to see two police boats speeding out of port. We'd beat them to Kampos, but not by much. "We have company," I said, indicating the boats.

He turned the wheel, aiming for the rickety pier that jutted into the turquoise water beneath the pointed gray roofs of the castles. The last time I'd been to the Palaces at Kampos was during my illicit weekend with Noah. The development was only recently abandoned at that point, but I still remembered how creepy the hulking shells of empty McCastles had seemed to me. "There are hundreds of them; how are we gonna know where she is?"

"The only one with running water or electricity is the model home. If I were Garrett, that's where I would hide out."

"You think it still has electricity and running water?"

"It did when I was here a year ago. We looked at it as a location for the film I just wrapped in Rome. That's why they keep it on—sometimes they rent it out. Some movie used it a few years ago for a huge fight sequence between superheroes."

Waves from our wake slapped the pylons as we pulled alongside the pier. He hopped out and I helped him tie the boat up before accepting his hand onto the wooden planks, turning back to look at the approaching boats.

"This way," Benny said. "There's a break in the fence."

We jogged across the rocky shore to the path that wound up the rugged hill, navigating cacti and fallen rocks. Between the boulders and brush, we were out of sight of the pier, so I wasn't sure how far behind us the police were.

"Here it is," Benny said.

We crawled through a gap in the chain-link fence, into the backyard of a house that looked like a bite-size version of a Disney castle, complete with stone balustrades and blue-gray steeples. There were gaping black holes where the windows and doors should be, and the ground was littered with old construction detritus, pieces of concrete and steel that no longer had any visible function.

The grid-like pattern of the deserted village spread across the valley before us, rows upon rows of identical three-story faux castles standing right next to one another, each with its own turret. They were in different stages of completion; those nearest to us seemed to be in the husk phase, with their exteriors all but completed, but farther down the overgrown gravel road, the homes were concrete block, their turrets not yet installed.

Alone, the castles were oddities, together they were postapocalyptic. There was a lesson to be learned here—something about greed, capitalism, and conformity—but I didn't have time to mull over what it might be.

"Come on," Benny urged, turning back to make sure I was behind him as he raced through the yard of the castle across the street and up the alley behind it. "It's at the top of the hill."

My heart pounded as we zigzagged through the maze, cutting

through mounds of gravel and around piles of pipes, uphill toward the model home. As we drew nearer, I saw it was identical to the others, but for the intact windows and doors and lone electrical wire hooked up to the side of it.

The call of an unseen bird drew my attention to the roofline of the house. Or was it something else? The noise came again, this time sounding chillingly human.

"Did you hear that?" I asked.

He nodded and we both stood still in the shadow of the looming house, our heads cocked as we listened. After a moment, the silence was broken by a muffled cry, this time almost certainly human. "I'm going in there," Benny said.

Before I could protest, he'd bolted up the steps and through the arched doorway, leaving it open behind him. My blood rushing in my ears, I darted up the stairs and through the doorway, into the shadowy marble entryway of the sparsely furnished house, where a dusty crystal chandelier hung overhead.

"Gia!" he called as he charged up the curved staircase.

I started to follow, but it struck me that rather than rushing in behind Benny, I should wait. If Garrett was there and armed, I could be Benny's backup, could make sure the police found us in time. I stood moored in the empty foyer, undecided, listening to the sound of Benny's footsteps as he ran along the hallway upstairs, opening doors and calling out.

Was I being a coward, or was I being smart?

Years ago, Gia had rushed to my defense. Hadn't she?

"Oh my God," I heard Benny cry. His words became muffled before he raised his voice again, shouting, "Abby! Get up here!"

My heart in my throat, I took the stairs two at a time, running toward the sound of his voice. As I reached the top, Adrianakis and Paros burst into the foyer with four other officers. "Up here!" I called to them.

"Stay there," Adrianakis said.

But I didn't listen. I turned and sprinted to the open door at the end of the hallway, rushing into what appeared to be the primary bedroom of the house. Like the rest of the house, it was sparsely furnished, with a simple wooden bed against the back wall, a chair in the corner, and a dresser across from the bed. On the bed was Gia.

She was thin, her long hair matted, dark circles beneath her eyes; but she was alive. She trembled as she looked up at me with a mix of shock and relief, tears rolling down her face as Benny undid the rope that bound her hands together. On the bed beside her was the dirty handkerchief that must have been in her mouth. "Abby," she croaked. "Thank God."

I ran to her, encircling her bony shoulders in a hug. Benny enveloped both of us in his arms, and that's how the police found us when they came in. "She's alive," I said, turning to them.

"Please, back away," Paros said, waving for Benny and me to move. "And don't touch anything," she added, exasperated. "This is a crime scene." She looked at the other officers and said something in Greek.

"Come with me," one of the younger ones said to us.

"We want to stay," I said.

He shook his head. "Is bad for evidence. Please." He gestured to the door.

"We'll be right outside," Benny called to Gia as we left the room.

In the corridor, we wrapped our arms around each other as we shed tears of joy, overcome with relief.

The nightmare was over. Gia was alive.

ABBY

CHAPTER 18

I SAT ON THE FRONT STOOP OF THE POLICE STATION, SHADING MY EYES against the noonday sun with my hand, while Benny paced up and down the sidewalk, periodically checking his phone to see whether Leon had sent confirmation that he'd reached Theodoropoulos.

"This is ridiculous," Benny said, checking his watch. "She's been in there nearly two hours. It's gotta be ninety degrees in there."

The air-conditioning in the building had broken, and though it was balmy outside, at least the wind made it more bearable than the stagnant heat inside.

"I've had enough of this," he said, marching toward the door of the police station, his mouth in a hard line.

"Where are you going?" I called after him.

"To give them a piece of my mind."

"That's not how— Benny, wait—" I shot to my feet but was unable to catch him before he'd blasted through the glass door and into the stuffy waiting room.

The young officer Primos froze behind the front desk as Benny stormed toward him. "What the fuck is going on here?" Benny asked. "Where's my sister?"

Primos stared at him, agape. "We—we are asking questions," he stammered.

"She needs a hospital, not an interrogation," Benny hurled. "She's been in there two hours. What can they possibly want from her? Where is Theodoropoulos?"

I gripped Benny's bicep, giving it a warning squeeze. Now that we'd found Gia in one piece, my confidence had returned. "What he means to say is that Gia has been through a lot already," I said apologetically. "She needs medical attention. Can she not finish answering questions tomorrow?"

"It will be over soon," Primos promised. But I could tell he didn't know that.

I leaned my elbows on the table, my face serious. "Is Gia under arrest?"

Primos shook his head, his eyes unsure.

I took out my wallet, extracted one of my fancy business cards, and slid it across the table with a perfunctory smile. I wasn't a criminal lawyer, and I knew nothing about Greek law, but it was the only card I had to play. "I'm Gia's attorney, and I need to speak to my client."

He picked up my card and looked from it to me, hesitant. "One moment."

As he disappeared through the door that led to the back offices, Benny appraised me with admiration. "Nice move," he whispered.

After a moment, Primos returned, gesturing for me to enter. "This way, please." As I started for the door, Benny followed, but Primos held up a hand. "Just her."

Benny started to protest, but I stopped him with a sharp glance. "I'll be here," he said.

Wishing I'd played the attorney card earlier, I followed Primos inside, past the empty waiting area, into a windowless white room with fluorescent lighting that could be construed as either a conference room or an interrogation room, depending on your point of view. A plastic fan rotated back and forth, pushing the air around but doing little to cool it.

"They were wearing plastic gloves," Gia was insisting as I entered the room.

She was seated in a metal folding chair at a table across from Adrianakis and Paros, as well as another burly officer in his forties who had been at the Palaces this morning and seemed to be in charge.

"I am Officer Papadopoulos," he said, rising to extend his hand.

"Abby Corman," I said, noting his damp palm as I gave my firmest handshake. "What's going on here?"

Gia's eyes were sunken, her lips cracked, her hair matted with sweat.

"Has she had anything to eat or drink since she arrived?" I asked, an edge creeping into my voice.

"She has water," Paros answered, gesturing to an empty paper cup on the table.

"It's empty," I said. "This place is an oven."

"We are all here together," Papadopoulos returned, wiping sweat from his mustache. He had wet rings beneath his armpits.

"But you didn't spend the past few days kidnapped," I said, my temper flaring. They were doing the same shit to Gia that they'd done to all of us twelve years ago, treating us like defendants. "Do you see the state she's in? She needs a doctor. She is a victim, not a suspect. Why do you still have her here?"

"We just have a few more questions," Papadopoulos said.

"Is she under arrest?" I asked.

"No," Adrianakis said, raising his hands.

"Then we're leaving," I said, pulling her up to stand with me. "We'll be happy to come by and answer your questions tomorrow, once she's had a chance to eat and sleep. Or better yet, you can come to us."

"Please," Adrianakis said, rising. "We will be waiting here at nine in the morning."

I stopped and turned back to them. "Please send someone to watch our house tonight. Her kidnapper is still on the loose."

Adrianakis and Papadopoulos exchanged glances. "Okay," Papadopoulos said. "We will send a man. He will escort you here in the morning."

That seemed fair enough. "Okay," I said.

I flung open the door and steered Gia by the elbow through the back office and into the waiting room, where we found Benny, who leaped to his feet when he saw us. "What the hell?" he demanded.

"We're going," I said, pushing open the door to the street.

Gia cringed in the bright sun like a vampire.

"The boat's in the port," I said to her. The port was less than half a mile away, all downhill, but Gia looked like she was about to collapse. "Do you think you can make it that far?"

She nodded.

"The closest hospital is on Naxos," Benny said as we started walking.

"I'm fine," Gia said. "I don't need a doctor. I just need a shower and to sleep."

"We really should get you—"

"No." She stopped in her tracks, tears springing to her eyes. "Please. I want to go home."

Benny and I looked at each other. "Do we need to see a doctor for the investigation?" Benny asked me.

"It couldn't hurt," I said. "But it's not necessary unless—"

"I wasn't raped or tortured," Gia said. "I was tied to a bed for a few days. Please let me go home."

"Okay," I said, relenting. I couldn't stand to see her in distress. "Let's go home."

We each slipped an arm around her waist, keeping her steady as we walked down the cobblestoned street toward the port, ignoring stares from passersby. When we reached *Icarus Flies,* she collapsed onto the padded seat and stayed there unmoving until we pulled up to our own dock.

Benny drove her up to the house on the ATV while I climbed the steep path, still fuming over the way the police had handled her. By the time I reached the house, she was bathing in the primary suite with the door closed and Benny was in the kitchen making prosciutto and mozzarella sandwiches.

"I made her eat a slice of bread before she went to shower," Benny said, sliding a plate toward me.

I went to the sink and washed my hands, then splashed my face with cool water. "It's so fucked up they treated her like that," I grumbled, drying my hands on a kitchen towel.

"Theodoropoulos will be here tomorrow," Benny said.

"You talked to Leon?"

He nodded. "Apparently Theodoropoulos was happy to help. Said he owed his career to my dad." He caught my eye and smiled. "That was pretty dope, the way you got her out of there."

I snorted. "Dope, huh?"

He shrugged, sheepish. "You shut my dumb ass up and handled it."

"Well, thank you," I said, more pleased with his praise than I wanted to admit. "Did she say anything?"

"They were asking her what happened, but it sounded like they were trying to catch her in a lie or something, grilling her about inconsequential details."

"Did she mention why they thought she was lying?"

He looked up from his sandwich and shook his head.

"I wonder how the team looking for Garrett fared," I said. The one thing Gia had told Benny before the cops came in this morning was that Garrett had been there with her and had fled when he saw the police boats on the horizon. He had his own rental boat hidden in a cove on the far side of the small island that wasn't visible from the pier where we'd docked. He could be anywhere by now.

"I get the feeling they won't be sharing that info with us. Leon's working on getting her a Greek attorney, though. He told me not to let her talk to them again until that's in place."

"We should never have let them take her. It's my fault. I should have known."

"Stop," he said, laying a hand on my shoulder, his brown eyes steady. "None of this is your fault."

I nodded, placing my hand over his. I still didn't know what the emails meant or who had sent them, but I felt silly for thinking it could have been Gia, that her disappearance could have been somehow linked to my betrayal all those years ago. She couldn't have read Noah's note in the book. She'd greeted me with open arms this morning, told me she loved me and thanked me for rescuing her. Everything was going to be okay.

ABBY

CHAPTER 19

G IA FINALLY EMERGED BLEARY-EYED FROM HER ROOM AT AROUND five to find Benny and me on the couch in the great room, once more reading through her manuscript. Her color was better now, her cracked lips were coated in lip balm, and the dark circles beneath her eyes weren't so pronounced.

"I'm starving," she said.

"We picked up takeout earlier," Benny said. "I'll heat it up."

"How are you feeling?" I asked her as we followed Benny into the kitchen.

"I think I'm in shock," she said, sliding onto a stool at the breakfast bar.

"That makes sense," I said. "Do you want anything to drink?"

"God, I would love a G and T. And I should probably have some water."

"Coming right up," I replied, glad to have something to do. I set a cup of water in front of her, then pulled three cut glass tumblers from the cabinet and filled them with gin and ice, adding a splash of tonic and a lime, just how she liked it. "We read your manuscript," I said. "Is it all true?"

She nodded. "You were right, Abs, I never should have married him so fast."

"I'm so sorry, G. That's not something I ever wanted to be right about." I passed her drink to her, and we clinked glasses.

Benny raised his glass from the island, where he was slicing bread. "Cheers."

"I'm so glad to have you back," I said. "We were really worried."

Her eyes misted. "Without you guys"—she paused, her face contorting to hold back a sob, and I put my arms around her—"they would never have looked for me," she said, her voice cracking.

"Did he hurt you?" I asked.

"Not physically." She let out a strangled sound. "I'm just . . . Can we talk about it later? I just want to be here with you guys right now."

"Of course," I said, stroking her hair. "You're safe now. You're here."

"But am I safe?" she asked, pulling back. The low sun shone through the windows, illuminating her tear-streaked face. "We don't know where Garrett is. He could come looking for me. He has the gun. He got bullets for it, I don't know where."

"The doors are all bolted and there's a cop out front," I said. "He'll be there all night."

She snorted. "A cop. Great."

"Were they hostile with you?" I asked.

"They were treating me like I was the suspect. Like I was lying. I was so tired, I couldn't even think straight."

"That may be our fault," I said, looking at Benny. "We gave them your manuscript."

She furrowed her brow. "You did?"

"We thought it might give them clues to help them find you," Benny added.

"But they couldn't find anyone matching the name or description of Dimitrios or Aristea," I said. "Did you make them up?"

"Dimitrios was a fantasy," she admitted. "A little eye candy for my readers. But Aristea worked here. You met her," she said to Benny.

"Do you know where she lives?" Benny asked.

She snorted. "Garrett did. But no."

Benny took Gia's plate from the microwave, and we moved to the kitchen table, Gia settling into one of the cushioned seats on the end while Benny and I slid onto the benches on either side of her.

"How much of the manuscript was fabricated?" I asked.

"Just the stuff about Dimitrios. I mean, I embellished a little here and there, and changed a few names, but most of it was pretty accurate." She picked up her lamb skewer and looked at it longingly. "I haven't had real food in so long," she said, taking a bite.

"What was he feeding you?" I asked as she chewed.

"Not much," she said with her mouth full.

Benny and I related our end of the events of the past few days to her while she inhaled her food, pausing only to take sips of her drink. When she finally pushed the plate away, I pulled a bottle of wine from the refrigerator while Benny grabbed glasses, and we retired to the great room, settling into the big white couch.

"I could fall asleep again right now," Gia said as she tucked her feet beneath her.

"You've been through a lot," I said. "And I don't want to make you talk about anything you're not ready to, but can you give us some idea of what happened?"

She leaned her head back on the cushions with a groan and closed her eyes.

"Come on, G," Benny said as he filled each of the goblets with wine. "We know it's been a long day, but throw us a bone. We've been so worried about you."

She held out her hand and he placed a glass in it. "That's better," she said, taking a long draw of her wine.

The sun was setting over the ocean, casting long shadows and turning the white walls of the room orange. "How did Garrett kidnap you?" I asked.

She sighed, running her finger around the rim of her glass. "It was the night the sale of the house closed."

"Last Friday," I specified.

"Right. I was home, packing for Sweden, when Emelia showed up, out by the pool. I hadn't seen or heard from any of them for nearly a month, but she looked like shit, and said she needed to talk to me. I didn't want her in my house, so I stepped outside to talk to her. The next thing I knew, I was waking up in that room you found me in, tied to the bed."

"Wait, *Emelia* knocked you out?" I asked.

She shook her head. "She said later it was Garrett. That he made her lure me outside. But who knows whether that was the truth. She played it like he was the bad guy, and he did the same to her."

"So they knocked you out and took you to Kampos," I said.

She nodded.

"Where was Timeo?" Benny asked.

"He was there in the beginning, but he and Garrett got into a big fight and Garrett pulled his gun —the gun from the library—on him, fired off a warning shot. The next day he was gone. I haven't seen him since."

"But how did he leave, if there was only one boat?" I asked.

"I don't know," she said, taking another slug of her wine. "I was tied up in that room. I could hear them arguing, but not everything they said. I only know what Emelia told me, but it may not even be true. Garrett may have shot him, for all I know. I was more worried about making it out of there alive."

"Of course," I said, thinking of Timeo banging on my door back in Sweden. Why had he been there? What if he'd come to alert us to what had happened to Gia? I wondered if Benny would mention him, but he didn't, so I didn't either. There was no use upsetting her now.

"How were the three of them related?" I asked.

"At first Emelia had me convinced that Timeo was the con artist and she was just along for the ride. But she later admitted it was her and Garrett from the start. They tried to fleece my mom with a fake charity scheme, but when she didn't bite, Garrett decided he wanted to target me instead." She took a sip of her wine. "This is all from Emelia, so take it with a grain of salt, but she said she didn't want him to target me because she knew he'd get involved with me romantically. But eventually she agreed. Once he got into it, though, he stopped contacting her, and she worried he'd actually fallen for me, so she convinced her ex-boyfriend Timeo to pose as her husband to come with her here to keep an eye on things."

"God, where do these people come from?" Benny asked.

"The dark web," she said seriously. "Emelia said there are forums for hustlers where they team up with each other to do jobs and share tips. Emelia and Timeo went to high school together, but she met Garrett on one of those forums, and they fell in love—or at least she did."

"What did they want from you?" Benny asked.

She rolled her eyes at his question. "Money. From what Emelia said, they usually pulled smaller jobs—they were only going after my mom for a hundred K, which was big for them. Emelia wanted Garrett to leave me once I'd given him the first three hundred, but he got greedy."

"So he was planning to steal the proceeds from the sale of the house?" I asked, trying to follow.

"I don't know what his plan was, exactly. I'm sure he wanted to take whatever he could, and once I asked for a divorce, he saw his prospects dwindling. But he knew I'd be worth a lot more once the sale of the house went through, so he waited that long to kidnap me. They took my computer and phone, texted you guys as me, made me log in to my bank accounts—but there was a hold on the money, so they couldn't get it." She paused, fear in her eyes. "I don't think any of them were killers before, but once there was fourteen million at stake . . . I'm pretty sure Garrett would have gotten rid of me once the transfer went through."

"We weren't gonna let that happen," I said, squeezing her hand.

"What happened to Emelia?" Benny asked.

She swallowed, her face grim. "I think Garrett killed her."

My hand flew to my mouth as I gasped. "Why?"

"He didn't want to share the money with her."

"Fuck," Benny said. "What happened?"

"All I know is they went out on the boat and only he came back. When I asked him where she was, he said *That greedy bitch won't be coming back* and he'd do the same to me if I got any smart ideas." She waved her hand over her head in the general direction of the water, where the sun had set, leaving the sky lavender in its wake. "I'm guessing he took her out there in the boat, shot her, and dumped her body in the sea. But that's just a guess."

"Jesus," I said. "And they were a couple?"

Gia nodded, staring into her wine. "They were together, but I didn't get the impression he was any more faithful to her than he was to me. The engagement ring he gave me, he took off her finger. Emelia said he'd stolen it from a rich widow he seduced."

"How romantic," Benny said dryly. The light outside was failing now, the shadows at the edge of the room deepening. Benny rose from the couch to light the candles in the fireplace. "And how did Timeo fit in?"

"Emelia promised him ten percent of her cut if he did the job with her. She chose him because she trusted him and thought Garrett would be jealous she'd brought her ex along, but it backfired when Timeo became enamored with Garrett and started making mistakes." She reached out to smooth the lines between my brows. "You're frowning."

"I'm thinking," I said. "It's a lot to process." It all made sense, so why did something still seem off? "Why did she tell you all this?"

"I don't know," Gia said, swirling the wine in her glass before taking the last sip. "Maybe she was bragging. Maybe she was lonely. Maybe she figured it didn't matter, since they were going to kill me anyway. I don't feel the need to psychoanalyze the woman who was complicit in my kidnapping. Not right now, anyway." She winked at me. "Maybe later, when I finish my book. Did you like it?"

"Yeah," I said. "It was really well written. Like your last one."

"Good." She sat up and stretched, setting her empty glass on the coffee table. "That's about enough trauma for one night. I'm tired," she announced, rising from the couch with an exaggerated yawn. "There is a time for making speeches and a time for going to bed."

My heart leaped to my throat. The quote was from *The Odyssey*.

She blew us kisses as she strode toward her room. "Love you guys."

It was probably a coincidence. It didn't mean anything. She might not even have realized what she was quoting.

"The attorney Leon hired will be here at noon tomorrow," Benny called after her. "He said we're not to talk to the police until then."

"I'll be up by then. Thank you guys for everything. 'Night."

She waved over her shoulder as she shut the door to her room behind her. I looked over at Benny, biting my lip.

"You're frowning again," he said.

"I just . . ." I paused, trying to figure out how to formulate what I was feeling without mentioning the book or sounding accusatory. "I know everyone processes trauma differently, but doesn't she seem kind of . . . casual for someone who just went through what she went through?"

He nodded in acknowledgment with a half-shrug. "You're not wrong. But it's not the first time she's been through something traumatic. Maybe she's desensitized."

That was certainly true. And she had been incredibly resilient after Noah's death. To be able to write about it in such detail so soon after it happened . . .

"I noticed you didn't mention seeing Timeo in Sweden," I said.

He shook his head. "It didn't seem like the right time."

I nodded as though accepting his answer, but I had a feeling it went deeper than that. That he was as guarded as I was about trusting Gia. I knew why I was wary. But why might he be?

"I'm gonna grab a glass of water," I said. "You want one?"

"Sure, thanks."

On my way to the kitchen, I paused to look through the walls of glass toward the mountains silhouetted against the starlit sky. Out on the deck the pool glowed an unearthly blue, and spotlights lit the branches of the citrus trees down the hill.

As I gazed toward the horizon, one of the tree lights suddenly flickered, as though a large shadow had passed over it. I froze, the hair on the back of my neck prickling.

"Benny," I called, keeping my voice low.

"Yeah?" He turned, looking over the back of the couch.

"I think I just saw something on the hill."

He sat up. "An animal?"

"Maybe."

He climbed over the back of the couch to stand next to me. "Where?"

I pointed down the hill at the citrus tree where I'd seen the movement, but all was still. "It was a shadow. Something big." I shook my head, trying to shake it off. "Maybe it was nothing. A dog or something."

"This house is like a glass box," he said, looking out. "Do you wanna alert the cop?"

I hesitated. "Yeah," I said finally. "Better safe than sorry."

It was probably nothing, I told myself. But again I thought of Timeo in Sweden. Finding Gia was such a relief, it was tempting to think of the case as closed. But it wasn't. Someone out there had sent me those emails, and Timeo had followed us all the way to Sweden. Why?

I was quiet as we walked back to the house after sending the cop chasing after shadows at the periphery of the yard.

"What is it?" Benny asked once we were inside. "You're still pensive."

"It's just . . . we still don't have an answer as to why Timeo followed us to Sweden, or who's been sending me those emails."

"I know," he said. "But we're worn out. I don't think we're going to figure anything else out tonight. Let's sleep on it?"

He was right. Neither of us had slept last night, and we'd had a long, emotional day. But as I lay in bed, so tired I felt drunk, I found that once again I couldn't drift off. The emails had to be about Noah, which meant that someone knew I'd lied about the nature of our relationship. If it wasn't Gia . . . then who?

Had someone seen us leaving the full moon party together? But even if they had, that didn't mean he hadn't attacked me. Too many dates that started off well ended badly; too many men didn't know the meaning of the word "no."

But Noah wasn't one of them.

A chasm of shame opened inside me, thinking of what I'd done to protect myself. He might have been a player, but he wasn't the monster Gia made him out to be, a characterization I'd confirmed with the split-second decision not to challenge her version of events, which had spiraled into a lifetime of guilt.

What had Benny said about the family trying to reopen the case? They knew Noah's character, and he might well have mentioned something to a family member or friend in Germany about us. Hearsay wouldn't have been seen as evidence by the police, but it might have been enough to convince someone close to him to seek revenge. Why now, though? After twelve years? And at the exact same time Gia was kidnapped? It was too remarkable to be chance.

Could Garrett have been related to Noah somehow? Garrett's attempts to swindle first Caroline and then Gia certainly felt targeted. But Noah didn't have a brother, and Garrett was too young to be his father. Was he Noah's friend? Was Timeo? Or . . . Emelia.

Emelia.

She was German, blond, the right age. Why hadn't I thought of it before?

My pulse quickened as I unplugged my phone from the charger and opened Instagram, navigating to Gia's page, where I landed on a picture of Gia and the girl Benny had identified as Emelia, smiling on the beach, their arms wrapped around each other. The picture grew blurry as I zoomed in on her face. It was hard to tell, but maybe . . .

Noah didn't have a brother, but he did have a sister. A much younger sister. She'd been only thirteen at the time of his death, which would mean that now she'd be twenty-five. Like Emelia.

I scrolled through Google looking for an image of his grieving family, finally pulling up a picture of his mother and the awkward thirteen-year-old I'd known as Claudia. Claudia had been a child then, with mousy brown bangs, braces, and gangly legs. You'd never make the connection to the beautiful woman standing next to Gia unless you were specifically looking for it. But with a little imagination, I could visualize the woman that little girl might grow up to become, and the resemblance to Emelia was strong enough that I would have no trouble believing it if someone told me they were the same person.

I rushed out of my room and into Benny's, not bothering to knock. His room was dark, and he sat up in bed, disoriented, as I burst in.

"Benny," I whispered, thrusting the phone into his hands, the screen glowing with the picture of young Claudia.

"What's this?" he asked.

I sat next to him, enlarging the picture. "Emelia is Noah's sister."

ABBY

CHAPTER 20

Yeah, i know," gia said with a sigh, sliding my phone across the kitchen table to me.

It was nearly noon. As desperate as I'd been to share the potential bombshell I'd discovered, I'd waited patiently for Gia to wake up on her own. But this indifferent response was not what I had expected.

"You know?" Benny asked, as thrown as I was.

"Why didn't you tell us?" I overlapped.

"Because I didn't want to trigger you," she said gently, her eyes fixed on me. "It's why she and Garrett targeted our family. They wanted to make us pay for Noah's death."

My mind reeled. "But you didn't mean to kill him."

She snorted. "You think they care about what I did or didn't mean to do? I took her brother's life. She told me she's been plotting her revenge for years. She just waited until Dad was dead to exact it because she knew it would be easier without him around."

"But . . . Garrett killed her?" Benny prodded.

She shrugged. "Maybe. Probably. I can't be sure. Like I said, I think he got greedy when he saw how much money was at stake."

There was a knock at the front door, and Gia rose, stretching. "That's gonna be my attorney."

Benny and I exchanged a weighted glance as we followed her into the foyer, where she opened the door to a serious-looking man in an immaculate suit, his hair streaked with gray, the dramatic arch of his brows giving his face a permanent scowl.

Leon had managed to push Gia's police interview to give her time with this attorney he'd selected for her, and while he hadn't shared the guy's full résumé, he had mentioned one notorious case he'd won in which his client had been accused of dealing arms to the Syrians. Leon didn't elaborate on why he believed Gia needed this kind of pit bull to defend her, but the man was hired, and as we walked him into the living room, he made it clear he needed to talk to Gia alone.

"We'll head into town," Benny said. "You want anything from Aíolos?"

She shook her head. "I'll see you guys later."

On the road to town on the ATV, Benny and I agreed it was strange Gia hadn't told us about Emelia's connection to Noah. "Emelia must have been the one sending you those emails," Benny offered.

"Yeah," I agreed, unsettled. "Though if Garrett killed her, I don't know if the timing—"

"We don't have a timeline for any of this," he reminded me.

"True," I said. But something was still nagging at me. Something didn't fit. I just couldn't pinpoint what it was.

I WAS SITTING ALONE AT a table on the sidewalk of the harborside restaurant where we'd just finished eating, waiting for Benny to return from the restroom, when I felt eyes on me. Chills ran up my spine as I turned slowly, trying to look casual behind my sunglasses as I swept the scene before me, my gaze roving over the smattering of patrons until I landed on a man with only a bottle of Perrier before him, staring intently at me.

A pair of Wayfarers was perched on his prominent nose, a Yankees baseball hat pulled low over his shiny black hair, but I'd recognize him anywhere. He was the same man I'd seen three days ago in Sweden.

Timeo.

Adrenaline shot through my veins as I rose from my seat and made my way to the back of the restaurant, where Benny was just emerging from the bathroom.

"What is it?" he asked when he saw my face.

"Timeo's here," I said in a low voice. "On the patio. He was staring at me. He's probably watching us now."

He put on his sunglasses to look over my shoulder. "Yeah, that's him."

"I bet that's who was in the yard last night, too."

He nodded. "What do you want to do?"

I chewed the side of my cheek, mulling over our situation. We could call the police, but that would ruin our opportunity to talk to him. And I needed to know what he wanted. "We're in a crowd, so we're relatively safe. I say we confront him, turn the tables. He'll be surprised and might reveal something he didn't mean to."

I thought I detected a hint of admiration in his gaze as he nodded. "Lead the way."

My palms were sweaty as I threaded my way through the restaurant toward Timeo's table, my heart in my throat. As we approached, I noted that one of his arms was in a sling, though it didn't appear to be bandaged. He trained his eyes on his phone until we landed at his table, directly in front of him.

"Hi, Timeo," Benny said.

He looked up, pretending to just notice us, his mouth slightly ajar as though he wanted to speak but wasn't sure what to say. I'd been right, we'd caught him off guard.

"Why are you stalking us?" I asked point-blank.

"I'm not—" he started to protest.

"So it was a coincidence you were in Sweden earlier this week, banging on my door?" I asked.

His mouth opened and closed.

"What do you want?" I demanded.

"I need to talk to you," he said finally.

"If you're going to try to extort us, it's not going to work," Benny said.

Timeo rose, casting a glance around at the patrons of the restaurant who had begun to take notice. "I just want to talk. Please."

Benny looked to me, and I indicated a picnic table in the shade of an olive tree about fifty yards away, overlooking the water near where the ferry docked.

We walked in silence, an awkward trio, Benny and me on either side of Timeo. Despite the mild temperature and strong sea wind, I felt a bead of sweat trickle between my breasts, settling into the bodice of the sundress I'd borrowed from Gia.

When we reached the picnic table, Benny and I sat across from Timeo, who took a slug from the water bottle he'd brought with him.

"How did you know where to find us in Sweden?" Benny asked.

"Gia talked about the trip, she showed us pictures of the hotel and the suite she'd reserved. I needed to talk to you in person and I knew I could find you there. Only the place was fully booked, and they don't allow anyone who's not a guest past the gate. I didn't mean to scare you, but I didn't know how else to reach you."

"You've got a lot of nerve being out in public with the cops looking for you," Benny said gruffly.

Timeo drew back, seemingly startled. "What?"

"What do you mean, what?" Benny demanded. "You kidnapped my sister and tried to steal fourteen million dollars from her. Just because you ran off doesn't mean you're not guilty."

"I didn't," Timeo protested. "I didn't do anything to your sister." He gestured to the shoulder on his injured arm. "She shot me."

"What?" Benny and I said in unison.

"That's what I wanted to talk to you about." He pulled the collar of his shirt down, displaying a large white bandage that encompassed most of his shoulder. "I'm lucky she didn't kill me."

Benny narrowed his eyes. "My sister *shot* you."

"When I was trying to get Emelia out of there."

"Out of where?" I asked, my blood pressure skyrocketing. What-ever element of surprise I'd thought we had was flipped on its head. Now I was completely bewildered. "What are you talking about?"

"Out of her house. She'd knocked her out somehow and shot Garrett. She—"

"I'm sorry, what?" Benny asked.

The story was unspooling so fast, I felt like I was on a merry-go-round spinning out of control. I held up my hands, stopping him. "Hold on, slow down. Timeo, please start from the beginning."

"Emelia went up there to talk to her—"

"Up where?" I asked, my prosecutor instincts kicking into gear.

"To the house."

Get the facts. "When?"

"A month or so ago, not long after you left," he said, nodding at Benny. "Maybe two days after Gia kicked us all out? She had just gotten back, I don't know where she'd gone. We were all staying in a hotel down by the marina—"

"Who do you mean by we all?" I asked.

"Garrett, Emelia, and me."

"What was Emelia going to talk to her about?" I asked.

He sighed. "I'll get to that. Let me finish."

I held up my hands in surrender as he took another swig of his water.

"Garrett and I were waiting in the boat while she went up to the house," he went on, "but after half an hour she hadn't come back, so Garrett went after her. Ten minutes later, I heard gunshots, so I followed to see what had happened."

He pushed his sunglasses up on his nose, and I noticed his hand was trembling. "When I reached the patio, I saw Emelia crumpled next to the pool. I heard something around the side of the guest-house, so I crept over there, and I saw Garrett's body lying on the ground in a puddle of blood. Gia was standing over him with a gun in her hand. I panicked and ran." He shook his head, regretting his choice. "That was a mistake."

"Wait, you're saying Gia shot Garrett?" Benny asked, unbelieving.

He nodded. "She heard my footsteps and ran after me. I tried to rouse Emelia, but she was out cold, so I picked her up. I was half dragging her, trying to get us out of there when Gia caught up with us. I begged her to let us go, promised we would keep quiet." He swallowed. "She shot me in the shoulder. There was so much blood, my arm was just dangling. I didn't have a choice, I had to let go of Emelia and run. Gia fired at me a couple more times as she chased me to the boat, but she didn't hit me again."

Silence fell over the table as he finished his story. I felt like I was staring into a broken mirror, the picture of what I thought I knew shattered, the jagged pieces reflecting a distorted image that no longer made any sense. I glanced over at Benny, whose brow was as furrowed as my own. "So let me get this straight," I said. "You're telling us Gia killed Garrett?"

"I mean, I didn't take a pulse, but . . ."

"And what about Emelia?" I pressed.

"She wasn't dead when I was there, but I haven't been able to reach her since. I can only assume . . ." His voice trailed off, his face pained.

"And you didn't go to the police?" I asked, incredulous.

"And say what, the woman we were extorting shot my friend? None of us are on good footing with the authorities. That wasn't an option."

"Okay," Benny said, eyeing him. "This is all just kind of hard to believe because yesterday we rescued Gia from the Palaces at Kampos, where Garrett was holding her hostage."

Timeo shook his head emphatically. "That's not true. It can't be true. I saw him, he's dead."

"So what do you think happened?" I asked.

"Gia killed Garrett and Emelia, then faked her own kidnapping to cover it up," he said, as though it were the most obvious thing in the world.

I closed my eyes, breathing through my nose to keep the dizziness at bay as I tried to sort out my thoughts. It couldn't be true. Could it? Anger frothed inside me. I'd spent the past few days in despair, thinking Gia was dead. And now Timeo was saying she'd faked the whole thing to cover up a double murder?

No. Surely he was lying.

So why did it seem so plausible?

My conscience whipsawed back and forth, leaving me disoriented.

Maybe it was self-defense. But that didn't change the fact that if what he claimed was true, she'd killed two people and faked her own kidnapping, then lied to our faces about it.

Surely Timeo was the liar, trying to clear his name somehow. But if he'd simply stayed away, no one would ever have been the wiser. What was the upside for him? It had to be money.

"Why are you telling us this?"

"I haven't gone to the police," he answered. "I wanted to come to you first. Emelia was supposed to be giving me ten percent of her cut, but now she's gone, and I don't have anything."

Bingo.

"But you just said you couldn't go to the police," Benny pointed out.

"I can tip them off anonymously," Timeo answered. "Send them the evidence I have."

"So you think we're gonna pay you how much not to tell this crazy lie to the police?" Benny asked, incredulous.

"Seven hundred fifty thousand." He took a breath. "And it's not a lie. It's the truth. I have evidence."

"And what might that be?" Benny asked.

Timeo shifted on the bench to reach into his pocket, extracting a small plastic bag containing the casing of one bullet. "The bullet she shot me with, which I'm sure ballistics can match to the gun she used. The antique gun from the library." Benny reached for the bag, and Timeo jerked it away. "No way."

"Kinda hard to match the bullet to the gun if the gun is missing," Benny said.

That was true, but I knew from a friend who was a criminal lawyer that even without the gun, the type of gun could be determined from the casing. Not to mention that Timeo's story alone would likely cast enough doubt onto Gia to open an investigation.

"I also have pictures of the letter Emelia wanted to show to Gia."

"What letter?" I demanded.

Timeo pulled out his phone and scrolled through the pictures until he found what he was looking for. "It doesn't matter if you delete it," he said as he handed his phone across the table to me. "I have it backed up."

I looked down at the glowing picture on the phone in my hand and my blood ran cold.

"She was only thirteen when your sister killed him," Timeo said.

"Killed him while he was attacking Abby," Benny returned hotly.

"Not according to that note," Timeo said.

"What's this?" Benny asked, his eyes roving across the screen as he looked over my shoulder to read an arrangement of letters cut from magazines, like a ransom note from a nineties movie:

NOAH WAS NOT A RAPIST.
HE DID NOT DESERVE TO DIE.

"I've seen this," Benny said. "It was sent to the police years ago and rejected as a fake. Anyone who didn't like Gia could have sent it. And there were plenty of people that didn't like her, especially after the notoriety she brought to the island. Not to mention, she wasn't always as kind to the help back then."

Timeo shook his head, swiping to the next picture. "It was attached to this."

My heart plummeted as I recognized the yellowed paper immediately, but Benny stared at it, confused. "What is this?"

"It's the back cover of the paperback copy of *The Odyssey* Noah's dad gave him before he went to prison." He indicated the name printed in faded ink at the top. "See, that's his name there."

"What does this prove?" Benny asked.

"Noah and Claudia—that's Emelia's real name—talked on the phone every Saturday. The day he died, he told her he'd finally cut his last tie to his dad, who they both had a fraught relationship with, by giving away his copy of *The Odyssey*."

"And?" Benny demanded.

"He gave it to the girl he was into, who he'd spent a wild weekend with the week before. This girl was the best friend of the crazy heiress he'd been seeing earlier in the summer." Timeo's sharp eyes landed on me and I felt like I was going to be sick. "Claudia knew it was Abby, but no one would listen to her when she tried to tell the police they were involved, and she believed Gia killed Noah intentionally. They dismissed it as hearsay, from a thirteen-year-old."

Benny looked from Timeo to me, thrown, expecting me to say something to defend myself. But I couldn't. It was true.

"Two years later, Claudia received this letter," Timeo went on. "It was unsigned, but postmarked here in Miteras, with the back cover of the book attached. It was proof of what she'd believed all along. She's been plotting her revenge on your family ever since."

I pressed the heels of my hands into my eye sockets until I saw stars, trying to stop the earthquake within me. I could say now that the letter didn't prove anything. That even though Noah and I had been consensually involved, he'd attacked me that night when I turned him down.

But I couldn't lie anymore.

"Why did Emelia risk going back up to the house to show this letter to Gia?" I heard Benny ask.

"She knew they likely weren't going to get any more money out of Gia," Timeo replied. "But she wanted to confront her."

They continued going back and forth, their voices sounding farther and farther away as the walls I'd erected to keep the demons at bay collapsed on top of me.

I'd been convinced all these years that I was the liar and Gia was the hero. While I'd known that Noah had been innocent, I had confidence that Gia at least believed she had been defending me when she hit him. But I had to admit that Timeo's accusation felt oddly familiar, as though somewhere in the dark recesses of my mind I'd been preparing for something like this to happen. Something that would make me face up to the truth.

I couldn't look away from it anymore. As much as I wanted to deny it, I had a horrible feeling that the instinct I'd dismissed when I'd first discovered the copy of *The Odyssey* beside my bed was likely right: Gia had been the one to take the book out of my bag all those years ago; she'd known about Noah and me all along.

Which would mean she'd known she wasn't defending me from her stalker when she brought the lamp down on Noah's head—she'd killed him intentionally, in cold blood, and now she'd done the same to Emelia and Garrett.

I didn't want to believe any of it. But the pieces I'd been trying so desperately to fit together in the past few days had finally clicked into place.

Like the email said, *The truth will out.*

ABBY

CHAPTER 21

THE LEAVES OF THE OLIVE TREE RUSTLED OVERHEAD AS BENNY AND I watched Timeo walk away, his outline growing smaller as he moved down the boardwalk. Where was he going? He'd exchanged phone numbers with Benny but hadn't given us a timeline, had made no specification about where or when we should pay him, and we hadn't asked. Should we have asked? I'd never been blackmailed before; I didn't know the rules.

At any rate, it was out of my hands. I certainly didn't have the better part of a million dollars lying around; it was up to Benny.

"What the fuck, Abby?" Benny muttered once Timeo was out of earshot. "Was that true?"

I sighed, resigned. If Benny and I had ever had a chance, my answer would end it. "Yes."

He shifted on the bench of the picnic table to look at me, disappointment written across his face. "Please explain."

"Noah wasn't who Gia made him out to be." I took off my sunglasses and looked him in the eye. "He never stalked her or threatened her, he only told her he didn't want to be exclusive. The rest was a misunderstanding she blew out of proportion."

"So what, then he started seeing you?"

"It wasn't like that. I'd met him first, he'd asked me out before Gia ever laid eyes on him. But then she swooped in and told him I had a boyfriend I was in love with. So yeah, after they broke up, I hooked up with him. And yeah, part of it was to get back at her for not playing fair."

Saying it out loud sounded so lurid, so petty.

"Jesus," he said.

"I know, it was stupid," I said, contrite. "But we were both eighteen. Not that that excuses any of it. The whole thing was dumb, and the fact it turned out the way it did . . ." I shook my head. "It never should have turned out that way."

"So, the night of Bacchanalia . . ."

"Noah was there, we were both on molly and not thinking clearly. He was leaving the next day for a charter, and I was heading back to the States, so we knew it was the last time we'd see each other. Gia was dancing with a bunch of other people, so he and I snuck out of there. We went to the guesthouse instead of the house because I figured that if she came home early for some reason, she would never go in there."

"But she did."

I nodded. "You know the rest."

My heart was heavy with regret as we sat in silence, staring at the sunlight dancing on the white-capped waves.

"Did Gia know he wasn't attacking you?" he asked finally.

"At the time, I believed she didn't, that she was telling the truth about defending me. But now . . ." I sighed. "Noah gave me his copy of *The Odyssey*, with a note tucked inside. I had put it in my bag, but later I couldn't find it. I always wondered what had happened to it, but it never turned up—until a few days ago, on the bedside table of my room here, with the note still inside."

"But why would she rip off the back of the book and send that message to Emelia, incriminating herself?"

I paused. "That was two years later, the book could have fallen into other hands by then. Or I could be wrong about the whole thing. It could have been put on my bedside table by a housekeeper who found it somewhere. Still, if Gia did read that note back then, she knew about me and Noah."

"Which would mean she didn't accidentally kill him trying to defend you," he said wearily.

"Exactly." Our eyes locked, an entire universe between us. "It's a lot easier to believe my best friend accidentally killed a guy while trying to defend my honor than that she murdered him in cold blood for sleeping with me."

"Tell me about it. She's my sister." He bit his lip as his eyes searched mine, and I felt a hole open up inside me. "I can understand why Emelia wanted revenge."

"I know," I said, my voice quivering. "I'll never forgive myself for what I did to them." I swallowed the lump in my throat, realizing how foolish I'd been. "I should have explained immediately when Gia killed Noah—"

"Why didn't you?"

I blinked away tears, emotion welling inside me. "You don't understand. Everything I had, I had because of Gia. Your dad was paying for my college education. If she'd known the truth about me and Noah, she would have stopped him . . ." My voice caught in my throat, overwhelmed by a tsunami of shame. "I was terrified to end up like my mom. I had the rest of my life ahead of me, and no matter what I said, Noah would still be"—I choked back a sob—"still be dead."

I broke down then, my shoulders shaking as the tears came.

Benny didn't reach out to comfort me, his eyes fixed on the water as though he couldn't stand to look at me. I'd never felt so alone.

"It tore my heart out, having to tell the world that Noah was a rapist," I said once I could speak again. I wiped my eyes with the back of my hand. On some level it was a relief to tell someone the secret I'd carried around with me for twelve years, but that didn't make the secret any less hideous. "I've hated myself for it every day."

"It was self-preservation," he said after a long moment.

He was looking out at the approaching ferry, not at me, and I couldn't tell whether his observation was indictment or absolution. But I had to tell him the rest, in the hope that maybe he would understand and find it in his heart to forgive me.

I took a ragged breath. "You know, before my mom came to work for you guys, we lived in this little apartment in the Inland Empire. She was always fighting for scraps to be able to take care of us. She put on a brave face and tried to keep things positive for me, but I overheard her talking to her girlfriends late at night about how her boss at work would touch her, how without his recommendation she couldn't get another job. I remember our electricity being turned off when the owner of the restaurant she worked at didn't pay the staff for a whole month because he'd lost their wages gambling in Vegas."

He looked at me in silence, his eyes full of sadness.

"People who have money seem to think that people who don't must not be working hard enough," I went on. "But when the odds are stacked against you . . . it's not easy. When you have no money, your entire life is dictated by the whims of others. By paying for my education, your family gave me the opportunity to break that cycle—for which I will forever be grateful. But I got too comfortable, started thinking I was one of you. I forgot my place and jeopardized my entire future, all over a guy I'd likely have forgotten the moment I returned to the States. Gia effectively reminded me where I stand, I guess."

"Fuck, Abby," he said. My heart sank even further as he buried his head in his hands, overcome. "Fuck."

"I'm sorry," I said.

He ran his fingers through his hair. "I need some time to think."

"Okay."

He rose from the table. "I'm sorry, this is just a lot all at once."

Watching him walk away felt like falling, the blue-sky day at odds with the storm inside me. I'd gone to Sweden thinking I would re-connect with Gia and Benny, and now I'd lost both of them.

This was all my fault. What I'd done with Noah had been reck-less, my lies opportunistic. I was selfish, and I knew whatever came my way, I deserved it.

"Abby!"

At the sound of Gia's voice, the hair on the back of my neck prickled. I quickly put my sunglasses on to hide my bloodshot eyes and turned to see her striding toward me in jean cutoffs no longer than the ones she'd been wearing the day we met Noah.

Was it possible Timeo was lying about her? He *was* a professional liar—one who stood to gain nearly a million dollars from our believ-ing his story.

"Where's Benny?" Gia asked as she slid onto the bench beside me.

"I don't know," I said. "He said he had to take care of some things."

I pictured her standing over Garrett's body, blood on her hands. Was he as violent with her as she wrote in her book? If she did kill him, could it have been self-defense?

But Emelia . . .

"How was the lawyer?" I asked.

"I think it's safe to say he's a little smarter than those cops I had to deal with yesterday," she said. "He's gone to talk to them now to set up a meeting for tomorrow and get private security for the house. I didn't want to be there alone, so I came down here." She displayed the red, raw skin on her wrists. "Also, I needed Neosporin for the rope burn on my wrists, and headache medicine. I have a crushing migraine. I think I'm still dehydrated. And I missed you."

I stared at her, unsure what to say, how to handle her. Should I confront her about what Timeo said? Or keep my mouth shut?

Tears welled in her eyes as she reached over to take my hand in hers. "I don't know if I said it enough yesterday, but thank you. Thank you for caring enough to find me. Before you came into that room . . ." She took a shaky breath. "I didn't know if I'd ever make it out of there."

"Of course," I said.

As she brought my hand to her cheek, I wondered how she could possibly know about my transgressions and still behave so warmly toward me.

"I should really get back up to the house, I've got some work emails I need to answer," I fibbed.

"It's like eight in the morning on the East Coast," she protested.

"I know, but—" *But I don't want to be alone with you, knowing what you're capable of.*

"Please," Gia said, her face tear-streaked. "Don't leave me. I don't want to be alone."

I wanted so badly for her version of events to be the truth. And it still could be. It was entirely possible Timeo was the one lying, not Gia. At least about the parts that mattered. It was possible that Garrett had kidnapped her in an attempt to steal the proceeds from the sale of the house; that Gia had truly thought Noah was attacking me that awful night twelve years ago.

Possible, but not probable.

"Okay, I'll go with you to the store," I acquiesced. There would be other people at the store, and it would give me a chance to observe her, to get a grip on how to handle her.

She squeezed my hand and nodded, wiping her tears with the bottom of her T-shirt. "Thank you."

Hopefully, by the time we returned to the house, Benny would be there.

ABBY

CHAPTER 22

THE SMALL CONVENIENCE STORE WAS DARK AFTER THE BRIGHTNESS of the day, its shelves stacked with the necessities but nothing more. I located antibiotic ointment and ibuprofen while Gia chatted up the guy behind the desk, purchasing Nutella and a few avocados. She seemed relaxed as we exited the shop, looping her arm through mine to tug me toward the gyros stand.

We sat outside as she ate, tzatziki dripping down her chin. "So good," she murmured, pausing to take a sip of her Coke. "Tell me about Sweden. I was so sorry to miss it."

She said it more like she'd had a hair appointment she couldn't skip than like she'd been kidnapped and nearly killed. Or was that my prejudice, expecting her to behave a certain way?

"The hotel was stunning," I said. "We saw the northern lights, too. They were incredible. But we were so worried about you the whole time, it was hard to enjoy it."

She gave me the side-eye. "Anything else?" she insinuated.

I shook my head. "Well, there was one thing."

She raised her brows and my heart beat faster as I considered the possible repercussions of what I was about to say.

"We saw Timeo."

She frowned. "Timeo?"

I nodded.

Gia set down the end of her sandwich and wiped her mouth with her napkin. "What was he doing? Did he talk to you?"

"He tried to. It was strange, he approached our room from the woods while I was alone on the deck. It really freaked me out, and I went inside."

"So, you never talked to him?"

"The hotel staff chased him off," I answered, careful to be ambiguous, should the conversation we just had with Timeo come up later. "Can you think of any reason Timeo would have followed us there?"

"He probably wanted money. I'm sorry he scared you." Gia balled her trash, rising. "I left the boat in port."

"I'll meet you at the house, I have the ATV."

"Leave it for Benny," she returned. "Come with me."

I hesitated, looking toward the spot under the trees where the ATV was parked.

"How's he supposed to get back up to the house if you take it?" she reasoned.

She was right, and I wasn't quick enough to think of another excuse.

My legs grew heavy as we walked side by side down the wooden planks of the pier to where she'd tied *Icarus Flies*. My mouth was suddenly dry, everything inside me screaming not to get on a boat with her. But I saw no plausible way around boarding the boat without tipping her off to my suspicions, and I wasn't ready for a confrontation, not without Benny.

I stepped onto the deck, unwinding the stern rope as she undid the bow. As we pushed away from the pier, Gia froze, her gaze fixed on something in the distance. I followed her line of sight to a man of Garrett's coloring, height, and build who was talking with another man on the far side of the port, his back to us.

"It looks just like him," she whispered.

She seemed so authentic, her face drained of color. If she was pretending, she was a fantastic actress.

"Surely he wouldn't be stupid enough to come back to Miteras with the police looking for him," I reassured her.

"Right," she said shakily, but she didn't take her eyes off the man until he turned.

It wasn't Garrett.

I stood beside her at the helm as she fired up the engine and we slowly pulled away from the pier, leaving no wake in the turquoise water as we puttered out of the marina.

"What happens if you can't find Garrett to divorce him?" I asked.

"Then I can serve him by publication, which basically means I post a divorce notice in the paper. Which would be terribly embarrassing if anyone still read the paper."

"And you won't have to pay him anything?"

She shook her head. "I have video of him cheating. Besides, he kidnapped me. I'm not sure, but I'd be willing to bet that that negates anything I'd owe him."

"Can I see the video?" I asked, hoping she wouldn't see through my obvious ploy to confirm there was in fact a video.

Gia nodded, taking her phone from her back pocket and scrolling through the videos while we cruised toward the open water. She handed it to me as she punched the gas, and I sank into the captain's chair next to her and pressed Play.

On the screen, the living room of the house was candlelit, but bright enough that I could clearly make out Garrett bending Camila over the corner of the couch, Timeo in her mouth. "Smuttiest scene Camila Delgado's ever done," I muttered.

She snorted. "Benny's girlfriend. Can you believe that shit?"

I watched as the video zoomed in on each of their faces and down their naked bodies.

"Jesus," I said, returning the phone. "You could have a future as a porn director."

"Except I didn't do any directing," she answered. "Amazing what the people you think you know best will do behind your back."

I let my hair whip into my face, keeping my gaze trained on the horizon. If that barb was meant for me, I couldn't acknowledge it. She didn't know I'd spoken to Timeo today, I reminded myself. She still thought I believed her side of the story.

Didn't she?

The boat skipped over the tops of the waves as Gia circumnavigated the island, the spires of the palaces reaching up from behind the cliffs of Kampos on our left, Miteras Town giving way to rocky, barren hills on our right.

"You really think Garrett killed Emelia?" I raised my voice over the sound of the motor.

She gathered her hair into a ponytail as she glanced over at me. "I can't be sure," she said. "But I think so."

"When did she disappear?"

She slowed the engine, bringing the boat to a crawl so we could hear each other better. "I don't know, all the days kind of blended together."

The sea between the two islands was always a wind tunnel and today was no exception, the boat rising and falling sharply with the rolling of the waves as our forward motion idled. "Do you think it was on the earlier or later end of while they held you captive?" I pressed.

"Later, I think. Why are you asking?"

But I wasn't about to mention the emails to her now. "No reason," I said as nonchalantly as I could muster. "It's just so fucked up."

She shrugged as the water slapped the side of the boat and I caught the railing, my stomach flipping. While I wasn't exactly seasick, I'd never been great on a boat, and the anxiety frothing inside me didn't help.

"Are you okay?" she asked, unfazed. "You're looking a little green."

I nodded. "Let's go. I'm better when we're moving."

She cut the wheel, revving the engine as she pointed the bow of the boat toward Kampos.

"Where are we going?" I asked.

"I thought we'd drop anchor at Kampos beach, have a beer."

I wanted to be alone on a deserted beach with Gia even less than I wanted to be in this boat with her right now. "Benny is going to be waiting for us," I protested.

"Let him wait. I haven't gotten to spend any one-on-one time with my bestie in forever."

"Gia, I'm tired and I have work emails I was supposed to be responding to—"

"Come on," she pleaded. "One beer. For old times' sake."

"Why don't we go get Benny and I can do what I need to do at the house, then we can come back for sunset?"

"One beer," she pouted.

Build goodwill, I reminded myself. *The same way you would with a witness.*

"One beer," I relented.

I crossed and then uncrossed my arms, staring at the golden ring of sand as it grew closer. Was she fucking with me, or was she just being Gia, impulsive and insensitive to everyone else's needs? I'd been so grateful to her for taking me under her wing when I was younger, so spellbound by her dazzling personality. I was so blown away that this brilliant creature wanted to be my BFF that I'd looked past her glaring flaws.

"Looks like we have it all to ourselves," she said as she cut the engine twenty-five meters from shore.

Looking at the unchanged beach, I was flooded with memories. The first time I ever got drunk was on Kampos beach, drinking warm rum and Coke. There were picnics and bonfires and campouts, Gia's presence beside me a constant, her head tossed back with laughter, always the first to take a dare and the last to go to bed.

Could she really be a ruthless killer?

Gia's shortcomings didn't mean she'd done what Timeo claimed.

Everyone had flaws, didn't they? Myself included. We'd been through so much together. She deserved the benefit of the doubt.

She opened the small refrigerator to take out two beers. "An eye for an eye," she said, tossing me a beer.

Thrown, I missed the pass and the beer landed at my feet with a thud, fizzing as it rolled on the bottom of the boat. "What?"

"It's what Emelia said, when she told me who she really was."

I bent down to collect the beer, taking the moment to plot the best way to reply.

"I thought she just wanted your money," I said carefully, holding the beer out over the water to open it.

"Money is a salve for all wounds," she said bitterly. "Or so you'd think, until you have a full bank account and a broken heart." She looked at me, her eyes sad. "I loved him, Abs. And I thought he loved me. That's the most fucked-up part of all of this. I'm such a fool."

And there she was again, my best friend, broken-hearted. A killer? Or a fool? Perhaps both.

"Love makes fools of all of us," I empathized. *And killers out of a select few.*

She evaluated me, her dark eyes probing. "Do you know something you're not telling me?"

The cove was isolated; no boats on the waves nearby, no sunbathers on the beach. Kampos Bay was not the place to have this conversation.

I shook my head. "No. What do you mean?"

"You seem . . . on edge."

I forced a laugh. "It's been a stressful week."

She stripped off her shirt. "A swim always helps."

"I didn't bring a suit."

She rolled her eyes, shucking off her shorts. "There's no one around for miles."

Even more reason not to get in the water with her.

"How can you be sure Garrett's not still there?" I asked, scanning the cliffs of Kampos.

"He won't be back," she tossed over her shoulder as she climbed over the side of the boat and splashed into the water. "Come on!"

"I'm good. I don't really want to get wet right now."

I fished my phone from my pocket and stepped out of Gia's line of sight to quickly type a text to Benny:

Gia showed up right after you left. Made me take the boat back with her. Now she's swimming at Kampos Bay.

"The water's perfect," Gia called.

I perched on the side of the boat, looking down at her as she treaded water, my phone in my hand. Beyond Gia, a school of fish agitated the surface of the water. "Where do you think Garrett went?" I asked.

"Somewhere he won't be found."

"You're not scared of him?"

"Of course I am. I'll always be looking over my shoulder, until he's caught."

My phone dinged with Benny's reply:

Are you OK?

I stepped away from the edge of the boat so that Gia wouldn't observe me typing:

I don't want to be here but she won't take us back.

Immediately, my phone began to ring.

"Hi, Benny," I answered.

"Tell my stupid brother he should be out here with us," Gia called.

"Can she hear me?" Benny asked.

"No," I answered.

"Tell Gia the lawyer wants to meet her at the house."

"Does he?"

"No, but we can tell her he canceled when you get here."

I watched as a flock of gulls dived squawking at the school of fish. "You're there now?" I asked.

"I came back looking for you. We need to talk."

I swallowed, mentally preparing myself for the hammer to drop.

"What does Benny want?" Gia asked, climbing over the side of the boat and wrapping herself in a towel.

"Let me talk to her," Benny said.

I passed the phone to Gia. I couldn't hear what Benny was saying, but her brow furrowed as she stepped into her shorts. "Okay, fine," she said finally. "We're on our way back."

She hung up before returning the phone to me and pulling her shirt over her head. "My lawyer wants to talk with me at the house."

I breathed a sigh of relief as she fired up the engine and pointed the boat in the direction of Miteras.

ABBY

CHAPTER 23

Benny was waiting for us at the end of the pier when we pulled into the cove beneath the house, his feet dangling into the water. He grabbed the rope I tossed him as we approached and secured the bow, then offered me his hand, pulling me close to him as I stepped up onto the dock while Gia secured the stern.

"You okay?" he whispered.

"She knows we saw Timeo in Sweden but not here," I said under my breath.

Benny nodded slightly, then reached past me to offer Gia his hand.

"So gallant, brother," she teased as she climbed up beside us. "Where were you?"

He took her beach bag and swung it over his shoulder as we walked down the pier. "I had to mail Camila a book she left here."

"What book?" Gia asked.

"*The Odyssey,*" he said casually.

I tripped over the step down to the sand and he caught me, holding my eye as he steadied me with a look I read as *Trust me.*

"I'm shocked Garrett didn't steal it with the rest of them," Gia said just as casually. "Was it valuable?"

"It was just an old paperback," Benny answered as we started up the dirt path that led to the house. "But she had some notes in it she wanted, for an adaptation she's acting in. You didn't see it lying around?"

She shook her head. "But I hardly ever go upstairs."

Benny laughed. "How do you know it was upstairs?"

"I assumed because that's where she stayed," Gia said, giving him a curious look. "What's the story with you two, anyway?"

"I've hardly talked to her since she slept with your husband."

"Good riddance," Gia said.

As we came around a bend in the path, I froze. A dead snake lay flat on its back in the dust ahead of us, its white underbelly exposed to the sun.

"What are you doing? It's dead," Gia said, starting to move forward.

But Benny held out his hand, stopping her. "Maybe. Just give it a minute. Some of them play dead to fool predators or lure prey."

"They're everywhere this year," I said with a shiver, casting a wary glance at the underbrush on either side of the trail.

"They're always there; you just don't always see them," Gia said.

Just as Gia lifted her leg to take a step, a small brown mouse darted out of the underbrush. The snake flipped and struck with lightning speed, sending us all scrambling backward just as quickly.

"Holy shit!" I cried, gripping Benny's arm.

"That could have been your ankle," Benny said, reaching out to bite his sister with his hand.

Even after the mouse had disappeared down the snake's gullet, I wasn't eager to walk past where it had slithered into the grass.

"Hop up," Benny said, bending to offer me his back.

I didn't need to pretend to be brave. I gladly hopped up, allowing him to carry me the rest of the way while Gia walked ahead of us, turning back to snicker at my cowardice.

When we reached the top of the hill, I climbed down from Benny's back and we stopped for a moment for him to catch his breath. The breeze was cool on my skin as I gazed out at the horizon, watching a falcon circle overhead. "This view never gets old," Benny said. "I'm gonna miss it."

Above us, the falcon suddenly dived like a torpedo, murderous talons extending as it disappeared beyond the lip of the hill with a flap of its powerful wings.

"Is my lawyer here yet?" Gia called over her shoulder as she cut across the patio toward the back door.

"He canceled," Benny said, eliciting an exaggerated sigh from Gia. "Sorry, I should have mentioned. Something came up. But he'll be here tomorrow morning."

"Fine. In that case, I'm grabbing a cold beer and heading back down to the beach. Who's with me?"

Benny and I exchanged a glance. "I think you're on your own," he said.

As we turned to follow her into the house, I heard a squawk and looked up to see the falcon rising into the air, a limp snake dangling from its talons.

"Oh my God," I said, swatting Benny and pointing at the sky. "You think that's the same snake that was on the path?"

"Maybe," he murmured, watching in awe.

Gia stood by the pool, shading her eyes as she looked up at the sky. "Get Benny to tell you about the food chain sometime," she teased, turning her back on the spectacle to open the sliding door to the kitchen. "He's an expert."

Once the bird had vanished over the top of the hill, Benny and I followed Gia inside, where we found her standing in front of the open refrigerator. "What the hell, we have no beer?" she asked.

"There was some on the boat," I offered.

"Those were the last two." She groaned. "I'm not going back into town."

"Guess you'll have to go without, then," Benny said.

She grabbed a bottle of white wine and poured it into a refriger-ated mug, then added a copious amount of ice, splashing the wine onto the countertop. "Problem solved," she said. "Anyone?" she asked, holding out the bottle.

Benny and I shook our heads.

He caught my eye behind Gia's back as she returned to the re-frigerator for a bottle of water. "I saw you filled in the well," he said.

The well. With all that had happened in the past twenty-four hours, I'd nearly forgotten her obsession with closing it in her manu-script. But Benny's pointed mention of it now sparked a flash of the three of us pacing the guesthouse the night of Noah's death, arguing over whether to call the police or throw his lifeless body into its deep stone shaft.

Clearly Benny had also made that connection. I could hear in his question that he was wondering whether Gia had disposed of Emelia and Garrett in the way we'd discussed doing with Noah.

But she seemed oblivious, popping a handful of blueberries into her mouth before shutting the fridge. "Yeah, finally," she returned when she'd swallowed the berries. "Dad should have done that years ago. I can't believe he didn't after the goats died."

"I don't remember the goats," Benny said.

She looked at him, incredulous. "At all?"

"I vaguely remember having them at some point, but I didn't know what happened to them."

"It was super traumatic for me. I was only ten. I'd been feeding the goats every day, I'd given them all names—then one day I went out there and they were all dead, just lying there bloated in the sun, flies buzzing around."

"That's so awful," I said. "I didn't know about it either."

"You didn't?" She looked genuinely surprised. "We made offer-ings to the woman in the well. That's why I always went out there and poured wine down it."

I nodded, although I didn't remember dumping offerings into the well more than the one time.

"Anyway, it's taken care of now," Gia said. "I didn't want anyone else making stupid mistakes with it."

"I would have thought you'd be delighted at Melodie accidentally killing her crops, or her cats," he said dryly.

"Melodie's a bitch, but I'd never hurt her kitties," Gia said. She took a swig of her wine and grabbed her beach bag from where Benny had left it on the dining table. "I'll be at the beach if you need me. Don't do anything I wouldn't do." She smirked, casting a glance around the room. "Well, I guess that's easy, seeing as I've done things on pretty much every surface in this house. Later."

She gave a little wave as she slid open the door and stepped into the sunshine.

I STOOD AT THE WINDOW watching as she hiked down the trail to the beach, her towel slung around her neck.

"Hey," Benny said.

I turned to him. "Hey."

"What happened while you guys were out there?"

I shrugged. "I tried to press her, but she was pretty consistent. She said something about how the people you think you know best will betray you—but we were talking about Garrett. She said some other strange things too, but contextually—I don't know. She did seem confident Garrett wouldn't be back."

He ran his fingers through his hair, taking a seat at the dining table. "I wanted to talk to you."

My heart skipped a beat as he gestured for me to sit opposite him and I perched on a chair, anticipation raising my pulse. "Yeah?"

He caught my gaze, holding it as he spoke. "I'm really sorry, Abby."

"For what?" I asked, not understanding.

He took a breath. "What you said about your mom earlier, about your circumstances. I knew you didn't grow up with the money I did, but I never really thought about it, I guess. You were just you, if that makes any sense."

I nodded. I'd always seen the difference between Gia and me, but when it came to Benny, it felt like we lived in our own world. "That makes sense."

"I'm sorry I never realized you were playing by different rules." He shook his head, contrite. "That's the thing about privilege, it's blinding. The way I put you on the spot with my professions of love that summer, my God I was such an idiot. How unfair—"

"Don't," I stopped him. "Nothing I said earlier was about you, Benny. I've never had anything but love for you. I see what's in your heart. You're an incredible person, an incredible brother and friend."

"I'm sorry if I ever pressured you—"

"You didn't." I held his gaze with a small smile. There was no point in holding back now. "And I can't say your feelings were totally unreciprocated. But you were my best friend's little brother, and I was going to college on your family's dime. It was too much of a risk to take, to get involved with you in that way, we were too young. Things got . . . confusing after we kissed. It was one of the reasons I didn't go to Switzerland with you guys, one of the reasons I jumped in headfirst with Noah."

He studied me. "I had no idea."

"And then, years later, when I read the screenplay you'd written . . ." I closed my eyes. "The compassion you had for your characters, your forgiveness for the mistakes they made—"

He took my hand and squeezed it, and I opened my eyes to see his were filled with understanding.

"I'll never forgive myself for what I did," I continued. "But your screenplay helped me channel my anger with myself, to strive for justice in every other area of my life. It's why I became an attorney.

"Benny . . ." I didn't know whether he'd ever talk to me again, so I might as well say everything I needed to say now. "I know it's been a long time since you were the boy who loved me, and I won't blame you if you never want to see me again after this." A hummingbird batted its wings inside my throat, making it hard to speak. "But I want you to know that I love you."

His lips parted in surprise, his warm brown eyes searching mine for context.

I took a breath. It was now or never. "Not like a friend," I clarified. "I mean, you are my friend, but I . . . I'm in love with you." I dropped my gaze, unable to bear what would certainly be a look of pity on his face. "I have been for a long time—since I read your screenplay, really—but I was able to convince myself otherwise until this week, being with you."

A second went by, two. So this was it, then. Without looking at him I began to rise.

His chair scraped on the floor as he pushed it back in haste. "Abby," he said, coming around the side of the table to take my hand. "What happened to you was fucked up." He gently tilted my chin up with his fingers so that I was forced to meet his eyes. The tenderness in his gaze took my breath away. "You were put in an impossible position and yes, you made mistakes. But I can't say that I wouldn't have done the same in your situation."

Hope blossomed inside me, chasing away my anxiety, if only for a moment.

"We're about to have some more hard decisions to make," he went on, "but we're older now, and, I think, wiser. And this time, we'll have each other."

Have each other? He paused, his gaze steady, as I stared at him in astonishment. This was not at all how I'd thought this would go, but I wasn't protesting.

"The past decade, I tried and tried to talk myself out of loving you," he said. "I'd think I'd gotten over you, then I'd see you again—and you'd have some boyfriend, or I'd have some girlfriend, or both—but it didn't matter. Every time I saw you, I was always right back where I started."

He moved closer, his gaze dropping to my lips. "This week, being with you as the woman you are now," he continued, "it's taken every ounce of willpower I have not to do this."

He dipped his head and pressed his lips to mine. His kiss was surer than it had been at sixteen, his stubble rougher. But his lips were just as soft, igniting a blaze within me. I buried my hands in his hair, pulling him closer, hunger building with every breath. It felt like I'd waited a lifetime for this moment, and his acceptance of me, knowing my secret, only made his kiss that much sweeter.

"I know we have a lot to discuss," he said, coming up for air. He pushed aside my hair and lightly kissed my neck.

"We do," I agreed, lit up by the feeling of his lips against my skin. "And we can't talk in front of her."

"We can't do any of the things I want to do with you in front of her," he whispered, his breath hot on my ear.

My body flushed with desire. "We'll talk," he murmured. "I promise. But I am not letting my sister steal this moment from us."

He pressed me up against the patio door, his hands on the glass as he kissed me deeply. The rush of lust that came over me was overwhelming. As long as I'd been fighting my feelings for Benny, I hadn't allowed myself to properly fantasize about him. Yes, sometimes when I was with another man I'd see a flash of his face, but I'd push it away so quickly I could pretend it didn't happen. I hadn't permitted myself to think about us together, hadn't imagined what it would feel like to have his body against mine, his breath coming faster as our kisses became more passionate.

But here we were, his hands roving over my skin, our hips pressed together, the straps of my sundress slipping, his eyes full of ardor as we tugged at each other's clothes. The love I felt for Benny was solid, dependable, enduring; but this raw hunger was new. It was a revelation to see him like this, to feel him like this, to be the object of his desire.

"Come on," I said, threading my fingers through his as I tugged him across the living room toward the stairs.

When we reached my room, we locked the door behind us.

AFTERWARD, BENNY LAY IN BED, watching with a grin as I threw on his T-shirt to go to the window and look out. The sun was low in the cloudless sky, the sea a deep blue. At the bottom of the hill I could make out Gia lying on a towel in the golden sand, a sunhat over her face.

"I think she's asleep," I said as I returned to sit on the edge of the bed.

"What are you doing way over there?" he teased, beckoning to me. "Get in here."

Though we'd just finished dousing the flames that burned between us, the flicker in his eyes lit a fresh spark in me. "I'm afraid if I get any closer, we won't talk about the things we need to talk about."

"Fair," he said, his lips quirking into a smile.

My heart tugged, and I inched closer. Images of his body intertwined with mine flashed before my eyes. I tried to push them away so we could focus on the problem at hand.

"What are we going to do about Gia?" I asked.

"You believe Timeo?"

His face was grim as he held my gaze, and I could tell he was as conflicted as I was. "I don't want to, but . . ." I sighed. "We have to consider it."

"What does your gut tell you?"

I winced. "That he's telling the truth. Yours?"

He closed his eyes, leaning his head back against the headboard. "Same." After a moment, he lifted his head, his brow furrowed. "What about those threatening emails you received, though? It would make sense for Emelia to have sent them, but if Timeo is telling the truth and she's been dead for weeks, she couldn't have."

"I thought about that too."

"Did you see the email that came in from Leon today?" he asked.

I shook my head. "What did it say?"

"His guy looked into the server location of the threatening messages sent to you, and it was the same server as the emails sent to us from Gia's account while she was ostensibly kidnapped on Kampos."

"Or, if Timeo's right, the emails Gia sent, posing as Garrett posing as her."

"Regardless, Timeo definitely couldn't have been the one to send you those messages, because he was in Sweden when you got the second one."

I nodded. "I never thought it was him. But it could have been Garrett or Emelia, if Gia's telling the truth, or Gia herself if she's not."

"But why?"

A cloud passed over the sun, darkening the room. "Emelia must've hated me for backing up Gia's story when she killed Noah. I told the world he was a rapist, and that's how he'll be remembered. I don't exactly have a blackmail-worthy fortune, but I did lie, and I could see her wanting to scare me. And Gia— If what Timeo said is true, she also had reason to want to scare me, to remind me of how intertwined our fates were. In case we started to question her story, the way we are now."

He groaned. "I wish it didn't all make so much sense."

"Maybe Timeo is the one lying, and we're the assholes for thinking otherwise," I suggested hopefully. But we both knew that seemed increasingly unlikely.

Benny laced his fingers through mine. "I don't want this to be true any more than you do." He broke off, shaking his head. "Hell, if Garrett was as abusive as she claimed, I could almost understand it . . ."

"But Emelia and Noah," I said. "We can't—I can't—justify that."

He studied me, his dark eyes somber. "What are you suggesting?"

"If we don't tell the police everything we know, we're complicit in whatever she's done."

"*If* she's done anything."

I frowned. "I thought we were on the same page."

"We are," he assured me. "I'm just— She's my sister, Abs. I want to at least give her the benefit of the doubt."

"You're right." I exhaled through pursed lips. "We don't have any evidence either way."

"So, let's give her an opportunity to defend herself to us before we tell the police what Timeo said."

"You want to confront her?" I asked.

"It doesn't have to be a confrontation," he said. "We just tell her what Timeo said and see how she responds. I have to be sure." He leaned his head back against the pillow, thinking. "I'll have to move some money around to get it all in the same place, but I'll figure out getting the payoff to Timeo tomorrow."

I stared at him. "Wait . . . you want to pay off Timeo?"

"If he comes forward with his story, it exposes you, too. I don't want to make you suffer through that," he said.

"That's very generous of you," I said. "But . . . I don't know. I . . . I was thinking maybe I should come clean, finally tell the truth."

He sat up straighter. "Abby, if you do that . . ." He shook his head, his face solemn. "You could lose your career, possibly even go to jail."

"I know," I said. I'd thought about it nearly constantly for the past twelve years, looked up all the consequences of my actions. "But maybe I should."

"Abby, no." He ran his fingers through his hair, distressed. "You made a split-second decision—that, yes, was the wrong decision— but you didn't kill Noah. You were just a kid, in a terrible situation."

"But it's because of my testimony that his death was never investigated further."

He shook his head, taking my hands in his. "If you believe that, then you don't know my family as well as you think you do."

"What do you mean?"

"Whether or not you admitted to the police you were involved with Noah, and whether or not Gia knew about it, she would always have maintained she knew nothing about your relationship, that she believed she was saving you from a rapist. Maybe that defense wouldn't have worked for someone else, and if the note in that book had surfaced, it might have made things harder for her, but with my family's influence . . ." He sighed. "Shit, you work in the legal system, you should know better than anyone it's set up to favor some people over others." He looked at me meaningfully. "Why do you think The- odoropoulos said he owed his career to my dad?"

I nodded, absorbing that. "But your dad's gone now."

"Which is why Timeo's threat holds any water at all." He evaluated me with sympathy "Why is it that you want to confess?"

"Because I'm sorry," I said, emotion welling in my chest. "I want to be a better person."

He opened his arms and I fell against him, my tears staining his skin. "You are a good person," he said, kissing the top of my head. "But Noah is dead. His mother is dead. If Timeo is right, so is Emelia. Confessing will do no one any good, but it might destroy your life."

"I know, but . . ." I took a shaky breath. "I don't want to carry this around with me anymore."

"It's heavy for you," he said, stroking my hair.

"Yes."

"Did you ever think that maybe carrying it *is* your penance?"

"I'm not sure it's fair that I get to decide my own fate when Noah couldn't decide his."

"Life isn't fair, I'm living proof of that."

He was right, but I'd all but made up my mind. I wanted to be part of the solution, not part of the problem. I wanted to finally make this right.

ABBY

CHAPTER 24

I N ACCORDANCE WITH OUR PLAN, THAT EVENING BENNY ROSE FROM THE outdoor dining table after dinner, announcing he had some work to finish up, and would be in the library if we needed him. He topped up our drinks and cleared our plates as he went inside, leaving Gia and me alone. The sun had set but it was still warm and the sky wasn't quite dark yet, the stars beginning to twinkle as the moon rose over Kampos.

The minute the sliding glass door had closed behind Benny, Gia cut her eyes toward the kitchen with a smirk. "So. You and my baby brother finally did the nasty."

I winced. "Gia, please—"

"What?" She grinned. "I'm happy for you guys. He's been in love with you since he was a teenager, and I've seen the way you looked at him in recent years. It's been a long time coming." She waggled her eyebrows, accentuating the obvious pun. "How did it happen?"

"I don't know," I said, feeling the color creep into my cheeks. Gia was the last person on earth I wanted to talk about this with. "It just happened."

"And?"

I looked at her levelly. "Do you really wanna hear about your brother's sex life?"

She drew back. "Well, when you put it like that."

"That's what it is," I said, exasperated. "He's your brother. Where are your boundaries?"

Her face fell. "You're my best friend. We've never had any boundaries before."

I reached across the table and took her hand. "*You've* never had any boundaries."

Tears welled in her eyes. "We've always told each other everything."

I withdrew my hand to take a sip of my wine, considering how to respond to that. It was the perfect opening for the conversation we needed to have, though I'd hoped it would start on a friendlier note. So much for the good cop routine.

"Have we?" I finally said.

"Yes," she answered emphatically. "We've never kept secrets from each other."

"We have, though," I said quietly.

"Abby, what the hell? You're scaring me."

I took a breath, trying to figure out where to begin. "I talked to Timeo."

She drew back. "You said you didn't talk to him."

"No, I said I didn't talk to him in Sweden. He's here now. He found us earlier today when we were in town."

"What did he want?"

I eyed the serrated knife on the empty cutting board in the center of the table. I didn't see how I could move it without drawing her attention. But I didn't really need to worry about her threatening me with a bread knife, did I?

"He tried to blackmail us for the amount Emelia was supposed to pay him for doing this job with her," I said.

"Blackmail you with what?"

"The bullet he says you shot him with."

"He said I *shot* him?" She guffawed. "When? How?"

"He said Emelia had come up to the house to talk to you, and when she didn't come back to the boat, he came up to check on her and found you standing over Garrett's dead body with your dad's antique gun in your hand, and Emelia knocked out by the pool."

"Wow," she said. "That's . . . just, wow."

I waited for her to meet my gaze, wanting to see the truth in her eyes, but when she finally did, her irises were pools of black. "So, you didn't shoot him?" I asked.

She sprang to her feet. "No, Abby! Jesus!"

"Or Garrett or Emelia?"

"Fuck no," she avowed. "Are you crazy?"

I held up my hands. "I had to ask. He seemed pretty adamant. He claimed Noah's death wasn't an accident either, that you killed him on purpose."

"No wonder you were acting so weird on the boat this afternoon," she said, pacing the patio. "He's grasping at straws, trying to get money out of somebody."

"Okay," I said.

"Okay?" She threw her hands up, exasperated. "You accuse me of murder, and all you have to say is *okay*?"

"I'm just trying to figure out what's going on," I said.

"I thought you were on my side."

"I've always been on your side." I paused, plotting my next move as I watched her tread back and forth over the flagstone. "I've gotten a couple of threatening emails recently," I said finally.

She stopped and turned to me, one eyebrow arched.

"Messages calling me a liar."

She crossed her arms. "What?"

"Did you send them?"

She drew back. "No. Why would I—"

"Because it's true." I swallowed. "I am a liar."

She sat in the chair opposite me, her keen eyes locked on my face. "What are you talking about?"

"I think you know," I said quietly.

She shook her head, her face a mask of bewilderment. "I really don't."

I steeled my nerves. "The copy of *The Odyssey* on my bedside table didn't belong to Camila."

"What the fuck does that have to do with anything?"

I hesitated, asking myself again if it could be possible that she really didn't know. That Timeo was the liar, not Gia. I'd gone into this conversation hoping that might be the case, but strangely, the more vehement her denials, the less I believed them.

"The book was mine," I confessed quietly. "Inside was a note Noah had written to me."

"Noah?" She seemed sincerely baffled. "What did it say?"

The words I'd hoped never to say to her: "That he'd enjoyed our weekend together, and he hoped to see me at Bacchanalia."

"Your weekend together?"

I took a breath. "Did he really stalk you?"

"Yes! You were there!"

"No. I wasn't," I said, doing my best to keep the emotion out of my voice. "I only saw what you wanted me to see, until I heard Noah's side of the story."

She narrowed her eyes. "Noah's side of the story."

"The weekend you were in Switzerland, we ran into each other, and he told me how you'd told him I had a boyfriend back home—"

"What? No—"

"You said it because he was into me, and you wanted him for yourself."

"For fuck's sake, Abby, we were eighteen," she snapped. "If I did that, which I don't remember, I'm sure it's not the only dumb, selfish thing either of us did back then."

"Which is why I let it go."

"Regardless of what he told you, I was genuinely afraid of him. He was a mean drunk and got violent with me—"

I leveled my gaze at her. "Really, Gia? No one besides you ever saw him get violent."

"You saw the bruises!"

"He told me—"

"Whatever he told you, it was to get into your pants," she cut me off. "Which I'm guessing worked, from the way you're talking about him. Congratulations, you fucked my stalker."

The hurt in her eyes was raw, her anger searing. But as painful as this conversation was, I still hadn't gotten to the truth. I had to strike deeper. I gathered my courage, knowing the next thing I said would change us forever. "And when you found out, you followed us home from the full moon party and killed him."

There it was. One sentence to dissolve seventeen years of friendship.

She gasped, her eyes wide. "You let me think he was raping you so I wouldn't know you'd gone behind my back."

"Yes," I admitted. "In the moment, that's what I did. It was wrong, and I'm sorry. But this week I realized you knew all along we'd gone off together."

"That's bullshit."

"He wasn't obsessed with you, you were obsessed with him. You found the book that mysteriously disappeared from my bag days before Bacchanalia, read the note from him, realized we'd been together, and murdered him in a fit of jealousy. We both lied about what really happened that night because it was better for each of us."

"I *didn't* know!" she insisted. "I never saw your stupid book. You think if I'd known my best friend was fucking my stalker behind my back, I would have just let it go?"

"No," I said. "You certainly didn't let it go."

"Shit, Abby. What kind of horrible person do you think I am?"

A part of me wanted to back down, to apologize and make up. But the damage was done. She wasn't the person I'd thought she was.

"Noah isn't the only person you've killed, is he?" I asked.

"What?"

"Where's Emelia?" I pressed.

"I don't know—"

"Where's Garrett?"

"I told you, he ran off when he saw the boats coming."

"Not according to Timeo."

"Timeo is a professional liar! I can't believe you believe him over me." She shook her head sadly. "Jesus, Abby. You were supposed to be my best friend. I've never been anything but loyal to you. We gave you a place to live, an education—a life you never could have afforded without me—"

"I'll always appreciate everything your family has done for me," I interjected.

"—and now I find out you'd been screwing my stalker behind my back and you think I killed him in cold blood? I can't even . . ." She paused, realizing. "You stayed friends with me, thinking I murdered the guy you were sleeping with. That says more about you than it does me."

"I convinced myself you didn't know—"

"Because I fucking didn't!"

"But when Timeo told us what you'd done to Garrett and Emelia, it all clicked into place."

"I didn't do anything to Garrett and Emelia!" she cried. "You psycho bitch! They kidnapped *me*."

I dropped my head to my hands, rubbing my temples. Was I wrong? Was I in fact a psycho bitch, throwing my best friend under the bus on the word of a hustler?

But it was more than that. It was the book on my bedside table, the note in Emelia's possession, the threatening emails. Timeo's story simply tied it all together.

I knew what Gia was doing, planting seeds of doubt in my mind. And she was so convincing, it would have been easy to believe her. But I'd been down this road before. I knew her tricks, and this time I wouldn't play the fool.

"You should know I'm going to confess tomorrow," I said.

"Good for you. Do the right thing." She pumped her fist. "I guess it's your life to ruin."

"I'm also going to tell the police what Timeo said," I warned.

She reached out and unceremoniously lifted the bread knife from the table, spinning it in her hand. "You know, if you really believe I killed all these people, you should probably be more afraid of me."

I stilled, adrenaline flooding my veins as I watched her, determined not to give her the satisfaction of scaring me. But I flinched as she suddenly thrust the knife into the tabletop, leaving it protruding from the wood.

She laughed. "Boo."

"Please," I said, my heart beating erratically. "This isn't about us."

"It wasn't," she agreed. "But it is now."

"You can't just go around killing people, Gia."

"Like I said . . ." She placed her hands on the table, pushing up to standing to lean toward me over the bread knife, her eyes hard as diamonds. "I haven't killed anyone."

"Okay."

She withdrew, crossing her arms. "What does my brother think of all this?"

"You'll have to talk to him about that."

"So he knows what you've done. Interesting." She pursed her lips. "He always did like the crazy bitches." She shrugged. "But he'll take my side in the end, you'll see. Blood is thicker than . . . semen."

She hurled the word over her shoulder like a rotten tomato as she stormed into the house, leaving the sliding glass door open behind her. I grimaced, disappointed in myself for failing to keep that conversation from going off the rails, never mind elicit a confession from her.

She was wrong about Benny, though.

At least I hoped she was.

ABBY

CHAPTER 25

AFTER MY CONFRONTATION WITH GIA, I WAS SO FULL OF RIGHTEOUS indignation that I couldn't stand the idea of even being under the same roof with her, so Benny suggested we hike to the old well to see whether she'd really filled it in. The moonlight coated the olive grove in silver as we made our way along the dirt path, our squat shadows bouncing after us. Slowly, the night air and exercise cooled my rancor as I unloaded the details of our conversation on Benny.

What had I expected? That she would roll over and tell me everything? Cop to three murders and turn herself in? Or give me some proof that Timeo was lying? Gia had never behaved the way she was expected to. "Maybe I shouldn't have confronted her," I muttered.

He shook his head. "You confronted her because you wanted an answer. *We* wanted an answer. Even if she didn't give us the answer we wanted, we still got one, didn't we?"

"I guess some ridiculous part of me was hoping she and I would come out of this still friends."

"I'm sorry." He wrapped an arm around my shoulders and kissed my forehead. "I'll try to talk to her in the morning, see if I can get any more out of her."

When we reached the clearing, we found the grass crushed and mounds of dirt scattered around, marked with the tracks of some kind of farm machinery. The four-foot-high circle of rocks that had once stood in the center was nowhere to be seen. "This should be it, right?" I asked, confused. "But where's the well?"

"Yeah, this is definitely where it was," he confirmed. "It looks like she didn't just have it filled, she had it completely removed."

"Seems like an unnecessary expense."

"Yes." He met my eye. "Yes, it does."

IN THE MORNING, BENNY AND I were stationed on the couch in the living room when Gia finally emerged from her locked bedroom fifteen minutes before she was due at the police station. He rose as I darted into the kitchen so that he could attempt to talk to her alone.

"Gia—" he started.

"Not now," she said without slowing.

Hidden behind the cabinets, I listened through the open door as he chased after her.

"We need to talk."

"I'm on my way to the police station," she returned.

"I'll come with you."

"Please don't," she snapped. I could tell they'd stopped in the foyer. "I've already heard everything you and your *girlfriend* think of me, and I don't need that kind of negativity in my head right now."

"I want to hear your side of it," he said calmly.

"Later," she said. "Enjoy fucking her now, because once you realize who she really is, you're not going to want anything to do with her."

That stung, as I knew she meant it to. But her threats were empty. Benny knew all my secrets now, and he still loved me; he'd told me so not five minutes ago. He still didn't believe that I should confess my lies to the authorities, but he recognized that it was my choice and promised he would support me, whatever I decided to do.

Which was how I found myself in the stuffy lobby of the police station at two in the afternoon, sitting on a metal folding chair with Benny by my side, waiting to speak to Theodoropoulos.

We'd been there for nearly an hour when Gia finally emerged from the back, accompanied by her Greek attorney. She looked the part of the proper lady, wearing a pale pink blouse and a knee-length white skirt, her hair pulled back in a ponytail. She avoided our eyes as she walked through the waiting room and out the glass door, and in spite of everything, my heart felt heavy with the loss of my friend.

"Miss Corman?" Primos called, looking at me from behind the front desk as he hung up the phone. "Follow me."

I rose and Benny started to as well, but I placed a hand on his leg. "I got this."

He nodded reluctantly, sinking back into the chair. "I'll be here."

I followed Primos through the door into the back workroom, where Officer Paros looked up from her desk with interest as he led me to an office at the rear. The door was open and Theodoropoulos was inside, bent over a laptop on the desk positioned before an open window with a view over the tops of the buildings of town toward the bay. He looked more than twelve years older than the last time I'd seen him, his formerly salt-and-pepper hair almost all gray now, the wrinkles on his long face deep as canyons.

He rose as I entered, still thin and surprisingly tall, and extended his hand. "Abby," he said, gesturing for me to take a seat facing the desk. "You look well."

"It's been a long time," I said, sitting as he settled into the chair behind the desk.

Primos hovered above me, unsure what to do.

"You can shut the door on your way out," Theodoropoulos said to him. "Thank you."

As Primos exited, I unscrewed the cap of my water bottle and took a sip, preparing myself for the task ahead.

"It seems they are younger every year," Theodoropoulos said to me as the door closed behind Primos. His eyes settled on me. "It is terrible what happened to your friend."

"That's what I wanted to talk to you about," I said.

He raised his formidable brows, gesturing for me to go on.

"I don't know what she's told you, but the version of events she told us . . . I don't believe it's true."

"Oh?"

The breeze through the window made the office cooler than the rest of the station, but still the heat was oppressive. "Timeo came to me and Benny yesterday. He had a bullet wound in his shoulder and a different story about how everything went down."

Theodoropoulos listened intently as I relayed Timeo's version of events, scribbling notes on a yellow legal pad with a pencil every so often but never interrupting. I remembered that about him from the investigation into Noah's death. Most cops interrupted so much that you couldn't keep a train of thought on track, but Theodoropoulos let you talk, asking questions only when you were finished.

"Why do you believe Timeo's story over Gia's?" Theodoropoulos asked when I'd imparted all Timeo had told us.

"He had a gunshot wound—"

"Did you see the wound?"

"I saw the bandage; his arm was in a sling." I realized as he scribbled it down that a bandage meant nothing. I took a deep breath, steeling my nerves. "But more than that . . ." I forced myself to meet his sharp eyes. "Noah and I were involved. The night Gia killed him, we were together. It was consensual. He wasn't attacking me."

My heart stopped as I waited for the hammer to drop, for him to tell me this meant jail time, a public announcement, some definitive punishment for my actions. But he simply nodded, unruffled. "Do you believe Gia knew that?"

"I convinced myself for years that she didn't, but with this new information . . ."

He evaluated me. "What evidence do you have that she knew about your relationship with Noah?"

"He'd written a revealing message to me inside a book that went missing a few days before he died," I said, aware that that wasn't evidence. "I found it beside my bed when I arrived earlier this week. I think Gia had it all along. She knew about us. She must have seen us leaving the full moon party and followed us."

"You have evidence of this?"

"Not specifically." I paused, my confidence slipping. "She lied in her memoir. Noah didn't stalk her, and I don't believe he was ever violent with her. I thought at the time it was a misunderstanding, but now I wonder whether she was ever afraid of him, or just pretending."

"Lying in a memoir isn't illegal, unless it violates someone's rights," he said, not unkindly.

"I know," I replied, frustrated. This wasn't going at all as I had expected. I could feel the interview getting away from me like a tennis ball bouncing downhill, and I didn't know how to stop it. "What I'm trying to say is, I believe she's doing the same thing now that she did then, using her manuscript to cover up a murder."

"Why do you believe that?"

"You've read it?"

He nodded.

"Okay, for example, take what she wrote about the well. Neither Benny nor I remember anything happening to any goats. She makes out that it was some big deal as a reason to close the well, but she'd never mentioned it before." I took a breath. "I believe she made all that stuff up so that the fact she had it filled in right after her husband disappeared would be less suspicious."

"The husband she alleges kidnapped her after the well was filled in?"

"Yes," I answered emphatically. "I think she faked her kidnapping and made up all that stuff about Garrett's shady business partners to take the spotlight off her."

"And what evidence do you have of this?"

I sighed, hamstrung. "I believe their bodies are at the bottom of the well."

He appraised me for a moment before speaking. "I can't dig up the well without probable cause, which I don't have without evidence."

I chewed my lip, disheartened.

"What do you want me to do, Abby?" he asked calmly.

"I want justice," I said. "I'm willing to pay for what I've done, and I want her to do the same."

He nodded. "But there's no evidence she's done anything. All I have right now is your confession that you lied to the police twelve years ago. That changes nothing."

"You're not going to prosecute me?"

"The case is closed, Abby." He sighed. "This isn't enough to re-open it. It might have been twelve years ago, but that ship has sailed."

"So, nothing happens to either of us?"

He leveled his gaze at me. "Not without hard evidence."

"And if Timeo were to come to you?" I asked.

"I hope he does," Theodoropoulos said. "He might be able to give us information that could lead to the discovery of actual evidence."

We sat in silence for a moment before he rose. "Thank you for coming to see me."

"What do I do now?" I asked as I stood.

"Go back to America. Go back to your life." He paused, his hand on the doorknob, looking down at me from beneath his eyebrows. "Do you know of the remora fish?"

I shook my head, not following.

"It's a fish about this big"—he held his hands three feet apart—"with a suction cup it uses to latch on to sharks. The remora keeps the shark clean, and the shark provides protection and food for the remora. But if the remora becomes too annoying, or the shark is particularly hungry, it will eat the remora."

I drew back. "Are you saying I'm a . . . parasite?"

He shook his head. "It's a mutually beneficial relationship between the shark and the remora, but the shark always has the upper hand. Do you understand what I'm saying? A shark may provide for you, but it will never be your friend. This would be a good time to find new waters to swim in."

"HE CALLED ME A REMORA," I said, picking at my salad. The restaurant on the harbor where Benny and I had stopped for lunch was uncrowded, the umbrellas overhead blocking the afternoon sun. A cooling wind blew off the bay, fluttering my napkin in my lap.

"The fish that swims with sharks?" he asked.

I nodded. "He warned me that the shark eats the remora if it's too annoying."

Benny raised his brows. "So he did believe you."

"I don't know," I said. At the end of the jetty on the other side of the marina, the ferry had pulled up and was letting off a trickle of passengers. "I mean, maybe? But he was very clear there was nothing he was going to do without evidence."

"Maybe he doesn't want to get eaten either," Benny suggested.

It was funny, I hadn't thought of Theodoropoulos as a remora. He had power over me; to me he was a shark. But the fact that Benny so immediately identified him as a remora reminded me that Benny himself was a shark.

He smiled. "Well, I can't say I'm not relieved he refused to arrest you."

Had Benny spoken to Theodoropoulos? Persuaded him somehow to turn a blind eye to my transgressions?

I narrowed my eyes at him, keeping my voice playful. "You didn't tell him not to arrest me, did you?"

"No. You made it pretty clear you didn't want me to. Anyway, I don't know that it would have done much good. I don't have the kind of power my dad did."

The ferry's horn bellowed, echoing over the water as a cluster of waiting passengers climbed aboard.

"I should have approached Gia differently," I said, resigned. "If I could have stayed friendly with her, she might have eventually told me something."

He shrugged. "Maybe she'll tell me."

"Are you going to stay on good terms with her?"

He looked at me, resigned. "Abby, regardless of what she may have done, she's my sister."

I bristled. "*May* have done?"

"I'm not saying I believe her; I have all the same doubts you do. But as Theodoropoulos said, we have no evidence."

"So, what, are you just going to pretend nothing happened?"

"No. I'm just as wary of her as you are," he said carefully. "But I'm also not going to dedicate my life to proving she murdered her asshole husband and the woman that fleeced her."

"Noah wasn't an asshole," I pointed out.

"I know this may be hard to hear, but I didn't know that until yesterday. You did, and you remained friends with her for twelve years after she killed him."

"I didn't know she'd killed him intentionally!"

"I know." He sighed. "Let's assume she did find the book, that she did know about you guys. That doesn't have to mean she killed him intentionally. She may have thought she'd teach the two of you a lesson, and it went terribly wrong."

I drew back. "Whose side are you on?"

"I'm on your side." He leaned across the table, taking my hand in his. "I'm just saying, we've reported what we know to the police. Let's move on with our lives."

I averted my gaze to stare at the line of passengers boarding the ferry, attempting to quell the riot inside me. I knew he was right, that this wasn't my fight, and I'd done what I could, albeit twelve years too late. But still it was hard to walk away. "You're not really going to pay off Timeo, are you?"

"No. In fact, I was planning to encourage him to go to the police."

I nodded, relieved. "And what about Gia?"

He shrugged. "I'm not going to ignore her, but I'm also not going to invite her into my life. Gia's blood, and I'll always love her. But after what we've learned, I don't know that I'll ever fully trust her again."

The ferry bellowed its warning of departure and I glanced over to see that the crowd of passengers was all aboard. I watched idly as one last traveler unloaded a carry-on-size roller bag from the back of an ATV parked beneath the trees and slung a backpack over their shoulder. As the passenger stepped into the sunlight, I saw it was a woman, a baseball hat pulled down over her face, her long dark ponytail protruding from the back of the cap.

My breath caught in my throat.

"Benny," I said, indicating the woman.

We watched her cross the gangplank to board the ship, finally turning her face toward us as she took her place at the railing, scanning the port as if looking for someone.

Benny and I rose at once and ran, leaving our things behind.

For a moment Gia stood still, her face inscrutable as she watched us sprint down the boardwalk and along the jetty, closing the two hundred yards that separated us. The gangplank lifted and the engines fired to life. I had the sensation of running through water; as in a nightmare, we seemed to be moving in slow motion, unable to reach the ferry before it departed.

As we drew closer, Gia turned away with a swish of her ponytail, disappearing through the doorway without a backward glance to be swallowed up by the dark interior of the ferry as it chugged out to sea. Benny and I stood panting at the water's edge, our hands on our knees, the waves churning against the rocks below us as we watched the boat grow smaller and smaller until it faded into the horizon.

ABBY

EPILOGUE

EIGHTEEN MONTHS LATER

PAST THE SPRAY OF FUCHSIA BOUGAINVILLEA, THE SAPPHIRE SEA sparkles, the horizon still blurred by the dissipating morning fog. This is my favorite time of day in Montecito, when the sun has just burned through the gray marine layer and the world is revealed in all its vibrant color. I can hardly believe Benny and I live here now, in the Spanish-style villa where we met as teenagers, atop a hill facing the vast Pacific Ocean.

It took us a year to straighten out our lives after everything that happened in Greece. I quit my unfulfilling job and moved back to California, where I started working as legal counsel for the charity Papa Hugo ran—the one, ironically, that Gia had wanted to take over. It had fallen into Melodie's hands after Papa Hugo died, but she wasn't passionate about it and was glad to turn it over to Benny and me. I felt finally that I was doing something positive for the world, which made moving across the country from my mom easier. She comes to visit regularly now, and I think she enjoys returning to

California, staying in the guesthouse where we lived for five years and showing her wife around Santa Barbara, especially when the weather is cold in D.C.

AFTER BENNY AND I WATCHED Gia vanish on the ferry that September afternoon, we returned to the house, where we found a handwritten note on the kitchen counter:

Benny,

I'm taking off for a while. I don't feel safe with Garrett out there, so I'm gonna lay low until all this blows over or he turns up. Please don't worry about me or look for me. I've taken pains to cover my tracks so that Garrett won't be able to locate me.

I've answered all the questions asked of me by the police, and they've given me the okay to leave. Leon knows as well, though like you, he doesn't know where I'm going. Please tell Melodie she can have everything in the house (unless there's anything you want).

I'll turn up when I'm ready.

Until then,
Gia

I knew that had the note been left the day before, it would have been addressed to me as well, but our friendship would never recover from the accusations I'd levied at her.

Even with my suspicions about the terrible things she'd done, I still felt sad at the loss of our friendship. Turns out you can know someone's a terrible person, even a murderer, and still miss their laugh.

Benny verified with the police that they'd given Gia the green light to leave, then called Leon, who confirmed that she'd transferred all her money into accounts only she could access. He would continue to manage her investment accounts, but she'd insisted on taking control of her own finances. When we shared with Leon our suspicions of Gia's duplicity, he politely but firmly declined to get involved in speculation about her personal life.

Melodie was a different story. She had never liked Gia and harbored her own suspicions about Gia's book. The police couldn't demand the well be dug up without a warrant, but as the owner of the property, Melodie could do whatever the hell she wanted. And after hearing us out, she was as anxious as I was to see what was down there.

After Gia sailed off into the sunset, Benny and I stayed an extra couple of days in Greece, waiting for the excavation team. They thought we were crazy for opening it up when it had just been filled in but were happy to take our money. Dig day was pleasantly cool with a hint of fall in the air, and we lingered around the edges of the clearing as the men worked, nervously waiting to see what their excavators turned up.

The sun was setting by the time they hit the rocks at the bottom of the well.

Rocks were all that was at the bottom of the well.

I couldn't name the emotion I felt that evening as we sat on the patio for what would be the last time. Disappointment, relief, regret, and confusion all swirled inside me as I downed my Sancerre, zipping my jacket against the autumn evening chill.

"What if we're wrong?" I asked Benny, staring across the bay at the spires of the Palaces at Kampos, silhouetted eerily against the darkening sky.

"Do you think we are?"

"I don't know anymore."

"We may never know," he said.

"Just because she didn't bury them at the bottom of the well doesn't mean she didn't bury them somewhere." I gestured to the sea, lit by the nearly full moon. "There's a whole ocean out there."

BENNY EMAILS GIA EVERY NOW and then, keeping her up to date with the goings-on in his life, but she's never replied. Nor have we ever heard from Timeo again, after Benny left him a message begging him to report everything he knew to the police.

In April, Benny took me to Paris for my birthday, where we stayed at a luxurious hotel just off the Champs-Élysées and ate croissants and chocolate and sipped champagne at all hours of the day. Our room was sumptuous enough that we didn't feel guilty about the amount of prime touring time we spent tangled up with each other between the sheets, the Eiffel Tower watching us through the window.

In retrospect, the lavish vacation in the most romantic city in the world should have tipped me off, but I was completely shocked when he dropped to his knee on our balcony the morning of my birthday and pulled out a ring. The diamond solitaire in an Art Deco setting was a family heirloom, and nearly a year later now, with our wedding in a few months, my heart still leaps when I look at it.

That evening, we were strolling around our neighborhood before our dinner reservation when we wandered into a charming little shop that sold books and chocolates, paired together. The red-carpeted store was a maze of curated shelves and cases, each designed to surprise and delight, and before long, Benny and I had lost each other in the crowd of shoppers exclaiming over white chocolate in the shape of a tomb paired with *The Fall of the House of Usher,* or yellow chocolate in the shape of a Rolls-Royce paired with *The Great Gatsby.*

I was inspecting a dark chocolate silver-frosted mirror paired with *The Picture of Dorian Gray* when I caught a whiff that stopped me in my tracks. An intoxicating blend of orange blossom, vanilla, and musk that I'd know anywhere.

Gia.

I spun around, knocking into a mother shopping with two teenagers, who all gave me dirty looks.

"Pardon," I muttered as I edged around the case they were bent over.

I worked my way through the labyrinthine store as quickly as I could, dodging around shoppers, my heart in my throat as I scanned the faces and shapes of the customers, looking for Gia. She could look different now, I reminded myself. Her hair could be shorter, lighter. She could be wearing a hat and glasses, or a bulky coat to hide her slim frame.

I grabbed Benny's arm when I found him perusing a shelf of chocolate bars named after authors, and his face immediately shifted from amusement to concern when he saw me. "Are you okay?" he asked.

"I smelled Gia," I said, glancing over my shoulder as I pulled him toward the door. "Her perfume. I'd know it anywhere."

Outside the night was cool, the scent of blooms on the breeze erasing her aroma. I swept the sidewalks on both sides of the one-way street with my gaze, rattled.

"Did you tell her we were coming here?" I asked.

He nodded reluctantly. "And that I was going to propose. I wanted her to know I'd chosen you. That we were a team."

"So she could have followed us," I said. "She could be here."

I shifted my weight, clocking a group of twentysomething women as they exited the store.

"What are you gonna do if you catch her?" Benny asked.

I opened my mouth to answer, but like a dog chasing a car, I didn't have a plan for if I caught her. "I don't know," I said, deflated.

He wrapped me in his arms and kissed the top of my head. "Come on," he said. "Let's go to dinner."

I was as sure Gia had been in that store as I was that she'd killed Garrett and Emelia, which was to say . . . oh hell, maybe ninety percent sure? I wavered sometimes, especially when I went back through old pictures, and I knew Benny did as well. As much as I held on to some shred of hope that she was innocent, I wished sometimes that there had been bodies at the bottom of that well so I would know for certain one way or another.

It wasn't until we returned to the hotel later that night and I was going through my purse looking for my lip balm that I found the white chocolate bust. It was packaged in a clear plastic wrapper with a notecard inside indicating the chocolate was made in Switzerland and was meant to be the bust with which Tom had killed Freddie in *The Talented Mr. Ripley.*

"Benny!" I called, holding it up.

He wandered in from the bathroom in his boxers, flossing his teeth. "What's that?"

I handed it to him. "I found it in my purse just now. You didn't put it in there?"

Our eyes met as he shook his head.

"It was her," I said. "I knew I smelled her."

"It couldn't have fallen into your bag?"

"It's a miniature of the damn murder weapon from the book she mentions in her manuscript. She wants me to know she's watching me."

"Maybe it's her way of congratulating us on our engagement," he said dryly, handing it back to me.

"Maybe," I said warily.

I'M WORKING IN MY HOME office when Benny comes in, sweaty from a run, with a book-shaped package tucked under his arm. "This came for you," he says, tossing it onto my desk.

I rip open the paper to see Gia's face staring up at me from the back of a paperback. "What the hell?" I say, pulling the book from the package.

Beneath the ADVANCE READER COPY label, the front cover features a rendering of a silhouetted couple kissing at sunset with the sea in the background while a girl watches from behind them, her arms crossed. Scrawled in a chalky typeface is *Ladykiller: The True Story of How I Married a Con Man / by Gia Highsmith Torres.*

Benny comes around the back of my desk chair to look over my shoulder as I open the book, flipping to the dedication page. *"For anyone who's ever been burned. I see you,"* I read.

"Interesting," he says flatly. "What's the epigraph?"

I turn another page. "It's from *The Talented Mr. Ripley:* 'They were not friends. They didn't know each other. It struck Tom like a horrible truth . . .'"

I look up at Benny and raise my brows. "Am I a narcissist if I think this might at least in some part be about me?"

"You're not the narcissist here."

I flip through the pages of the book. "I'm almost afraid to read it."

"Do you want me to read it first and give you trigger warnings?" he teases, reaching for it.

"Hell no." I pull the book away from his grasp and stand, brushing past him as I exit the room, my work forgotten. "I'll be by the pool if you need me."

BUT GIA, IT TURNS OUT, has not spilled my secrets in her book. Instead, she's written me out of it nearly entirely, save a mention of my attempt to warn her against Garrett before they married. In her version of events, Benny flies from Sweden to Greece alone to look for her, while I return to the United States. After he rescues her, Gia overhears him on the phone with me, explaining that I was right about Garrett and begging me to come see her, but I make excuses and stay away, too wrapped up in myself to care about her.

It stings, but it is, I realize, better than the alternative, and leaves me feeling begrudgingly grateful.

The book ends on a high note with Gia reuniting with Dimitrios in Barcelona, culminating in multiple graphic sex scenes set on a boat and in the bell tower of a church, among other places. They rent a humble home in a rural part of an unspecified country and he works with wood while she finishes the book, determined to live a simpler life than she had before.

At the mention of his woodwork, I call to mind the live-edge coffee table in the living room of the house in Greece, and how similar it was to the tables she described as having been made by Dimitrios. Benny remembers it too, and recalls another table, a glass one, having been there when he visited with Camila the month before. It could be that Gia simply found the table in a shop and was inspired to attribute its creation to Dimitrios. But it does make me wonder.

The critics are split about her book; some call it a tale of redemption, others call bullshit. Gia's a "sexy, sailor-mouthed heroine for modern times, unashamed to put herself first," or she's "a dangerously narcissistic and often intoxicated antihero with no moral compass." Her perspective is "fresh," or it's "privileged," the book a "dazzling breakthrough," or "pure trash." Regardless, it's a hit, and everyone has a theory about who the movie star Gia christened Yasmin in the book might be in real life.

Though Gia has still not reappeared, her refusal of all media requests is all the press she needs. Her publicist must be a magician, because within a week of the publication, the headline on Page Six reads WHERE IN THE WORLD IS GIA HIGHSMITH TORRES?

All the other tabloids follow.

Two weeks later, the book hits number fourteen on the *New York Times* bestseller list.

WAS I WRONG ABOUT HER?

The question often keeps me up at night. As Theodoropoulos said, there was never any evidence that she knew I was dating Noah, just as there's no evidence that what Timeo told us is true. Gia's truth is hidden somewhere within her, bent by her conscience into a shape she can accommodate, just like mine. Whatever terrible things she may or may not have done, I can't fault her for protecting herself; it's only natural.

When did she learn she couldn't trust me? Was it my first betrayal, when I slept with Noah behind her back; my second, when I lied to her about it; or my third, two years later, when I sent the letter to Emelia that sparked her quest for revenge?

Yes, I was the one who sent the letter.

Driven by guilt, I'd cut out the letters to spell the message and put the note into an envelope with the age-worn back cover of the copy of *The Odyssey* that had been left in my bag after the book itself disappeared, carrying it with me all the way to Miteras to mail it so that it wouldn't be traced back to me.

I had the chance to confess when Timeo brought it up, but I didn't, and now it's too late. Funny, how it's easier to forgive her for protecting herself than it is to forgive myself for doing the same.

I hope I'm mistaken about her, that my own guilt is what makes me convinced of hers. But I can't deny I still believe she's guilty. One passage in particular from her book stands out to me, a passage that reads differently in light of what I know now. It takes place shortly after she's fled Miteras, when she's in the airport in Athens:

I've nearly reached the front of the line when I spot a tall, sandy-haired man in a white button-down at the magazine stand across the way. His face is angled away from me toward a rack of books, but the slope of his shoulders, the slight tilt of his head is so familiar, my blood runs cold. I watch, frozen, as he runs his fingers through his hair the exact same way Garrett does, then takes a book off the shelf and sets it in front of the woman working the cash register, who flashes a flirtatious smile as he says something to her.

"Miss?"

I whip around to see it's my turn at the coffee bar, and apologize, my eyes darting toward the magazine stand as I order a coffee and pastry. But I can't see past the bulk of the men waiting at the end of the bar for their drinks, and once I've paid, the Garrett look-alike has disappeared.

It wasn't him. It couldn't have been. How could he possibly have followed me here?

My coffee and pastry in hand, I dart across the corridor to the magazine stand, where I smile at the girl working the register. "Do you speak English?" I ask.

She nods. "A little."

"The man who was just here, tall, light brown hair and a white button-down, I think he's a friend of mine." I flash my most winning smile. "Did you maybe catch his name?"

She shakes her head.

"What did he buy?"

She types something into her computer and reads from the screen: "An English translation of *The Philosophy of Protagoras*. We carry all the Greek philosophers."

The knot in my stomach tightens. An obscure book of Greek philosophy is exactly what Garrett would buy. *"Man is the measure of all things?"* I quote, trying to call any more information about Protagoras to mind.

She shrugs, looking at me blankly.

"I'll buy the same book."

I sweep the corridor with hawk eyes as she rings me up, then take a seat at the gate with my back to the window, scanning the faces of everyone who comes and goes. I flip over the book to read the back, which reminds me that Protagoras believed that the truth was relative, because what one person might consider to be true, another might consider to be false. Certainly prescient, and a theory I can easily imagine Garrett using to justify his lies.

I'm somewhat calmer by the time my boarding group is called, not having seen the man in the white shirt again. Surely it was simply a look-alike, with similar reading tastes.

It strikes me that I'll always be looking over my shoulder from now on, waiting for the jack to pop out of the box. Even at my most relaxed, I'll forever be slightly on edge, prepared to flinch if someone claps too loudly or turns too quickly. I'll sleep lightly, watch my back, be more careful who I trust.

Or will I?

Time is like water; some of it is clear and some of it is murky, but the more that stands between you and the past you've buried, the less you can see it. Once the memory of Garrett has been swallowed by the depths of the sea, perhaps I'll learn to be careless again.

I look forward to that day.

THE BRILLIANCE OF GIA'S WRITING is the truth in it, hiding in plain view. Her choice to use the word *careless* instead of *carefree*. One could read the passage as she's intended, to relay her enduring fear of her vanished husband; but I read it a different way.

Gia will live on the razor's edge until the lies she's printed about her latest crime are read so many times that they're accepted as truth. She'll be waiting for Garrett's body to wash up on shore until enough time has passed that his skeleton has been swallowed by the depths of the sea.

Perhaps then she'll be careless enough to take the life of another friend or lover who crosses her.

I hope it won't be me.

ACKNOWLEDGMENTS

I am so grateful to everyone who helped bring this book to life. To my husband, Alex, who supported me through the good days when the words flowed like a river and the bad days when the words were more like rocks. To my parents, for giving me a love of reading, and to my darling little girls, my sun and my moon, who are my biggest fans regardless of the fact they're not quite old enough yet to read my work.

To my incredible lit agency, Levine Greenberg Rostan Literary, and especially to my personal champion, Sarah Bedingfield, thank you for all your encouragement, patience, knowledge, and for always making time for our marathon phone calls. I'd be lost without you! To William Morris Endeavor and my extraordinary film agent, Hilary Zaitz Michael—you continue to amaze me. Thank you for navigating the ever-changing television landscape to bring this book to the screen.

To my spectacular editor, Anne Speyer, thank you for your keen eye and for shaping this manuscript with the finesse of a sculptor to make it the book it is today. To all the amazing team at Bantam

Books, thank you for believing in this book and all your hard work to bring it into the world. Special thanks to editorial assistant Anusha Khan; Jen Garza and Sarah Breivogel in publicity; Quinne Rogers and Kathleen Quinlan in marketing; leadership team Kara Cesare, Jennifer Hershey, Kara Welsh, and Kim Hovey; Carlos Beltran and Susan Turner respectively for the beautiful cover and interior design; production editor Ted Allen; and head of subrights Denise Cronin.

Last but not least, thanks to you, dear reader, for reading! Readers like you make the world a better place.

ABOUT THE AUTHOR

KATHERINE WOOD is a graduate of the University of Southern California and a native of Mississippi. She lives in Atlanta with her husband and two children, a ferocious kitty, and a naughty pug.

thekatwritesbooks.com

ABOUT THE TYPE

This book was set in Fairfield, the first typeface from the hand of the distinguished American artist and engraver Rudolph Ruzicka (1883–1978). Ruzicka was born in Bohemia (in the present-day Czech Republic) and came to America in 1894. He set up his own shop, devoted to wood engraving and printing, in New York in 1913 after a varied career working as a wood engraver, in photoengraving and banknote printing plants, and as an art director and freelance artist. He designed and illustrated many books, and was the creator of a considerable list of individual prints—wood engravings, line engravings on copper, and aquatints.